MW00423091

Skin of the Night

By C.K. Bennett

The Night series

Skin of the Night
Into the Night

SKIN
OF THE
NIGHT

C.K. BENNETT

Third edition

Editing by Natalie Bolderston

Artwork by Caracolla

https://ckbennettauthor.com

Instagram: @ck.bennett

To C., for your support, and so much more.
I know we're cool.

ACKNOWLEDGEMENTS

In light of how you will always come first in my life (in all areas apart from one), I would first and foremost like to give a special thanks to you, A., my beloved boyfriend, for your continuous and invaluable support. I am especially grateful to you for being willing to wake up in the middle of the night to listen to my, supposedly, pressing ideas, only so that I might – finally – be able to sleep, too. Health and fitness freak that you are, I know how precious those eight hours of sleep are to you, so I truly don't take it for granted.
You are the best thing that has ever happened to me.

I am also grateful to you, my dear family members, who are not allowed to read this series for obvious reasons. You'll get a better acknowledgement in the next instalment.

When it comes to you, my dear readers, words fall short. I am so grateful to you for joining and supporting me on this journey, some of you since the very beginning, from the very first chapter I uploaded of *Skin of the Night*. In terms of writing, I would be nowhere without you guys. You're the ones who showed me that I can actually do this – if not for me, then for you. Your feedback has been invaluable and has taught me so much.
I'd also like to thank you for your kindness towards each other. Truly, I'm astounded by what a constructive and positive community we are. You are all so kind, not just to me, but to each other – your debates in the comment sections have always been remarkably constructive and respectful. Instead of attacking each other, you try to understand each other's perspective, and that's been such a moving thing to witness. I know Will & Cara have a knack for lighting the fuse and sparking debates in the comments, but I am so impressed with how you've handled them.
I really am so humbled by your attention and support, and most

of all by your patience. It's been a bumpy ride, but finally, I have taken the necessary steps to give you my characters once and for all. Now, they are yours to keep, for as long as you'll have them. I love you all so much. I am extremely honoured to have you as my readers.

Thank you, author Darla Cassic, for inspiring and helping me in more ways than one. You are an incredible writer in your own right, and I cannot wait to see where your works will take you in the future. You have quickly become my closest confidante in bringing *The Night* series to life. I am so humbled and grateful for your astute feedback and insights (as well as humour), but most of all, I am grateful for your friendship. While it bloomed under peculiar and unexpected circumstances, getting to know you has been an intense and rewarding experience. You are such a precious individual, and I am so glad to have stumbled upon you (as well as your Romance works). I cannot wait to continue completing each other's sentences for years to come, and I promise I'll stop converting you into a nocturnal creature like myself. That office is looking more and more promising, though. (Check out https://darlacassic.com to find out where you can read Darla's books)

To you, Natalie Bolderston, my editor, I want to give a massive thanks for bringing *Skin of the Night* to the next level. You've helped me make it the best version it could ever be. Your talent with words is outstanding, and I am so glad you wanted to bless my work with it. You are such a sweet soul, and it's been an honour to work with you. Thanks for taking part in bringing this dream of mine to life.

CHAPTERS

There is always some madness in love.
But there is also always some reason in madness.

– *Friedrich Wilhelm Nietzsche*

APRIL 12ᵀᴴ, 2019

GOOD TERMS

"I T SHOULD BE HERE," I TOLD OLIVIA AS I TURNED LEFT, into a small alley, to find the secluded bar. Looking up, I saw a white and gold sign that was shaped like a hexagonal prism, though cut in half, which overhung a green door. *Disrepute,* it said. It was a members' club, but I was aware it welcomed walk-ins. Still, to be on the safe side, I had booked a table a few days in advance.

When I halted in front of the entrance, Olivia and I were greeted by a polite doorman who opened the door for us. Walking in, we journeyed down a narrow staircase leading into an underground cavern with a barrel-vaulted ceiling. Since it was still relatively early on a Friday night, there weren't that many people here yet. Our arrival attracted a few glances, but none of them lingered. I considered that to be a positive thing, as it meant we didn't stand out.

After we had stored our coats in the cloakroom, the staff showed us to our table and handed us the cocktail menu. Sinking onto the settee, I gazed around. The interior was reminiscent of the sixties, with plush colours and lots of velvet furniture. Comfortable and electronic lounge music played in the background.

Upon closer inspection, I noticed that the average age of the clientele was a little older than we were used to. Most of the people present looked like they were well-established men and women in their thirties and forties, so I doubted that students frequently went here.

Taking a seat beside me, Olivia wrinkled her small nose. Her plump, light pink lips formed an uncertain line.

"Was this the place Jason recommended?" She was referring to the man I considered to be my very best friend, and who had – just a few days ago – also become my flatmate.

"Yes."

She leaned closer to murmur, "It's very posh, isn't it?"

"You sound surprised."

"Well, I'm worried I'll stand out."

I studied her from head to toe. In her deep-red dress, Olivia resembled a magnificent rose. She was truly a gorgeous young woman. If anything would make her stand out, it was her beauty, and that alone.

"I wouldn't worry if I were you. You definitely look like you belong."

A heartfelt smile spread across her face. "Really?"

"Absolutely. You look stunning."

Touched by my compliment, she placed her hand on her ample bosom. "Thank you, Cara," she said, "but so do you."

I shrugged and reached for the deep-green menu on the small table in front of us. The velvet material was adorned with the letters D.R.P. in gold. "Should we have a look at the menu?"

Olivia scanned our surroundings once more before she leaned closer again. "Well, are you absolutely sure that lawyers frequent this place?"

"Judging by the look of it, I'm positive."

"It's just that I'd hate to waste my time here if it isn't the case."

"Well, this was Jason's recommendation, and since his father established a law firm, I took his word for it. Mentioned something about his brother favouring this place as well, and he's a solicitor, too, from what I've gathered."

I had yet to meet a single one of Jason's family members. Since he no longer lived with them, the opportunity simply hadn't presented itself yet. I was vaguely aware that they were filthy rich, thanks to Jason's father being the founder of Day & Night LLP – a firm offering legal services – and that they were a busy bunch, since each individual had a demanding job that took up most of their time. But that was as far as my knowledge about them went. In fact, aside from his father, who was called John, I didn't even remember their names.

However, now that I had secured a vacation scheme at Day & Night to be completed over the summer, and had moved into Jason's flat in Notting Hill, that reality was about to change. Eager to meet the new tenant and upcoming trainee, his father had already invited me for dinner on Sunday two weeks from now, and I was sincerely looking forward to it.

As I returned from my thoughts, I saw that Olivia was on the fence, so I continued, "If you're having second thoughts, we can always find a new place, but perhaps we should give this one a chance first?"

She brushed a lock of her angelically blonde hair behind her ear while she continued to assess our sumptuous surroundings. Since her hesitation was blatant, I sighed.

Olivia could be quite impossible to deal with. If she didn't get her way, she transformed into a whiny brat that I couldn't be bothered to babysit. It didn't help that I was already beginning to suffer from a guilty conscience at the constant thought of my neglected coursework. Seeing as I was a law student in my third year at UCL, it was not a matter that I took lightly. Besides, my reasons for being here were purely selfless. I wasn't the one that had wanted to go out tonight. She was. So, if she was going to be a pain in the arse, I'd leave her to prowl on her own. However, I had already warned her of said fact, so she had been surprisingly compliant today.

Upon hearing my sigh, Olivia returned her attention to me. "Fine. Let's give it a chance."

I released a groan. "Took you long enough."

"Yeah, sorry. It's just been so long since we've had a girls' night out that I want everything to be perfect."

My lips twisted with amusement. "Like you're actually here to spend quality time with me," I replied with a note of sarcasm.

"Hey, I'm here for that, too," she argued. "It's just that, ever since I broke up with Colin, I haven't had sex."

I couldn't help grinning. "What – so you've had a dry spell for three months? Poor you."

Three months without sex? I'd be going insane. No wonder she had been so eager about this night.

She gave me a scowl. "Yeah, well, unlike you, I haven't got a fuck friend, Cara. I need to satisfy my libido somehow."

"Vibrator not doing the job?"

"Not even close. I need a man."

"And preferably one with a heavy wallet at that." I couldn't help myself.

A chortle escaped her upon my playful remark. "Hey, you know I'm not like that. I just thought it would be nice to find a lawyer, since I'm a law student and all that. We'd have something in common."

"Aside from sexual desperation, you mean."

She slapped my arm, gently. "Stop teasing me."

"Sorry, love. I couldn't help myself." I released a sadistic laugh. "Anyway, we're in the right place, then." I shook my head. "I still don't understand how you managed to persuade me into joining this."

Olivia snorted. "Cara, even though you may come across as aloof, you've actually got a fairly warm and large heart in there – that's how I managed to persuade you. A heartbroken best friend isn't something you have the capacity to ignore."

"Lesser of two evils, perhaps."

"What's that supposed to mean?" she replied, bewildered.

I smirked. "Perhaps tending to your needs is my way of making you shut up sooner."

Olivia scoffed. "If that's your attitude, you'll make a rubbish parent."

Humoured, I allowed my eyes to wander around the space. "I suppose it's a good thing I don't want children, then."

Did I want children? I'd always said I didn't, but Mum always told me that the right man would change my mind. Because I was one for keeping an open mind, I didn't argue with her on that. She had wisdom in her years that I could only dream of. My perspective today was no guarantee of tomorrow's.

"Have you settled into your new flat yet?" Olivia asked. Steering my attention back to her, I saw that her eyes were the ones wandering now, and it amused me. She surely wasn't wasting her time locating a target, and I appreciated that. As soon as she sealed the deal with someone, I'd be heading home.

"Not yet. I've been so busy with coursework that I've hardly had time to unpack just the essentials. I mean, I had to search for an entire hour before I found the dress that I'm wearing tonight." I gazed down at the purple material. It was my favourite cocktail dress because it clung to my slim and curvaceous figure like glue. In it, I felt opulent.

I continued, "But I've booked a date with Jason tomorrow to finish unpacking."

Jason and I had met at a pub three years ago, where a live band had been performing songs by Arctic Monkeys, which was among my favourite bands. Our encounter had been perfectly coincidental and, in retrospect, rather comical. I had been returning from the bar with a new round of drinks for my younger sister Phoebe and myself when a drunken idiot had bumped into me, and the impact had made me spill the pints I was holding over Jason, who had been walking past me just then.

I had been mortified, but thankfully, Jason hadn't failed to notice that it hadn't been my fault. After telling off the lad that had bumped into me, he had offered to buy me a new round. I'd been so charmed by him at that moment that I had struck up a conversation with him, and soon enough, I'd learnt that he also studied at UCL, although he wasn't on my course. Instead, he was about to finish his first year of studying medicine back then.

After a few minutes of effortless and invigorating conversation, I had invited him to join my sister and me. Since he was there with a couple of mates, he brought them along, and ever since that fateful moment, we had formed an irreplaceable and platonic friendship. These days, he was much like an elder brother to me. I'd always wanted a brother, even if I did adore my sister Phoebe.

So, when Jason's previous flatmate had decided to move in with his girlfriend instead, Jason had asked me to take his place, and I hadn't hesitated to accept.

The memory made me smile to myself. I was still wearing it when I eventually lifted my eyes to regard Olivia again, but it faded as soon as I recognised the look on her face. Already?

Looking in the direction of her gaze, I saw the profiles of two men seated by the bar, and since they were frowning rather angrily at one another while they spoke, they looked to be in a heated debate about something.

The next thing I noticed was how attractive they were. Late twenties, perhaps? Early thirties? Both had neatly trimmed stubble and short hair that was immaculately groomed. The man I found most comely was brown-haired, and the other dirty blonde, like Jason. However, I'd always had a kink for dark and tall.

"Which one?" I enquired.

"Brown-haired."

"Let's head over then, shall we? I'll mind his friend," I proposed and ascended from my seat to approach them, confident. I always had been.

Hesitant, Olivia said, "Cara, maybe not. They don't look like they want to be disturbed."

I scoffed. "So what? You won't know unless you try, Livy – and I can handle rejection. Can't you?"

Her warm brown Bambi eyes turned towards me, and they were filled with a vulnerability that I hated to witness. Colin had really done her in, hadn't he? When he cheated on her time and again?

"Livy," my tone was unusually strict, "Colin is a bastard that never deserved you, but just because he is, it doesn't mean every man is. You can't give him that power, and you shouldn't let your past ruin your future."

Olivia inhaled deeply before she offered me a firm nod of her head, and I was slightly surprised at how quickly she absorbed my pep talk. Her libido must indeed be desperate, I gathered. Either way, I gave her no time to change her mind. Confident in my strides, I approached the two men while Olivia trailed behind me.

The dirty blonde man noticed me first, and the look on his face affirmed my ego. With slightly thin lips parting, he turned his whole body towards me. Just like his brown-haired friend, he had a strong, lean build.

"Hi," I greeted and presented my most lascivious smile as I held his gaze. His eyes were large and a warm shade of brown, like melted chocolate. I loved chocolate.

He appeared speechless, so I continued, "I'm sorry to interrupt your conversation, but my friend and I were—"

"We're not interested," a dreadfully sensual voice interfered from my right.

Looking towards its source, I locked eyes with the man Olivia had laid her favour with. They were light-blue and eerily familiar. Dark brown eyebrows ran in nearly straight lines above them, and the shadow they provided augmented his alluring and mysterious aura.

Had I met him before?

A frown formed on my face. I could have sworn I'd seen him somewhere.

At that moment, I was so preoccupied with trying to put a name to the face that I neglected the chance to admire it, but Christ, had I ever seen a man more gorgeous than him? Prominent cheekbones highlighted the shape of his strong, square jaw. It was clenched, I saw, but I gave no thought as to why.

Below a proportionate, straight, and masculine nose rested a pair of full, delectable lips. They pressed together, forming a brooding line, while he continued to study me in his annoyance. He was easily the most physically attractive man I'd ever encountered, and he wasn't remotely interested.

"Where are your manners, man?" his friend scolded before his eyes darted in my direction again. "Please excuse him. He's a bit blunt."

Puzzled, I persisted in staring at the dark-haired stranger.

I must have met him before. I was certain I'd seen him somewhere. However, would I have forgotten an encounter with such a beautiful man? I doubted it. Where had I seen him, then? Was he a celebrity?

"I'm sorry – have we met before?" I blurted out in my bewilderment.

His eyebrows arched before a condescending chuckle slipped out of his mouth. A look of sardonic amusement etched through his riveting features.

"Honestly, you're interrupting our conversation, and you couldn't be more original than that, Miss? At least you could have compensated with a better chat-up line. I'm disappointed. And like I said, we're not interested, so move along, would you?"

Bewitched by the sound of his sensual voice, it took me a few seconds to process the content, but once I had, I frowned, offended. Meanwhile, his friend groaned and shook his head beside me, clearly despairing of his companion.

Could they be gay partners?

Since I was struck by mild shock at his impertinence, I asked, "I beg your pardon?" Then, as soon as it subsided, I snapped back, "I was being serious, you utter twat."

His eyebrows furrowed while his arresting eyes – twice – travelled up and down my body, and once they'd returned to mine, a crooked smile crept across his tempting mouth. From the way they had devoured my body, I eliminated the option of him being homosexual. Only a straight man could regard me with such a gleam in his eye.

"Perhaps we've slept together. But, if we have, you weren't worth remembering," he finally answered. My lips parted with my eventual gasp. What a complete arsehole!

Shame to think he'd piqued my interest earlier when he obviously didn't deserve it. That was quite an insolent way to treat another human being. His arrogance was off the charts. Who did he think he was? So yes, I had interrupted them, but there was a polite way to reject me. There was no need to step on my dignity.

Rigid, my stare transformed into a pure glower. "As if I'd ever get so lost and desperate that I would wind up in a bed with *you*. You're a sorry excuse for a man. Tell me, was it the lack of your mother's affection that made you grow up to treat random women like shit?"

He blinked at my ruthless insult, perhaps a little gobsmacked, and beside me, his companion burst into poorly stifled laughter. Olivia's existence was lost on me, but knowing her, she was probably a breath away from withering.

"I can assure you that my mother and I are on good terms," came the handsome man's calm reply.

I folded my arms and scoffed. "Too good, I wager," I countered. "Heading home to spend the night in her bed, then? That why you're not interested?"

Before he was able to respond, Olivia gasped and clasped my hand to drag me away. While observing their shocked facial expressions, she said, "Please excuse us."

"Excuse *us*?" I echoed in disbelief while she tugged me away from them. "Didn't you hear him just now? How bloody rude he was?"

"Choose your battles, love! He's obviously not worth our attention," she retorted.

Seeing as she made a valid point, I simmered down somewhat. Only now did I notice that her body was trembling with irritation. Just like the rest of us, she was rattled. Well, that was something I quite excelled at – rattling people. It was definitely a flaw, but then everyone had flaws, I consoled myself.

After pushing me onto the settee again, Olivia dumped her body next to mine, folded her arms and glared away from me. "Cara, honestly! 'Have we met before?' What was that?"

Seeking reconciliation, I pouted at her. "I'm sorry. I honestly thought I'd seen him before. Worst part is that I still think I have."

She frowned and turned to catch a glimpse of them. Mirroring her, I saw that they were laughing, clearly at my expense. Well, they could laugh all they wanted. Personally, the only thing I found laughable was how attractive I had initially found them to be. Instead, they were ugly souls with nasty tendencies. How dare they laugh at my decision to stand up for myself?

"Yeah, you know, now that you mention it, maybe he does look a bit familiar," Olivia stated and faced me again with a puzzled expression.

Where had *we* seen him, then?

"Order us a round, please, would you? Strongest cocktail they've got," I said while averting my eyes from the two men. I wondered to myself whether the encounter with them had ruined my chance for a pleasant night.

The sound of Olivia's subsequent chuckle assured me that I was already forgiven for the strife I had caused a moment ago. "Sure," she obliged and pushed herself up from her seat. Impressed, I watched her graceful strut as she returned to the bar like she hadn't a concern in the world.

Olivia had always been great at rising above things. Less could be said for myself. I had much to learn from her in that respect.

Throwing another glance at the two men, I saw the dark-haired man turn his head once Olivia reached the bar. It was obvious from how consciously he regarded her that he desired her attention. However, with her chin raised high and her gaze fixed straight ahead, she refused to acknowledge him, and the satisfying view made my lips twitch into a devilish grin.

If only Jason had been here. Right about now, he would have laughed his lungs out while repeatedly patting my back, but he'd had coursework to do, which I had respected. Nevertheless, I could have used his moral support, so I decided to send him a text.

20:58

> You didn't warn me about dickheads when you told me about this place x

Thought that was a given? You wanted a place with lawyers. You can't have one without the other x

> You twat. I'm not a dickhead

You're not a lawyer

Yet x

> I just accused a man that Livy wanted to get off with of sleeping with his mum. Doubt your coursework is more entertaining…

Lmao you did what?

Did he deserve it?

> 100 %

By the time Olivia returned, it felt like only a minute had passed. As she placed an espresso martini on the table, I looked up from my phone to find her smiling. Caught by it, I grinned back and put my phone aside. She had brought me my favourite cocktail.

"Next round's on me," I said.

"I didn't pay for it." She pressed her lips together in a poor attempt to hide her smile.

My cognition lagged. "What?"

"The guy you insulted did. Asked for your name, too, but I

didn't give it to him. Gathered I'd leave that choice to you."

Instantly, the floor summoned my jaw. Had he really bought me a drink? After all that?

Responding to impulse, my gaze travelled in his direction. Spellbinding blue eyes met mine, and I was immediately captured by them. Wearing a complacent smirk, he raised his glass at me and gave me a wink, leaving his friend to snigger beside him as he shook his head.

"Seriously? What's his problem?" I grumbled, irritated, and broke out of his spell to focus on Olivia. Sinking into the spot beside me, she raised her cosmopolitan to her mouth.

After a sip, she reflected aloud, "I think you changed his mind, acting the way you did. While I waited for our drinks, you were all he asked about. I told him nothing, though."

Bemused, I blinked back at her. "You had a conversation with him?"

Olivia frowned. "He insisted on paying for our drinks, Cara. What was I supposed to do?"

Ignore him? I would have. "I'm so sorry you had to go through that."

Laughter poured from her mouth at the obvious humour I'd spiked my reply with. "You can have him," she assured me with a grin, and her tone clearly implied that she harboured no bitterness and genuinely meant to give me her blessing. "He put me off with his attitude," she continued to explain. "His friend, though – Andrew – he seems nice. He apologised on William's behalf. William's the arsehole."

I scoffed. "Thanks, but no thanks. I'd rather he pissed off."

Olivia chortled and browsed the room again, probably to locate new targets. Meanwhile, I stared at the cocktail Mr Arsehole had bought me. I wanted it, but it seemed wrong to accept it. So instead, I just continued to stare at it, conflicted.

"Oh, for heaven's sake, Cara. Consider it an apology. Drink it," Olivia scolded and rolled her eyes.

"You do realise that if he sees me drinking it, he'll consider himself excused?" I countered. "I won't allow that. I'd rather buy my own." I stood.

"He's going to speak to you, then," she warned. "Is that what you want?"

"Who says I've got to reply? I might as well return the favour – not interested," I stated cheekily and headed for the bar. Eyeing Olivia over my shoulder, I found her grinning at me, silently commending my fierceness.

I was halfway there when I sensed his eyes upon my figure, and it demanded every ounce of my willpower not to meet them. To signal that I did not want to be approached, I ensured that I would arrive at the far end from both men once I reached the counter.

Spreading my hands across the dark surface of it, I searched for a bartender, but both of them were busy serving other customers, so I waited somewhat vigilantly. I could sense that Mr Arsehole continued to stare at me, and it made me feel strangely uneasy. Hyperaware of myself, I shifted my weight onto my right leg and resorted to studying the wall of myriad bottles behind the bar.

When his muscular and bare forearms suddenly entered my field of vision, I recoiled a small step. From the corner of my eye, I saw them rest against the counter beside me. He'd rolled up the sleeves of his white shirt, and the grey waistcoat that he wore on top clung to his robust anatomy, serving as an unfair reminder of his tantalising masculinity.

"I'm sorry about earlier, Miss. You're right. I was very rude."

Since I refused to acknowledge his existence, I pretended not to have heard anything while I waited for a bartender to notice me.

"If you'd give me a second," he continued once he realised that I wasn't going to respond, "I'd like to explain why."

Just then, a bartender spared me from having to respond to the imbecile. Blonde with green eyes, he looked positively Nordic. An alluring grin decorated his mouth when our eyes locked.

"What can I get you, Miss?" he enquired politely, and judging from his strong accent, I thought he might be Swedish.

Leaning slightly forward, I smiled back. "An espresso martini and a gin and tonic, please, thank you."

Nodding, he extended to me the payment terminal he'd just typed into, and I was just about to grab it when Mr Arsehole beat me to it. After snatching it away from me, he inserted his own card.

"No!" I admonished and stared at his large hands. Prominent veins branched across the back of them, and a few climbed a small distance along his fingers, although they stopped long before they reached his neatly trimmed nails. They were undeniably male hands, and they were a beautiful pair at that. The experienced look of them wasn't something I would forget anytime soon. During a brief moment of weakness, I wondered what it would feel like to have them caress my naked skin.

His eyebrows arched at my harsh response. Through a lopsided smile, he said, "Now that I've got your attention—"

"You had my attention earlier, Oedipus," I interrupted, "and you wasted it," I reminded him as I snatched back the device.

"Oedipus?" he echoed with a titter of amazement. "How astute."

I merely rolled my eyes and was just about to withdraw his card when his loud sigh made me look at him.

"If you withdraw my card," he said, "dear Philip will have to restart the whole process. Do you really mean to make his job any more difficult than it needs to be? Just because you can't swallow your pride?"

I could hardly fathom the audacity of this man. I had never met someone quite so irritating in all my twenty-three years of life.

When I looked at the bartender, whose name I supposed was Philip, I saw a flicker of humour cross his face.

"You should have a sign on the door that warns of arsehole clientele," I told him.

He pressed his lips together and winked at me. Then, glancing at the pest beside me, Philip asked, "What have you done to deserve such a characterisation, Will?"

William chuckled. "Well, I acted like an arsehole, naturally."

"That's unusual."

"Yes, she caught me at a bad moment."

Philip smiled. "Then you ought to apologise to the lady," he teased and cocked his head in my direction.

"I'm trying, but she's not letting me."

"Try harder."

The source of my annoyance faced me again. "Andy – my friend – has got a girlfriend. Or, he used to. They split up just today, but I expect it's only temporary. So, you've got the wrong end of the stick, love," he explained. "I'm the nice guy. Now, unless you'd like to get in the middle of that, I reckon I did you a favour."

I pressed my lips together and despised the fact that I found his reason valid. Then again, it could as well have been a lie. I didn't know the man. What's more, if it had been the truth, he could still have treated us more politely.

Scepticism coloured my tone as I replied, "Why should I trust what you're saying?"

He gestured towards the payment terminal. "Let's settle this first. May I buy your drinks for you?"

Finally, I met his eyes, and they were smouldering. The sight made a lump gather in my throat. I hadn't noticed it before, but the man was rather intense – everything about him was.

Struck speechless, I nodded my head.

"Thank you," he said before giving me a look of wonder. Puzzled by the expression on his face, I frowned back.

"So," he said while completing the transaction, "what's your name, then?"

"Oh, so you actually *are* interested," I replied sarcastically as I watched Philip perform his magic. "How funny. I haven't been bullied by a boy who fancies me since primary school."

Stealing a glance at William, I saw his mouth bend into a winsome grin before an incredulous laugh slipped out of it. In front of us, Philip pretended not to exist, although he failed at disguising his amusement. From his pursed lips, it was obvious that he was struggling not to laugh. Seeming to realise the same, he walked away to finish my drinks further away from us, probably to give us some privacy.

"Yes, well, I'm glad I could treat you to some nostalgia," William replied.

"More like trauma."

Glancing over again, I noticed that William had turned slightly away from me to hide his reaction. From my limited view of his face, I saw that his grin persisted, but he was now biting on his lower lip while looking at the floor as though he could hardly contain himself.

"Listen," he said and turned to face me properly again. "If it's not obvious already, I seriously regret my behaviour. I hadn't thought you'd be so…" His eyes narrowed faintly. "Intriguing."

I snorted. Did he really consider that to be a legitimate excuse for his behaviour? What if I hadn't been intriguing? What then? Would he have considered his conduct justified?

He was obviously a conceited idiot. Why was I wasting even a breath on him?

Condescension was etched on my face when I finally turned towards him. Even though I was wearing heels, he towered over me. Since I felt small and vulnerable this close to him, I wondered how tall he actually was. Taking my own height into account and adding it to the fact that I was wearing heels, I reckoned he was at least six-foot-four, maybe five.

He was strong, too, which I could tell from the way his shirt and waistcoat strained against his body, as well as the general width of him given his broad shoulders and back.

"Who would have guessed? How to seduce an arsehole – accuse him of sleeping with his mother. Turned you on, did it? The idea of her?" I cheekily responded.

Frightened, I turned rigid when he suddenly leaned towards me. Hardly an inch separated our noses. He was so close that

I could smell the alcohol on his breath as it fanned against my face. In my momentary fear, my eyes locked with his, and I was immediately hypnotised by their dominating gleam.

Perhaps this wasn't a man to be trifled with. He didn't strike me as the sort of man who allowed others to walk over him. On the contrary, he looked to be in the habit of performing that deed himself. I felt walked over. To be honest – under the burning heat of his gaze – I felt vanquished.

"*You* did," he replied firmly.

THAT'S MORE LIKE IT

IS BOLD REPLY TOOK ME ABACK. I HADN'T FORESEEN that he would be so direct with me, but it was oddly refreshing. Suddenly nervous, my heart started pounding in my chest.

"Well," I murmured as I mustered my remaining courage to say, "you got what you wanted – something original."

His lips tucked into a smile. "Without a doubt. Although, is your name as original as your personality?"

The astute method he employed as he made a third attempt to fish out my name impressed me. He was obviously a cunning man, so I reminded myself to exercise caution. However, it amused me that he wasn't one to give up without a fight, so a faint smile nested on my mouth while I shook my head.

"I'm afraid I'll have to disappoint," I said.

"How so? It's not Electra, is it?"

I couldn't possibly suppress the giggle that escaped my lips, because the reference was remarkably shrewd. Clearly, he had read and enjoyed his fair share of Greek tragedies, too. Electra was, in some ways, Oedipus' female counterpart after all.

Momentarily inspired by the current theme, I lied, "No, but you're not far from it, actually. It stems from Greek."

"Really?" He looked intrigued.

"Yeah. Name's Cassandra, but everyone calls me Sandra." Since I wasn't naïve enough to trust him on a whim, I didn't feel like giving him my real name. Besides, he hadn't proved himself remotely deserving.

"Sandra," he echoed with a nod. "Well, I'm William, as you may have already gathered, but you can call me Will."

"Or Oedipus. Tomato tomato," I countered.

Genuine amusement twinkled in his eyes. "So you're a fan of Sophocles and Greek tragedies, then? Or are you merely a disciple of dear Mr Freud?"

His evident intellect irritated me somewhat because it led me to like him more than I wanted to. He was retaliating with precisely the same sense of humour and with force equal to my own. It wasn't often that I encountered people who could keep up with my sharp wit, but this man seemed to be up to the task. Despite his lack of affability, he clearly stored a quick and well-functioning brain behind that annoyingly handsome face of his.

I was still contemplating whether to reply when Philip interjected, "Here you go, Miss," and presented two lush cocktails. "An espresso martini and a gin and tonic."

"Thank you." I was about to grab them when William beat me to it.

"I'll give you a hand," he said as an explanation.

"I've got two already. Three aren't required, as you can see."

He chuckled. "You've got quite the witty mouth, haven't you?"

"Well, at least one of us has got some wit," I challenged. "Poor man can't even count right."

William shook his head at me but, nevertheless, persisted in carrying my drinks away. With a pout on my face, I trailed after him. How had it come to this? I hadn't meant to attract him earlier. Had I known my insult would prove so counterproductive, I'd have bitten my tongue.

"Andy," he called and cocked his head in the direction of Olivia's lonely figure. Struck by evident surprise, Andrew's brown eyes widened before he stood from his seat.

When I fixed my gaze on Olivia, I found her smirking. The sight extracted a groan from my mouth. Unlike Andrew, she wasn't the least bit surprised, and I didn't appreciate it, because it spoke of her impressions and expectations of me.

"It's Olivia, right?" William asked once we reached her.

"Yes, but everyone calls me Livy."

"Livy," he echoed as he placed my drinks on the table. "Well, Livy, would you mind if Andy and I joined you?" he enquired politely as he stretched back up. His sudden gallantry made my eyebrows furrow. How was it possible to host both a gentleman and the Devil himself in the same vessel? Flummoxed, I watched him.

"No, of course not," Olivia answered with a dazzling grin.

"I mind," I declared.

Immediately, William turned towards me with a sardonic smile. "You don't get a say, I'm afraid."

"Pardon?"

He faced Olivia again while pointing his thumb at me. "Is she always such a handful?"

In turn, Olivia studied me with clear humour in her eyes. "Takes one to know one?" she replied cheekily. As thanks for the support, I wanted to kiss her entire face like an excited dog.

William laughed. "I suppose I deserved that."

I rushed to grab the available seat beside her on the small sofa so that I wouldn't be forced to sit next to him, and after leaving my purse on the floor beside my feet, I leaned next to her ear.

"I don't know what he wants, but my name's Sandra, okay? Short for Cassandra," I whispered.

Olivia pursed her lips. "He wants you, but alright."

I scoffed before I continued in another whisper, "Andy split from his girlfriend earlier today. Just thought you should know – unless William was only telling a lie, of course."

She gave me a nod to confirm that she'd heard me.

"So, Sandra," William said as he fetched a chair over, "now that you're done whispering about me, why don't you tell me a bit about yourself?" Descending into his seat, he sat at a right angle from me. Intimidated, I instantly recoiled towards Olivia.

That was what he was – intimidating, and immensely so.

"I'd rather not."

He chuckled. "Are you students? You look a bit younger than the average woman here," he probed, eyes shifting between Olivia and me.

"We are," Olivia confirmed, and I was immediately alarmed.

Worried she would inadvertently expose my real identity, I hurried to say, "Livy's studying law at UCL."

A glance passed between William and Andrew then.

"Are you?" Andrew asked her.

Catching on to my deceit, she glanced in my direction. Nevertheless, she proceeded with honesty, "Yes. I'm in my third and final year now."

"And how do you like it?" Andrew followed up while he brought a stool over to sit across from her.

"I love it, but it's very demanding."

A chuckle escaped both men and, again, a message I couldn't quite decode passed between their eyes.

"What's funny?" I asked.

While directing his attention to me, William struggled to suppress his grin. "Well, both Andy and I are lawyers, so it's just a bit charming to hear a student's perspective."

Points for Jason. Lawyers did, in fact, frequent this place. "Are you barristers?" I asked.

William shook his head and folded his hands together. "Solicitors. Corporate kind."

"I see. So you're colleagues, then?"

"Yeah."

"And how's working with corporate law? Is it compelling?" I had a personal interest in whatever he had to say now. Was I networking unknowingly?

William smiled, and I thought it was because I was finally expressing signs of interest. "Certainly. Initially, I wanted to specialise in human rights, but my father swayed my mind. I'm glad he did."

I was taking mental notes. Like William, I aspired to be a solicitor rather than a barrister, regardless of whether the latter weighed heavier in matters of prestige.

As I looked diagonally across the table, I caught Andrew's eye. Seeing an opportunity to taunt William, I deliberately gave him a seductive smile before I asked with feigned interest, "How about you, Andy? Have you always wanted to practise company law?"

Noting my behaviour, his eyes flickered in William's direction. "I was never really sure until I completed the LPC."

"But I'd like to know more about you," William insisted and leaned forward to demand my attention.

I frowned. "You can't always get what you want."

While scrutinising me, his eyes narrowed somewhat. "Since you specified that Olivia is a law student earlier, I think it's fair to assume you're studying something else. Otherwise, you'd be more likely to say, 'we're studying law'. And considering the nature of your earlier insults, I'm going to take a wild guess and say psychology."

A giggle surged out of me. "Well done, Sherlock."

He didn't look convinced. "No," he murmured as he continued to analyse my reaction. "That was too easy – I was wrong. It's something else, isn't it?"

Olivia nudged my arm then, and when I looked over, I saw disapproval in her features. It would seem that William had managed to stir her sympathy to some extent, and now she was asking me to share her sentiment.

After a sigh, I returned my gaze to William's. "I study medicine,"

I lied. I knew enough about the coursework from Jason to be able to make it convincing.

His eyebrows climbed higher up his forehead. "Really? Here in London?"

"No, in Edinburgh. I'm only visiting Livy for the weekend," I continued to lie.

While it was hardly detectable, I noticed that his eyebrows twitched. In fact, if I hadn't known better, I would have thought he looked a bit disappointed. "Oh. Edinburgh," he repeated to himself. "Well, medicine – that's impressive. Decided what to specialise in?"

I shook my head. "No. Not yet."

William nodded and leaned back again. All the while, he continued to stare at me as if he were observing every corner of my soul. His gaze was remarkably piercing – penetrative, as if he could catch a glimpse into my core with a mere glance. It made me wonder if he hadn't already discerned all my lies.

"Well, the mother I love to sleep with is an oncologist," he eventually said.

I blinked. "Oh. Well, that explains everything. You've clearly got a type."

My joke extracted a laugh from him. "And you clearly embody all the necessary characteristics of said type."

"Just my luck."

His eyes gleamed with amusement. "Anyway, are you in your third year as well?"

I groaned. "Is this an interview or something?"

He stood no chance of hiding his grin when he turned to his colleague. "She's lovely, isn't she?"

Andrew smirked. "Indeed."

Taken aback, a blush emerged on my cheeks. Were they patronising me, or were they sincere? Olivia sniggered beside me, unwilling to come to my aid. Meanwhile, William faced me again.

"I'm worried I might have fucked up my chance completely," he said, although he seemed to be speaking to Andrew still.

"You have," I assured him.

"How do I change your mind?"

I scoffed. "You're the lawyer. Shouldn't you know how to sway one's opinion?"

I heard a strange sound beside me then, much like a strangled laugh, and when I looked over, I saw that Andrew was looking anywhere but at me while he tried to fight back a massive grin.

"You're quite right," William replied, summoning my attention again, and once I fixed my gaze on him, I could have sworn his eyes were aflame with something I had no experience dealing with.

"I'll start with this," he continued. "We have definitely not met before. There's not a chance I wouldn't remember you, for several reasons."

Sceptical, I raised a brow. "Such as?"

"Aside from the obvious?"

"What's obvious?"

"Well, the obvious is that you're really quite stunning, physically speaking, but then that's seldom enough to capture my interest, much less my memory. You see, beauty isn't in short supply in this world, but yours is.

"What's not so obvious at first sight – regarding any person, really – is your admirable integrity, sharp wit and keen intellect. Ultimately, you're a rather bewitching woman, and quite impossible to forget, I expect."

My breath caught in my throat at his climactic declaration. Meanwhile, Olivia and Andrew stilled beside me, awaiting my reaction. Since my mouth appeared to have disconnected from my brain, I merely stared at him while I tried to process his memorable confession.

Seeming to realise that I had completely lost track of space and time, Olivia quickly nudged my arm to help me reconnect with it. Returning to my senses, I gave William a genuine smile to express my gratitude. His earlier insult, where he had accused me of not being a memorable encounter, had angered me more than

I'd expected it to. It was the way he had phrased it, as if I were an escort offering my services.

I struggled to form a decent reply. "I appreciate that, but I meant what I said earlier – you do look familiar. Livy thinks so as well."

Visibly reluctant, he gave Olivia his attention. "Do I?"

She nodded. "No idea why, though. Have you been on telly?"

He chuckled. "No."

"Newspaper?" I asked.

William cocked his head. "Once or twice. Work-related, though."

I narrowed my eyes at him. "How old are you?"

"Now who wants to know?" he countered, humoured.

I rolled my eyes.

"Tell you what," he said, "for every question you ask, I get to ask one as well."

"No deal."

"Oh, come on, love. What have you got to lose?"

"My dignity."

He burst out laughing, and it occurred to me that I wasn't going to get an answer from him anytime soon.

"How old is he, Andy?" I enquired and turned towards him. Hoping to resemble a version of a puppy, I pouted at him, but his responding scoff proved my efforts ineffective.

"Sorry, love, you're on your own."

I sighed. It was worth a shot.

Wearing a sly smile, William sent his friend a nod of gratitude before he said, "Looks like Livy's finished her drink. Perhaps you could get her another one, Andy?"

Grinning back at William, Andrew stood and then turned to regard Olivia. "It would be my absolute pleasure."

"I'll come with you," Olivia offered, enthused, and pushed herself out of the sofa. Immediately, colour reduced in my face while my heart skipped a beat.

Was she blind to the fact that this was precisely what William had intended? Or did she mean to go along with it? Was she going to abandon me to the care of this dreadful man? This horribly intriguing creature that I did not want to succumb to?

"Don't leave me," I pleaded.

Visibly amused, she directed her eyes to mine. "You're a grown woman, Sandra. You'll be alright. We've all seen that you can fend for yourself."

From the faint pink in her cheeks, it was obvious that she desired time alone with Andrew, but it would cost me severely. William had piqued my interest to the extent that I considered it morally wrong. He wasn't right in the head. He was rude, and he was bloody attractive.

Lethal combination.

As I continued to entreat her with my eyes, William conceitedly asked, "Yes, I wonder what you're scared of. Starting to get under your skin, am I?"

My gaze dashed to his at once, and I proceeded to glare at him while Andrew and Olivia headed for the bar. "You will not be getting anywhere near my skin. What's the matter with you?"

He shrugged. "Right now, you."

"What do you want?"

"I'd like to get to know you better. Isn't that what you wanted in the first place? I mean, you approached us first."

"Specifically your friend," I reminded him tersely.

His head tilted, and even though he concealed it well, I thought I recognised hurt somewhere deep within his eyes. I must have bruised his ego. "Oh, so that's what this is?" he queried flatly. "I'm not cutting it?"

Since it was far from the truth, my conscience suffered at the impression I was clearly giving off. Blowing out my cheeks, I leaned forward to grab my gin and tonic, and while I was raising it to my lips, I hurriedly said, "No, that's not quite it."

Since I wasn't looking at him anymore, William leaned forward again to attract my gaze, and once he captured it, he scoured it thoroughly. Meanwhile, he folded his hands between his thighs and allowed his thumbs to rub together. "So, I do make the cut?" he asked then, ever slick.

I couldn't fight my smile. "There is no 'cut' to make, Will. I'm not here looking for anything if that's what you mean."

"Then how come you approached us to begin with?"

My eyes darted in Olivia's direction, but since I didn't want to expose her, I was quick to avert them again. Alas, he didn't fail to notice my wandering attention. As soon as he turned his head to observe Olivia and Andrew by the bar, he stated, "Right. I get it now. You were winging her."

When he looked back at me for confirmation, I merely returned his gaze so as not to reveal anything. Suddenly, a grin claimed his mouth. I frowned in puzzlement.

"It's been a long time since I've gone on the prowl," he said, "but if I'm not wrong, you approached him because she was initially interested in me." He leaned back. "What a textbook performance. Didn't work, though."

I had to give it to him – the man was remarkably perceptive. His aptitude for reading social situations was outstanding. Nevertheless, he still hadn't detected my lies – or at least it seemed that way.

I scoffed. "Doesn't matter. As soon as you opened your dreadful mouth, her interest shifted onto your friend instead."

William laughed wholeheartedly. "I'm not even slightly upset. She's not my type."

"You mean she doesn't remind you of your mother?"

He rolled his eyes. "Either way, she's clearly not interested anymore, so there's nothing holding you back. You've got a green light to get to know me."

"I'm sorry, didn't you hear what I just said? I'm not interested in anything other than helping Livy out."

He surprised me when he suddenly stood. "Right, well, if that's the case, I'll just head over to them if you don't mind. Shame if that sabotages Olivia's chances."

"Wait, wait – fine!" I urged and raised my hand to halt him.

"I'll entertain you."

Releasing a satisfied sigh, he sank into his seat and folded his hands just above his crotch. "That's more like it," he said, and I desperately wanted to tear the smirk off his face.

"You're insufferable," I grumbled.

"You're only upset because I've outwitted you."

"Why are you so determined to get to know me?"

"Because you've seriously piqued my interest."

Again, his directness caught me off guard, and just like before, my heart began to pound harshly. Each thump of it pressed against my ribcage to the extent that a keen eye could probably see it. Because of it, I was starting to realise that my body wanted something quite different from my mind.

"I commend your grit at least," I muttered and placed my drink back on the table. Folding my arms, I hoped to hide my vigorous heartbeats.

Another smirk climbed to his annoyingly kissable mouth. "Thanks. I'm quite pleased with that attribute myself," he said while moving off his chair to grab the vacant spot beside me on the sofa.

I stiffened when he draped his arm over the back of it, across my shoulders. It wasn't that I minded the intimacy. On the contrary, I seemed to fancy it more than I was willing to admit.

"Listen, let's start over, yeah?" he proposed. "I realise it's a poor excuse, but I've had a rough day at work. To make it worse, Andy and Chloe have been together for an entire decade. She's practically my sister. So, when I heard the news – two minutes before you arrived – I wasn't in the right frame of mind to handle you well," he continued to explain. "I'm very sorry. I truly am."

He brought me closer to him, and as I mellowed against his warm body, the scent of him struck me hard. He smelled intoxicating. Drugged, I inhaled the fragrance deep into my lungs. I picked up testosterone, something dark, something sweet, and plenty of challenge.

My Achilles' heel.

"You smell amazing," I blurted out without thinking. "What fragrance is that?" Indeed, he smelled remarkable – even better than Jason did.

Soft laughter poured out of him as he leaned forward to grab one of my drinks. "Stick around, and perhaps I'll tell you. And you smell rather amazing yourself." As he leaned back again, he continued, "On another note, you've got three of these to finish."

He raised my espresso martini towards my mouth, and he did not stop until he had placed the glass to my waiting lips. Consequently, my lips parted not because of the cold and solid material against my skin, but rather because of his surprising gesture. Wearing a complacent smile, he tilted the glass and carefully poured a portion of the cocktail into my mouth.

I watched him the whole time, overwhelmed by his sensuality. I had never met a man quite so slickly domineering before. I had an inkling he was in the habit of getting his way.

He lowered the glass to allow my swallow, and as I did, he watched me intensely. Meanwhile, the expression on his face was strangely erotic. Was he imagining me swallowing something else?

"I guarantee you, Sandra, that had we slept together, I would not have forgotten. So, where you might have seen me before, I don't know – but I wish it were in bed."

3

WON'T YOU COME IN?

ALL AIR WAS EXPELLED FROM MY LUNGS, AND I COULD NOT look away from him. He had me trapped in his gaze.

Astonished, I asked, "Are you always this crude?"

"Sorry," he apologised insincerely and placed my cocktail back on the table. "I can't seem to think straight in your presence. My tongue travels before my mind."

When the edge of his mouth tucked up to form a crooked smile, I recognised it as the one he'd already presented several times. It was unique to him, and a testament to his cunning and calculating persona. The shape of it whispered tales of his intellectual conquests, of how sublimely he outwitted any opponent. Anyone could have been fooled by the invincibility it exuded, and yet, despite this, I thought I detected a hint of veiled vulnerability, and it intrigued me.

"Anyway," he interrupted my analysis, "though I haven't been acting my age, I'm twenty-eight. How old are you?"

Since I saw no harm in sharing this detail about myself, I replied, "Twenty-three."

"So you're in your—"

"Ah-ah," I interrupted. "My turn," I said while pointing my finger to my chest. His eyes dropped towards it, and it dawned on me then that I had directed his gaze straight to my cleavage. Immediately, a wave of heat flooded my face, causing a crimson blush to penetrate my faint layer of makeup. I rushed to entwine my fingers in my lap. When I glanced at William, he looked equally bothered, his gaze veering to Olivia and Andrew instead.

Was it possible that he harboured at least a modicum of respect for me? I had just provided him with a golden opportunity to ogle my breasts, but instead, he'd hastily looked elsewhere. It increased my faith in him. Perhaps he wasn't so terrible after all.

"First impressions," he muttered. "They can be surprisingly difficult to disprove."

I chuckled. "Spoken like a true solicitor."

He gave me a wry smile. "Your turn, you said. What would you like to know?"

Where to begin? Glancing at Olivia and Andrew, I was reminded of his companion. They seemed like good friends, and that made me curious. "How long have you known Andy for?"

"My entire life. My turn." He grinned. "What are your interests, aside from medicine?"

That was a substantial question. "Um, I have eclectic tastes, so I find that question too vast to answer. You'll need to filter it down."

He sighed, and I thought it was in despair. "What do you spend your leisure time doing?"

I scoffed. "Leisure time? What leisure time?"

"Have you got a boyfriend?" he suddenly tossed at me.

I stiffened. "That's none of your business."

A lascivious gleam entered his arresting eyes, and it captured me wholly. All I wanted was to explore the dancing blue depths. In so many ways, he seemed like a promise of pleasure. Given his level of self-assurance, I couldn't imagine that he'd disappoint between the sheets, so why did I deny myself the chance to explore his potential?

His smile turned crooked again. "I assure you, darling, it is."

Unsure of his insinuation, I looked away. I had a faint idea, but I wanted to be certain. Frankly, I wanted to hear him confess it. "How so?"

There wasn't a trace of a smile present on his face when he answered, "Because I'd like to see you again. So, if you've got a boyfriend, I'll need to know. I'll have to reassess my tactics, then."

I gaped at him. "Reassess your tactics?" I echoed disbelievingly. "Are you trying to say that if I do have a boyfriend, you won't respect it?"

"No, I'll respect it – physically." He glanced away before murmuring, "But I'll try and tempt you to leave him."

"You're ruthless," I accused. Was he drunk?

"Which you need," he claimed with a smirk.

I frowned. "You don't even know me."

"No, I don't, but I've got a vague idea of what I'm dealing with. My intuition tends to serve me well."

"You're so cocky it borders on madness," I exclaimed. "Are you drunk, William?"

His eyebrows furrowed. "What makes you think that? No. I've had two cocktails."

"Because your head is messed up."

"You've messed it up."

I snorted. He'd have to do better than that. "That's ridiculous. What a rubbish line."

"Better than 'have we met?', though."

I glared at him, and he glared straight back.

After a brief while, he tilted his head and watched me as though he were trying to solve an enigma. "If you actually had a boyfriend," he said with narrowed eyes, "I doubt you'd allow me to keep my arm around you like this – much less let me pour your drink into your mouth. Then again, you could just be a partner liable to cheating, but I seriously doubt you're the type."

I leaned forward to grab my espresso martini. "I don't see

why we're even entertaining this question. You said you want to know because you'd like to see me again, but in case you've already forgotten, I live in Edinburgh."

"Sure, but for now, you're still in London. How long are you staying?"

"Will," I shook my head, "I'm not going to set aside time to see you. I'm here to visit my friend."

"Who is obviously interested in getting laid," he replied, head cocking in her direction. Looking over, I discovered her laughing at something Andrew must have said. "I'm sure she'd appreciate it if I took you off her hands, at least for tonight," William continued.

While it had been on the cards, his proposal still took me by surprise. As soon as I turned my head to regard him again, his eyes blazed into mine – two blue flames, wild in their craving for me.

In the orange light of the place, he resembled something of the divine. A Greek god, perhaps, and I was only a mere mortal. How was I supposed to resist such celestial temptation? I was submitting to his power more by the second.

I struggled to fathom the reality that I had only met this man mere moments ago. Our chemistry was clearly off the charts.

When I had spent too long contemplating his offer, his impatience got the better of him. "Listen," he said, "we can either spend all night bickering, or we can spend this ridiculous energy in my bed. It's up to you." His voice was terse and to the point while his gaze burrowed into mine. "Either way, you would be doing both yourself and your friend a favour by joining me back at mine."

Pink and breathless, I looked away from him. This man surely didn't beat around the bush. He hadn't even kissed me yet, and now he was suggesting sex? What sort of a scene was he into? No-strings-attached, I reckoned. That notion filled me with relief, because I didn't have the capacity for romance at this point in my life.

To buy more time, I raised my drink. "I'm not nearly drunk enough for this," I replied and then filled my mouth with the liquid courage. Humoured, William watched me drain the remaining contents.

"I fancy my women responsive, Sandra, so please keep the intake to a minimum," he warned.

"You're speaking as if I've agreed," I countered and placed my empty glass back on the table. Just as I was about to reach for my next drink, a large and unfamiliar hand took hold of my jaw. Turning my face towards him, William leaned in so close that our noses touched. Only then did he pause his advances.

My breath abandoned me at once. Within me, my heart throbbed with bittersweet delight. It was begging me to give in – to allow myself a night I would never forget. Besides, it wasn't like I hadn't had a one-night stand before. Hell, I often preferred them. The less they knew, the better.

I wasn't at a point in my life where romantic companionship was even remotely appealing. It was far too time-consuming a venture. I had my studies to mind – my ambitions to realise. I was a millennial woman, and fiercely independent at that. Intellectual pursuits were my main priority.

However, I was still a sexual creature. I had needs. While I had Aaron to fulfil them, my casual arrangement with him allowed me to have one-night stands, which I occasionally indulged in. Tonight, William wanted me to treat myself to another one. So, why was I being so difficult? Because he'd been an arsehole at first? What did that matter if I wasn't going to see him again? Plus, he had apologised, and now he wanted to make amends – properly.

The light-blue colour of his eyes struck through my defences while he gently released my jaw. Trailing his thumb across my cheek, he then buried his large hand in my long, wavy brown hair.

His voice was as mollifying as a lullaby when he said, "I want you to know that if you decide to join me, I'll have no expectations. I'd be happy just to talk all night."

My heart throbbed again. Seduced by the sensual promise that basked in his eyes, I gave him a faint nod.

"I'm going to kiss you," he warned.

Utterly at his mercy, I swallowed. I couldn't move another

muscle. He had me completely spellbound.

"Okay." It was barely a whisper that escaped my mouth.

After a lopsided smile, he pressed his soft mouth to mine, and I marvelled at the taste of him. Only seconds into it, I knew he was the best kisser I'd ever encountered. His lips moved tenderly across my own – gentle at first, until his lust overruled his resistance. With his hand in my hair, he brought me closer, and his remaining arm moved to sweep around me.

While pressing me tightly against him, he kissed me like I'd never been kissed. It set my heart on fire. No words could ever match the immense feeling. Kissing someone had never felt so right.

The mere motion of his lips overwhelmed me. So simply, he made me feel like the most precious thing alive – as if he couldn't bring himself to stop until he had devoured all of me. Untamed and famished, he pushed his tongue into my mouth to explore the rest of me, and I, rather earnestly, welcomed him.

It was only when blood rushed towards my sex that I realised why this particular kiss affected me so. For the first time in my life, kissing someone didn't feel like a mandatory part of seduction. I actually wanted this. I wanted to kiss him – I was desperate to. In fact, I never wanted to stop.

But he pulled away far too soon. Breaking away, he leaned forward to grab my drinks for me. He shoved them into my hands, impatient, while he stared intensely into my eyes.

Breathless, he ordered, "Neck these. Then we're leaving. Non-negotiable. I'm not wasting a second longer."

I obeyed without protest. Afterwards, he clasped my hand in his and stood while dragging me up with him.

But all of a sudden, something was off about him. His gaze was fleeting, and he looked a bit lost, even dazed.

It surprised me. He didn't strike me as the type of man who would respond so profoundly to a mere kiss. Taking his expertise of the art into account, I was confident he'd kissed his fair share of women.

So, was it possible that the same flame that had spread through my system like wildfire had also touched him? I found that hard to believe. He was too much of a stoic for it, much too nonchalant and arrogant.

He started towards the exit, meaning we'd have to pass the bar where Olivia and Andrew sat chatting. Once we reached them, Olivia studied us bewildered. Was it the look on my face? It had to be.

"We'll be off," William announced and released my hand to wrap his arm around my waist instead.

Olivia released a laugh. "Sandra, you devil."

"Devil, indeed," William confirmed and shot me a look that I didn't understand.

"Will you be alright by yourself, love?" I asked Olivia, concerned. There wasn't a chance I would leave her behind if she didn't approve. If that meant losing my one shot at a sensational night, then so be it. My duty as her best friend would come first.

She eyed me shrewdly. "Will you?"

"I'll take good care of her, Livy. You have my word," William assured her, suddenly the gallant man again, rather than the greedy, libidinous and domineering man I'd just been kissing. I quite fancied them both.

"You better. I know who you are, should she happen to disappear by the morning," Olivia threatened.

"She might be sleeping until dusk, seeing as she won't be getting much rest tonight, so don't be concerned if she doesn't answer her phone first thing in the morning," William informed her.

Andrew chuckled beside my gaping blonde friend. "He's a bit of a character, but you get used to him. Very blunt, is all."

"Blunt, indeed," I mumbled under my breath.

"It was lovely to make your acquaintance, Livy. I hope we'll meet again," William stated before he leaned in to offer her cheek a peck. "You're a sweet girl. Again, I'm sorry about earlier."

"Y-yeah. Me too," she stammered and met my eyes with evident concern, and I knew why. 'I hope we'll meet again.' I hoped it was only his courteous side speaking, because as far as I was aware, this was a one-time arrangement. Had I jumped the gun by assuming that no-strings-attached was mutually understood?

"I'll see you Monday, Andy," William continued to his friend, who responded with a perceptive smirk.

"Looking forward to it. Have fun."

Without replying, William dragged me towards the cloakroom, and his impatience was clear from his long strides.

"Do you live nearby?" I asked on our way there.

"Yes," he answered before I heard him mutter under his breath, "and thank fuck for that."

§ § §

"Have you got the time?" I wondered aloud when he had guided me along the streets of Soho for a few minutes. Raising the hand that wasn't holding mine, William eyed his wristwatch. I swallowed as I recognised the brand – a Rolex.

Glancing up at his profile, I realised that he reeked of upper-class wealth, and I wasn't ensnared by it. Rich people could sometimes be dreadfully arrogant with their aristocratic tendencies. However, since I wasn't one for prejudice, I wouldn't let his potential fortune define my impression of him. Besides, Jason came from a wealthy background as well, and he was as close to an ideal human being as could be.

"Ten to ten," William said and tugged me closer.

"Ten to ten? I was only there for about an hour?" I replied, astounded. Had he managed to seduce me that fast? How licentious of me – and I wasn't even tipsy!

Seemingly amused, he glanced at me from the corner of his eye. "If it's any consolation, I didn't leave you much choice," he said and rounded a corner to enter Wardour Street.

I frowned at myself. Was I really so desperate for him that I couldn't last much longer than an hour? Poor Olivia. I hoped I hadn't ruined her evening.

"Do you think Andy will take good care of Livy?" I enquired worriedly. "I feel like I'm being a rubbish friend."

"Again, I didn't leave you much choice."

I halted promptly. "We ought to head back."

William chuckled. "I'm afraid I disagree. You're really doing her a favour, Sandra."

"But what if I'm not? What if Andy rejects her and she ends up alone tonight?"

From the wrinkle that formed across his nose, I got the impression that he could understand where I was coming from but – for selfish reasons – felt disinclined to oblige.

Since he struggled to form a reply, I retrieved my hand from his grasp and continued to argue, "You said yourself that you expect Andy will get back with his girlfriend. Don't you think he'll reject Livy because of that? He's probably not ready to be with someone else, especially so soon after spending an entire decade with his ex."

A sigh poured from his mouth while his shoulders sank, and he proceeded to study me for a brief while. Appearing to reach a conclusion to his contemplations, he confessed, "I'm tempted to lie because I'd like to be alone with you. But, at the same time, I wouldn't want it to bite me in the arse later on, so I'll be honest. Andy's unlikely to sleep with your friend. He's still in shambles over Chloe."

It was my turn to sigh. "Right. Well then," I mumbled and dropped my gaze to my feet.

Had we really met our end already? It seemed so abrupt. "It's just," I said, "I'd like to be alone with you as well, but I don't think it's right to—"

"I get it," he interrupted with a nod. "You're a good friend. I'd have done the same."

After sighing again, I directed my eyes to his and pouted. Since I was unsure of how to proceed, I resorted to admiring his beauty for a while. I could hardly believe I was about to turn him down. Then again, for the sake of friendship, there were few sacrifices I was unwilling to make.

"I'll walk you back," he said after a short silence.

"That's not necessary."

"I insist. London's not safe at night, especially for women

like yourself."

A blush surfaced in my cheeks at his courteous behaviour and indirect compliment. Then, all of a sudden, an idea occurred to me. "You know what?" Reaching into my purse, I fished for my phone. "I could always just call her."

"A perk of the twenty-first century," William joked and earned himself a smile.

I hurried to locate Olivia's number. While she was slow to pick up, at least she did.

"Hello? Is everything okay?" she immediately asked.

"Hi, love. Quick question."

"Yes?"

"Are you absolutely sure you won't mind if I—"

"Oh, for heaven's sake. We've already been over this." I could hear her eyes roll.

"It's just that—"

"Are you still with him?"

"Yes."

"Then don't keep the poor man waiting!"

"But Livy, there's something you ought to know first."

"What?"

"I don't think Andy's interested in the same as you."

She was quiet for a beat before I heard her murmur to someone, "I'm so sorry. Please excuse me for a minute."

A few seconds of silence elapsed before her voice returned. "Hello, Cara?"

"Yes, I'm still here. Did you hear what I said?"

"Yes, but so what?"

I frowned. "What do you mean 'so what'?"

"Why should that matter?"

"Wasn't your aim tonight to..." I paused to steal a glance at William. Lowering my voice, I continued, "find a man?"

"Oh my God. Cara, I'll have plenty of opportunities to find a rebound in the future. I love you for caring so much, but I wouldn't dream of getting in your way. Besides, I'm genuinely enjoying myself. Andy's a really sweet guy, and he's actually hilarious. To be perfectly honest, I started friend-zoning him even before you called to warn me."

Unsure of her sincerity, I asked, "Really?"

"Really. In fact, it dawned on me while we've been chatting that I don't need to sleep with a stranger to reinstate my status as a single woman. What I need is an actual connection with someone. A one-night stand isn't going to provide that, and it's not going to help me get over Colin, either. Frankly, I think sleeping with Andy would've made me feel like shit. I'd feel used again, which is the last thing I need right now. Only a new, genuine connection is going to help me move past Colin."

Impressed with her rationale, my eyebrows arched. "Points for introspection, Livy. I'm glad you've got such a healthy mind."

"Are you being sarcastic?"

I tittered. While I had a habit of being sarcastic, I wasn't now. "No. I'm being sincere. I'm impressed."

"Thank you! Honestly, I'm a bit impressed myself if I can say that."

"You can," I chuckled.

"Well then. With that out of the way, you can stop worrying about me. I'll be fine. Get back to your man. I'll want to hear every single detail in the morning."

"Okay. Speak soon, then."

"Yes. Love you."

"Love you too."

As soon as I rang off, I gave William a grin while stuffing my phone back into my purse. "She doesn't want him that way either, apparently."

His responding grin far outmatched mine. "Problem's solved then, I take it?"

"Seems that way."

"Brilliant. She say why?"

"Well, like Andy, she's recently split from her partner as well."

"I see."

"Now, then. Where to?"

"Right this way," he said and reached for my hand again. As soon as our skin made contact, my heart contracted in the most peculiar way. In fact, I couldn't recall having experienced a similar sensation in all my life. It was almost painful in its intensity.

"Besides," I said once we started walking, "I'm sure she could use a sympathetic shoulder to lean on, which Andy can provide. I've no idea what it's like to endure a break-up, so I'm sure she appreciates speaking with someone who understands, even if they don't go into it."

"You've never had a boyfriend?" William enquired, seemingly astonished.

I shook my head. "Nor am I looking for one."

"Why not?" he queried, and I found his tone slightly odd, as if he were feigning nonchalance towards the subject.

"Because I don't have the time that's required for a happy one."

"Please elaborate."

"I'm very dedicated to my studies," I explained. "So, firstly, I can't afford to be preoccupied with a man, as I'm sure it would divide my attention. Secondly, he wouldn't deserve to get only leftover scraps of my time, which is what would happen."

Glancing up, I thought William looked quite impressed with my reasoning. "Is that the real reason you're reluctant to see me again?"

Yet again, his directness caught me off guard. "You're very forward," I commented.

"Don't digress."

My heart slowed while I gazed blankly ahead. He was putting me on the spot, and it was uncomfortable. I worried my honesty would change his mind, but I decided to share it anyway.

"Yes."

I could, of course, have resorted to a lie, but I wasn't in the habit of mistreating people. If his feelings were under threat of being toyed with, he deserved to know. I would have wanted as much for myself.

"I see." William nodded. "And it's never occurred to you to let your suitors be the judge of that?"

"Of what?"

"Of whether they'd be content with only 'leftover scraps' of your time."

Facing him, I lingered on a step. "I – no. Why should I? Wouldn't that involve inviting the risk in the first place?"

He shrugged. "I suppose. Then again, the reward you'd reap would be invaluable."

"But the odds of achieving that are astronomical." I shook my head. "I really don't think it's the best tactic."

"And there's no way I can convince you otherwise?"

Stealing a glance at him, I noticed that he was consciously keeping his gaze from meeting mine.

I sighed. He might be the most alluring man I'd ever met, but I was a rational woman. I knew meeting him again would be sealing my doom. He was a little *too* alluring.

I could manage one night without getting attached to him, but another was a different story entirely. My attraction to him was too immense to ignore. I'd never been so captured by another individual before, and surely not so fast. It made me fear his power over me. If we met again, I didn't trust that I'd be able to resist growing fond of him. I didn't trust myself not to give in to temptation. I would want to explore more of him – every corner of his enigmatic mind, and every fibre of his mouth-watering anatomy.

I couldn't have that. Not now. I didn't have the capacity for it. I was a top student. Becoming infatuated could ruin that, and I wasn't about to take the risk. To add to that, I wasn't interested in making a commitment to someone when I knew I'd fall short of their expectations – and, even in the event that I didn't, my reverence for them would tell me they deserved better than what I could offer.

"I'm afraid not."

William chuckled, but it was a humourless sound. "Well,

I'll try either way. For starters, I both admire and respect your dedication to your studies. If you agree to meet me again, you'll find that out for yourself. I wouldn't dream of getting in the way of your education."

Somewhat surprised, I looked up at him. "I appreciate that, but I'm afraid it's out of your hands. You don't get to decide how I respond to something. This is what I've spent the past three years doing, and I'm not inclined to change my ways for you."

Faint irritation swelled in his eyes upon my rejection. With a clenched jaw, he glared away. "I must admit," he said, "I'm a bit shocked your sole intention tonight is to use me for your own sexual benefit. What the hell is that all about?"

Guilt flooded my body. Unsure of what to say, I fell silent while he continued, "Please don't tell me it's due to some discreditable idea of feminism, because that's nothing short of toxic feminism, and you're doing every feminist – myself included – a great dishonour and disservice by acting like it's not."

He couldn't have been more wrong. With eyes that sought acquittal, I replied vehemently, "No, of course not. I just assumed that sex with no strings attached was mutually understood and agreed upon."

"Well, you assumed wrong," he retorted. "Fuck's sake. You could have warned me."

Wearing a pout, I sighed. "Well, I'm warning you now – and I'm sorry. I do—" I paused and motioned towards him—"fancy you. I'm just not interested in anything more than one night."

He was silent for a beat, contemplating. This was it, I realised.

"I suppose I'll just have to fuck you so well that you'll change your mind," he finally asserted.

Air stormed out of my lungs like someone had just punched me in the gut. I doubted I'd ever get used to the shocking – yet somehow arousing – effect of his vulgar tongue. Frankly, I wondered at that moment just what else his tongue was capable of.

"But if you don't mind my saying," he continued before I could catch my breath, "I think you're being ridiculous. Law isn't an easy path of education either, and I completed my degree at Cambridge. Even so, I still found time for romantic endeavours. That should speak volumes."

I gaped. He'd studied at Cambridge? No wonder his intellect had impressed me earlier.

Smirking, he placed his index finger below my chin and closed my mouth. "Something to consider," he added. "You can gape later, when we're naked in my flat."

The mouth of this man rendered me speechless. It must have earned him a slap or two during his lifetime.

He didn't bother waiting for my response. Instead, he started towards the entrance of an elegant white building with warehouse-style windows. A Starbucks resided on the ground floor. Was he a regular there?

He entered a code on a keypad to unlock the front door that was next to the Starbucks, and after pushing it open, he stepped aside to let me enter. As if I'd walked into a past era, I gazed around the splendid reception area where marble made up the floor and walls. "Nice building," I remarked.

He didn't respond. Instead, he guided me towards the lift and pushed the button. The doors opened immediately. After ushering me in, he joined me inside and pressed the digits of a code again. We watched the doors slide shut, and as they did, I mentally thanked myself for having shaved earlier that day.

Gravity gently tugged my gut as we rode up, but it was nothing compared to the magnetism the man beside me exuded. He seemed electric, and it was making me increasingly nervous. Looking over, I saw that he was completely composed. Was I the only one struggling to resist sexual urges? It seemed that way. That notion bruised my ego so much that a pout dominated my face.

"I hope you're not a Patrick Bateman," I murmured, hoping to lighten the atmosphere. From the corner of my eye, I saw his lips twitch.

"An American psycho? How could I be? I'm not a Yank."

"Ha-ha."

He grinned to himself. "I'm afraid the only thing I've in common with Mr Bateman is a taste for the finer things in life," he replied and, for emphasis, lowered his hand from my back to gently pat my bum.

A second later, we arrived at our destination, which I noted was on the top floor. The doors parted to reveal a vestibule where a dark brown entrance door interrupted the wall straight ahead. With a gentle push, he encouraged me to approach it.

Here as well, a code was required to unlock the door, and he entered it quickly. Turning the handle, he revealed a marvellous and spacious flat. Complementing the exterior door, solid dark brown wood served for a floor. Surrounding it were cream-coloured walls decorated with a fair number of contemporary paintings. The interior was undeniably modern, though with a touch of old-fashioned moments.

He stepped in first to hold the door for me, and when his eyes met mine again, they were lit with desire alone.

"Please, Sandra. Won't you come in?" he asked, and his voice was an invitation in and of itself.

SATISFIED?

WITH MY BREATH STUCK IN MY THROAT, I WALKED IN and was just about to remove my heels when William clasped my wrist to tug me harshly towards him. As I slammed into his robust body, the little air I had left was knocked out.

"I'd rather you kept those on," he purred and then dipped down to engulf my mouth. Wide-eyed, I mellowed against him, utterly at his mercy. The effect this man had on me was beyond my comprehension. I felt like a snake hypnotised by its master's flute.

While his mouth demanded possession of mine, he shut the door. The sound of it being locked made my heart skip a beat. I was both literally and figuratively trapped, and yet I harboured no desire to escape. Then, was I truly trapped? Perhaps I was suffering a mild case of Stockholm syndrome, because I was surely in favour of my captor.

The taste and scent of him was intoxicating. How had it come to this? I definitely hadn't been expecting his attention earlier tonight. And yet, here I was, about to ravish him while I explored every bit of his tantalising body.

He didn't waste a second. Impatiently, he slipped his tongue into my mouth and reached for the sash of my coat to untie it. As soon as it came undone, he spread it apart and grabbed my waist to press me against him. Without breaking from his mouth, I shrugged out of my coat and let it fall to the floor behind me. The second it landed, he pinned me forcefully against the wall, and the impact caused me to groan into his mouth. Upon the sound, his smile interfered with our passionate kiss.

"You know…" he cooed as he moved to trace soft kisses down the slope of my neck. When he found my throbbing pulse, he gently sucked and nibbled on it. The sensation of it made my eyes close. So quickly, he'd located one of the most sensitive areas of my body. "Despite the sorry excuse for a man that I am, you seem to find yourself so lost and desperate that you've wound up in my bed after all."

Using my own words against me, he riled me.

"Is that supposed to arouse me?"

"No. However, it certainly aroused me," he countered with a smug chuckle. When he suddenly thrust his crotch against me, my lips parted. His erection strained against the lower part of my abdomen as a silent promise of pleasure. The anticipation was thick and dense in the air between us, and it revealed itself in how increasingly erratic our breathing became. Meanwhile, his large hands trailed down my waistline to grip my hips.

"The shape of you should be illegal, love," he stated admiringly and leaned slightly away to get a better look. A moment later, his gaze struck mine like a bullet.

Caught by his allure, a groan leapt over my tongue before I flung my arms around his neck to bring his tempting lips back to mine. As the delectable flavour of him exploded in my mouth, I closed my eyes to savour it. Like an addict, I craved more of the drug-like sensations he evoked. Under his influence, I felt ecstatic.

Expertly, his tongue teased mine with gentle flicks. I'd already fallen victim to his remarkable way of kissing, but that didn't prevent it from mystifying me. How was it possible to be so tender, and yet simultaneously so forceful? He wasn't eating my mouth, and yet I had never felt so devoured. His lips moved according to the bliss-point – the brink between too much and too little.

Needing air, I pulled away, albeit reluctantly. "Where did you learn to kiss like that?"

My question prompted his smirk. "Unfortunately for me, you weren't there."

Pink climbed to my cheeks. When I was about to reply, he distracted me by dropping to his knees.

Puzzled, I wondered, "What are you doing?"

As a response, he folded his hands over the pale skin of my bare knees and brought them over his shoulders. Thinking I was about to fall backwards, I squealed inwardly, but thankfully, the wall behind me served as support.

In silence, I commended his original move. It left me even more curious about what scenes he could orchestrate. So far, he hadn't proved particularly conventional.

At the sound of my stifled squeal, he grinned up at me, and the look in his eyes completely paralysed me. Through long dark lashes, he watched me intensely. Held by his wilful gaze, I didn't object to his next advances. Slowly but confidently, his hands smoothed up my naked thighs, warm and soft, before moving inward. His touch left tingling sensations in its wake, making me pant loudly. Raw arousal flooded my veins the closer he drew to my soaking sex, and all the while, my heart thundered in my chest.

Only then did I realise the state of my black lace knickers. Blushing scarlet, I stared at him bashfully. Not once had he broken eye contact.

When his slow fingers reached the fabric of my wet underwear, he placed the pad of his thumb precisely against my throbbing clit. Acute and sharp, the sensation shot up my spine all the way to my nose. My back arched away from the wall while my hands gathered in his dark brown hair.

My eyes shut.

Holy shit.

"Ah," I groaned as he rubbed gently.

"Sandra… You're drenched," he informed me smugly.

Batting my lashes apart, I was caught yet again by his smouldering stare. He had beautiful eyes. They resembled a serene ocean surrounding a warm paradise. How ironic. He was anything but that.

"No, please. Have me already," I pleaded, high-pitched, and dragged my hands through his hair. It was soft and thick between my fingers.

"Oh, I intend to, darling," he assured me softly. While observing me intently, keenly attuned to any response, he pushed up the fabric of my purple dress to reveal my bum. Appreciative of my bared flesh, he smoothed his hands across the firm curve of it and, carnal in his methods, squeezed my cheeks before he gave my right side a quick, harsh spank. I nearly jerked away from him, but his hold on my hip prevented me.

"Ah," I hissed as the sting of his palm burnt a mark into my skin.

"That's for being a bloody pain in the arse earlier," he growled and gripped my knickers. "Now, how much do you care for these?"

Confused by his question, I watched him. It was difficult to keep up with him. I was much too aroused to stay focused on anything but his hands on me.

"I'll just have to find out then," he murmured after my failure to reply. Shocking me, he ripped my lace thong to shreds between his strong fingers. Overwhelmed by how arousing I found his action to be, I gawked at him.

After discarding the ruined garment by his front door, he leaned in – ever so slowly – to trace the inner side of my thigh with soft kisses.

"Do we need protection?" he murmured as he trailed the tip of his nose across my skin.

"I'm clean," I assured him breathily. "Are you?"

"I am."

I swallowed while I considered whether to trust him. "Good. But I'd prefer if we used a condom either way."

I tensed as his lips grazed closer and closer to my bundle of nerves. Just before he reached it, my fingers formed a fist in his hair to halt his advances.

Noticing my reluctance, he replied, "I'll respect that. However, the scent of you is driving me mad, so I'm willing to risk it. May I?"

I blushed at his vulgar statement. I wasn't used to verbal lovers, but William appeared to be one. Though, surprisingly, it only made him all the more alluring.

If I went along with this, I'd finally discover just what else his tongue was capable of, and that idea was slowly but surely seducing me.

"If you give me anything, I'll have your balls on a platter," I warned.

The cool breath of his chuckle spread across my wet folds, and my jaw clenched.

"I've no doubt you will. However, I won't give you anything other than bliss," he claimed.

I looked at the ceiling as I contemplated whether to surrender to temptation. The desire to feel his tongue on me was too immense to ignore. I badly wanted to assess his talents with it, especially since I was confident it would bring me pure ecstasy. Besides, it seemed unlikely that he'd lie about being clean just for a chance to please me. In the end, what he intended to do was entirely selfless. He wouldn't derive any physical pleasure from it himself.

"Fine. But I'd still prefer to use a condom later on, to diminish the risk."

"You have yourself a deal, love. I can't wait to sample your taste," he answered lustfully and placed a gentle kiss on the spot just above my clit.

For quite some time, he continued to circle it with soft kisses. Rigid and enthralled, I watched his head between my thighs. This teasing was driving me insane. I'd never endured such agonising lust before. He was tantalising to a fault. In fact, if he didn't pick up the pace soon, I'd have to take matters into my own hands.

"Will," I prompted.

Again, he chuckled against my folds, letting his breath fan across them. I inhaled sharply and squeezed my eyes shut.

"All in good time, darling," he reminded me and placed a tender kiss directly on my throbbing bud. God, it felt good. The friction was divine. My legs tensed.

"Again," I begged.

Then, a slick and warm sensation circled my clit, expertly sensitising it. It was his tongue, and it was astounding. My mouth formed a circle as my breath abandoned me.

Lowering his focus, his tongue lapped across my folds to collect my fluids. "Mm. Even better than I'd imagined," he claimed while savouring the taste of me.

What an unbelievably erotic man – novel. Blushing at his words, I opened my eyes to watch him again. He sent me a wink and, while making his return to my flesh, held my gaze.

"Oh," I whined as his tongue drew slow circles. Deliberately, he avoided making direct contact, and it was driving me wild. My blood felt like it was on fire.

Hot and bothered, I pleaded, "Please, Will."

Finally, he caved in. As he swept his tongue directly across my clit, my head jerked back into the wall, but the pleasure he provided numbed out the pain. Resolutely, he increased the speed of his flicks, and his pattern was out of this world – a combination of up and down and round.

He was blowing my mind – literally left, right, and centre – and masterfully crafting a sensational orgasm within me. Never, in my life, would I forget the climax I was about to endure. I was certain.

The tension raged through my veins, and my entire body flexed as I struggled to withstand it. It centred in my lower abdomen, growing larger and larger. When it reached the verge of unbearable, I cried out his name.

Determined to drive me over the edge, he persisted. My toes curled first. Then my shudders started. *Oh no.*

"Ah!" I gasped as the most powerful orgasm I'd ever experienced flooded my body. Convulsing away from the wall, I crouched over him while I tugged his beautiful hair, overcome with relief and a sense of liberation.

Oh, my God.

While I drowned in my pool of bliss, he shoved my legs off his shoulders. Next, he grabbed my waist to hoist me up against the wall. Only vaguely did I hear the undoing of a belt. I was much too sated to mind reality, but when the crest of his erection swept across my soaked folds, I made a swift return to it.

"Condom!" I chided and opened my eyes to glare at him. I was religious about my practice of safe sex.

With a look of disdain on his face, he frowned back. "What do you take me for?"

Confused, I directed my attention to his erect member between us and blinked, surprised. He'd already sheathed his length in the latex, and I noted to myself that I'd never come across such a perfect shaft, both in length and girth.

"Right."

"Satisfied?"

Meeting his eyes again, I gave him an inveigling smile. "Almost." I lowered my hand to trace the length of him with my fingertips – all while I held his gaze. "Get inside me and I will be."

Lust and wonder danced in his eyes while he chewed on his lower lip. Meanwhile, the rest of his mouth curved into his increasingly familiar crooked smile.

"Careful what you wish for," he warned. Pushing his hips forward, he reached between us to align himself with my entrance again. While he coated the tip of himself in my wetness, he continued roughly, "You'd better muster your strength, love. By the time I'm finished with you, you won't be able to walk."

Saliva amassed in my mouth upon his carnal warning. While I stared into his striking eyes, my heart throbbed in the same alien manner that it had earlier this evening. Although the sensation was sweet, it was also devastatingly profound. Seeing as I'd never experienced anything quite like it, I couldn't fathom the nature of it.

Indeed, he was devastating, but before I could contemplate my strange heartbeat further, he thrust powerfully into me.

"Ah," I whimpered when he shoved past my walls until he reached the very end of me. It hurt, albeit faintly. Gripping his broad shoulders, I clawed at the fabric of his shirt and further into his skin.

"Shit," he breathed, "you feel fucking amazing. The pressure of you—" He cut himself off by demanding my mouth, and while kissing me as though I were his salvation, he withdrew from within me.

"Be gentle, please," I mumbled against his lips. "You're very large."

I felt, rather than saw, his responding smile. "You'll survive," he countered smugly and pushed forcefully into me again. His thrust was of such strength that I was pushed slightly up the wall.

I hissed into his mouth and locked my legs around his strong waist. "Fuck."

He started a punishing rhythm – in and out, and so bloody deep, but the friction he provided was nothing short of exquisite. This man was clearly an expert in the art of fucking.

"Oh," I panted. My brows furrowed as I was submerged in the intense look in his eyes. I'd surely scored myself a ten out of ten tonight, hadn't I? I must have been storing up some serious karma when I'd consoled Olivia through her heartache. Nothing else could explain this uncanny encounter. Then again, I'd never believed in karma.

I was just lucky. It was that simple. To express my gratitude, I would savour this beautiful man.

My eyes closed when his large hands began to roam across my body, exploring and caressing every curve. Ruled by zeal, he grabbed the fabric of my dress above my breasts to liberate the aching mass. Pushing the material downwards, he grinned at the view now unveiled.

"Just when I thought you couldn't get any more perfect," he

stated and lowered his head to engulf my left nipple with his mouth.

My face flushed at his sensual compliment, and further when he harshly sucked my erect nipple. Groaning, I buried my breast deeper within his possession and relished the delicious sensations that rippled throughout my body.

He was well on his way to obliterating all of my defences. Would one night with this man truly be enough? I worried it wouldn't. Truly, if this was what it entailed, it was tempting to submit to him.

Moving away from my breast, he kissed his way across my sternum and up my neck to reach the line of my jaw, all while he continued to fuck me into oblivion against the wall. We hadn't even made it to his bed, I realised.

Upon a particularly perfect thrust, I gasped and hugged him against me. He'd struck precisely against my front wall, a spot that was especially sensitive. Seeming to notice this, he repeated the same motion, again and again.

"Oh my God," I mouthed, because I lost my breath.

"Come on, love," he growled under his breath. "Give in to me," he commanded, voice excitingly authoritative.

Now holding my breath, I squeezed my eyes shut and felt the tension border on unbearable. A few more of those thrusts and I would come undone whether I wanted to or not.

"Ah!" I wailed as my toes curled again. "No," I whined. I didn't want to climax so soon.

Burying his hand in my hair, he tugged my head back to expose my neck. "Yes," he panted and thrust expertly into me.

Fuck!

Immediately, I was sent over the edge again, reeling straight back into bliss.

I pushed against him, desperate for space. I was so overwhelmed that I feared I'd implode. My entire body was convulsing, but he confined me to him, strong arms becoming a cage.

"Stop, please," I uttered through a desperate pant.

"You're exceptionally sensitive," he remarked, voice full of wonder. He wasn't the first to tell me that, but that didn't make it less true. I'd always been like this. Perhaps that was why I enjoyed sex so much. I rarely had it without coming at least once.

"Yeah, well, for better and for worse," I hoarsely responded.

He chuckled and, to my relief, stalled his thrusts. Instead, he brought us away from the wall and carried me into his living area. Locating his dark brown dining table, he lowered us onto it before he propped himself on his strong arms, which were placed on either side of me.

In silence, we stared entranced at each other – both overawed by the chemistry between us. I'd never experienced anything quite like this before, and certainly not with a stranger. The mere magnitude of it was uncanny. Was this the sort of encounter that would only happen once in a lifetime, if at all? Was I currently staring at the right one, or was he just another fool among the crowd of imposters? My gut whispered he was different, but I was scared to listen.

With a look of amusement, he leaned back a little, but he remained buried within me, which my vagina was hyperaware of. The tissues of it throbbed around his shaft.

"Your sexual stamina could use a remedy," he murmured as he busied himself with undoing the buttons of his waistcoat. Offended, I gave him a scowl.

"Fuck you."

"You are. Right now, as it happens," he fired back, thoroughly amused, and thrust gently into me again.

"Ah," I complained and looked grumpily away from him.

He chuckled. "We'll have to practise, I suppose."

"In your dreams."

"There as well, I'm sure," he teased. "But I've got to say, after watching you come – twice already – I'm not the least bit inclined to adhere to your wish about not meeting again. I'm confident I could watch you come for a lifetime without growing bored."

My face turned red. I refused to debate this with him. I wasn't changing my mind. However, like the solicitor he was, he surely drove a hard bargain, both sexually and figuratively.

When I heard something soft drop to the floor around his feet, my eyes darted in his direction again. Presented to me was a stunning view that made me salivate. Clearly, the man worked hard to stay healthy. He was easily the fittest man I'd ever slept with. I could wash my clothes on his stomach, for crying out loud.

I couldn't resist ogling him. While his muscles were prominently defined, they weren't too much. They were athletic and proportionate – exactly my taste.

Groaning, I turned sideways and tucked my face into the palm of my hand. This wasn't fair. I didn't deserve this. Why were my willpower and dedication to my studies being put on trial like this?

"Either way, we're nowhere near finished," he said and reached for my arm. Gripping it, he dragged me off the table and slipped out of me in the same moment.

Now towering in front of me, he dropped a sweet and extended kiss on my mouth and then whirled me around and reached for the zipper at the back of my dress. While studying my surroundings, I heard it come undone beneath his skilful fingers.

When I noticed a staircase leading to another floor, I realised that his penthouse was even more spacious than I'd thought at first, especially if he lived alone. Did he live alone? Considering how neatly the interior design was put together, the man evidently had excellent taste. However, it was dominated by darker shades of the masculine variety, which led me to doubt that he had a female housemate, if he had one at all.

"Do you live alone?" I asked just before my dress fell to pool around my ankles.

"No. I'm expecting my girlfriend back in about an hour, so we'll have to be quick," he replied flatly.

My heart faltered. Slowly, plagued by dread, I turned my head to regard him over my shoulder. A sardonic smile welcomed me.

"Tosser," I insulted him, annoyed. He'd been pulling my leg.

He laughed, and his eyes creased with his amusement. "Yes, darling, I live alone. Do you?"

"No. I've got a flatmate – best mate."

"Mate?" he echoed, perplexed. "You mean you live with a man?"

"Yes."

"That's a bit unusual, isn't it?"

"Maybe." I shrugged. "He's like a brother to me, though."

"Poor guy," he tittered. "Is he aware you think of him that way?"

"Of course – it's a mutual thing."

He looked sceptical. "I'm sure. You haven't slept with him, then?"

Facing forward again, I laughed at the preposterous idea. "Of course not."

"I can't imagine he'll be happy with my future visits," he continued conceitedly. Visits? What did he mean visits? Had he forgotten that I apparently lived in Edinburgh?

I was about to murder his hope when he placed his hand on the small of my back and pushed me forward quite tenaciously. Spread flat across his dining table, I felt his nails claw down my back.

"Mm. You are a sight to behold," he claimed after he'd left a kiss on my shoulder blade. While stretching up to his full height behind me, he smoothed his hands across my buttocks. "This," he squeezed, "is more enticing than I could possibly express."

I swallowed a lump in my throat and closed my eyes to prepare for his intrusion. Soon enough, the tip of him lapped across my folds, possibly to lubricate himself in my fluids. It was a careful action, and yet the sensation made me shiver. I was overly sensitive now, which convinced me that I'd be coming again in record time.

And then he pushed into me with a groan that joined my own. Searching for something to hold onto, I spread my arms to grip the edges of the table, and when he grabbed my hips upon his steady retreat, I perceived it as a warning. His next shove wasn't going to be merciful.

However, his following thrust proved me wrong. Unlike earlier, he was deliciously delicate in his treatment this time around. He didn't plough into me. Instead, he settled into a steady rhythm that massaged my front wall in the most pleasurable manner. In all fairness, this pattern was far worse, because it seemed to trigger me more swiftly.

"Oh my God," I whimpered and gathered my arms to lift my upper body. Using his hold of my hips, he manoeuvred me to meet each of his thrusts, which led him to reach so blissfully deep.

I'd never been penetrated so well.

"You like that?" His voice was sexier than any other I'd heard, and particularly when he used that tone. It made him irresistible.

"Mm, yes. Don't stop," I answered breathlessly.

His warm mouth placed a loud, hungry kiss on the spot between my shoulder blades. As the tip of his nose trailed up to the nape of my neck, he murmured sensually, "If I could, I'd fuck you forever, darling. You feel that good." And then, a single harsh thrust.

"Oh!" I shook my head from side to side.

Would I survive this?

AGAINST YOUR BETTER JUDGMENT

INEXORABLE, HE CONTINUED, SEEMINGLY DETERMINED TO ruin me. But all of a sudden, he pulled out and grabbed my arms. After hurling me onto my back, he knelt between my legs and tucked them over his shoulders again. My face paled when I understood his intention.

"No. Please," I begged and sat up to grab his jaw. "I've had enough. I just want you to come."

While soft laughter poured out of his mouth, he gripped my wrists and locked my arms by my sides. "Well, that's not what I want," he contended with a gleam in his eyes.

"Will!" I writhed against his hold on me, but he was much too strong. I tried to close my legs, but his mouth had already reached me. Pleasure bolted through me at once, merciless in its force.

"Shit!" I cried out as his tongue continued to torment me. Crouched over him, my toes curled again. Breathing erratically, I felt the tension rebuild within me, impossibly strong. A tearless sob escaped my mouth, and I failed to inhale again. All I could focus on was the unbearable tension that engulfed my entire body. Desperate for release, I tried to break away, but he wouldn't have it. While maintaining his grip on my wrists, he smothered my legs with his arms to hold me in place.

And then it unfurled. Shuddering against him, I wailed his name until I collapsed onto him, limp as a corpse. Only vaguely did I hear him chuckle.

Gently, he moved me onto my back. My eyes had been shut, but when I reopened them, I discovered him hovering above me. A soft expression dwelled in his features, and I hoped it included sympathy. While he brushed a lock of my hair behind my ear, his eyes roamed across my flushed face.

"Women as beautiful as you shouldn't be allowed to wear clothes," he then brought himself to say.

Unimpressed, I only frowned back. What an unbelievably shallow compliment. As if it ought to be a beautiful woman's duty to please the male eye. As if an attractive woman shouldn't be allowed to decide over her own body.

Bewilderment entered his face upon my silence. "What?"

"That was a rather shit compliment, even though I know you were only trying to be nice."

His eyes widened. "What—? How was it shit?"

"Because it sounded a bit sexist."

He gaped for a short beat, struck by disbelief as he tried to see from my perspective. Then, at last, he shook his head as if heading back to reality. "For the record, I'm not a male chauvinist. I find sexism outrageous. Besides, you're living proof of how amazing women are." With a pleading gaze, he continued, "If you give me your number, I'll prove to you all of the above."

My lips twisted with amusement. Damn it. I didn't want to be smiling right now. It was giving me away, and I worried he'd misread a smile as actual – albeit disguised – interest.

"No."

He sighed, head dropping. "Give me at least your surname then."

I groaned, despairing of him. "No, Will. I wish you'd give it up already." Considering his persistence, I realised this had been a mistake. "I should leave," I said with a sigh and tried to shove him off, but he wouldn't budge. "Will," I prompted.

"Fine," he grumbled. "Have it your way."

Since he didn't move, I wasn't sure what he meant. "Sorry?"

Lifting his gaze, he studied me for a brief moment while his lips formed a brooding line. "When you leave tomorrow, that's it. But I'm going to have you all of tonight. If you're still determined not to meet again by the morning, I'll respect that."

I swallowed, and while I struggled to string together a coherent response, he leaned away and dragged me with him. Once I was seated on top of the table, he bent over to heave me across his shoulder.

Wide-eyed, I stared at the floor beneath my head and wondered what I'd set into motion. "What are you doing?"

"I'm ensuring my end of the bargain," he muttered and kicked open the door to another room. After stepping into the darkness of it, he dropped me off his shoulder.

I squealed in fear of meeting the floor, but confusion silenced me the instant my skin met soft material. His bed?

After shutting the door, he switched on the lights. I found him grinning at me, clearly amused by my earlier squeal.

"What – did you think I'd resort to violence?" he asked.

"Maybe. For all I know, you could still be Mr Bateman in disguise," I countered through protruding lips.

That made him laugh. "I can assure you I'm not. I'm merely a man who's grossly intrigued by you."

I snorted. "I'm sure your mother would be jealous, had she heard that."

He shuddered. "What? No. Way to kill the mood."

I arched my brow at him and directed my gaze to his ever-present erection. How potent was he, truly? "You don't seem affected."

"That's thanks to the glorious view," he explained and gestured towards me.

Blushing, I observed my new surroundings. His bedroom was really quite big. I noted three doors leading into it, and we'd arrived through one of them. So, what was hiding behind the other two? A bathroom, I gathered, as well as a closet, or perhaps a private office?

"Even for a corporate solicitor, your flat's rather big," I remarked. "And seeing as you're only twenty-eight, I'm struggling to understand how you could've amassed such a fortune already."

"Well, you'll never know, and you've got yourself to blame," he countered cheekily and approached the bed. "Shame you're not a gold digger, Sandra. Had you been, I'd have you on your knees in a heartbeat."

His comment made me face him again. Unimpressed, I stared at his lopsided smile while he reached for my heels to peel them off my feet. Once he had placed them on the floor, his mouth dived for my calves, and I watched as he slowly kissed his way along them. He really was remarkably sensual. Truthfully, it demanded all my willpower not to submit to his wish about meeting again.

I wondered if I'd regret it. Then again, if I did, I knew where he lived. He – the poor man – didn't even know my real name.

While I'd been worrying, he'd made his way to my throat. Covering it with soft, amorous kisses, he extracted another groan from my mouth. Meanwhile, I seemed to have wrapped my limbs around him subconsciously.

After roaming across my moist skin, his hands closed around my upper arms. Then, he shoved me onto my stomach beneath him. With my eyes fixed on the black headboard of his bed, I felt him lift only my derrière.

"I'll be coming with you this time, but it won't be the last," he warned.

Without further ado, he pushed forward until he reached the very end of me. Hissing and grinding my teeth, I fisted his bed sheets so hard that my knuckles grew numb and white. As he made his retreat, he leaned over me, and the intimacy of his action struck me hard.

Strong as a fortress, he hovered above me while his lips blessed my neck. Making his way towards my ear, he whispered, "This is going to get a bit rough, love. Tell me to stop if I'm hurting you."

My eyes widened and I swallowed. Just what did he have in mind?

Sneaking his hands under my body, he found my wrists, locked them within his grip, and dragged my arms behind me, successfully lifting my torso from his colossal mattress. When he thrust again, I realised what he'd meant. I barely managed to stifle my whimper. He was using my arms to balance out his weight. With each thrust, he dragged me towards him, and it made him reach a depth that no man before him had.

How it was possible to fuck anybody so well was beyond me. He must have been designed to pleasure women into insanity. Though it hurt faintly, it was undoubtedly a pleasurable pain. Never in my life had I been dominated like this, and I relished it. Granting him power over my pleasure was easily the best decision I'd ever made, sex-wise. He knew exactly what to do in order to unravel my erotic demons. Since he was introducing me to a whole new dimension of sex, I feared I'd never be satisfied with anything less again.

"Ah!" A bottled-up cry spilled out of my mouth as he continued to slam into me. This tension was intolerable. I couldn't last much longer. It was far too powerful. *He* was far too powerful, and so my shivers started. Oh no.

"Not yet," he chastised and released my right forearm to spank me. The sting of his palm made me hiss. What he'd done had been counterproductive, because my drenched, quivering walls clenched down on him as if to reject him. Even so, he forced past them.

"Don't you dare," he growled. "We're coming together this time."

The sound of our flesh parting and meeting echoed through the room – the most erotic thing I'd ever heard.

"Please," I begged and shook my head. An entire night of this was out of the question. I wouldn't last – I was sure.

"Nearly there," he consoled me and released my left arm as well. Instead, he grabbed my hips to hold me in place. Desperate to release at least a portion of the tension within me, I tugged my own hair while I silently pleaded for him to come.

Finally, his thrusts switched rhythm. They grew slower, but harder.

"Fuck," he groaned through grinding teeth and dug his fingers into the flesh of my lower cheeks. "Come for me," he commanded, and I instantly obeyed.

Allowing myself the release, I shuddered through my intense climax, lost to the world. He closed over me immediately, confining me to him. With strong arms wrapped around me, he performed his final thrust and spilled himself within me.

Lost in oblivion, I fell limp in his arms and heaved for air. I barely noticed that he rolled us onto our sides where he withdrew from within me.

We recovered in silence. Though I couldn't speak for him, I was not only recovering from my row of orgasms, but from mild shock as well. Surely, I'd never had better sex, nor met a man more compelling.

His eventual sigh broke the silence. While squeezing me against him, he planted a firm kiss on my neck, and afterward, he nuzzled his face in the crook of it. "I'm gutted you don't want to do this again some other time," he murmured against my skin.

I didn't reply because I couldn't find my voice. I was much too overwhelmed.

An invisible fire in the form of his hand travelled up and down the curve of my waistline. "You're fucking gorgeous, love. Do you know that?"

I cleared my throat and turned to look at him. Hoarsely, I replied through a smile, "Now that's how you pay compliments, William."

He smiled lopsidedly. "I'm a quick learner."

I tittered. "You're conceited, is what you are."

"And how would you know?" he challenged, unimpressed. "You hardly know me."

"Cocky, at best," I insisted and faced away again.

"Well, you're rather irritating."

"And yet here I am," I teased.

"Against your better judgment."

I laughed. "If you want me to leave, I will."

He tensed against me. "Don't."

"Alright, then. All part of the deal, I suppose."

Propping himself up on his arm beside me, he studied me for a while.

"Sandra, I'm curious. You don't strike me as sexually inexperienced. Frankly, you come across as being on the liberal end of the spectrum. That makes me wonder how frequently you do this sort of thing. I realise it's none of my business, but…"

I smirked to myself. "Well, how often do you do it?"

"Random one-night stands? Every leap year, maybe."

I faced him disbelievingly, but there was no hint of a lie in his eyes. "I find that hard to believe. With your talents, as well as stamina, you must be getting your fill somehow."

He chuckled. "Right. If I answer, will you?"

I narrowed my eyes. Again, he drove a hard bargain. I was desperate to know now. "Fine."

He looked away. "I have regular sex, but with the same partner—" his eyes darted towards me—"usually."

"Elaborate."

He scratched his stubble for a moment, thinking. "I'm not in a relationship, but I've got an agreement with another woman. A sexual one."

"Ah," I uttered as I understood. We were in similar situations then, I supposed. I had Aaron for that. However, regardless of my arrangement with Aaron, I didn't shy away from the occasional one-night stand. The only condition was that I used a condom so that Aaron wouldn't have to, and frankly, I'd do it anyway. Collecting sexually transmitted infections was not a hobby of mine.

"Your turn," William reminded me.

"Well, same as you, I suppose. Though, when it comes to one-night stands, I might indulge a couple of times a year. All depending on the person, to be honest. I don't go all out to sleep with a stranger."

"Like I did tonight," he added with a leer.

"Right." I grinned, but my amusement suffered a sudden death when something occurred to me. "Is your partner going to mind?"

He scoffed. "She hasn't got a right to know."

"That's not an answer, William."

He sighed. "I'm not sure. It's implied I'm allowed to do this sort of thing, but predicting a bruised ego can be surprisingly difficult."

Right. That made sense. In the end, that was exactly why Aaron and I had agreed not to mention other partners to each other.

Suddenly, a frown occupied his face. "Wait, did you say 'same as' me? You've got a regular partner?"

I blinked over at him, surprised by his sudden display of disapproval. "Yes?"

Gripping my jaw, he glared into my eyes. "Then what's the problem, exactly? Clearly, you have got time. Reject that wanker. Instead, you can reserve that energy for me."

My jaw clenched in his hold. "Of course I won't do that. The arrangement I've got with Aaron is perfect. I hardly ever pay him a thought. He's so low maintenance that he might as well be air, and I've got a funny feeling you won't be, Will, but it's not your fault. It's just that you're new. Aaron's familiar. New, right now, is bound to mess with my head for a while, and I don't want that."

He moaned and collapsed onto his back beside me. "You've got to be kidding me."

His dramatic reaction made me pout. "I'm not. I'm sorry."

"How about this, then. Give me your number, and I promise I won't reach out to you till you've completed your exams – so in about two months."

Frustrated, I frowned to myself. It became apparent that I would need to be brutally honest with both him and myself, so after drawing in a deep breath, I mustered the courage to place myself in a vulnerable spot. I'd never been this transparent with a mere stranger before, but William surely made it difficult to avoid.

"William, I'm sorry, but you're not casual sex material. You're *boyfriend* material. I'm a bit too compelled by you. Meanwhile, Aaron doesn't intrigue me that way at all. He's just there – platonically."

"I can't believe this." He moaned to himself. "Are you honestly saying I'm *too* interesting?"

I grimaced. "Well, sort of. I'm not at a point in my life where 'too interesting' is worth risking my attention for. I'm very sorry, but I've got to be rational about this. What I'm doing is damage control."

"Fuck this," he muttered. "I'm done."

I tensed. "'Done' as in you want me to leave?"

"No, but I'm forfeiting. You're clearly not going to change your mind."

I sighed and crawled towards him. With my hands folded under my chin, I rested across his muscular chest and held his gaze. "Sorry."

"I'm over it," he assured me nonchalantly.

"I'll give you a blowjob, if you want, for compensation."

"You'd do best to stay silent, I think," he muttered, but there was an erotic twinkle in his gorgeous eyes. It hurt to look at him now. He had better be worth rejecting.

"I don't know what your partner is into, but I don't tend to speak much when I'm performing fellatio. It might have to do with having a cock in my mouth, but what do I know?" I teased and trailed soft kisses down his torso. The slabs of muscle flexed beneath my mouth, causing me to grin. Was he ticklish?

Reaching forward, he buried his hands in my hair and dragged me back to his face. "What are you? The Devil?" he asked and glared into my eyes.

I smiled wryly back. "It's your night. I'll be whatever you want."

"Mine, then," he said, making my heart falter and my lips part. Had he truly just said that? Again, the strangest feeling poured through my chest, but I couldn't fathom the nature of it.

"Oh, but you already are," he teased and reclaimed my mouth. Irked, I pushed him away. "I'm not."

"You just said it yourself. I'm boyfriend material," he argued, amused.

"You're also an idiot."

His left eyebrow arched. "My degree begs to differ."

"Cambridge," I muttered with a roll of my eyes. "Quite the card, that is."

"Yes." He tucked his arms under his head. Lying beneath me, he studied me, seemingly fascinated. "I hope I'll forget you."

Struck by his brutal words, I frowned. "Why?"

"Because if not, I'll go mad." He chuckled and wrapped his arms around me to fling us around. "But for now, I intend to take full advantage," he continued and reached over for his nightstand. When I saw him withdraw another foil packet, my eyes widened. Already?

"I assure you, though, Sandra, I won't give you a single reason to ever forget *me*."

§ § §

An internal alarm woke me the following morning. My eyes opened at once, whereupon the sight of the black and unfamiliar nightstand prompted me to remember where I was. To allow the initial shock to subside, I continued to lie there for a few seconds, wide-eyed. One after the other, memories of last night paraded into my mind until there was an abundance of heat in my face. I smiled in spite of it, for it had been dreamlike.

Returning to the present, I noticed that there wasn't a sound around me – not even of a body softly drawing breath. Was he still lying behind me? I remembered I'd fallen asleep in his arms sometime after midnight, but nobody was holding me now.

In case he was still present in the bed, I turned carefully and slowly, but he was nowhere in sight. Relaxing somewhat, I groaned to myself and rubbed my face. I despised the inevitable next phase – the awkward conversation and forced small talk that always occurred the morning after a one-night stand, unless I'd snuck out before the guy woke. There was always that dreadful question hanging in the air and spilling between the lines: what's next? Should we go back to being perfect strangers, as if we hadn't just enjoyed each other more intimately than most, or should we embark on a journey that was bound to end in tragedy once I failed to live up to his expectations?

Considering what a paradigm shift William represented in my expectations of men, I decided to remain for a while longer to muster my courage. I'd need every drop of it if I was going to be able to stick to my rules and leave without any intention of a reunion.

Gazing around, I wondered what time it was. Last night, I'd brought my purse into his bedroom, so I reached down the side of the bed for it and took out my phone. As the screen lit up, I saw that it was half ten and that I had two missed calls from Jason, as well as a text from Olivia that had been received just a minute ago.

Since I had plans with Jason today, I decided to call him before I did anything else.

"Morning, love," he answered after a single ring.

"Morning, Jason," I replied hoarsely and proceeded to clear my throat.

"Glad you're not dead," he said with a chuckle. "Whose bed did you fall asleep in?"

"The bed of the guy I insulted," I mumbled, embarrassed.

"No way. You're joking."

"Am not."

Laughter burst out of him. "Oh my God. Course you did. Was it worth it?"

"Yeah, actually. Best I've ever had," I admitted.

"Really?" he queried, amazed.

"Really."

"Damn. Will you stick to your rules, then?"

I sighed. "That's the plan."

He was quiet for a beat. "You don't sound too happy about that."

A knock on the door interrupted our conversation, and my heart contracted with a thrill upon the sound.

"Yeah, I know. But listen, I've got to go. I'm about to get dressed and leave. I'll be home soon, alright?"

"Right. Later, then."

"Yeah." I hung up. "Yes?" I called out and watched the doorknob turn. Once the door swung open, I was presented with the view of the gorgeous man I'd managed to seduce last night. I must have been wielding some black magic. Nothing else could explain this. For better or for worse, he was precisely my type, both physically and mentally. Dressed into beige trousers and a simple white shirt, he leaned against the doorpost and smiled.

There wasn't a chance I could keep myself from blushing.

"Morning," he cooed and tucked his hands into his pockets. "Sleep well?"

"I did. You?"

"Same."

"Have you been awake for long?"

"About an hour." He shrugged. "Anyway, I've made you breakfast. If you'd like a shower first, there's a bathroom through that door," he said and cocked his head towards it.

My eyebrows arched. I hadn't expected this level of hospitality. "Thanks. You're very kind."

My compliment didn't appear to affect him. "You'll find fresh towels on the shelf beside the shower. There's shampoo and conditioner for women there as well, should you want to use it."

I grimaced. "Why have you got that? Is it your regular partner's?" If it was, I wasn't inclined to even touch it. It would feel wrong – like I was trespassing on her territory.

His smile transitioned into a grin. "No. I shopped for it this morning, when I went out for coffee."

"Oh." My blush intensified at his thoughtfulness. "That wasn't necessary, but I appreciate it."

He shrugged again. "I left a T-shirt for you as well. If there's anything else, let me know. I'll just wait in the kitchen."

As soon as he closed the door, I pushed the duvet aside, climbed out of the bed and approached the bathroom. Upon entering, I felt like I'd walked into a spa. Like I'd expected, it was rather spacious. He even had a tub.

Although it was tempting to stand under his rain shower for ages, I was quick to step out because I meant to respect Jason's time. In the end, he had reserved the day to help me unpack, so I ought to get home as soon as possible.

As I looked in the mirror, I was grateful to discover that there wasn't much makeup left on my face. The remaining traces were nothing the wipes I kept in my purse couldn't get rid of.

Once I'd finished rinsing my face, I dressed into the plain white T-shirt that I found resting on a chest of drawers inside the bathroom. The size of it made it work like a dress, which I appreciated. Grabbing my towel, I wrapped my hair and decided to face reality.

The smell of bacon hit me first. Exiting his bedroom, I heard London hum in the background through a window he'd opened in his living room. As I walked through, I looked towards the front door and noted that my knickers were gone. He'd probably thrown them in the bin. Heading past the staircase leading to another floor, my eyes landed on his square dining table, and the memory it triggered made my vagina throb. As I thought of it, I noticed how sore I was. He'd had his way with me three times before he'd let me sleep. To let my vagina heal, I'd be sexually inactive for at least a week.

Passing the dining table, I turned a corner and came upon the door to his kitchen. It was open, and the scent of bacon was concentrated here. Lingering on a step, I drew in a deep breath for courage before I walked in and found him seated by the island, reading on his iPad.

"It smells amazing," I said the instant he looked up to acknowledge my arrival. When my eyes landed on a pan containing scrambled eggs, saliva amassed in my mouth. While I was certain they'd be no match for Jason's recipe, I could hardly wait to fill my mouth.

"Oh my God, you've pulled out all the stops, haven't you?" I commented appreciatively while I hesitated to hop onto the stool beside him. Seeming to notice, he smiled, charmed, and patted the top of it as an invitation.

"Please," he said after I'd sat down, "help yourself."

Hungrily, I scanned the options in front of me and was about to grab a croissant when I noticed the Starbucks cup standing next to my plate. My eyes zoomed in on the black ink on the side. *Electra*, it read. Laughter surged out of me at once. Pointing at it, I turned to face him.

"Is that for me?"

Wearing a smirk, he reached for his own cup and turned it so I could read the name on the side. *Oedipus*, it read, which made me laugh even harder.

"You're certainly something else," I remarked. "That's brilliant."

"Glad you've noticed."

I got the feeling there was another dimension to his response, but since I wanted to avoid ruining the mood by introducing the conversation that would ultimately lead to rejection, I pretended not to have registered it while I reached for a croissant.

"I wasn't sure how you take your coffee, so I opted for a regular black. If you'd like any milk, it's in the fridge," he said while I helped myself to some scrambled eggs.

"Like I'd have the nerve to complain," I countered, amused.

"What's your usual order, though?"

"At Starbucks?"

"Yeah. Or just in general."

"Flat white. But I often opt for black coffee as well. Depends on my mood."

"I see."

"And you?" I had no use for this information, but I thought it polite to ask anyway.

"Black, nothing added. Always."

I nodded as I raised a forkful of scrambled eggs to my mouth. The minute the flavour exploded on my tongue, my eyes widened with disbelief. It tasted precisely like Jason's, if not even better.

Observing my reaction, he queried, "Everything alright?"

I paused chewing and turned to frown at him. Stowing the

eggs in my cheek, I covered my mouth and declared, "This is absolutely delicious. What's your secret? I've never tasted better scrambled eggs in my life."

A grin formed on his face before he fixed his gaze on his iPad again. "I'm glad. If you decide to stick around, perhaps I'll tell you."

My heart sank. It was clear he was waiting for me to share my verdict, and he wasn't going to like it. There was simply too much at stake. While I couldn't deny that he might be a diamond in the rough, the problem was that I couldn't know for certain. I had no guarantee that we'd turn out to be compatible, and I wasn't willing to explore the potential when I already had countless obligations to mind that were vital for my future.

With a sigh, I put my fork aside and folded my hands in my lap. "Will, I've already told you. I don't have the capacity for anything other than a one-night stand – especially now with my exams round the corner."

Stealing a glance at him, I saw his jaw clench while he locked his iPad. After shoving it away, he faced the windows and stared out at the rooftops of London. "And like I've said before, I'm willing to compromise. Focus on your exams. Once you're done, let me know."

Unsure of what to say, I merely continued to look at him. Eventually, his impatience got the better of him and he faced me again. Perplexed, he asked, "Why won't you just give me a chance? That's all I'm asking – a single chance to prove myself worthy of your attention."

Unsettled, my lips pursed. "I've already explained why."

"Well, to be perfectly frank, I find your reason rather pathetic."

Groaning, I placed my elbows on the island to bury my face in my hands. "Is it really so hard for you to accept that I'm just not interested in anything more than this?"

"Yes, actually."

A certain lie I'd told him earlier marched into my mind then, and I intended to make use of it. Perhaps reminding him would moderate his zeal. "Will, I live in Edinburgh. There's no chance we'd work out."

"Why so pessimistic? Edinburgh is but a mere flight away," he argued, shocking me.

While gawking at him, I probed, "Are you implying that you'd be willing to fly to Edinburgh only to see me again?"

He frowned. "I'm not implying it. I'm professing it."

Stunned, I could only stare at him.

"I realise how crazy that sounds," he murmured after a while and waved his hand in the air, "so allow me to elaborate. What I'm saying is that I'd like to keep in touch. If that proves rewarding enough, I'm not closed to the idea of flying over to see you. Besides, have you got ties in London aside from your friendship with Olivia? Does your family reside here, for instance? Judging by your accent, you sound like you might have grown up around here. If so, I'm sure you'll be visiting London again soon enough."

Since I could hardly believe what I was hearing, I remained speechless.

He sighed and faced the windows again. "I see it as a win-win situation. You said you're reluctant about dating because you haven't got time to spare for it. Obviously, I won't be able to demand much of your time while you're in Edinburgh. And, like you, I've not got much time to spare either. I'm an ambitious man, so I spend most hours of the day at work anyway. It'd be mutually beneficial. Don't you see? Our needs are compatible. What's it going to cost you to keep in touch while you're in Scotland? I just don't understand how that's asking too much."

After a while, he added, "Had you said it's because you don't fancy me that way, I'd of course respect it. But that's not the case, is it?"

Conflicted, I swallowed a lump in my throat. The solution was simple, and yet I couldn't bring myself to utter the lie. "No," I barely mumbled, "it's not."

He groaned loudly and tossed his head back to stare at the ceiling in despair. "Women," he complained under his breath.

I realised at that moment that I'd misread him. He wasn't an arsehole at all. In his own way, he was instead a rare breed of a gentleman. Upon recalling what he had told me last night about how rarely he indulged in one-night stands, he didn't strike me as a man who chased skirts merely for the thrill of it, or because he was looking to boost his ego. On the contrary, he seemed rather fastidious about whom he blessed with his time and attention.

And here I was, wasting it.

I'd studied him for some time when I said, "I'm sorry, William. You deserve better." I wasn't sure exactly what had caused me to say it, but it was like my heart had governed my tongue.

He sighed and reached for his iPad again. "Well, I agree – I deserve at least a chance."

I nodded and focused on my plate again. "I really am sorry."

After that, I suspected he succumbed to disgruntlement, because neither of us said a word for the remainder of breakfast.

When it was time for me to leave, I'd at first meant to hand back his T-shirt, but he insisted that I should keep it. To go along with it, he provided me with a pair of his white Calvin Klein boxers since I had no knickers to wear after he'd ripped them to shreds last night. I laughed wholeheartedly while I pulled them on, but they served the purpose, nevertheless. In fact, they were quite comfortable – like wearing hotpants.

While I got dressed and collected my things, he called for a black cab, and I had only just finished brushing my hair when he arrived in the doorway of his bathroom to announce that it had arrived downstairs.

"I'll walk you down," he added.

Once we were down on the street, we approached the black cab that was parked along the kerb. Taking advantage of his long legs, he strode to reach it first so that he could open the door for me. I couldn't resist grinning at him.

"Thank you," I said and halted in front of the open door to face him. "I had a wonderful time, and you're an excellent cook."

The smile he offered took my breath away. It would have turned most women into blind fools. Wearing that, he could do whatever he wanted and get whatever he desired, apart from me.

Hesitation radiated from his behaviour when he lowered his head somewhat. Realising what he wanted, I smiled wryly and stretched up on my toes to meet him. His warm mouth moulded against my own, but it felt different this time. There was a vulnerability behind the motions of his lips, as if he were holding back to protect himself from harm, when what he truly wanted was to consume me. While part of me wished the moment would last forever, a larger part demanded I pull away.

"You know where I live," he said and proceeded to cup my cheeks in his hands. "So, if you change your mind, you'll know where to find me," he added and quickly stole another kiss. When his lips parted from mine, I was mesmerised by the urgency in his eyes. "Do change your mind," he implored.

I gave him a faint smile and turned away from him. With a sigh that came straight from my heart, I headed into the car. Once he'd shut the door for me, he tapped the window on the front passenger side. Curious, I leaned over to see what he wanted. The driver rolled down the window, and through it, William extended a few notes to cover the fee for my trip. "Drive safely," he stressed.

"Of course, sir," the driver replied.

"Thanks. Have a good day."

"You too." With that, the driver rolled up the window again and pulled out on the street.

It was tempting to glance through the rear windshield, but I didn't. Instead, I pouted to myself while I wished him all the best. Right man, wrong time, was what it was. So, in the end, he wasn't really the right man at all. Had he been, he would have arrived later, when I'd be ready to commit to someone.

6

———◆•◆•◆———

SOUNDS LIKE YOUR TYPE

URING THE TRIP, I OPENED OLIVIA'S TEXT.

> You alive? x

> Just left. Can I call you? x

A moment later, she called.

"Hi," I greeted.

"How was it?" Olivia wasn't beating around the bush.

Heat prickled my cheeks. "He was brilliant – all around."

"I knew it!" she cheered. "You had so much chemistry, Cara. I've never seen anything like it. I'm so happy for you."

"Yeah, suppose we did," I mumbled as I studied my nails, and I wondered to myself whether there were remnants of his skin still underneath them. In the end, I did recall clawing down his back several times.

"What are you going to do, then? How were things this morning?"

"They were a bit awkward, mainly because I rejected the chance to see him again."

Olivia groaned loudly. "Cara, why? Why would you do that? If you liked him, why not give the poor man a chance? I seriously don't think you'll ever come across a better model of the male specimen in your life. I know I won't."

I chuckled. "I'm sorry, but that's just stupid. I won't think like that."

"Why not?"

"Because I hardly think it's right to start seeing someone based on that premise. Grabbing the chance merely because I don't think I'll come across something better? Please. He deserves better than that."

"So you didn't tell him your name, then?"

"No."

"Poor man."

I sighed. "Yeah, he was quite remarkable. I wonder if I'll regret it. Then again, I'm not one to wallow in the past. Besides, I've got far too many obligations to mind as it is, so I'm sure it was for the best."

"Just don't come complaining to me when you end up alone."

I looked out the window. "Well, there's a difference between being lonely and being alone. I seriously doubt I'll ever be discontent with being alone. You see, I rather enjoy solitude. It's my best friend. We get on so well."

She groaned again, and I knew that if she'd been here, I'd have seen her eyes roll.

To change the subject, I asked, "Anyway, how was your night?"

"I had such a blast, Cara." I could hear the smile in her voice. "We left the bar after a couple of hours and went to play table tennis. Some random lads joined us, as well as a couple of girls, and it just turned out to be a really fun night. I made so many friends I'll probably never see again."

Her last comment made me laugh. "I'm glad, Livy."

"Yeah. But you know, Andy did tell me something after you left last night, about William."

Dread made my chest contract. "What did he say?"

"It's nothing bad, but I just think you ought to know."

"Know what?"

"Apparently, Will's not one to have one-night stands very often. Andy was quite shocked about it after you left. Mentioned it had been years since it last happened."

I'd already inferred as much, but that didn't prevent my heart from clenching in that same unfamiliar manner. All I could think was that it was the last thing I needed to hear. "Are you saying this to make me feel special? Because I don't require an ego-boost."

"Oh, Cara. I think you know why I'm saying it. Just something to consider."

"There's nothing to consider," I corrected curtly. "Anyway, I'm nearly home now. Speak later, yeah?"

"Yeah. Tell Jason I said hello when you see him."

"Will do. Love you."

"Love you too."

§ § §

Upon unlocking the front door and pushing it open, I discovered Jason exiting the bathroom just behind it, wearing nothing but a towel around his hips. With his dirty blonde hair and light-blue eyes, he resembled Apollo himself – especially with that towel that could have doubled as a fustanella. Any other woman would have taken the opportunity to ogle his impressive physique, but since I'd witnessed it countless times by now, I hardly noticed.

"There she is," he greeted once our eyes locked. "How are you feeling?"

"Tired."

"I bet."

"Livy says hello."

He frowned, as if he'd suddenly recalled something. "Whatever happened to her last night?"

"Well, the guy I slept with was there with a friend, so she spent the rest of the night with him. Went to play table tennis apparently."

"Sounds like fun. They end up in bed?"

I shook my head. "No. She wasn't feeling it, and neither was he. Like her, he was fresh out of a relationship."

"But I thought the whole reason you went out last night was to find her a rebound?"

"Yeah, but she's changed her mind. Told me a one-night stand isn't going to help her get over Colin, so she'd rather wait till she makes a new genuine connection with someone."

Jason looked impressed. "Good for her."

"Yeah, I thought so, too. Anyway, I'm sorry for making you wait."

He scoffed. "No worries, love." Folding his arms, he tilted his head and smirked. "Well?"

"Well what?"

"Did you stick to your rules, then?"

I sighed as I undid the sash of my coat. "Yeah."

He shook his head in comical despair. "Poor man. Was he gutted?"

Upset at the reminder, I pouted. "Quite."

He tutted. "Again, poor man. I'm so glad I've never fancied you that way when you're as unattainable as they come."

I snorted. "Don't be silly, Jason. Besides, I'm not sure you would have liked him much, so you shouldn't feel bad for him. He was very forthright – and opinionated."

Jason was far too idealistic in his nature to tolerate a brutal force like William. If there existed a single person who could make Jason lose his temper, I was confident that William would be that person.

"Sounds like your type," he teased.

I chuckled. "Definitely was."

Jason's eyes widened considerably then. "What are you wearing!" Laughter spilled out of him.

Glancing down at myself, I sensed my embarrassment reveal itself in my face. "He tore my knickers apart. Gave me a pair of boxers to compensate, as well as a T-shirt."

"He did what?" Though he continued to laugh, he sounded more shocked now.

"Yeah, he was something else."

"Jesus Christ, what a brute. Were they expensive?"

"No. Besides, it was honestly quite arousing."

Disbelieving, Jason shook his head. "What else did he do? Who is this guy?"

"I don't want to talk about it."

His ensuing smile was sympathetic. "You never do."

I nodded. "Just easier to leave it in the past that way."

"You know best." He gestured towards the mountain of boxes standing outside my bedroom door. "Anyway, shall we crack on with it, then?"

"Yeah."

§ § §

The following Monday, I walked into Bentham House alongside Olivia, where we had planned to meet Aaron in the social hub before our lecture in Advanced Contract Law. It was the only module I had in common with her now that we had completed the compulsory ones of the first and second year. While she was ambivalent about the module, I found it nothing short of riveting, and the same applied to Aaron, which wasn't all that surprising when considering the fact that Aaron and I had selected all the same ones. While Olivia preferred areas of public law, Aaron and I favoured private law.

Upon entering the social hub, I scanned the people present until I located him next to a girl named Cassie. I had nothing against her, but I had a funny feeling she rather disliked me, and I suspected it was because she had developed feelings for my regular bed partner. Aaron denied it, but I wasn't convinced.

"She doesn't dislike you," he'd always say, "and she doesn't fancy me that way."

"Ah, Cassie," Olivia murmured from beside me. "Of course."

I chuckled. Olivia absolutely could not stand the poor girl after she'd overheard her gossiping about me in one of the common rooms two years ago. I hadn't minded because I was aware that I came across as aloof and therefore tended to give off a terrible impression.

"Retract your claws, Livy," I joked and adjusted my bag on my shoulder.

"I can't believe he doesn't see it. She's so taken with him – it's almost painful."

"He insists she isn't."

Olivia raised a brow and faced me. "Would you be cross if he ever sleeps with her?"

Dumbfounded, I replied, "It's far too early for this, but no, of course not. He can sleep with whomever he likes. We're not in a relationship."

"What if they start dating?"

"Then he'll have my blessing." I shrugged.

While it was true that a small part of me worried that he'd fall in love with someone else, it was only because it would mean that I'd ultimately lose him as a bed partner, and I didn't think I'd ever find another Aaron. He truly was the ideal fuck friend. I'd be gutted if I lost him before I was ready for it to happen. However, I'd been aware of that risk ever since the beginning of our arrangement, so of course I wouldn't be so selfish as to get angry over it.

If he fell in love, I'd be the last person to stand in his way, because while I didn't love him romantically, I loved him as a friend, and that meant I'd put his happiness first.

"You're so rational it should be criminal." Olivia smirked.

"Hardly."

"Do you even have an ego?"

"A huge one," I joked.

"Oh, he's seen us," she warned and turned her head to give him a smile of acknowledgement. Once I looked over, I saw him walking towards us, and behind him, Cassie stared daggers in my direction.

Tall and lean, Aaron Myers was easy on the eyes. His dense Afro-textured hair was cut short, and I had a habit of clawing through it whenever he claimed my body. In the comeliness of his face resided eyes that were nearly black in colour, and they regarded me with tenderness as he approached.

Ambitious and strategic, Aaron was one of the cleverest men I'd met, and his introverted nature complemented mine. His presence was profoundly comforting. He'd listen in silence and contemplate whatever I had to say before he'd offer unique insights and impressive reflections.

We had met during our first year at UCL at a social event that the university's student union had organised to provide students with an opportunity to make friends and start networking. He had been seated with a group of lads, but he'd looked far from interested in whatever they were discussing.

Across the room, our eyes had met. Instead of looking away, I'd given him a small smile, which he'd immediately returned. Excusing himself from the others, he'd approached me, somewhat shy in his demeanour. I was easily the more socially confident one, and he seemed to have appreciated that, because once I'd started talking, he'd expressed no desire for me to ever shut up.

That night, we'd wound up in my bed, and from there, our casual arrangement had been set into motion. In fact, one of the things I fancied most about sleeping with Aaron was that his schedule was aligned with my own, so finding time for a sensual round was never much of a challenge.

We'd done it in the lavatories on campus several times – generally whenever we required a quick break from studying. Another bonus was the fact that Aaron wielded skills that were above average. He was keenly attuned to my needs and always prioritised them, just as I made a point of prioritising his.

Alas, the expertise of a certain man I'd met this past weekend forced him into the shadows. William possessed what I considered to be an X-factor. Aside from his outstanding talents between the sheets, there was something remarkably compelling about him. However, I couldn't put my finger on precisely what it was. He was just so assertive and self-assured – seemingly unshakable. I admired his apparent resolve about things. He knew what he wanted, and he didn't waste a second trying to seize it.

Like a breath of fresh air, he'd been exceptionally stimulating. That was just it – he was exceptional.

"Hiya," Aaron greeted and successfully distracted me from the dangerous lane of thought I'd entered. I reminded myself at that moment not to think of William. It wasn't fair to Aaron, and it wasn't good for my sanity. William was the past. Aaron was the present, and I would keep it that way.

"Did you have a nice weekend?" he continued and managed to steer me right back onto the thought of William.

"It was quite dull, to be honest," I lied. Olivia gave me a knowing glance, but I ignored it as I continued, "I finished unpacking most of my things, but had to order a new wardrobe from IKEA since there wasn't enough space for all my clothes. Bought a desk while I was at it."

Aaron chuckled. "I'm not even slightly surprised. Jason help you out?"

"Yeah."

"Good of him. You could've asked me, you know."

"I know, but I wanted some quality time with him since neither of us has got much time to spare with my exams coming up and his current placement at the hospital."

"Understandable. How about you, Livy?"

"My weekend was great. Spent it with my mum."

"Weren't you and Cara going for a drink on Friday?" he probed her then, but she didn't so much as twitch.

"We did." She smiled. "Was great fun, but we decided to head home early because of exams coming up," she explained with a nonchalant shrug.

"Responsible of you," he commented, amused. "So, I take it your plan to find a rebound failed, then?"

"I cancelled the quest," she replied with a chuckle.

"Oh. How come?"

Since I'd already heard this part, I zoned out of their conversation and started towards the lecture theatre. I was adamant about sitting at the front, which was why I always arrived early.

§ § §

With a few other classmates, we were sitting in the café for lunch after our lecture when my phone notified me that I'd received an email. I wasn't usually one to look at my phone when surrounded by my friends, but since I wasn't particularly involved in their current discussion, I decided to take the liberty.

As soon as I identified the sender my heart jolted. It was from Day & Night LLP where I was set to complete a vacation scheme this summer. Alarm ruled my body as I rushed to open it. I hadn't expected to hear from them during this time, so I was worried it contained bad news regarding my work experience placement. While I waited for it to load, I prayed to the god I didn't believe in that they weren't going to terminate it. Once the text showed up, I was at first met with a polite greeting from Theresa Ainsley, who was the woman I'd been both interviewed and hired by.

As I read on, I was pleasantly surprised.

"You okay, Cara?" Aaron suddenly asked, and it occurred to me that he must have noticed my apprehension.

Lifting my gaze from my screen, I replied, "More than okay. I'm brilliant, actually."

Everyone fell silent around me.

"What's up?" Aaron probed with a frown.

"I've just received an email from Day & Night."

"And?"

"Well, it appears one of their paralegals is pregnant and is going to take maternity leave this summer, so they've asked whether I'd be interested in extending the length of my work experience placement. They've offered me to shadow one of their solicitors instead, as a paralegal slash legal assistant. Essentially, they're offering me to be a trainee for a few months."

Aaron's lips parted while Olivia gasped beside me.

"You're kidding!" she exclaimed.

"Am not."

"No doubt due to your excellent marks. For how long, though?" Aaron queried.

"Three months."

"Three months!" Olivia echoed, astonished. "That's amazing! That's bound to be a positive contribution to your resume, Cara."

"I know. I'd be a fool not to take the offer."

"You've got to take it," Aaron urged.

"I will, I will," I assured him with a smile. "If you'll excuse me, I need to write back."

"Well, there go our plans for the summer," Olivia murmured. "Can't say I'm upset about it, though."

I chuckled. "Me neither."

§ § §

It was nearing time for dinner when Olivia decided she'd revised enough for the day. Shortly after she'd left, Aaron leaned back in his chair, and I sensed his eyes on me.

"Have you heard back from Day & Night yet?" he asked after another while.

Looking up from my computer screen, I met his eyes and nodded. "Yeah. I've got to sign a new contract, so I'm stopping by on Monday next week at ten."

"I'm very happy for you, Cara. This is big."

"It is, and I wouldn't have managed it without you."

"What do you mean?"

I arched a brow. "You know what." I focused on my screen again. "My marks wouldn't be half as good without your help."

"You're giving me too much credit. You're helping me just as much."

"Our brains were made for each other."

"They were," he agreed, and his tone was conspicuously fond.

I'd thought our conversation was over, but since I sensed him continuing to observe me, I asked, "What?"

"Have you got any plans tonight?"

My blood slowed in my veins. Since I knew where he was going with this, I kept my eyes on my computer screen.

For the first time in my life, I dreaded sleeping with him again, and it wasn't because I felt like I was keeping him in the dark. I had faced him the day after sleeping with someone else several times before, and it had never posed a problem. Not once had my conscience suffered. Besides, for all I knew, he could have scored last weekend as well.

The truth was that I dreaded sleeping with him again because William had left a lasting impression. I hadn't yet recovered from the power of his attention. Because of that, a quick fix with Aaron wasn't something I had the mind for. Moreover, I didn't want to ruin my experience of Aaron's talents in bed. However, if we slept together so soon, it would inevitably result in that.

"I'm just not feeling up to it today. I'm sorry," I declined.

"Fair enough," he replied with a nod and focused on his textbook again.

Even though I knew I could only delay it for so long, I puffed out a quiet breath of relief.

§ § §

Finally, it was Monday the 22nd of April, which meant I was about to sign my new contract. I was tense as I waited for Ms Ainsley in the grand reception area of the Day & Night building on Cannon street, but to my surprise, she wasn't the one to collect me. Instead, a middle-aged man exited the lift and called my name.

"Ms Darby?"

"Yes?"

His piercing light-blue eyes – which was the first thing I noticed about him – locked with mine, and something about them struck me as familiar.

As he made his way across the floor, I admired his elegance, as well as the power of his strides. He had a level of class I could only dream of managing. Scattered throughout his otherwise dark brown hair were silver strands. Neatly shaven, he looked years younger than he was. Physically speaking, he was one of those men who made age his friend. Mirroring his grin, I wondered who he was.

"It's a pleasure to finally meet you. I've heard great things," he said just as he halted in front of me. He extended his hand, and I was quick to take it. His grip was firm, and I appreciated that.

"Have you?"

"Indeed." He chuckled. "You must be wondering who I am."

"Well, we've not met before, have we?"

"No, I'm afraid not. I'm John Night, Jason's father."

Awestruck, I gaped. Was I really looking upon the legend himself? To what did I owe this honour? In fact, was it normal for a CMD to welcome insignificant trainees like this? I was well aware that my purpose here wouldn't be to serve directly under him. So, why the special treatment? Was it because I was his son's flatmate?

"It's an honour to meet you, sir," I immediately said.

Genuine laughter rumbled out of him. "Please, call me John."

"Then you must call me Cara."

"Cara," he echoed, delighted. "Theresa told me you were coming in today, so I gathered I ought to welcome you myself. It's a shame we haven't met till now. I know Jason's very fond of you."

I grinned. "Well, I'm rather fond of him too."

"I'm happy to hear that. Anyway, thanks for being motivated to move things around on such short notice. I hope you didn't have to cancel any plans for the summer."

"I'd happily cancel my entire social life for this opportunity, John."

He laughed. "Then you'll make an excellent solicitor when the day comes. Are you anxious to start?" he asked and ushered me towards the lifts.

"Definitely."

He chuckled and gently landed his hand on my back. "You'll fit in perfectly, I'm sure."

"I hope so." I hadn't had colleagues since I'd quit my job at Starbucks three years ago to focus on my degree.

"How was my son this morning?" John asked while he ushered me into the lift and pressed the button for the tenth floor.

The mention made me smile. "Groggy, but grateful for the breakfast I served him in bed."

"He has mentioned that you're an excellent chef."

"Has he?" I queried, surprised.

"Indeed. Hasn't he told you?"

I was grinning while I shook my head. "Must have slipped his mind."

"I'm sure he was just too busy devouring your cooking to think of commenting on it," John responded, amused. "Wherever he lost his manners, I don't know, but I'm sure my parenting is free of any blame."

I laughed wholeheartedly and was grateful to learn that John was obviously a witty man with a great sense of humour.

"My office is on the top floor," he said, "but yours will be on the tenth floor, with the M&A department. That's where the solicitor you'll be aiding has got his. If ever there's anything at all, don't hesitate to stop by."

I nodded.

"You'll be shadowing my eldest son during your time here, so he'll be in charge of overseeing your work. He's a good man, I like to think, and one hell of a solicitor. I couldn't be prouder of his achievements. Hopefully, you'll learn a great deal from him."

My eyebrows climbed up my forehead. I'd be shadowing Jason's elder brother? I hadn't expected that. Though Jason had mentioned him several times, and always with a tone of brotherly affection, I'd never met him.

"If he's your son, I'm sure I will," I replied sincerely.

The lift halted on our floor and the doors parted. Presented to me was the view of an open-plan office which closed offices surrounded. Lush and light shades of seemingly expensive interior beckoned.

Placing his hand on my back again, John guided me out of the lift, past the curious faces of a few future colleagues of mine, and then further towards the dark brown door of an office that seemed to be rooted in the corner of the building. I wondered what the view from it was like. In a few seconds, I'd find out.

While raising his hand to give the door three gentle knocks, John sent me a wink. "He may bark, but he never bites."

A short, nervous laugh escaped me.

Then, an eerily familiar voice called from inside, "Come in."

Upon hearing it, I frowned. I was certain I'd heard it before, but where? Opening the door, John stepped through first and brought me along with him. The sight that met me rendered me paralysed, overcome with emotion. Confusion, despair, as well as fear and unbelievable joy seeped through my heart all at once, causing it to twist rather painfully.

With parted lips, I watched him lift his gaze from his desktop Mac and onto my figure beside his father. Upon recognising me, his eyebrows climbed up his forehead while his eyes widened beneath them.

Seemingly speechless, William – erotica in the flesh – stared back at me.

HAVE WE MET?

F OR A MOMENT, ALL I SAW WAS HIS NAKED BODY, BOTH ON top of and within me, while he pleasured me into the celestial. I could hardly believe my eyes.

This was why I'd thought he'd looked so familiar back then; he was Jason's elder brother! How had I not connected the dots? Jason had even mentioned him several times, but never in my wildest dreams would I have thought them to be one and the same.

Paling where I stood, I recoiled a step, struck by the overwhelming power of his presence. By now, I had almost managed to tuck my adventure with him into the depths of my memory. These days, I hardly ever gave him a thought because I was sure I'd never see him again. Yet, here he was, in the flesh, regarding me as though he'd just been punched in the gut. The odds of this happening were astronomical, and it made me question my own convictions. Did coincidences truly exist, or was everything written in the stars? If so, what tales did they hold of my future? And why on earth had they included *him*?

I was still trying to comprehend the truth of my circumstance when John started speaking. "Will, this is Cara Jane Darby, the new trainee. She's also Jason's flatmate, so be good to her. I've spoken highly of you, and I wouldn't like to be disproved."

Paralysed, William continued to stare at me. I didn't blame him for struggling so hard to compose himself. Not only had I arrived like lightning from a clear blue sky, but I was also being introduced under an entirely different name. However, when John cleared his throat, seemingly puzzled by his son's behaviour, William charged up from his seat.

Marvelling at the beauteous view of him, I blinked twice as he made his graceful approach. For the life of me, I couldn't locate my lungs or my tongue, so, out of breath, I watched him draw nearer. Only he could hypnotise me like this. I simply could not look away.

"It's a pleasure to make your acquaintance, Miss Darby. I'm William, but you may call me Will like everyone else. I'm looking forward to working with you. I hear your marks are impeccable. I'll personally ensure that you'll get to put theory into practice during your time with us." He extended his hand to me.

The same moment his voice addressed me, it dawned on me that I had actually missed it. Deep, authoritative, and oddly soothing, it whispered of sensual pleasures. How strange it was, to find myself having missed a person I'd only encountered once before.

A crimson blush painted my cheeks when I directed my gaze to his waiting hand. Staring at it, I remembered how it had completely dominated me. A particular memory, of when he'd used his grip on my arms to balance the weight of his powerful thrusts, flashed through my mind.

This was outrageous. What was I supposed to do? I couldn't work here, under the leadership of a man who had fucked me into oblivion. How was I supposed to look him in the eye without being reminded of that? How were we supposed to take each other seriously, as professionals, when our current acquaintanceship was composed of carnal indulgence? Would we be able to overlook it? Start anew?

I found I wanted to cry. This was the worst possible thing that could have happened. I'd worked so hard to prove myself eligible for this work experience placement, and now I'd quite literally fucked my chance at it.

"Murphy's law," Dad's voice chimed in my head. "Anything that can go wrong will go wrong. In other words, whatever can happen, will happen." Well, I was currently witnessing evidence of that theory. Lesson learnt, Dad, albeit too late.

"Y-yeah," I stammered and, while breaking contact with his striking eyes, grabbed his familiar hand. His grip was firm around my own, as if he was worried I'd disappear if ever he let go.

"Well, I'll leave you to it, then," John said with a sigh. "I've got a meeting in less than two minutes. If there's anything I can help you with, Cara, do let me know, but I expect my son will take good care of you."

"Of course," William assured him, and there was a gleam in his eye when he finally released my hand.

After giving my shoulder a supportive squeeze, John headed for the door and closed it behind him. The sound made me jump.

"Well then, *Cara*," William said, emphasising my real name, and strode away to find a seat on his matte black desk. After folding his hands above the crotch of his light-grey trousers, he studied me with the same crooked smile that I had worked so hard to forget.

"Have we met?" he asked and successfully knocked all the air out of me. The bastard was using my own words against me. How dare he toss that line at me at a time like this?

"I'm quite sure we have," he continued and narrowed his eyes. "I could have sworn I've seen you before. Have you been on telly? In newspapers?" Not a hint of sympathy was present in his piercingly blue eyes. Lost for words, I couldn't dodge even an ounce of his wrath, so instead, I merely gawked.

"Right, it's coming back to me now," he said, nodding to himself. "I know where I've seen you. It was in my bed, wasn't it? While I fucked you senseless? Yes, I believe so. Now that I think about it, how could I forget? Must have been your lies that have got me all confused."

Overwhelmed, I took a sharp breath and looked away. Stringing together a single coherent thought proved impossible. I'd never been this shocked.

"Please, have a seat." He gestured towards one of the two black chairs in front of his desk. As I fixed my gaze on them, I noted that his office was rather big. Against the wall to my right stood a white leather sofa, along with a coffee table made of transparent glass. Behind him, London revealed itself.

Incapable of ministering any muscle of my body, I remained in the same place. Seemingly impatient, he leaned back to fetch a document from his desk.

"I gather you're here to sign the contract establishing your temporary role here."

My gaze dashed towards him again. His composure bewildered me. Was he feigning nonchalance? Of course he was. We both knew what we'd done to each other, naked and lusting.

I swallowed a huge lump in my throat. It might have been my heart. However, since it was currently thundering like a bloody orchestra within my chest, perhaps not.

"I..." Averting my eyes, I adjusted my purse on my shoulder.

"You?" he prompted, audibly amused.

"This is...I'm sorry, I'm just..."

"Shocked?" He filled in the blanks. Since I still couldn't bring myself to look at him, I only nodded. Frankly, the mere sight of him was unbearable.

"Cara, take a seat," he ordered, reminding me of his domineering attitude. Obeying – because I didn't know what else to do – I approached the chair that stood furthest away from him. As I went, I sensed him watch me with interest.

I was about to sit when he slid off his desk to descend into the chair beside mine. Freezing, I met his eyes and watched him recline into it. He smirked up at me and gestured towards my chair again, inspiring me to mentally curse his confidence.

After I'd slowly found my seat, he turned his chair towards me and queried somewhat bitterly, "Is it Cara? Or do you prefer going by Sandra?"

I pursed my lips. "I didn't think I'd be seeing you again."

"I realise that, and yet, here we are."

I grimaced and begged my heart to calm down. From the speed of its beats, I had to be shortening my lifespan. "I don't quite think that this is a good idea."

He was quiet for a second. "What? The placement?"

I nodded.

He scoffed. "Don't be ridiculous. It's far too late to apply for a spot somewhere else. I can guarantee you won't get it. The competition is intense. This isn't an opportunity you should cast aside merely because you've coincidentally fucked your boss."

My breath hitched at his blunt phrasing. I'd nearly forgotten about his vulgar tongue, but not quite. Beside him, I blushed blood red.

He leaned forward, towards me, and it perturbed me. The tension between us was thick and dense in the air, and it made me feel like I was suffocating. Having him so close wreaked havoc on my emotions. Suddenly, I made no sense to myself. All I knew was that I wished he would back away so that I might be able to think clearly.

His eyes zoomed in on my blank facial expression. "I seem to recall you having a dreadfully sharp tongue. Have you lost your bravado?"

"Are you at all able to be quiet for longer than a second? I need to think!" I snapped, growing increasingly annoyed with his scrutiny. I was trapped in a clusterfuck of a situation, and he wasn't allowing me any mental room to sort it out.

"I honestly can't believe you're Jason's flatmate. All along, you've been within my reach. I'm furious. Had I known, I'd have hunted you down," he declared momentously.

Horribly uncomfortable, I tensed in my seat. At the very best, this was wildly inappropriate. If he was still adamant about getting me into bed with him, things were going to end in chaos.

He sighed and tossed the contract onto his desk. "When Theresa told me whom she'd hired for the position, she mentioned a girl named Cara, studying law. Not Sandra, studying medicine, in fucking *Edinburgh*." He leaned back. "At least I've got your number now."

"What do you want me to say?" I retorted defensively.

"I'd like an apology, for starters," he calmly replied.

"Well, I'm sorry, Will. It wasn't personal."

He nodded. "Thank you."

My eyebrows furrowed as I met his arresting eyes. "You've got to see why this won't work. Surely, you're not that daft, are you?"

He glared at me, and I nearly withered under the heat of it. "Well, I must be, because I don't see the problem. You'll only be here for three months. Had it been indefinite, we'd be having a different conversation, but it's not. We're also adults, meaning we should be able to work our way round it."

"How do you think John would react if he knew? Or Theresa?" I countered in my scepticism. To my satisfaction, he grimaced at the very idea.

"Exactly," I said and folded my arms together.

"There won't be a reason for concern unless we behave in a way that warrants it. If you can manage, I guarantee I will, too. I'd hate to see you waste an opportunity like this, especially when knowing it'd be my fault."

Mustering whatever courage I had left, I stared at him with eyes of steel. "If we're going to do this, I'd like to make one thing abundantly clear. I will not have sex with you again. Do I need to explain why, or are you on board with that?"

I couldn't believe what I'd done. Never in my life had I managed something so outrageous before. I had slept with my best friend's brother. Not only that, but he was also going to be my boss for three months. If there had been even a slim chance that I'd want to sleep with him again, it had been completely obliterated in the wake of this.

I wondered whether I ought to tell Jason but immediately decided that I wouldn't. Since it had only been a one-night stand, I thought he'd be better off not knowing. Informing him was simply unnecessary, as it wouldn't happen again.

Aloofness spilled from William's eyes, and his heart-shaped lips formed a straight line. Added together, his facial expression made it impossible to gauge his thoughts.

"Who says I'd want to?"

My breath hitched, and my eyes widened. Right. I hadn't thought of that. For a moment, I considered myself despicably conceited. He was the professional here. Of course he'd abandon the idea now that our circumstances had changed.

"Right. That should make things easier." I'd managed to sound stoical, but behind my pretence, I was hiding a rather bruised ego. Rationally, I appreciated his rhetorical insinuation, but irrationally, I didn't. Being a woman that William Night desired was the most significant boost I'd had in a long time. Alas, the time for that was long gone. However, I had meant for it to turn out this way, so why did I feel so slighted? My feelings weren't justified, nor did they make any sense.

He sighed. "Well then. Shall we move along? We can't really afford to spend more time on this matter. I'm a busy man, and people are counting on me to perform according to schedule. On that note, you should prepare for three intense months."

It hadn't been necessary to tell me that. I was strapping up for the most challenging three months I'd probably ever have to endure, and it wasn't strictly due to the tasks I'd be delegated. It was also because I'd be facing intensity in the flesh for the better part of ninety days.

I nodded as I guided myself into a more professional frame of mind. "Yes."

Reaching forward, he fetched the contract he'd presented earlier and leaned towards me. Now close again, the scent of him struck me with merciless force. Immediately, I was sent down memory lane and into his bedroom, where his alluring scent was etched into the walls, and where his naked skin caressed and guided mine.

I was certain my pupils were dilated when I looked at the contract, though I could barely make sense of a single letter. I was much too distracted by my lust for this testosterone-bomb beside me.

I realised at the same moment that there were two dimensions to this. I was divided. Part of me wanted to fuck him into eternity. The other was adamant about remaining sensible, and sensible did not favour erotic thoughts of William Night when taking our new circumstances into account.

However, I wasn't deluded. There was no point in denying the fact that I was drawn to him like a moth to a flame. Anything else would be an absolute lie. My whole body tingled where I sat, aching for his sexual attention. He was the sexiest man I'd ever encountered, both in mind and body, and he was my best friend's brother, as well as my future boss. He surely was Satan in a Sunday hat.

Fuck.

He started speaking again, and like a male siren, his voice summoned me to my doom. "Your tasks will mainly include that of a paralegal's. Although I'll be your supervisor for the span of the placement, Elisabeth will be teaching you the basics of your tasks the first few days. She's a full-time paralegal, close to your age – twenty-five – and very kind and patient. I'll make the introductions once you've signed your contract.

"For now, I gather I'll guide you through it. If you have any questions, don't be shy. Tell me to stop, and I'll explain the implications to the best of my ability. Understood?"

He was awfully authoritative, and although I didn't like to admit it, it had a hotline to my libido. When I had thought things couldn't possibly get any worse, he proved me wrong. William, when focused and professional, was devastatingly attractive. As he was now, I could watch him for a lifetime, endlessly aroused and fascinated.

Since I failed to provide an answer, he turned towards me. Utterly susceptible, I looked straight back, and once he gauged my thoughts, his eyes noticeably widened.

"No, Cara. Do not look at me like that," he instructed impatiently.

"Like what?"

"Like you want me to claim you across my desk, right now."

My mouth dried as my breath left me. Though outrageous, the idea made my knickers grow damp while my heart raced. I would have loved every second of it, I was sure – until he surrendered his domination of me to remorse.

"What?" I whispered feebly.

"You heard me." He charged up from his seat. Walking round his desk, he reached for the black telecom and raised the handset to his ear. Shortly after he'd pushed a button, he requested in a chillingly strict tone, "Ellie, could you come in here for a sec? I've got a favour to ask of you." Once he rang off, he locked eyes with me and clenched his jaw.

I frowned in confusion. Wasn't he supposed to guide me through the contract? Before I had a chance to ask, there was a knock on the door.

"Come in," he answered and sank into the seat of his stylish, grey desk chair.

Turning my head, I watched a Black lady step in. Her Afro-textured hair was styled into twists that stopped just below her breasts, and she had the sort of smile that would make you turn your head after her on the street. She oozed maternal care. My first impression was that I'd come to adore her.

"You must be Cara," she said, and she had a voice that would suit a soft lullaby. What a remarkably soothing voice. Cooing was likely a constant for her.

A little chubby in her anatomy, she made her way over and extended her small hand. She was quite a short woman, but her breasts were huge. They strained against her dark blue satin blouse, and I couldn't help but steal a swift glimpse of her cleavage while I sized her up.

Eager to escape the heat of William's attention, I clasped her hand and ascended from my chair. In my heels, I was at least a head taller than her. "That's me, yes. You're Elisabeth?"

Her smile transitioned into a full-blown grin. "Please, call me Ellie. Elisabeth sounds so formal."

"Elisabeth is a lovely name," I remarked. "But of course, Ellie is, too."

"Ellie," William chimed in from behind us, "please see to it that Cara finds a space where she can read through her contract. I've got work that requires my immediate attention."

"Of course, Will. Whatever you need."

"Thanks. Did you manage to contact GreenPark for me?"

"Yes. I've sent you an email about it. The appointment should already be synchronised with your schedule."

Smirking, William looked to me. "Watch and learn," he said and then gave Elisabeth a fond wink.

"Certainly. But Mr Night—" it felt incredibly weird to refer to him that way—"what shall I do once I've signed?"

He frowned at how I'd addressed him, but I'd done it deliberately to create as much psychological distance between us as possible. It was purely a defensive mechanism to remind me of our professional relationship.

"I told you to call me Will, Cara," he murmured. While extending the contract to me across his desk, he continued, "If you've any questions, take notes and bring them to me once you've finished reading through. If you don't, simply sign and hand it over to me."

Nodding my head, I walked over to grab hold of it, but with each stride, the electric charge between us surmounted my heart. Once our gazes met, no words were required. I understood precisely what his eyes meant to convey.

He wanted to fuck me again, and he wanted to do it now.

Shocking myself, I realised that if our circumstances had been different, I would have succumbed to the desire.

However, while feigning obliviousness to the sexual mayhem he ceaselessly roused in me, I turned my back to him and said, "Thank you, Mr Night."

I thought I heard him curse under his breath, but I couldn't be sure.

MOMENTARY LOVER

A s soon as we'd walked out, Elisabeth was guiding the way to a vacant desk when warm brown eyes met mine across the room. The owner was walking straight towards us, seemingly on his way to William's office, but he came to an abrupt halt just before he passed. Visibly confused, his attention flickered between Elisabeth and me.

Startled by the memory of him, I stared up at him, wide-eyed. Could this day get any worse? If he learnt my true identity, it was only a matter of time before rumours about my prior encounter with William would flood the office. As their latest trainee, that was the last thing I wanted.

Elisabeth paused to regard him. Meanwhile, Andrew stared unashamedly at me with a bewildered expression on his face. Exerting every ounce of the self-discipline I'd harnessed over the years, I managed to remain composed. While feigning obliviousness, I returned his gaze with eyes that claimed innocence.

"Sorry, was it Sandra?" he eventually brought himself to ask.

Elisabeth came to my rescue. "Sandra? What on earth did you spike your coffee with this morning, Andy? This is Cara Darby, our new trainee."

Perplexed, Andrew's eyes did a sweep of my body. Faint pink claimed his cheeks while he frowned to himself. After clearing his throat, his eyes returned to mine. Since I sympathised with his confusion, I gave him a small smile.

"Sorry, I must have confused you with someone else," he murmured, embarrassed. "I could have sworn you were her."

Elisabeth giggled. While giving my arm a maternal squeeze, she smiled up at me. "Please excuse him. He's a delightful man."

"Yes, please pardon me." Andy extended his hand to me. "I'm Andrew Thompson, but everyone calls me Andy."

While nodding, I clasped his hand and gave him another small smile. "Cara."

"Are you showing her around, Ellie?"

"Sort of."

His attention shifted onto me again. "Why not William? I thought he was supposed to be her supervisor."

He was slick! I was certain he'd only asked to observe my reaction. Thankfully, my face didn't even twitch.

I said, "He had work to do. He seems delightful, though."

Andy tittered at my comment. "He seems delightful?" he echoed. "First time I've heard that. 'Delightful'." Another poorly stifled chuckle leapt out of him. "You're in for a treat, love. Just remember that even though he may bark, he never bites. Where other people might end a sentence with a question mark, Will usually finishes with a full stop. It's just who he is and always has been," he said. "But as long as you're aware of that, I'm sure you'll be fine."

I was almost tempted to say, 'No shit, Andy. I've already gathered as much,' but I refrained.

Elisabeth smirked. "I haven't briefed her on what to expect of her boss' general behaviour yet, so thank you for taking care of that, Andy."

He gave me a wink. "I've got your back, sweetheart." Directing his focus to Elisabeth again, he asked, "So he's busy right now? I've got something I'd like to run by him, preferably before his meeting with the lawyers from Lightning Charge this afternoon."

Nodding, Elisabeth replied, "While he's always busy, he hasn't got anything besides paperwork until then. I'm sure he could spare you five minutes if it's urgent and you ask nicely."

"Great, thanks." Steering his eyes back to mine, he grinned. "Pleasure meeting you, *Cara*."

"You too."

As he walked away, he shook his head to himself, and I had a suspicion as to why. I feared he would probe William about me in only a few moments. If he did, I prayed William would either tell him a lie or ensure his silence some other way.

"Appears you've got a replica out there, somewhere," Elisabeth remarked and started walking again.

"Would seem so," I replied, amused.

"I'm sure her freckles aren't as adorable as yours."

Her compliment made me flash her a grin. I'd always been grateful for the freckles that covered my nose, and they were in fact Aaron's favourite part of my face.

I paled as I thought of him. Now that I was bound to encounter William time and again, I was certain it would wreak havoc on the dynamic between Aaron and me. It had taken me a week to recover from my session with William, and Aaron had spent it growing worried about our arrangement. How was I supposed to manage this time around?

By not sleeping with William, I thought to myself as the obvious answer. I was motivated to manage that for several reasons: for the sake of my placement, for the sake of my friendship with Jason, for the sake of my arrangement with Aaron, and last, but certainly not least, for the sake of my sanity, my education and finally my career.

"Here we are." Elisabeth brought me out of my thoughts and motioned towards a free desk.

"Thanks," I replied, perhaps too eagerly, but I was in dire need of privacy.

I'd have to call Olivia as soon as I left. She was the sole person I could confide in about this, and I was desperate to talk to someone. I would use her as a soundboard to air my thoughts. Perhaps then, I'd be able to make sense of this dreadful mess.

As I went over my contract, I found nothing I'd like to discuss. Unsurprisingly, it was faultless. I hadn't expected any less of a law firm. However, I couldn't help but read the contract with William's voice in my head, because I could imagine that he had penned it. Authoritative and impatient, his otherwise sensual voice barked every single word at me. It caused a constant grimace to cover my face as I read through.

Bloody hell, he was everywhere – even in my head. I felt like I was suffocating.

"Cara," his voice suddenly called. That wasn't where I was in my contract? My head snapped up when I realised he was truly speaking to me. Whirling round in my chair, I discovered him standing behind me, slightly bent across my shoulder.

"Shit, you scared me!" I immediately recoiled towards my desk.

"Not my fault you're so oblivious to your surroundings."

"I was concentrating." My gaze shifted to his shoes. "I hadn't expected Bigfoot to move so quietly."

Amusement danced in his eyes before he closed them to refocus.

"I've got ten minutes to spare, should you want to go over your contract now."

"I was just finishing."

"Then let's continue in my office."

A normal human being would have said, 'Right. Shall we continue in my office?' But of course, he was everything except that.

Ascending from my seat, I gave him a scowl. Disobeying him in full view of the others was out of the question, regardless of how much I wanted to when considering that being alone with him wasn't good for my mental health. However, professional as I was,

I collected my contract to heed his command.

When I walked past him, his hand landed on my back, and I immediately stiffened. Did he think I required a compass to find his office?

"I can walk by myself," I muttered under my breath when we were out of hearing range.

Devoid of emotion, he quietly replied, "I'd prefer not to walk behind you. My eyes keep landing on your beautiful bum, and I'd hate to objectify you like that."

With cheeks hot and red, I charged into his office and watched him close the door behind him.

"You can't speak to me like that," I grumbled firmly. "I was actually considering signing a moment ago, but you just reminded me why I shouldn't!"

"Calm down."

I gaped. How could he, as an able lawyer, possibly find his comment justifiable?

"Calm down? Are you actually telling me to calm down when your comment clearly constitutes sexual harassment under the Equality Act of 2010?"

His eyes widened with his shock, and the sound of his sharp inhalation satisfied me profoundly. Since he appeared speechless, I continued, "Do you tell Ellie that you prefer not to walk behind her since you'll sexualise her if you do? As if that's not completely unheard of and therefore acceptable behaviour? I am utterly serious about this placement, and I ought to be treated as such."

Aghast, he blew his cheeks out and gripped his hips while he processed my tirade. At last, he had the decency to look thoroughly ashamed of himself. "You're right. It's completely unacceptable, and I'm sorry. It won't happen again."

"No, it won't," I retorted and folded my arms.

In silence, we stared at each other for a long while. Once he gathered that the storm had passed, he let out a loud sigh.

"Honestly, Cara, I truly am sorry. I didn't mean for it to come across that way. It's just – well, there's really no excuse, but I've got my roles a tad bit confused today. Give me some time to adapt, and I promise I'll do better. Seeing you again wasn't something I'd expected, and certainly not here. It's messed with my head, especially because it's you. I just need to readjust – to start regarding you as a colleague, rather than as my…" He paused, and I could tell he was searching for the appropriate label by his fleeting gaze.

"One-night stand?" I filled in.

His eyes shot to mine, and the sudden certainty they contained made it clear that my suggestion hadn't resonated with him.

"I was going to say momentary lover."

Since his phrasing was blatantly deliberate, I couldn't prevent the blush that surfaced in my cheeks. Without a doubt, he'd intended for it to sound more romantic than the label 'one-night stand' typically implied, and it made me wonder if it were because he'd experienced our night together as more meaningful than a mere session between the sheets. If that were truly the case, we shared the same view, and quite frankly, I found consolation in the fact that my subsequent interest in him hadn't been entirely one-sided. Like me, perhaps he too had required several days to recover from our last encounter.

After pursing my lips for a beat, I replied, "Yeah, well, you're not alone in that. How do you think I've experienced all this? Not only have I managed to fuck my flatmate's brother, but he also just happens to be my new boss. And yet I still manage not to sexualise you – outwardly, anyhow."

I wished I hadn't added the last part, but my mouth had spoken before my mind caught up. At once, his eyes shot towards me, leaving me to whimper. Why had I said that?

A smug smile crept across his lips while he propped his back against the door. Folding his strong arms across his chest, he studied me until I felt ready to expire.

"Outwardly, you say?"

"Mr Night." Menace filled my tone. I was not a woman to be

trifled with right now.

Smirking, he nodded to himself. "I admire your resolve, Cara, but why do you insist on calling me 'Mr Night'?"

"It's all part of the resolve you so admire."

"What?" he queried, perplexed.

"I'm creating psychological distance between us, and it's working, so I've no intention of stopping."

He burst out laughing then, and I found it awfully patronising.

"Fuck this," I grumbled and dropped the contract on his desk. I wasn't going to sign it. This would never work. The man wasn't taking me seriously at all, and I found it extremely offensive. I was serious about this placement. That meant I was determined to put our sensual past behind us, but he kept insisting on reminding me of it. As such, he wasn't treating me like every other employee at all, and that wasn't something I found acceptable.

I did not want his special treatment. I wanted to be treated like anyone else in this firm, like we'd never shared a bed. I couldn't fathom why he would assume it was alright to do anything else.

My action murdered his laughter. With the eyes of a hawk, he watched me approach him in front of the only sensible exit, but if he didn't move, perhaps the windows of his office would become sensible options, too.

"Cara."

I hated when he used that tone, because it exuded power not even I dared question.

"Sign the contract," he ordered.

While avoiding his eyes, I reached for the handle, but his hand intercepted. Grabbing my wrist, he guided my hand away, and then he completely shocked me. Entwining our fingers, he held my hand most affectionately and fixed his eyes on them.

Overwhelmed by the intimacy of his action, I followed his gaze. My heart thundered against my ribcage until its beats were of such strength that I wondered if it would burst within me. It felt like my whole body was vibrating.

What the hell was going on with me? Was this truly just lust, or was I growing infatuated with this imbecile? No, I couldn't be. I hardly knew him.

Without releasing my hand, he repeated, "Sign the contract, Cara."

Speechless, I continued to stare at his hand around mine. I was trying to make sense of my feelings, but fathoming the extent of his influence seemed impossible. I'd never felt like this, as if he'd set me on fire, and he was only holding my hand.

"I promise I'll be good to you," he murmured and, much to my regret, let go.

Paralysed, I watched him walk past me to fetch my contract from his desk. Upon his return, he withdrew a pen from his pocket and gave me a grave look.

"I won't let you waste an opportunity like this, and I'm not saying that because I want to get in your knickers. I'm saying it as one solicitor to an aspiring one. We'll work it out. We'll just have to communicate. This is a strange situation, but we're both adults. We'll work our way round it. Please don't squander your potential just because you happen to have shared a bed with me."

Again, I swallowed, hypnotised by his power. Still paralysed, I merely stared at him, undecided. I just couldn't decide!

With a sigh, he grabbed my shoulder to make me face the door again. Next, he shoved the pen into my hand and then retreated a step while holding the contract against the brown wood of his door.

"Three months, Cara. You'll survive, and you'll be thanking yourself – and me – for the rest of your life." He resembled the Devil, urging me to sell him my soul in exchange for perpetual success. Was I really going to take that deal?

I looked at him for some time, contemplating, until I finally decided that he was right. This placement would most definitely assist my career later on, and I wasn't about to waste it over an issue like this. Like he'd said, we were adults. We would work our way round it. If his behaviour escalated into being truly intolerable, I reminded myself that I could always notify the HR department of his relentless advances, even if I hoped it wouldn't come to that. Seeing as he was Jason's brother and John's son, I would rather avoid going to such measures, but if he didn't stop sexualising me, I'd be forced to. And so, since my career was in fact at stake, I finally decided to sign the contract.

My hand was shaking when I put the pen to the dotted line, but it stilled with revived confidence as I began to write my signature. Once I'd finished, he was quick to snatch the document away. As I embraced my new reality, air stormed out of my lungs.

I'd signed. I was trapped with him now, for three long months.

"Excellent," he murmured, audibly pleased.

My body was rigid while my eyes followed his. He was walking round his desk now, where he stored my contract in the top drawer.

"Now, then." He exhaled and dropped into his chair. While grinning up at me, he spread his arms apart in a jovial manner before enquiring, "Will you have dinner with me today?"

Grinding my teeth, I glared back. "Are you taking the piss?"

"Not at all." He chuckled. "Seeing as you'll be stuck with me for the better part of three months, I gather we should get to know each other better. Dressed, this time."

There he went again. I'd never admit it aloud, but the man had wit. However, I didn't appreciate the reminder it contained this time around. Despairing, I looked away while shaking my head. "You're unbelievable. Unless there's anything else, I'd like to leave now."

"It's a harmless dinner, Cara."

Nothing involving that man was harmless. "Goodbye," I muttered and opened the door.

"Tell Jason I miss him, will you? Ask him if I might come for dinner this week."

Appalled, I froze upon his bold suggestion. Nevertheless, I was grateful for the due reminder. Shutting the door again, I turned to face him and folded my arms.

"Speaking of Jason," I said, "I'd rather he didn't find out about us."

Identifying leverage, his smile grew cunning. "Is that so?"

"Can you promise you won't tell him?"

Bringing his pen to his mouth, he chewed on the end of it while he studied me for some time. "Depends."

"William, seriously." I was reaching the end of my tether. "How do you think he'd react if he found out? He'd be awkward around the both of us to say the least, and I'd like to avoid that. God knows, he might even get angry with me."

"Have dinner with me, then. If you do, I won't tell him."

I gripped my hips. "Are you listening to yourself? You're abusing your power. This is essentially blackmailing."

A smug chuckle leapt out of his mouth, and the sound made me realise that I'd rather have Jason find out than yield to his blackmail.

"You know, you really are a right arsehole," I declared. "Do what you want then, but if you have any regard for my feelings in all this, you won't tell him." With that, I turned to open the door again.

"Wait, wait," he called to stall me. With a sigh, he said, "I won't tell him, Cara. I promise."

Sceptical, I turned back around. "Really?"

He nodded gravely. "Of course. I respect you far too much to do such a thing. I was only taking the piss. I'm sorry."

"Ha-ha," I uttered sarcastically and opened the door.

"Hang on, I'll walk you out. I'm about to have lunch."

Reluctant to obey, I hardly slowed down as I approached the lift. Alongside Andy, Elisabeth was waiting just in front of it. Wonderful. Andy and William were precisely the two people I'd like to spend time with in a lift right now.

Much to my regret, William managed to catch up with me by the time the doors opened to let us in, and his pace hadn't failed to grab the attention of both Andy and Elisabeth.

"Christ, Will, you must be starving," Elisabeth commented.

"I heard they're serving pizza," William joked.

During the brief journey, Andy traded regular glances with William over my head. They sent each other cheeky smiles, but Elisabeth paid no attention, which made me think that the two men behaved like this on a regular basis. It wasn't surprising when taking into account that they were best friends, but it annoyed me nevertheless because I was certain I was the cause of their current amusement.

Stealing a glance at William through the mirrors, I wondered to myself whether he had misled me on purpose earlier. In the end, his statement had been rather ambiguous. "Who says I'd want to?'" didn't erase all room for doubt. He hadn't actually denied anything. Had he phrased it that way deliberately, to misguide me, and thereafter buy himself more time to analyse how to proceed? In fact, he might only have said it to retaliate for a bruised ego.

The possibility intrigued me. Did he truly intend to relent his efforts, or was he only weighing up which route to take in order to win me over, despite my convictions?

The impression I had of him was that he was not inclined to cease his pursuit when he had his eyes fixed on a prize. He was far too assertive. Last time we'd met, he'd ardently tried to persuade me to give him a chance. So, the question remaining was: was I still the prize?

"Oh my God, I just recalled – do you know what Andy did earlier?" Elisabeth suddenly exclaimed and whirled around to face William. While laughing, she continued, "He thought Cara was someone else, so he called her Sandra. You should've seen him. I've never seen him quite so confused."

"Did he?" William replied, and it was clear from his tone that he was highly amused. Too curious to stop myself, I stole another glance at him. He met it with a gleam dancing in his eyes, and I immediately grasped that they had talked about it behind closed doors.

Fuck.

Once we reached the ground floor, Elisabeth and Andy exited before William and I did, so when he grabbed my arm to stall me, they kept on walking.

With my heart in my throat, I faced him.

"Andy knows," he declared, leaving blood to drain from my head.

"Did you tell him?" I snapped, both irked and defensive.

He glared back. "He's a fucking lawyer, Cara. He can detect a lie when he hears one, especially from me – and he's not stupid. Of course he remembered you."

"Shit," I whined and stamped my foot.

Blinking, he dropped his gaze to it. "Did you really just stamp your foot?"

"William! If Andy spills, it's only a matter of time before everyone knows!"

His grip tightened around my arm. "He won't tell anyone, Cara. He's my best friend, and he's got my back. Always."

"Tell anyone what?" an exceptionally gorgeous woman probed just as she entered the lift. With raven black hair that cascaded down to the middle of her back, she took my breath away. Slanted, dark brown eyes that were complemented by long lashes met mine. Her full lips tucked into a wry smile beneath her small nose before she turned her attention to the man holding my arm. Once she saw him, it transformed into a grin.

"That's none of your concern, Violet," William quietly retorted and dragged me out with him. Casting a glance at her over my shoulder, I saw her fold her arms over the chest of her slender and curvaceous figure.

Intrigued, I asked, "Who's that?"

"Violet Rodriguez. She's my partner on a transaction I'm currently working on," William muttered.

"She's gorgeous," I remarked. When I looked back at him, I found him staring at me with an unreadable expression on his face.

Returning to our conversation, I pleaded, "Do you swear Andy won't tell?"

His jaw clenched. "Yes. But don't be surprised if he gives you any funny looks. He laughed until he cried earlier, in my office."

Well, at least someone was enjoying the chaos of our circumstance. Sulking, I looked towards the exit of the building.

"Suppose I'll be seeing you around, then," I muttered.

"Suppose so."

A week ago, I'd have kissed him goodbye. Strange to think of that. "Later, then. Enjoy your lunch," I said, and once I looked up, I discovered him regarding me with a strange sort of longing in his eyes.

He merely gave me a nod, and I sensed his gaze on my back the entire time it took for me to exit the building.

§ § §

"He's your boss!" Olivia practically shouted down the phone.

Trying to remain calm, I asked, "What am I supposed to do, Livy?"

"Christ, Cara! Is Jason aware?"

"Of course not," I growled. "Had it been serious between Will and me, of course I would have told him, but forgive me if I'm not inclined to tell my best friend, and flatmate, that I completely sexually exploited his elder brother."

"Yeah, don't tell Jason. I wouldn't want to know if I were him. But how did Will react when he saw you?"

Once I'd given her the scoop on my day, she puffed out a long, loud breath. "Shit. You're in it now, aren't you?"

"Livy," I whined, "do you realise what a clusterfuck of a situation I've got on my hands? And the bastard even tried to blackmail me into having dinner with him today – after I'd signed, and he'd promised to behave. Said he'd tell Jason about us if I didn't accept."

"That's outrageous! Please, don't tell me you agreed."

"Of course not."

"I can't believe he tried that."

"Me neither. I'm livid."

"He must be really taken with you."

"I don't care. It's completely out of the question. You'd think he'd realise that when *he's* the professional between us."

"Yeah, he was out of order. I'm so sorry, Cara. I honestly don't know what to say. I hope for your sake that he won't tell Jason."

"He promised me he wouldn't."

"Well, then I hope he'll keep it. But, aside from the shock of meeting him again in the role of your boss, have you considered what this means now that you're living with Jason?"

"Yes," I whined.

"We both know Jason's very close with his brother. To be honest, it's a wonder we hadn't met him sooner."

"I know."

"And now that you've just moved in with Jason, you're bound to see Will a lot more, even before you start work."

"I'm well aware of this, Livy," I reminded her brusquely.

"Sorry, Cara. I wish I could be of more help, but I've honestly got no idea what to say. It's a clusterfuck for sure, of epic proportions."

I sighed. "Well, I appreciate the moral support."

"It's the least I can do. I feel like you've been my acting psychologist for the past three years. About time I return the favour. Anyway, are you on your way here?"

Upon recalling my plans to revise with her and Aaron, I closed my eyes and stopped walking. "Fuck."

"Yeah, Aaron's here. Do you think you'll be able to act normal?"

I briefly considered going home instead, but immediately decided against it when I gathered Jason was likely to be there since his shift at the A&E department at the hospital didn't start till two o'clock.

"Well, it's not like heading home would be any better. Honestly, between the two of them, Jason's the one I'll have the hardest time facing."

"Yeah, I get what you mean. I wish there was something I could do."

I sighed. "Thanks. I appreciate the sentiment. Anyway, I'm sure I'm just overreacting in the aftermath of my shock. It's not like anything's really changed. Will and I aren't going to have sex again. The only thing that's different this time around is the inevitable continuity of my acquaintanceship with him. That's what's messing with my head, because I've never been in this situation before. I've never had to face Aaron while knowing I'm in touch with one of my previous bed partners, and I've definitely never had to face

SKIN OF THE NIGHT

Jason while knowing I've fucked his brother."

"Yeah, that's enough to mess with anyone's head."

"Right? And you know, the worst part is that I feel like I'm keeping them in the dark about something when, really, it's actually none of their business." I sighed again and rubbed my forehead. "Gosh, listen to me. William has promised not to say anything, so there's really no reason I should treat this as a problem."

"Again, Cara, your rationality astounds me. I wish I were half as level-headed as you."

I released a humourless laugh. "Honestly, I'm all talk and no trousers right now. Truth is I'm still all over the place."

"But the fact that you're aware of that obviously means you're slowly coming to terms with things. As you said, you've had quite a shock. Let it settle first. Once it subsides, I'm sure you'll be able to go about your business as usual."

Her words fuelled my motivation to move past this sooner rather than later. "You're right. Of course I will."

"That's the Cara I know and love."

"I don't know what I'd do without you, Livy. Thanks for listening to my rant, and for existing."

She laughed. "Right back at you, darling. I'll see you in a bit, then."

"Yes."

§ § §

I thought I deserved an Oscar for how well I'd handled facing Aaron. There was both a positive and a negative side to that, however, because while it had enabled me to maintain harmony, it also meant I was a skilled liar. The latter wasn't something I took pride in, because I despised dishonesty. However, I reminded myself that there was a difference between being honest and being open, and there was no need for me to be transparent, which meant being both. Had I been confronted by either Aaron or Jason, I'd have told the truth without hesitation, but to tell them unsolicited? I couldn't see what good it would do other than relieving my conscience.

It was nearing nine o'clock when the three of us decided to

leave campus. Olivia had stayed behind for longer than usual, and I suspected it was because she wanted to help me carry the burden of entertaining Aaron after today's events. She'd never know how much I appreciated that.

By the time we'd parted ways, Aaron had been in a delightful mood. It was clear he didn't suspect a thing. I hoped I would handle facing Jason equally well, but part of me doubted it. There was something about my friendship with Jason that was completely unique, because I genuinely regarded him as a sibling. Total transparency was something I'd practised in his company ever since the first time we'd met. To look him in the eye, while knowing how his actual sibling performed in bed – as well as against the wall, or on the dining table – wasn't something I looked forward to because of that. However, I would have to, and I hated it. This was the first time ever that I was keeping something from him, and I prayed it would also be the last.

Slight panic grabbed hold of me when I unlocked the front door to discover him right behind it. From his attire, I could tell he'd only just come home from work. Blinking in surprise, his tall figure turned towards me.

"Cara?"

"No, it's Santa."

Smirking, he knelt to untie his shoes. "Then I'll let you know I've been a good boy."

I chuckled and stepped in. "I already knew. First-hand experience. How was your shift at the hospital?" I closed the door behind me.

"Hectic, as usual."

"I can imagine." Apprehensive, I scanned his body language for any sign of veiled anger or disappointment but came up empty. He didn't look like he had the slightest clue. Had William kept his promise?

All of a sudden, a wicked smile claimed his mouth. With a mischievous twinkle in his blue eyes – eyes that were insufferably similar to his brother's – he met mine and stretched back up.

Perhaps William had told him after all.

"I heard you met my brother today," Jason began and slowly took off his shoes.

Had William told him that?

To hide from his gaze – and potential wrath – I faced the wall as I untied my coat. "Yeah, I did. Impressive man."

A short laugh escaped him. "Really? You'd call him 'impressive'? Perhaps I should have warned you, but he can be a bit of a dick. You get used to it, though, and if anyone can hold their own, it's you. Anyway, I wasn't aware you'd been hired for the job as *his* legal assistant. Dad told me just today." So it was John he had spoken to. I found relief in that.

"Neither was I," I replied. "Safe to say I was surprised."

"Well, you'll have plenty of time to get to know him before you start. We tend to hang out on the weekends to watch football together. He was actually meant to come over last Friday, but I had to cancel because I was asked to take a shift at the hospital."

Since I could only imagine the shock that situation would have made for, I counted my blessings. Jason would certainly have learnt the truth had it turned out that way, so I thanked the heavens for small mercies, because thus far, he seemed unaware.

"Right. Looking forward to it," I replied.

"He's a great guy. I actually think you'll get on really well." Far better than he knew. "You're sort of similar in a lot of ways."

"Yes, I got the same impression when I met him," I agreed. After hanging up my coat, I grabbed my bag and headed for my bedroom. "Anyway, I'm knackered, so I think I'll go to bed."

"Would you mind if I had a shower first?"

"Go ahead," I said as I shut the door between us. Leaning against it, I sank to the floor with a heavy breath. What a day. It was tempting to never leave my bedroom again. At least here, I was safe.

Or was I? With Jason as my best friend, would I ever truly be rid of William? I had a feeling he'd always be around, looming in the shadows.

"Fuck," I groaned and rested my weary head in my hands. I was definitely in need of my bed. Perhaps after sleeping, I'd feel better.

9

THE WAY OF THE WORLD

B Y FRIDAY, I WAS NO LONGER ANXIOUS ABOUT WILLIAM'S inevitable presence in my life. The process of coming to terms with it had been aided by the fact that I hadn't heard a word from him since Monday, and Jason hadn't shown any signs of being aware of our sensual past either. Clearly, William had kept his word so far. Besides, considering how busy Jason currently was with work at the hospital, I'd gathered I wouldn't be seeing his brother all that much anyway. In the end, Jason barely had time to catch his breath between shifts. The A&E department was clearly no joke. I hadn't ever seen him this exhausted.

"Shit," I muttered when I eyed the time. Lifting my head from Aaron's bare chest, I sat up in his bed and put my phone aside. "It's half six already. I should go."

"You might as well sleep over," he suggested and gently brushed his fingertips across my pale skin.

I shook my head and climbed out of his bed to recover my clothes from the floor. "No, I didn't bring my things. Besides, I've got to assemble my new wardrobe and desk. I'm in dire need of a quiet place to revise, and I honestly can't be bothered to head for uni every time, especially with our first exam coming up next Friday. I'd save so much time reading at home."

"Course you can't," he remarked amusedly.

Turning, I caught him admiring my state of undress.

"What do you mean by that?" I asked and pulled my blouse over my head.

He met my eyes as a smile climbed to his kiss-swollen mouth. "I mean you've always been a devout subscriber to efficiency. I'm sure you'd buy a new microwave if it meant you could save ten seconds heating your meals."

A laugh snuck out of me. "Well, who'd want to lie on their deathbed knowing they'd wasted hours that could have been minutes waiting for their meals to cook?"

"People who don't permanently reside in the future."

"I can live in the moment," I disputed.

He didn't look convinced. "If that were true, you'd spend the night."

My shoulders sank. "That's not fair."

He sighed. "Maybe." Pushing himself up, he crawled out of bed to reach for his boxers on the floor. "Mum was wondering whether you'd like to come for dinner on Sunday."

It had been over a month since I last saw his mother Mary-Anne, so I was slightly disappointed that I'd have to decline. After all, Mary-Anne was one of few role models in my life; I admired her resilience as well as her strength. Because of that, I adored spending time with her.

I'd met her for the first time over dinner two years ago, and I'd learnt then that Aaron's father had been both an alcoholic and an incorrigible gambler, so Mary-Anne had eventually been forced to leave him when Aaron was only four. While he hadn't been present in Aaron's life since then, I was vaguely aware that he had taken out substantial loans during their marriage to settle his gambling debt, and that he'd also spent a considerable amount of the sum that Mary-Anne had set aside to finance Aaron's eventual education on his troublesome habits.

With barely a penny to her name, Mary-Anne had raised Aaron to be the exemplary man he was today. Through hard work as a waitress, she'd given him the most comfortable life she could. Her story inspired me, and so did her character. In fact, upon meeting her, I'd quickly realised where Aaron had inherited his patient and constructive nature from, although Mary-Anne was slightly more forthright than her son.

As I pulled on the black stockings that I'd worn under my grey pencil skirt, I cast him a glance. "I'd love to, but Jason's parents have already invited me for dinner that day. If she's got time next week, tell her I'd love to come then instead."

"Right, I'd forgotten that. I'll ask her."

"Good."

After he'd pulled on his boxers, he sat down on his bed again and reclined to rest on his forearms while he watched me dress. "Suppose I won't see you anytime soon then, now that you'll be revising at home."

"Jason's working on Monday. His shift starts at two, so you could always come over and revise at my place then."

He nodded. "I'd like that."

"Mind if I invite Livy?"

"Of course not."

"Shall I invite Cassie as well?" My tone had been playful, but truthfully, I'd asked because I wanted to confirm that I wouldn't lose him as my bed partner any time soon.

"Don't be a tit," he grumbled, rolling his eyes, and that was all the reassurance I required.

§ § §

With a screw in my mouth and Foals playing in the background, I was sitting within the frame of my new wardrobe when I heard a key being inserted into the front door. Frowning, I placed the manual screwdriver aside. Was it half-past eight already? Reaching for my phone, I saw that it was only eight.

Leaving the screw on the floor, I called, "Hiya. You're home early." I stood. "How was work? I'd planned to cook dinner for you, but I started assembling the wardrobe I ordered from IKEA instead," I said as I walked towards my bedroom door to greet Jason, "so I thought we could just order something since—" I gasped as soon as I turned towards the front door. It wasn't Jason at all.

"What are *you* doing here?" I asked accusingly while my heart began to pound. Heat flooded my face all at once, and I dared not imagine its new colour. As adrenaline heightened my senses, I became hyperaware of his presence.

William was the last person I'd expected to see, so I hadn't been remotely prepared to endure the power he exuded, nor had I been prepared to regard the gorgeous view of him.

It really wasn't fair that anyone should be so attractive, and especially when considering our circumstances. In his navy suit, he looked nothing short of edible. To think I'd seen him stripped of it, naked in all his glory – I could hardly believe it.

All at once, the anxiety I'd managed to overcome since Monday recovered in full.

An amused and crooked smile emerged on William's mouth, and as I studied it, all I could think of was how masterfully it kissed. "It's lovely seeing you too, Cara. I've missed you."

I hadn't thought my cheeks could become any hotter, but he proved me wrong.

Since I remained speechless, he took the opportunity to add, "I'm charmed you thought to make me dinner. Work was fine, by the way."

"You're such a knob," I finally grumbled, but that only made him laugh.

"Sorry," he said, and when he raised his hands as if to claim innocence, I saw a keychain hanging around his index finger. "I didn't mean to startle you. I'm here to watch the match with Jason."

"Match?" I echoed, bewildered, and recoiled a step.

"Chelsea's playing at eight. I came straight from work, so Jason said to let myself in. He should be home soon, so you won't have to endure me on your own for long."

"You've got a key?"

Lowering his hands again, William proceeded to store the keychain inside his suit jacket. "I've had a key ever since he moved in."

With arched brows, I stated, "Good to know."

"He didn't tell you I'd be coming over?"

"No. Must've slipped his mind."

"He's been rather stressed lately," he justified.

"Clearly."

Unsure of what to do with myself, I folded my arms and glimpsed my bedroom door. "Well," I murmured, "make yourself at home then, I suppose."

"Thanks," he said and shrugged out of his jacket before he bent to loosen his brown leather shoes.

Though I was reluctant, I reminded myself of the hospitality he'd shown the morning after our first encounter, so I said, "I'll be in my room if you need anything."

Still bent over, he turned his head to glance up at me, and regardless of how much I hated to admit it, the smile he wore made my heart throb. "Really? I'd have thought you would bolt the door."

I'd wanted to seem indifferent, but his comment made it impossible not to smile, so I hurried to face away. While heading back to my room, I warned, "Don't push your luck."

"Is that Foals I hear?" he asked then. Surprised, I froze in the doorway before I slowly turned to regard him. Did he share my taste in music as well? If he did, I wasn't certain I'd ever discover a single flaw in him.

"Might be."

As he stretched up to kick off his shoes, he gave me a winsome grin. "You're into rock?"

"Among other genres."

"Which is your favourite?"

"By Foals?"

"No, genre."

Eyes darting, I shrugged. "Probably rock."

"And I thought you couldn't get any more perfect."

At this rate, red was becoming the permanent colour of my face.

"Have you got a favourite band?" he continued to query as he took the liberty of coming closer.

"What's it to you?"

His responding smile was playful. "Oh, come on, Cara. Don't be like that."

I pursed my lips in an attempt to suppress my smile, but it was ineffective. "It's hard to say. I've got several, and I can't choose between them. Though, right now, the band I listen to the most is probably Arctic Monkeys."

He came to a halt next to me and nodded. "Excellent choice."

"How about you?"

"Well, I feel similarly, but Pink Floyd is the band I always return to, so perhaps I should go with them."

I chuckled. "Old-school. Nice. They're at the top of my list as well."

"Really?"

"Really."

His lips spread apart into a full-blown grin, which revealed a straight row of pearly-white teeth. "Then I propose you come over to my place one day. We can listen to old vinyl records together over a glass of wine."

"Of course you'd propose that."

"Is that a yes?"

"It's a definitive no."

"Gutted," he jested, although I suspected he was slightly serious.

"You're relentless." I laughed in comical despair and entered my bedroom.

"I'm also shameless."

"Which I bet you use to your advantage." Glancing at him over my shoulder, my breath caught. A faint smile swam in the corners of his mouth while his eyes gleamed above, intensely.

"You've read me well. Though, I prefer not having to."

Gulping, I looked away. "Don't we all?"

Lingering in the doorway, his eyes scanned the chaos on my bedroom floor. "I see you've abandoned Sandra to become Bob the Builder instead."

The amount of wit his tongue ceaselessly whipped around was rather impressive, and it had a direct line to my sense of humour. Before I knew it, I was laughing from the bottom of my heart. "William, oh my God. Show mercy."

He smirked and tucked his hands into his pockets while he leaned against the doorpost. "Glad I amuse you." After glancing at the stacks of neatly folded clothes in the corner of my bedroom, he directed his attention back to me and asked, "Need any help?"

After finding a seat within the frame of the wardrobe again, I steered my eyes to his with a sceptical look on my face. Upper class as he was, I doubted he'd ever done similar work. "Do you even know how to use a screwdriver?"

From the expression that crossed his face, it was apparent that I'd offended him. "Of course. It's not exactly rocket science, is it?"

"Well, I appreciate the offer, but I'm alright."

"I'll leave you to it, then. Give me a shout if you get stuck."

"Won't happen."

Part of me definitely preferred him gone, but another wished he'd stay forever.

When I heard the characteristic sound of a crowd cheering on their team, I realised he'd switched on the TV to watch the match. Hyperaware of his proximity, I wondered whether to shut the door between us. Still, I decided against it, because part of me was desperate to maintain some level of control over his whereabouts so that I might predict a sudden arrival.

On edge, I continued to focus on my labour, but when half an hour had passed, the music that played in the background had swept me away into a state of mindfulness. Activities like these were thoroughly therapeutic. For the first time in weeks, I hadn't given my upcoming exams a single thought within the span of thirty minutes; even William's presence had faded into the background.

However, my state of relaxation soon transformed into frustration, because apparently, several screws were missing. While growling under my breath, I searched the floor for the assembly instructions, which was when I noticed a pair of feet in the doorway. Right in front of them, I discovered the document.

My heart skipped a beat as I lifted my gaze. How long had he been standing there for? Our eyes collided, and I saw humour basking in his. "Sounds like you've fucked up," he said and reached down for the assembly instructions.

Since I wanted to present myself as capable of the task, I retorted, "I haven't. A few screws are missing."

After eyeing me dubiously, he opened the instructions and skipped a few pages until he located the step I was currently stuck at.

"Give me that," I demanded. "Don't you have a match to watch?" I muttered as I stood.

"Half-time," he mumbled and approached to scan my work. Squatting next to me, he studied the various screws still in the bag and extracted one to compare it with the illustration in the instructions. "There are enough screws, alright. You've merely put them into the wrong holes," he said.

Mortified, I snatched the document out of his grasp. "How would *you* know?" I retorted defensively.

"I've got an eye for identifying holes," he said, looking at me sideways.

Meeting the licentious gleam in his eyes, I replied, "Me too – especially arseholes."

My witty response earned a chuckle, but his eyes strayed to search for something. "Here," he said and motioned towards the screwdriver behind me, "pass me the screwdriver."

I shook my head as I studied the instructions in detail. "I'd rather cast it into the fire."

His eyebrows arched at my unexpected reply. "Is that a *Lord of the Rings* reference?"

Since it had been exactly that, my lips pursed. "Maybe."

His head tilted while he studied me with a sense of wonder in his eyes. "Honestly, where have you been all my life?"

Snorting, I knelt to start removing the screws. "In hiding," I eventually muttered. "And I'm still not happy about being found, because I was never lost."

He tittered. "Love, you're so lost you don't even realise it," he claimed before he leaned past me to fetch the screwdriver. He lingered there for a second, and his proximity caused a bolt of ferocious electricity to course through my heart. Mindful of the memories his scent was likely to provoke, I held my breath and leaned slightly away.

"Am not," I insisted, but did not object when he began to remove the screws, because the sight of his beautiful hands distracted my attention. Steadily and patiently, they removed one screw after the other, and I thought at that moment that I must be going insane, because the view was oddly arousing. They moved so capably – so confident in their work. Those hands could make anything come undone.

In the dim light, his hair glistened faintly. My eyes journeyed along the tidy waves of it, down to where their darkness gently kissed his paler skin as they cradled his ears and neck.

As my gaze strayed further to admire the rest of him, that alien feeling crowded my chest again. It made me feel so full, like I hadn't sufficient space to contain it. It was dense and heavy, and yet simultaneously, I felt light as a feather.

Transfixed, I studied his beauty as though it were the most impressive constellation ever to have fallen into place. Indeed, he seemed out of this world. Like stars upon the sky, each gorgeous feature of his body connected to form a celestial masterpiece.

He was undoubtedly a work of art, and I marvelled at how many secrets each detail veiled. I wondered what his thoughts were, how far the alleys of his mind stretched, how vast their content. Could they be endless? He seemed like the embodiment of the entire cosmos – the skin of the night.

"The Devil's in the detail, darling," he suddenly said and glanced at me from the corner of his eye. "Something to bear in mind, especially if you mean to practise law."

Since I was still mortified over my display of incompetence, I folded my arms and looked away. "I'm just tired after revising all day. I've never encountered this problem before, and I'm a certified veteran when it comes to assembling IKEA furniture."

He was just about to respond when he was interrupted by someone unlocking the front door. Shooting up, I panicked at the thought of Jason discovering his brother in my room. A moment later, I reminded myself that the scene he'd come upon was entirely innocent, so in the end, there was no reason for concern.

"Hello?" Jason called while I heard a bag land on the floor.

"Hi, Jason," I greeted, although I didn't sound half as calm as I'd intended.

"We're in here," William informed.

Hearing his footsteps approach, I took a deep breath and begged myself to remain composed. I'd never been around the two of them at the same time before, and the reality of it was straining my conscience, because it intensified the notion that I was keeping Jason in the dark about my sensual history with his brother.

Once he appeared in the doorway, I forced forth a smile.

"What's going on here?" he queried curiously while he observed the current mess on my bedroom floor.

"I was just teaching your brother how to assemble a wardrobe," I said. In my peripheral vision, I saw William freeze before he slowly turned to regard me. Glancing over, I discovered a look of amused astonishment on his face.

"Yes," William said and directed his attention to Jason. "You see, I put the wrong screws in the wrong holes. I'd say it's because I'm tired after work, but the truth is that I was just too stupid and stubborn to realise it."

My jaw fell open at his playful insult, but before I could reply, Jason chuckled and said, "Sounds like you," to which William responded with an underwhelmed expression.

Speaking over each other, I said to Jason, "I love you," just as William replied, "No, you halfwit."

In perfect synchrony, we turned towards each other, but I was the first to speak. "I win," I declared.

A chuckle slipped out of his mouth while he shook his head. "Fake it till you make it, I suppose."

"Glad you seem to get along," Jason commented with a grin and folded his arms.

"You're late," William stated and returned his focus to my wardrobe.

"Yeah, I know. Chaos at the hospital today. Fridays, you know. Been keeping track of the match on my phone, though. Doesn't look like I've missed out on much."

"You haven't," William confirmed. "Anyway, have you had dinner?"

"No. I'm starving."

"Same."

"Have you had dinner, Cara?" Jason asked and proceeded to remove his shirt.

I shook my head.

"Right. Should we order something, then? I'm in the mood for sushi."

"When are you not?" William and I replied in perfect unison. Since I sensed him glancing at me, I resisted the urge to look in his direction.

"Right," Jason murmured with an arched brow, eyes flickering between us. While flinging his shirt over his shoulder, he continued, "Why don't you place the order while I shower? Half-time's nearly done."

"I'm busy slaving around," William said. "Cara, would you be so kind?"

I frowned. "I would, but given the size of you two, I've no idea how big of an order I should place."

"Order for a family of five," William suggested.

"Yeah, five is good," Jason agreed.

"Right, okay," I said and went to pick up my phone from the floor.

Not only had Jason finished showering, but the match had also started again by the time William returned the screwdriver.

"Please don't fuck up my work," he urged amusedly.

"While I appreciate your assistance, kindly piss off," I replied with equal humour.

"If it suddenly collapses in a few weeks, you'll be the culprit, not I."

"It won't."

From the gleam in his eyes, I could tell he was about to ridicule me, but Jason's sudden cry came to my rescue. "Fuck! Are you kidding me?"

The look on William's face made me giggle. I'd never seen his eyes quite so wide before. Horror-struck, he froze in front of me.

"Fly, you fool," I joked, and it earned me a smirk as he caught on to the reference.

Following his speedy exit, I got back to work with a smile.

To their great disappointment, Chelsea lost, and I hadn't needed to see the result with my own eyes to know that, because their constant whining made it obvious. The only thing that finally shut them up was the dinner that arrived. They'd invited me to eat with them in the living room, but since I was determined to finish assembling my wardrobe and desk before going to bed, I'd declined. Instead, I ate while I worked.

Though I wasn't usually one to eavesdrop, William's presence had piqued my curiosity to the extent that I had deviated from my normal pattern of behaviour by keeping my door slightly ajar so I could overhear their conversation. For the most part, it hadn't been that rewarding since they'd mainly discussed football and work, but when it was nearing ten o'clock, it took a different turn.

"I should probably think about leaving soon," William said.

"You heading to Violet?" Jason asked, and I wasn't quite comfortable with the way my heart reacted to the question, because it clenched and twisted before it sank in my chest. Given what time it was, a voice whispered in my mind that it was likely he'd referred to a woman who played a particular role in William's life – a sexual role.

The name echoed in my mind. Violet? I vividly recalled a beauty named Violet at his workplace. I'd encountered her in the lift with William just when I'd been about to leave after signing my contract. He'd said then that she was merely his partner on the transaction he was currently working on. However, was she his partner on other fronts as well? Was *she* the regular bed partner he'd mentioned the first time we'd met?

At first, the possibility intimidated me, but upon realising where my thoughts were headed, I frowned at myself. First of all, I had no claim on him, and secondly, I had no plans to ever sleep with him again. Ultimately, this information shouldn't have bothered me.

But somewhere deep within, it did.

"Just my ego," I reasoned in a whisper to myself. "Get a grip, Cara."

"Yeah," William confirmed after a while, and my heart proceeded to sink even lower.

"Why the hesitation?" Jason probed.

"No reason. Just wasn't listening at first."

"God, you're a tit."

"It's just my head has got a mute button reserved for your voice."

"Likewise."

"Anyway, yeah."

"How are things going with her?"

"What do you mean?"

"Has anything changed since we last spoke about her?"

I should not have been as relieved as I was when I heard William's responding laughter.

"Changed?" he echoed. "Are you asking whether things are

evolving into a relationship?"

"Considering your reaction, I gather they're not."

"Not even close. It's just sex, J, and always will be."

"What does that mean for Francesca?" Jason continued to probe.

Freezing, I stared blankly ahead. Francesca? He was involved with yet another woman? Somewhat repelled, I wondered how long his list of lovers actually was. Disappointment came next. For some reason, I hadn't thought him a womaniser. I'd thought him above that. Frankly, the impression he'd given me during the night I'd spent at his was that he was fastidious about his choice of partners. Clearly, I'd been naïve to think that. Then again, taking his unconventional charm and attractive appearance into account, it shouldn't have surprised me that he had a queue of women just waiting for scraps of his attention.

For the first time since I'd met him, I experienced a moment of sincere gratitude that I'd rejected him. To have to battle for his attention wasn't remotely appealing. I wouldn't settle for anything less than a man who recognised my worth from the start and treated me accordingly. To fight to persuade him to pick me, to urge him to see that he should favour me above the rest – my integrity would never let me sink so low. Just like every faithful woman, I deserved to be treated like I was the only woman in the world for him when it came to matters of romance.

Groaning quietly, I asked myself why I was even entertaining this lane of thought. A relationship with William was out of the question, so why should his conduct with other women matter to me? I should have been happy about this. He'd just solidified my decision not to pursue anything more with him ever again. And yet, despite that, disappointment still dominated my feelings, and I scolded myself for it. Who did I think I was? I had no right to be disappointed because he was seeing other women when I continued to reject his advances. In fact, it was only fair that he should seek out other women to help him heal his bruised ego and wounded feelings.

"Why should my arrangement with Violet have anything to say with regards to Francesca?" William replied, bewildered.

"So you plan to see her again, then?"

"I haven't decided yet."

"Because she's Kate's friend?"

Who on earth was Kate? Yet another lover?

"For example."

"What other reasons are there?"

"Well, she's not my type – too sensitive and emotional."

"Yeah, that's a bad match."

"And she seems rather keen, so I'm worried I'll end up hurting her."

"How shockingly empathic of you."

"Besides," William murmured, "there's another girl I haven't told you about."

Instantly, my heart climbed to my throat. Was it *yet* another girl, or was he referring to *me*? Panicking, my gaze dashed towards the door, and I dared not even breathe for fear of drowning out what would come next. Would he break his promise?

"What?" Jason replied, astonished. "Who?"

"I met her last Friday, at Disrepute. We slept together, but she rejected me quite brutally the next morning. Said she's not interested in dating, and I'm still a bit gutted about that, so it wouldn't be fair to Francesca if I start seeing her when I'm still hung up on someone else."

My heart was beating at such speed and strength that I could hear my pulse thump, and feel it pound in my throat. While I hadn't met him last Friday, but rather the Friday before that, I got the feeling he was referring to me. The similarities were simply too conspicuous. It couldn't be yet another girl, could it?

"Are you being serious?" Jason continued disbelievingly.

"Yeah."

"But you don't do one-night stands."

"Yeah, well, I made an exception."

"Shit. You must have really liked her."

"I do."

I stopped breathing. Lightheaded, I remained frozen and struggled to believe the implication of his statement.

"Damn," Jason said, astounded. "What's her name? Did you get her contact info?"

"No. I only got her first name – Sandra."

A quiet gasp stormed out of my mouth. Dropping the screwdriver, I sat back on my heels and stared at the door with shock. Had I actually just heard that? After taking a deep breath to compose myself, I wondered whether he was aware that I was eavesdropping and had therefore said it deliberately in an effort to trick me into his bed again, because he couldn't genuinely be that affected, could he? Then again, considering the current state of my own feelings, it wasn't impossible. I'd already acknowledged that he'd left a lasting impression, but I hadn't entertained the idea that I was guilty of the very same.

"Well, Sandra clearly doesn't know what she's turning down," Jason stated, unimpressed.

"Yeah, it blows."

"Have you tried hunting her down?"

"I did, but the mission failed. Besides, I think I should respect her decision. All I need is some time to get over it because she was... Well, let's just say that I seriously doubt I'll meet someone like her again."

"And she rejected you solely on the basis that she's not interested in dating?"

"Mainly. She studies medicine in Edinburgh, so there was that problem as well. Apparently, she just didn't see us working out."

He was definitely referring to me, and the reality of it completely obliterated the earlier disappointment I'd experienced.

"Well, I hope for your sake that she'll change her mind," Jason stated, and from his tone, I could hear he was displeased.

"Same. Anyway, I need to get a move on. It's getting late, and

Violet's a bitch about tardiness."

Jason laughed. "In general, or especially regarding this sort of appointment?"

"Both."

"Well, keep me posted on Sandra then, yeah?"

"Sure, but you need to stop living vicariously through me when it comes to women, J. You ought to get your arse on the market."

"There's no time for it."

"You sound just like Sandra now."

"Well, shit. Suppose it's a curse haunting every med student."

"At least *you* retain the decency not to fuck around."

When I heard the sound of chairs moving across the floor, I dashed towards my bedroom door to close it before either of them could round the corner and notice, and I'd barely managed to retreat a few steps by the time there was a knock at my door.

"Yes?"

It was William who had knocked, and when our stares collided, I wondered if he could tell that I'd overheard every last word while he'd confided in Jason. From the piercing power of his gaze, I got the impression he knew, but since his lips formed a brooding line, I wasn't certain. If he truly suspected me of having heard him, I would have expected him to present his typical crooked smile, as its cunning shape would reveal that it had never been unintended.

"I see you're nearly done," he said, relieving me of his attention to instead observe my new wardrobe.

I nodded. "Only the doors left."

"Good work."

"Thanks."

His eyes zoomed in on my bed then, and without asking, he walked in to approach it. Frowning, I followed him with my gaze and watched him lift my textbook in Advanced Contract Law from my bed.

"If it isn't Contract Law," he murmured to himself while he flipped through the pages. "I selected this module in my third year as well."

"Did you?"

He nodded, but his attention remained fixed on a page. "Which modules are you taking, exactly?" he asked then.

"Advanced Contract Law, Company Law, Commercial Law and Law of Taxation."

"Private law is your forte, I hear."

"Of course. That's why I should fit right in at Day & Night."

He glanced up then, and the smile he offered was small but sincere. "You certainly will." He shut the book and dropped it on my bed. "Well, give me a bell if ever you need any help while you're revising for your exams."

"That's very kind of you."

"I'd be delighted to help you out in whatever way I can." His statement triggered the memory of when he had insisted that he'd never get in the way of my education should I opt to give him a chance. He seemed to be recalling the same memory, as his gaze lingered on mine for a moment. "Anyway, just thought I'd say goodbye. I'm heading off. Good luck assembling the rest of your—" he paused to glance at the box containing my desk—"furniture."

I returned his smile, even though I wasn't quite comfortable knowing where he was headed. "Thanks for your help," I said. "I'll have you to thank if my wardrobe *doesn't* collapse."

He chuckled as he headed for the door. "Let me know if it does."

"You know I won't," I playfully replied and trailed after him to see him out.

While Jason and I watched him slide on his shoes, the younger brother asked, "Sunday, then?"

"Yeah."

"You're coming for dinner on Sunday?" I asked, enthused.

"Well, yes, but I think Jason was referring to the gym," William replied, eyes flickering to Jason's while he grabbed his jacket.

"I was. Speaking of, how about you join us, Cara? You're a gym rat just like us."

"You lift?" William queried, surprised.

A chuckle slipped past my smirk. "Yeah."

"Impressive. Too few women do."

"I know. It's a shame."

Jason embarrassed me by suddenly declaring, "She mainly trains lower body, though. In fact, the result is that Cara's bum is a magnet for attention, in the gym or otherwise. I've witnessed it first-hand."

"Which is why I like to cover it up when I'm training," I mumbled as blood sprinted to my cheeks.

A carnal memory flared in William's eyes when they landed on me. "I'm sorry you've got to go to such measures in the first place."

I shrugged. "Me too, but such is the way of the world."

"So you'll join, then?" Jason pushed, but I hesitated.

"Come on." William grinned. "It's important to work out when you're revising for exams."

Even though I knew I should avoid spending time with William whenever it was possible without raising suspicion, another part of me was eager for his company. Not only that, but I also felt I had to earn back some of the respect I'd lost after he'd caught me failing to assemble my wardrobe. I wanted him to find me competent because, for some ridiculous reason that I couldn't quite understand yet, I wanted to impress him. Besides, it wasn't like we'd be able to do much talking. We'd be there to train, not have tea.

Finally, my desire to see him again capsized my reason, so I said, "Okay. I'll join."

William's grin broadened even further. "Looking forward to it. Sunday, then?" He opened the door.

"Yeah," I sighed.

"Have fun with Violet," Jason said and gave him a wink.

Without looking at me, William murmured, "I'd rather it was Sandra, to be honest, but such is the way of the world."

Shocked by his bold declaration, I barely managed to remain composed while he closed the door between us.

While reaching forward to lock it after him, Jason turned towards me. "I knew he'd like you."

All I managed for a response was a faint smile, because my feelings were colliding into an unsolvable mess.

"I'm so glad you get on. Honestly," Jason continued. "My two favourite people in the whole world. What a trio we'll make."

"Me too," I replied, as I didn't know what else to say. "Anyway, I should finish my project." With that, I went back to my room without so much as a glance in his direction.

HUNT OF A LIFETIME

WILLIAM

ONE CANNOT CHOOSE WITH WHOM TO FALL IN LOVE. IT IS entirely primal and has been ruled by instincts as long as humankind has existed. Had I been a victim of the delusion that we had such a thing as free will, I would have believed that one could only choose whether to pursue or not. However, I was not. I knew full well that my reaction to her existence was embedded in my DNA, and that it was encoded in my genes that I would pursue her despite her rejection.

However, I was a strategic type of suitor – the calculating kind. Some would even say cunning. Unlike those who went straight for the kill, I preferred to lure my target into my web. In order to do that, I had to know my prey – how it operated, how it thought, how it could be seduced and finally overcome.

Indeed, the beginning of love is very much a hunt – thrilling, rapacious, and utterly instinctual. All at once, the brain and the body have turned towards one person, the senses have sharpened to perceive even the slightest sign of their existence.

However, when falling in love, one never realises in the very moment it happens. In retrospect, it's easy to identify the moment which triggered the revelation, but one cannot recognise it in the exact moment when love first begins to manifest. Because of that, I was entirely unaware of just how profound my feelings were on the verge of becoming. In fact, as I glanced at her across the gym, I thought all I was guilty of was fleeting interest or a rude curiosity that was based on primitive, reproductive urges.

I hadn't realised that the process had begun, that with each second that ticked by, I was losing my identity in hers, that my sense of self was slowly waning to create room for her, in favour of her. Instead, I was under the impression that I was mainly looking to sway her mind to repair my bruised ego. I was bitter that she hadn't found my offer sufficient enough, bitter that she had been able to remain sensible despite my ardent efforts to stir romanticisms in her, and I was bitter that she didn't seem as preoccupied with me as I was with her.

I simply hadn't grasped that how I reacted to her soft voice delivering sharp remarks was a sign of love manifesting, that her seductive eyes and the total fire they contained had instead lured *me* into their heat; nor did I, at the time, fathom the reason why I would gladly have made a fool of myself merely for the chance to hear her laugh.

Oblivious to the truth, I mistook genuine affection for an injured ego and assumed it was only my vanity that urged me to change her mind. I had no idea that it was the prelude to love. I was convinced that if I managed to change her verdict about us, I'd be able to exorcise her constant presence in my thoughts. I was aware it was a cynical motivation, but to spare my sanity, I considered it a necessary evil.

However, I was still contemplating which route to take in order to achieve my goal. Thus far, I had settled on the tactic of trying to befriend my foe, because if I did, I could perhaps locate her weakness and eventually strike it.

The trouble was that I'd never encountered an enemy quite so strong before. She seemed impossible to read, like she existed in a language entirely foreign to me. There was a mystery to her, like the suspense of a tale I'd never heard before and couldn't predict the end of.

She was whole all on her own, and frankly, I admired her for that. She didn't need anyone but herself, much less me. She wore her independence like armour, and it protected her to a fault. So then, how does one defeat an enemy boasting such a brilliant defence?

The Trojan way, I supposed. I'd have to trick her into letting me past her walls, and once inside, I'd make them crumble one by one until only she remained, stripped and humbled. Then, at last, my mind would be free of her – my ego restored.

Perhaps the extent of my determination should have encouraged me to suspect that something about my fascination with her was beyond the ordinary – had I truly not cared for her, then her rejection wouldn't have injured me as badly as it had.

But I didn't suspect. Instead, I'd gone blind and was desperately groping in the dark.

After a final pull-up, I released the bar and landed on my feet to glance behind me, but I was far from the only one to look in her direction. Jason hadn't lied – she was indeed a magnet for attention. Had she been mine I might have enjoyed it, but she wasn't.

While I knew she was perfectly capable of managing on her own, their hungry gazes still irritated me. From the little I'd learnt about her thus far, I was certain this was a far cry from the sort of attention she appreciated. Why else would she feel the need to cover up her derrière with that oversized black jumper whenever she did squats?

I also inferred a dimension of disrespect from their ogling. Her jumper might as well have been a sign begging her admirers to look away, and yet they all turned a blind eye to it and objectified her anyway. Quite frankly, I found their behaviour repulsive and uncivilised.

My contempt was further reinforced by my notion that they

were unworthy of her. Even the role as a mere spectator of her brilliance was above what they deserved. Indeed, I regarded them as filthy crooks molesting their unwilling queen.

The awareness summoned a strange urge to protect her from their sexualising stares, so without further thought, I grabbed my bag and bottle of chalk to approach her. I hoped my presence by her side would intimidate at least some of the men to look away. Their eyes would avert for the wrong reason, but at least she'd be spared from their ogling for now.

"Eighty kilos – not bad," I commended once I reached her.

"Just finished my last set," she replied breathily, and I had to smile at the sight of her flushed face. She wasn't holding back.

"So you won't be needing the rack?"

"No." She shook her head and wiped her forehead with her arm. "Dumbbell rows next."

"I'll take over this, then. Deadlifts."

"I'll help you remove the plates."

"You can leave two of them on." After giving her a nod of gratitude, I wondered what to say. It had been obvious from the moment she'd arrived with Jason that she was here to train, not chat. It was also plausible that she was deliberately trying to avoid me. However, that didn't align with my goal, so I needed to stall her somehow.

"Did you finish assembling your furniture on Friday?" In my hurry, it was the only thing I had thought to say, but after hearing it, I wished I'd remained quiet instead. What a dry start to a conversation. I hoped she wouldn't think me boring for that.

"My desk? Yes, I did." She tilted her head and smiled, and the view was rather enchanting. "Thanks for helping me out."

"Anytime. So your wardrobe still hasn't collapsed, I take it?"

She chuckled and gave me a knowing look while she pulled a plate off the barbell. "Not yet. Did you have fun with Violet?"

Her bold question took me aback. Unsure of where to look, I gazed around and vaguely noted that Jason was watching us from the bench press area. Once I'd recovered from the surprise, I turned my attention back to her and scoured her eyes for any sign of resentment, but I discovered nothing. She looked perfectly unfazed.

I sensed my bitterness beginning to fester. It was obvious I'd meant nothing to her at all, and that I'd be flattering myself if I presumed anything else. There wasn't a spark of envy in her, not a fragment of jealousy.

"Not quite as much fun as I would have had if it were you," I shamelessly confessed, because I hoped to provoke a reaction from her.

But none came.

"Is she the partner you mentioned?" she queried while she removed the last plate.

I studied her intently. "Yeah. Why?"

"I'm surprised you're comfortable sleeping with colleagues," she explained, and I thought I detected a hint of resentment in her tone, or perhaps it was only wishful thinking on my part. In fact, it might well have been general disapproval, which would make sense in light of her stated reservations about sleeping with a colleague.

"I'm usually not, but I can make exceptions. Something to bear in mind." My tone had been playful, but we both knew I'd meant it, which was why she didn't reply with anything other than a scoff.

At that moment, I wondered again whether she had overheard my conversation with Jason the other day. I'd meant for her to hear it, but I wasn't sure she actually had. The door had been closed before I'd knocked, and I knew she'd been listening to music. If she had, I wondered what she was thinking. That Jason had decided to interrogate me so thoroughly about my recent sexual endeavours wasn't something I'd anticipated, so I'd tried to shine a light on the fact that I'd much prefer to spend time with her than them. However, her favour still seemed far from my reach, so now I doubted she had eavesdropped at all.

"Impressive weights you're doing," I remarked to help myself think of something else. "I saw you hip-thrusting two hundred kgs earlier."

She gave me a complacent smirk. "Scared I'll put you out

of business?"

Her cheek never failed to entertain me, but she always seemed to forget that I was rather a proficient player in that game myself. "We both know I'm a capable thruster. I can still hear you moaning my name in my sleep. Quite the melody, that was." I hadn't been able to resist. There was something about teasing her that felt entirely necessary. She reminded me of an angry chipmunk whenever I flustered her, because her voice reached octaves so high that it frankly impressed me – and amused me.

Her mouth dropped open at once, and the fresh colour in her face contended with even the brightest of reds.

"You!" she spluttered, high-pitched, as predicted. "How dare you speak to me like that?" she continued, glorious in her anger.

I was sure my grin matched the Devil's. "It was only a joke, Cara. Just taking the piss while I still can. Can't be doing it once you start work now, can I?"

"You shouldn't be doing it now, either!" she insisted in a harsh whisper, clearly irate, and I noticed her hands had curled into fists by her sides. Alas, her anger didn't intimidate me in the slightest. On the contrary, it tempted me to continue.

"But you look so lovely with that colour in your cheeks – especially since I'm the one who put it there."

"You are unbelievable." She'd sounded despairing, and I realised I'd shot myself in the foot when she undid the belt around her waist, grabbed her bag and stormed off. As I gazed after her, I caught Jason in my peripheral vision, and once I looked over, he shook his head at me.

"Don't be a dick, Will!" he shouted across the gym, which earned us some curious glances from the few not listening to their own music.

I didn't bother replying.

§ § §

In the changing rooms, I was facing my locker when Jason enquired, "What did you say to Cara earlier?"

"Nothing really."

"Didn't seem like nothing."

"Made a bad joke, that's all."

"About what?"

"Nothing I'd like to repeat. I mean to apologise."

"You should."

After a glance in his direction, I gave a faint nod and reached into my locker for my shirt.

"Were you flirting with her?" he asked me then, but since I had expected the question, my equilibrium remained intact.

"No," I said with ease, but what I actually wanted was to tell the truth. In fact, I wanted to tell every single person in this room – the whole fucking world – that I'd slept with her, only so that I could deprive her of the excuse – the poor and pathetic excuse – which was but one among the several ridiculous excuses she had used to reject me. At least then, I'd have been one step closer to achieving my goal – she would no longer have been able to hide behind the erroneous conviction that people would care about whom she invited into herself.

But I'd made her a promise, and I intended to keep it. Besides, I could only befriend the enemy if she remained unaware of my antagonism. I couldn't imagine she'd want anything to do with me if I told Jason prematurely.

I frowned to myself when I realised I ought to be questioning Jason about why it should matter whether I was flirting with her or not. "Why?" I asked, and his potential answer filled me with dread. Had we, unwittingly, shared a woman? "Is there something I should know?"

It bothered me that he decided to pull on his T-shirt at that precise moment because it made me wonder whether he'd done it deliberately to veil his reaction, or whether it was merely because he didn't care all that much for the subject. Was it genuine or feigned nonchalance?

"What do you mean 'why'?" he asked, but his voice was muffled. "Are you asking whether I fancy her?" he continued as soon as his head popped out.

"Do you?"

Something strange happened inside my chest as I considered the idea. There was a contraction, and for a moment, I stopped drawing breath.

"Not really. She's hot, though – really hot. Or perhaps beautiful is a better word to describe her. I've never been able to decide – she's a good blend."

"Have you slept with her?"

Jason laughed. "No, we're not like that. I'm only saying she's attractive. Hardly think that's worth fucking up our friendship for. Pun intended."

I faced my locker again, and it demanded some effort to remain composed. He hadn't really denied anything – not as clearly as I would have preferred, anyway – and I couldn't keep probing him about this without raising suspicion.

Would he have slept with her if offered the chance?

"You don't agree?" he asked.

"On what?"

"That she's attractive?"

I hadn't the faintest idea why, but the question pissed me off. "Jason, she's your best friend. Quit sexualising her."

What I'd said gave the illusion that I had refused to speak further on the matter for moral reasons, but the reality was that I wasn't sure exactly why I wanted him to shut up. Perhaps it was because I felt nauseous at the thought of his potential sexual interest in her. The disgusting images were already feasting on my mind. Or perhaps it was because I wanted her for myself but didn't want to take her from him. He was my brother, after all – the person I cherished the most. If he wanted her, too, would I be able to let her go for his sake? Would he even desire her if he learnt the truth about our past?

Now more than ever, I felt the strain of keeping the truth from him. I wished she hadn't begged me not to tell. I wished she would have understood that while Jason might have disliked the news at first, he'd have come to terms with it within the span of a mere day – I was certain. Unlike me, he simply wasn't capable of holding grudges. But now that she had demanded my silence, I couldn't break it without shooting myself in the foot.

So, I supposed I'd said what I had as a last resort to inspire him to steer clear of her. If I reminded him of the platonic nature of their relationship, perhaps he'd reconsider his view on her.

His eyebrows jumped up his forehead. "Damn, someone's triggered. I wasn't sexualising her; I was admiring her. There's a difference. Christ."

"She's well fit," a random bloke commented behind us then. "The bird with the black jumper covering her arse, right? I'd do her in a heartbeat."

That sort of macho behaviour was exactly the reason why women frequently felt hostile towards our gender. Like them, I had no patience with it. However, that was only one among several reasons why his statement roused great ire in me.

I refused to acknowledge him. If I did, I worried I'd inadvertently get myself into a brawl due to the many insults my sharp tongue would launch at him. If there was one thing I'd learnt over the years, it was that my mouth was quite adept at getting me into serious trouble. It had earned me a black eye on more occasions than I cared to count, especially on the football field during my teenage years. So, with difficulty, I bit my unruly tongue and faced away.

Jason appeared to notice my riled state, so he merely gave the bloke a nod before he turned his back to him as well.

"What's got you into such a foul mood?" he mumbled very quietly after some time.

I lost it. "Men who constantly sexualise women, as if their primary purpose is to please us – as if their personality and intellect are of secondary importance. I wish they'd understand that – by behaving that way – they're doing us all a great disservice."

"Are you talking to me, mate?" the bloke questioned behind

me, menacingly.

I turned towards him, my muscles tensing as my stance grew hostile. I hated violence of any sort, but if he attacked, I was prepared to defend myself. "Well, since you ask, you must have identified with the men I'm referring to."

His brown eyes lit with anger, and I could tell he was considering whether to strike me. Judging by the width of him, I was confident he had steroids to thank for the size of his muscles. I was still stronger than him, however, and much taller. He'd be no match for me. Studying me from head to toe, he seemed to realise the same, so he took a step back and clenched his narrow jaw.

I growled, "Why do you think she was wearing a jumper to cover her arse?"

He pressed his lips together but said nothing.

"And yet you sexualise her anyway," I spat.

"Will," Jason intervened, grabbing my shoulder. "Calm down."

"Sorry," the lad murmured. "I meant no disrespect."

"Try thinking next time, yeah? With something other than your cock." I turned away from him and grabbed my bag. "I'm finished," I said to Jason. "I'll wait outside." Giving the lad a final glare, I headed out.

Prejudice led me to surprise when I discovered Cara there, leaning against the wall with her phone in her hand. In my experience, women tended to be slower than us when it came to changing and getting ready, but I supposed this was just yet another rule she was an exception to.

I knew I owed her an apology, so I drew in a steadying breath before I approached. I'd hardly managed three steps by the time she noticed me, and the look she gave me told me I wasn't forgiven yet.

The instant I reached her, I said, "I'm sorry about earlier."

"You're honestly such a knob, Will." She shoved her phone into the front pocket of her jumper. "I'm trying to put it behind me."

"Pun intended?" I joked, hoping to lighten her mood.

She gaped, and soon enough, an incredulous titter poured out.

"Okay, that was funny, but I'm being serious. You've got to let me move on."

I knew she hadn't meant to injure my feelings by saying that, but she did, nevertheless. "I'm having a hard time doing it myself. Perhaps that's why I keep bringing it up," I explained sincerely.

I thought I saw sympathy in her eyes, and she looked about to say something, but right before she could, Jason interrupted.

"Fucking hell, Cara," he said upon reaching us. "I was just telling Will that I find you beautiful, and he went and accused me of sexualising you. Do you feel sexualised? Because my conscience is seriously suffering right now, so I'd—"

"Jason – what?" She frowned, and I had averted my eyes by the time she searched for them. "You call me beautiful every day," she eventually continued, and I considered that to be valuable information. "Of course I don't think that."

"Right, good." He let out a breath of relief. "Will got me thinking, you see. Actually, he nearly got into a scuffle with another lad just now, defending you."

Though my intention hadn't been to defend solely Cara, but rather women overall, I was grateful he told her that. Perhaps hearing this would make her consider me in a favourable light.

"He did what?" Cara asked, astounded. Sensing her eyes on my profile, I looked over to meet them.

"Yeah." Jason nodded. "This random guy declared – unsolicited – that he found you hot, and Will lost it. I'm honestly quite proud."

I knitted my brows. Important details had been left out. I didn't want Cara to get the impression I was prone to violence either, because I wasn't. "It was the way he said it," I defended myself. "He sounded primitive. It pissed me off, especially when you—" I motioned towards her—"were wearing a jumper to hide your bum. It might as well have been a bloody placard, and he ignored it. I wasn't looking for a fight – I despise violence. I'd never hit someone first. I merely meant to rebuke him."

Cara's deep-blue eyes grew warmer, almost inviting. Seeing it, I forgot everything else. The effect it had on me was far more severe than I'd been prepared for. This wasn't normal, I thought, perplexed.

"Thanks, Will," she said, and I hated the smile she wore. She was supposed to grow weak for *me*, not the other way around – and yet, when I looked at her, I could sense that my strength was waning.

I gave her a faint nod. Looking between her and Jason, I found my situation quite intolerable. With too many thoughts to sort through all at once, I started towards the exit. "I'm heading off. I'll see you for dinner."

§ § §

There was quite the deluge outside, but I'd decided to walk home in spite of it, hoping to clear my mind. After fifteen minutes, I had got no further with sorting out my thoughts, so – eager for a distraction – I fished my phone out of my bag to check my messages. There was one from Andy and one from my good friend Alexander Winton. The three of us had been a trio ever since primary school, although I supposed Jason was an uncounted member of it as well.

I opened Andy's first.

I'm heading to Alex. Care to join?

Instead of replying, I opened Alexander's message.

Andy's coming over. I'd appreciate your moral support. I've no doubt he means to complain about Chloe, and you're much better than I am at putting him in his place

With a groan, I halted to reply to Alex.

You'll have to manage on your own. I've got dinner plans with the fam. Just tell him he's being an idiot. He knows it's true, deep down

Poor Chloe. I truly pitied her. Over the years, both Alexander and I had grown to regard her as a sister. She wasn't just Andy's girlfriend to us. Because of that, we had taken her side in the aftermath of their paused relationship. Besides, we both knew it was only a matter of time before Andy would come padding back to her, because his love for her was undying. Their issues weren't based on a lack of love, but rather on a difference of opinion on how to proceed in the future.

Chloe desperately wanted to conceive, and she was growing short on time. Four years ago, she'd been diagnosed with endometriosis, which was a condition that could affect her fertility. The older she got, the slimmer her chances of conceiving would become. Like Andy and Alex, she was twenty-nine now, and she had waited a whole decade for Andy to become mature enough to father a child. The trouble was that Andy didn't feel ready. The idea of children frightened him. He'd voiced concerns about whether he was fit for the role at all and frequently hid behind the excuse that he wanted to focus on his career for a while longer, which – understandably – Chloe had grown impatient with.

All she demanded was a clear answer: did he want children, or not? If he didn't, he had to let her go. But Andy did want children. He'd told me several times. However, he wasn't sure he was fit for fatherhood at this point in his life.

It was quite the dilemma, but I was convinced Andy was overthinking it. As soon as he held his baby in his arms, he'd settle into being a father without trouble.

A message came in from Francesca then, and I was immediately reminded that I still hadn't replied to her last text.

> Sorry if this seems clingy, but are we meeting tomorrow or not? I'd like to know so that I can make other plans if you've changed your mind x

"Fuck," I muttered to myself and resumed walking. I'd marked her text as read, something I always did because I favoured transparency, but now it had cost me the time I otherwise could have spent contemplating her offer. I'd have to respond soon.

I wondered if Kate knew about us. We hadn't spoken all that much since the end of our relationship five years ago. As I thought about it, I couldn't remember having spoken to her at all during the past year. She lived in Lancaster now with her new boyfriend, whose name was Matthew – an engineer like her.

Kate and I had met during my final year at Cambridge. We were only bed partners when I'd met Francesca for the first time. It wasn't until I was about to move back to London to complete the LPC LLM at the University of Law that we had agreed to try a relationship. At first, things had been stable, and I had often gone back to Cambridge to visit her. But, as time went on, my career had demanded more and more of my time and attention. In the end, our relationship had fallen apart, but I hadn't tried to save it either.

Following our split, I hadn't thought I would meet Francesca again, and I certainly hadn't thought that I would ever end up in bed with her. When we'd first met, there had been no spark between us whatsoever – at least not from my perspective. Since she was Kate's childhood friend, I'd been polite, but I remembered I had questioned how a bright mind like Kate's could endure the dullness of Francesca's.

Then, by some coincidence, I'd encountered her a few weeks before I'd first met Cara. She'd visited Disrepute with a few fellow models while I was having a drink with my colleagues. Violet had been there as well, but she'd left early to meet Clive – a man she was currently seeing unofficially and had yet to make up her mind about.

Nevertheless, her departure that night had made way for Francesca and me to rekindle our past friendship. She'd told me she had split from the boyfriend she'd had when we first met – Oliver, whom I had also met a few times – and that she had plans to move from Southampton to London in the near future.

As a precaution, I'd asked whether she still kept in touch with Kate, but she'd explained they'd drifted apart over the last couple of years, and that was the only reason I'd agreed to meet her for a date the following week. While I had never loved Kate romantically, I still had tremendous respect for her. For that reason, I would never think of courting one of her closest friends, and I especially wouldn't while knowing I had completely broken her heart. It would only have rubbed salt into the wound, and I wanted to avoid that.

However, since they were no longer close, I'd agreed to go on a date. I hadn't expected much from it, but the endeavour had turned out to be endurable, and I'd even gone so far as to end it with her in my bed. While she'd been recovering beside me, her naked body damp with sweat, she had confessed to lusting after me even while I was with Kate and she with Oliver, and that she'd been infatuated with me back then.

The news had upset me at first because I did not appreciate the disloyalty it implied towards Kate, but upon remembering that she was no longer part of our lives, I had put it out of my mind. Besides, she'd never acted on it, and I could hardly hold her human errors against her. We were all guilty of having thoughts and feelings that would be considered immoral if acted upon, but that was the critical distinction – they required the act in order to be punished as immoral.

We'd met six more times since then because – and it was an awful thing to admit – her presence in my life had become a matter of convenience for sexual purposes. Though she wasn't the brightest, she was a pleasant person – she could even be funny sometimes – and she was capable of arousing me, so I'd seen no reason to end it. Recently, however, I had sensed that her attachment was becoming stronger than I was comfortable with. While she was perfectly charming, I remained uncertain about whether to pursue things further, because our chemistry had never been effortless. Unlike Cara, she didn't fascinate me in the slightest, and I considered initial fascination a necessary requirement when it came to my romantic endeavours.

There I went again. Cara, Cara, Cara – as if I hadn't a life of my own, as if she were the only person worth my attention in the entire world.

I now compared every potential candidate to her. Ever since we'd met, she had become the standard I sought, and nothing else would suffice. I no longer enjoyed Violet's moans of pleasure because they weren't Cara's, and I seemed unable to admire Francesca's beauty because it wasn't Cara's.

The reality angered me to the extent that I acted on emotion and replied to Francesca that I'd be delighted to see her tomorrow. Foolish in my misery, I hoped I could fill the void that Cara had left behind with the attention of other women.

I was desperate to regain control because Cara's presence in my life made me feel powerless. In her audience, it was like I no longer reigned over my own mind, much less my body, and if there was one thing that frightened me above all, it was to be rendered powerless.

And yet, despite that, I experienced an incessant need to see her again. It was entirely compulsive, and I couldn't seem to resist it no matter how hard I tried.

Dinner couldn't commence soon enough.

§ § §

"I'm very sorry to hear about Chloe and Andy," Mum said after a sip of her favourite red wine. "Surely they'll get back together soon enough. This isn't the first time they've hit a bump in the road."

I said, "I agree. I'm convinced it's only temporary. Andy will see sense soon enough."

"I trust you and Alex will make sure of that," Dad commented, and as I looked at him across the table, I discovered a smirk on his mouth.

"We're working on it."

"Meanwhile," Jason chimed in, "I'm just minding my own business." A chuckle followed his statement.

"You've certainly got a knack for it," I agreed.

"How about you, dear?" Mum asked then, and from her gaze, I could tell her question was directed at Cara. "Have you got a special man in your life?"

I hadn't expected my stomach to sink the way it did when Jason wrapped his arm around her chair as if to mark his territory. "Only me," he joked and gave her a wink.

"Yes, only you," the target of my fascination replied while reaching for her glass of wine. "But on a serious note, I'm afraid not. I'm committed to my studies, and that's all I'm interested in maintaining at the moment."

The reminder irritated me. Hadn't I heard her pathetic excuses enough times by now? Would I ever see the day when she wouldn't rub them in my face?

"I'm sure a lot of men are very upset about that," Dad flattered her, amused. If only he knew he'd mocked his own son while he was at it.

As if his statement had prompted her, Cara's eyes slid briefly in my direction, but she averted them as soon as they collided with mine.

"I hardly think they're missing out on anything," she answered, and I was surprised by her humility. Did she not know the extent of her power? How effortlessly she rendered men senseless with lust? How far they would go for a mere second of her time?

"I'm really quite boring," she continued. "They'd grow impatient with my thirst for knowledge rather quickly, I expect, as it would probably come at the expense of their ego."

Dad leaned back, and I could tell from his gaze that her reply had intrigued him. "With all due respect, dear," he said, "I think you underestimate men – the decent ones, at least. In fact, I'm sure that spirit of yours is precisely what would attract your admirers in the first place."

I almost said "thank you" since he'd spoken my mind, but I resisted because it would have exposed our secret.

A smile surfaced on her plump lips. "I hope you're right."

"He's most certainly right," Jason insisted with a shake of his head. "You're remarkable, and you ought to know it."

His confidence led me to focus on my dish, because I suddenly couldn't stand the sight of him. Since I'd experienced it before – although never quite so intensely – I recognised jealousy when it unfurled within me, but never had my own brother been the target of it.

When I'd arrived here, I hadn't expected to feel this rigidity, much less this momentary resentment towards my brother which, if left untreated, could easily fester. Their familiarity triggered my envy because I yearned to know her like that. I envied him for having the freedom to wrap his arm around her shoulders without her shying away from his touch, and I envied him for having constant access to the enigmatic alleys of her mind.

While he'd told me that he didn't fancy her that way, he was still a man. He'd have to be blind, deaf and lack a cock not to feel even the slightest twitch in his pants around her. He might not view her in a romantic light, but I had no guarantee he wouldn't ever consider her in a sexual light. A couple of pints in, he could easily make the mistake. He'd done it before with my friend Harper.

Did I really have to count on Cara to retain the decency not to play us for fools? Did she even care about us being brothers? I knew she cared for Jason, but it wasn't with ease that I relied on her to do the decent thing. The impression I had was that she was perfectly – if not too – capable of separating sex from feelings. In light of that, there wasn't a doubt in my mind that she could sleep with Jason without giving further thought to it – unless he forced her to.

It was reasonable that I would experience discomfort at the thought of Jason entering her the same way I had, but what didn't make sense was my jealousy. Why did I yearn so desperately for her innermost secrets, for her body to invite my caress? And why did it bother me that other men could have the pleasure?

Resorting to silence, I continued along that train of thought for quite some time until the reality dawned on me all at once, and I was struck with a revelation. This wasn't mere lust. This wasn't a quest to restore a bruised ego.

I had fallen in love.

Under any other circumstances, I would have enjoyed the revelation, but since I knew Cara was nowhere near reciprocating my affections, I was instead rather upset.

"He's signed out," I vaguely heard Jason say just before Mum called for what I realised was the third time, "William, darling.

Hello?"

Like a deer caught in the headlights, I looked up.

"Christ. Are you quite alright, darling?" she queried worriedly, and I found it somewhat humiliating. Then again, I supposed that, to her, I'd always be no older than a boy. "You're as white as a sheet."

"What is it?"

"I wondered if you could fetch us another bottle of wine."

Grateful for the chance to escape the table, I pushed my chair out and stood. "Ripasso?"

"That'll do."

"He's been acting weird all day," I heard Jason comment as I left.

"Well, he's got a lot on his plate at work," Dad justified. "The transaction he's working on between GreenPark and Lightning Charge is a considerable one. GreenPark has got one of the largest networks of charging points for electric vehicles in the UK. Lightning Charge has been one of their competitors. You can imagine there's lots to go over and consider to ensure that the transaction happens smoothly and that the acquisition won't breach competition law – and I know Fred's pushing him hard."

While I appreciated his excuse, it was far from the truth. The transaction was indeed a considerable one, but unlike my feelings, I had it under control.

As I reached into the wine fridge for my mother's favourite Ripasso by Tommasi, I sighed to myself.

This was quite the conundrum. Given Cara's convictions, I doubted I stood any chance at all of earning her affections.

It didn't help that she commanded the attention of every man present wherever she went. It was only a matter of time before my successor would come knocking on her door. In fact, it was obvious that even Dad had fallen victim to her charm. So why should she favour me? It was clear our circumstances stopped her from entertaining even the thought of me, especially romantically.

Part of me wondered whether she would have been more amenable had I not been her flatmate's brother and her future boss.

At the same time, I knew I could never offer her anything else. These were simply the cards I'd been dealt, but I paused to wonder: could I still win with them?

I frowned to myself as I reminisced about our night together. She'd told me then that she considered me "boyfriend material". Surely she must have meant I possessed qualities she deemed desirable in a lover? So my personality wasn't the issue. Our incompatibility wasn't based on a difference of character, but rather on exterior factors, such as my future role as her boss, and my role as her best friend's brother. But surely those things could be overcome?

However, there was also Aaron to consider.

The moment I thought of him, my jealousy found another target, because her reasoning didn't make any sense. She'd told me she didn't harbour romantic feelings for him, that he might as well "be air" to her. However, I now suspected her of having lied, because nothing else could explain her desire to remain with him when she could instead have reserved that time for me. No one was that rational. No one had that much self-discipline. If she truly liked me as much as she claimed, if I were truly "boyfriend material", then surely she'd have chosen me over him.

As I continued to consider the possibilities, it occurred to me that it might well have been a lie she told herself, and thereby me, because she was in fact scared that Aaron would reject her – a defence mechanism, of sorts. Perhaps she actually loved him.

But that didn't explain why she had described me as "boyfriend material". Unless she had no conscience to speak of, it seemed too genuine a statement to be a lie. Had she told me that merely to shut me up? It would be a questionable method, but then again, it had worked at the time.

Delving deeper into thought, I recounted the scene in my office when she had signed her contract. The memory of her hand within mine remained particularly vivid because she hadn't shied away from my touch. On the contrary, I'd been under the impression she had welcomed the intimacy. Moments before that, she had confessed she was guilty of sexualising me as well.

Perhaps I did stand a chance after all. The question remaining was how. How could I make her see that I'd be worth risking her attention for?

I realised then that it was only my motive that had changed. I no longer sought to tear down her walls merely to humble her and retaliate for a bruised ego. Instead, I now sought to tear down her walls solely to earn her affections. My strategy would therefore remain the same. I'd need to befriend her before anything else, and since the strength of her convictions was considerable, I expected the process would require patience. Fortunately, I boasted quite a lot of grit, and I would rely on that to ensure her eventual surrender.

I was hatching the details of my plan as I returned to the table, and once I arrived, I could tell from the others' expressions that my smirk puzzled them.

"That's a different man to the one who left," Jason commented with a raised brow.

"I had a word with myself," I explained and walked over to where Mum sat while I opened the bottle to pour her a glass.

"Thank you, darling," she said and gave my back a fond caress.

"I'm sorry I've been such terrible company," I apologised and looked straight at Cara. "Had to solve a puzzle – that's all."

I thought I detected a flicker of trepidation in her eyes, but she looked away before I could be sure.

"Work-related?" Dad queried.

"Yes," I lied. "Anyway, I'm handling it."

"You always do."

Like I'd said, one can never choose with whom to fall in love. Now that I'd been struck, all I could do was gear up for the hunt – of a lifetime.

FRIENDS

TUESDAY MORNING, I WOKE AT EIGHT AND DRAGGED MY weary body out of bed to have a shower. My first exam, which was in Advanced Contract Law, was coming up on Friday, so I'd reserved every weekday till then for revising. Since Jason started work at two this week, I would have the flat mainly to myself, so I had invited Aaron and Livy over.

They wouldn't arrive till ten, however, and I was grateful for that because I was a fire-breathing dragon straight after waking, so I would've incinerated them in a heartbeat had they been here already. They both had first-hand experience with that idiosyncrasy of mine, so I supposed that was why they had suggested we meet at ten and that I should wake up at eight.

Half an hour later, I was sitting at the kitchen table, eating breakfast and reading the news on my iPad, when Jason walked past the open door. As expected, he hadn't bothered to put on a pair of boxers but instead covered his member with his hand.

"Morning," he murmured groggily, and I could tell from his

hair that he'd just removed the eye mask he always wore to sleep. In fact, that was the only thing he wore while asleep, and I'd learnt that last summer when we had spent a week at his family's holiday house on the Isle of Wight.

"Morning," I replied and smiled at the sight of his taut bum before he disappeared from my view on his way to the bathroom. Men – in my experience – often had better arses than women, and it was something I frequently envied them for. Jason didn't train his lower body half as much as I did, but judging from his derrière, it looked like he trained nothing else. Aaron was no exception, either.

An outsider would perhaps have found it strange that Jason didn't mind if I saw him naked, but the truth was that Jason was a bit of a naturist, and I was no different. To him, the naked body was the most natural thing in the world and therefore nothing to be ashamed of. Given his course of study, I supposed he had a rather clinical perspective on the matter, and I happened to share his view. Even so, I tended to cover up more often than he did, but I was rarely bothered if anyone caught me naked.

The fact that Jason and I had seen each other without clothes countless times was in fact something I appreciated, because it had led me to feel even more comfortable around him. Never during the three years we had known each other had he made me feel sexualised when he'd seen me undressed, and never had I felt at all judged for my appearance. On the contrary, his behaviour around my nude body had assured me his interest was strictly platonic.

I was aware it was unusual for two friends – especially of different genders – to frequently see each other stripped. Still, I couldn't fathom why that should matter when it had made me feel more comfortable in his presence than I otherwise would have thought possible. Somehow, our deviation from the norm had made me feel accepted in my entirety by him, and that was one of the reasons why I assumed his friendship was unconditional. Just like him, I knew I would treasure him as my most cherished friend till the end of my days because we were, quite simply, mind-mates.

I also happened to prize friendship over romantic relationships, and I supposed it had to do with the longevity of each concept. Most friendships could last a lifetime, and the unconditional aspect was something I found particularly inviting. In my limited experience, romantic love was complicated where friendship was not. Relationships also seemed to die more easily, and frequently, than friendships did.

Generally, however, relationships were something I struggled with because I had never been blessed with the ability to grow easily attached to people. I had very few, but very good, friends. I had plenty of people I considered acquaintances, though. While they regarded me as a friend, I couldn't return the favour. To me, 'friend' was an extremely precious title, as well as status, which I reserved for only a select few. In the few years I'd known him, Jason had somehow managed to climb to the top of that ladder.

For that reason, I imagined a prospective boyfriend would need to exceed my expectations of true friendship. He'd need to surpass even Jason, and frankly, I didn't think anyone ever could.

"When are Aaron and Livy coming over?" Jason queried upon his return from the bathroom. A towel was wrapped around his hips now. After dragging a hand through his damp hair, he approached the Nespresso machine to make himself a cup of coffee.

"Ten."

He nodded. "I haven't seen Livy for ages – not since she split from Colin."

"Yeah, she became a bit of a recluse while she licked her wounds. She's over him now, though, so you'll probably see her more often – especially now that we live together."

"She's over Colin?" He turned towards me. "Proper over?"

I reached for my cup of coffee. "I think so. Seems like it. She hardly ever talks about him anymore."

Jason faced away to grab his fresh brew. "Good for her. That bastard never deserved her in the first place."

"No, he didn't."

"Well, I'm looking forward to it. I've always liked her. I think she's my favourite out of your friends."

I smiled. Olivia was indeed adorable, and I'd always been thankful for her presence in my life even though we were quite different personality-wise. However, we'd known each other since we were only three, so our difference in temperament was something we'd learnt to appreciate over the years. She'd been my partner in crime for as long as I could remember, and because our ambitions had always correlated, we'd helped each other prosper. Our biggest difference in character was that Olivia was a hopeless romantic while I was more of a realist.

"She's fond of you too," I said.

"Is she?"

"Isn't everyone?"

He chuckled. "You flatter me."

"Just stating my view."

"Which is ever flattering."

§ § §

We'd been revising for nearly an hour when I received a call from Dad. To avoid disturbing Olivia and Aaron, I walked into my room before answering it. He mainly wondered how I was doing and whether I felt ready for my exams, so I complained about how stressed I was for a few minutes before he asked me to come for dinner on Friday. I declined because Mary-Anne, Aaron's mother, had already invited me, so we agreed on Saturday instead.

After hanging up, I stayed in my room to check my social media accounts, and Instagram had quite the surprise in store. I discovered a message request from none other than William Night, and it shocked me. It contained a meme of Leonardo DiCaprio biting on his fist from the film *The Wolf of Wall Street* with the text, 'When you see her loading up the barbell with forty-fives.'

I had to laugh. Of course he would opt for nothing less than a grand entrance. However, despite his impeccable humour, I didn't immediately accept. My first instinct was to decline, because I wanted to avoid interacting with him as much as possible. However, I couldn't deny the gross level of curiosity I experienced. It was further reinforced as soon as I clicked on his profile because it was of course private, so stalking it brought me no satisfaction. I'd have to follow him if I meant to have a peek, but my pride wouldn't let me, so I returned to his message request with some disappointment.

I'd already acknowledged that I was drawn to him like a moth to a flame, so accepting his request would mean speeding towards my potential doom. Had I learnt nothing from the mistakes of Icarus? Was I really going to fly too close to the sun?

Collapsing onto my bed, I contemplated my options, and as I did, I wondered why he'd wanted to contact me at all. A demon whispered in my mind that I ought to accept, if only to uncover his motive. Besides, if he proved troublesome, I could always block him.

So I accepted, and I responded with a fine meme of my own of a girl squatting with the text, 'When I hear, no man wants a girl that's stronger than him, and I'm like, ain't nobody looking for a weak ass man either.'

I waited one minute for him to see it, but since he didn't, I locked my phone and decided to head back to the others. I had only just returned to my seat by the time a notification lit up my screen.

Eager to see his response, I didn't hesitate to open it.

> Haha that's the spirit

> How's revising going? Getting frustrated yet?

His brilliant pun led me to like his message. There wasn't a doubt in my mind that he'd referred to the doctrine of frustration which was a common law doctrine relevant to Contract Law. After last Friday, he was well aware I was currently revising for precisely that module. Again, his impeccable humour triggered an uncontrollable giggle to sprint out of my mouth, which earned me a curious glance from both Olivia and Aaron.

"Sorry, just a meme," I apologised.

> Frustrated indeed. Nice pun

> I think having lunch with me today might help you out of said frustration

I rolled my eyes. So that was his motive, was it? I had to give it to him – the man had remarkable perseverance. How many rejections would it require for him to realise that it wasn't going to happen?

> Do you? I am shocked

> That would probably frustrate me more than revising ever could tbf

After I'd pressed Send, I paused for a moment to reflect on what I had just done: how natural the decision to reject him had seemed. It occurred to me then that it was actually becoming a habit. I'd hardly given a thought to it, and I found it fascinating. This was quite the contrast to the first time he'd asked to meet me again; I vividly recalled how difficult it had been for me to reject him back then. I hadn't been entirely certain that it was the right course of action. Now, on the other hand, I took his offer for granted. I was expecting him to ask again, and again, and again, until I perhaps – one day – changed my mind, although I wouldn't.

I couldn't be at all certain that his interest would be perpetual, and yet I conceitedly acted as though it would be. Perhaps this had been the last time he would ask, and I had wasted my chance without a second thought.

> You are ever pessimistic

> I could have a look at your notes, for example. Help you get a top score

> All I'm suggesting is a normal lunch between two friends

Friends. I stared at the word for a while, and I didn't appreciate the way my heart responded to it, because it took a deep dive in my chest, the beats growing stronger but slower. I read "friends" as a rejection in disguise. The fall from my high horse was certainly a painful one. Was he seriously friend-zoning me?

We could never be friends, I thought, embittered, and we couldn't for the simple reason that I didn't lust after my friends the way I lusted after William. I would never be able to view him in a platonic light, and I was offended by the idea that it wasn't mutual.

Or was it? It wasn't impossible that he was only being devious. After all, I'd already noted his sly tendencies.

What was his scheme? I couldn't read him. Was he writing to me in a genuine effort to befriend me, or was he looking to capture me once and for all? I really couldn't tell. It was plausible he sought to be my friend because of our relationship with Jason. In the end, it was inevitable that our paths would cross for the rest of our lives, so perhaps he was simply trying to make the best of it, and he thought pursuing a friendship with me would be the way to achieve it.

Since I didn't know what to think, I opted for an ambiguous, albeit humorous, answer inspired by one of my favourite comedies, *The Inbetweeners*. It was an image of the character Simon from the show, and he was holding his thumbs up while saying, 'Oh, friend.'

Haha Simon. What a legend

Not sure I can be friends with a briefcase wanker

Bus wankers only?

His wit really was flawless, and I was delighted he'd caught the reference.

"Who are you texting?" Olivia suddenly queried, and when I looked up, I found her regarding me with an arched brow. Her question drew the attention of Aaron, who paused typing on his computer to gaze in my direction. Looking into his kind eyes filled me with guilt all at once. I knew I hadn't done anything wrong – we weren't a couple – but since it was novel to remain in touch with one of my previous bed partners, it seemed immoral even though it wasn't.

"Phoebe." I uttered my sister's name as though it were the obvious answer.

"She's awake?" Aaron questioned, surprised, and blood rushed to my face upon his astute remark. "Isn't it like six o'clock in New York?"

"She's just woken up," I lied again.

"Right." He frowned, and I knew he didn't believe me, but he refrained from probing me further. "Tell her I said hi, then."

"Me too," Olivia said. "How is she liking Columbia?"

"She loves it," I said dismissively and focused on my phone because I wanted to avoid further interrogation.

> Lol maybe

> Anyway, I appreciate the offer, but I honestly haven't got time. Exam's on Friday

> I'm hardly allowing myself toilet breaks atm

Christ

You clearly need training in stress management

I'd be happy to tutor you in that as well. You'd get a 100 % discount

Since I sensed both Aaron and Olivia stealing glances in my direction, I pressed my lips together to hide my smile.

> Full-on life coach, aren't you?

Accept and you'll find out

Limited offer

> I need to get back to revising. Enjoy your lunch

> Seen

With a sigh, I put my phone aside and told myself not to check it again for the remainder of the day, but I failed every hour and was equally ambivalent every time I saw that he hadn't sent anything else.

§ § §

All through Wednesday, I'd checked my Instagram more than usual because I'd both dreaded and hoped to find another message from William. However, following my rejection on Tuesday, he hadn't initiated any contact. I'd opened our message thread several times throughout the day only to see that he'd been active now and then, but it hadn't been to message me.

So, by today, which was Thursday, I'd managed to recover some of my self-control and had hardly checked. He'd been active on occasion, but since I no longer expected to hear from him, seeing it hadn't bothered me all that much.

When the clock struck seven, I closed my textbooks, every tab in my Chrome window, and my Word documents to quit revising for the day. I was one of those students who always took the evening before my exams off to let the information process into my long-term memory, so I planned to do some wall-staring for the remainder of the evening before I would go to bed at nine.

Because I relished reflecting, wall-staring happened to be one of my favourite activities. I could lie for hours at a time just staring at the ceiling while I contemplated life. Consequently, boredom was an entirely foreign concept to me, and I'd always been grateful for that. My mind entertained me endlessly, so I'd never been one to depend on external stimuli. Being stuck in traffic or waiting for the Tube was actually something I enjoyed because of that. Dad liked to say, 'If you're bored, it's because you're boring,' and that statement resonated with me.

I wasn't sure how many minutes or hours had elapsed when I reached for my phone to check the time, but upon seeing my screen, my heart did a flip.

William had messaged me again.

Sitting up with some excitement, I unlocked my phone to open it.

19:57

Good luck tmrw. Not that you'll need it

168

My emotions were conflicted. While I appreciated hearing from him and was charmed he'd remembered my exam tomorrow, I also wished he'd leave me alone, because this was precisely what I had wanted to avoid. I'd been thinking about him most of yesterday, and I couldn't remember having checked my social media this frequently before, and it was only because of him. He'd become the distraction I had feared he would the first time we'd met, and seeing proof of it was only solidifying my desire to avoid him.

Nevertheless, I decided to reply.

> I do though, but thanks

Seen

A grin I hated surfaced on my mouth when he instantly marked it as read. He must have been waiting for my response. Soon enough, I was told he was typing a reply.

> You'll be fine

> You can't know that

When he sent an image of Bob the Builder with the text 'YES WE CAN' written across it, uncontrollable laughter burst out of me. His humour was frankly one of his most attractive attributes.

> Omg

> Make Bob proud x

> I'll do my best

I chewed on my lower lip when I realised that his back must be starting to hurt from always having to carry the conversation. On the one hand, that was what I wanted, because if all I offered were dry replies, he'd be more likely to grow bored with me. But on the other, I felt I owed it to him to return at least a portion of his interest. I convinced myself it was the polite thing to do, so before long, I started typing, although I had no idea what to say.

> Have you had a nice day?

C.K. BENNETT

I gasped when he instantly saw it and proceeded to like it. Too late to unsend it, I thought to myself. Fortunately, he didn't waste his time with replying.

> What's this? Are you actually showing interest in my wellbeing?

I already regret it lol

> Haha. My day was fine. Miss teasing you, though

He attached a cartoon of an adorable but angry chipmunk, which I stared at, nonplussed. What on earth was he implying?

The hell's that supposed to mean?

> It's you whenever I tease you

Was that really how he saw me whenever I got flustered? No wonder he couldn't stop himself from teasing me.

Omg

> Anyway, I don't want to distract you right before your exam, so I'll leave you to it

> Break a leg

I wondered if he were actually busy with something else, or perhaps even someone else, and had said it only as a cover-up to place himself in a favourable light. After all, shouldn't *I* have been the one to decide whether he was stealing my precious time or not? Knowing how many women he entertained, it was perfectly plausible that one of them had either just arrived or returned from the bathroom or something like that.

As soon as I heard my own thoughts, I frowned at myself. Why should it matter who he was with? He wasn't mine, and I had no intention of pursuing him either. Regardless of whether he was with someone else, he had set aside the time to send me this encouragement, and I ought to appreciate that gesture. One way or another, he was only being kind.

170

Thanks

Seen

By nine o'clock, he still hadn't sent me anything else, and I noted to myself that I disliked his habit of always letting me have the last word. For some reason, it made me feel inferior. So yes, he'd explicitly said that he didn't want to disturb me, but he'd done this last time as well. Knowing how sly he could be, I found it plausible that he was doing it deliberately, as some sort of strategic retreat. That was what bothered me about it. Was he playing games? Trying to attain some sort of psychological advantage? Unsure of what to make of it, I decided I would now pay careful attention to whether he would repeat this pattern.

After returning my phone to my nightstand, I settled for slumber, but I didn't feel the least bit tired. In the darkness of my bedroom, memories of our sensual night together feasted on my mind. One by one, they paraded into my thoughts, regardless of how hard I tried to suppress them.

My pulse spiked as I imagined him above me and within me, mouth forming dirty declarations while he stared intensely into my eyes. I couldn't breathe. Wide-eyed, I stared blankly ahead and felt an abundance of heat in my face. Hot and bothered, I writhed beneath the duvet, rigid.

"Jason!" I yelled when I'd spent hours chasing sleep to no avail.

A few seconds later, his familiar footsteps sauntered down the hall towards my bedroom. As he opened the door, I was presented with the view of his naked body, and I swallowed upon the sight. He would make a lucky woman very happy someday, and – hopefully – before his beauty withered with age.

"You called?" While rubbing his face, he leaned against the doorpost.

"Could you sleep here tonight? I can't sleep. I need cuddles."

A soft smile reached his lips before he nodded his handsome head and approached. "Of course, love," he said and climbed into my bed.

"I love you," I cooed.

"And I love you," he replied and hooked his strong arm around me to scoop me into his familiar embrace. "When have you got to wake up?" he queried drowsily.

"Alarm's set for half six."

"Okay, I'll make sure you wake up."

"Thank you."

"Sleep now."

"Yes." I snuggled closer and released a contented sigh.

§ § §

After completing our exams, Olivia and I were having dinner at Mary-Anne's place along with Aaron and Tyler – the latter was Aaron's flatmate of three years – when I boldly confessed to seeing little point in the Royal Family.

"That's actual heresy," Olivia remarked. She'd always been of the opposite opinion and fancied the tradition it entailed.

"I appreciate their charitable and diplomatic work," I said, "but that, as well as everything else, can be executed by elected officials. I can't stand the idea that people are born into roles like that. And how can we improve in the future if we won't let go of the past? The monarchy has served its purpose. It's outdated now. There's no reason to keep it around. I mean, merely for the sake of history? Please."

Olivia gasped as if I'd just cursed in church. "In times of need, we require one head at the top to gather the people," she argued. "One who unifies the people under a common goal. Politicians can't do that the same way the Royal Family can."

"Listen, I regard the Queen with the utmost respect," I insisted. "I think she's wonderful. What I'm questioning is the principle. I don't support the concept that people should be born into roles like that. And I also find it fairly ironic that they're not supposed to have a political opinion. They're supposed to be neutral. But isn't politics what royalty was built upon in the first place? Wasn't politics the reason monarchies came to be? I just think it's ridiculous. We can have presidents and elected officials. Look at

France, for example. They've managed superbly after abolishing the monarchy." I continued to rant, "I seriously think it's only a matter of time before we'll move away from the constitutional monarchy as well. It's outdated, to say the least."

Across the table, I saw Mary-Anne smirk to herself while she raised a spoonful of ice cream to her lips.

"Quite the diatribe," Tyler murmured and glanced at Aaron. "I can see why you like her," he proceeded to joke.

I'd always liked Tyler, and I could understand why he and Aaron had been friends ever since secondary school – they were quite similar. Both were shy of conflict and preferred a conciliatory approach to almost everything. I could oftentimes be quite the opposite, and it was certainly a flaw.

"I disagree," Olivia declared. "I think the Royal Family serves a unique diplomatic purpose, as well as an important general role in society. When or if a new war breaks out, the whole nation will be looking to Her Majesty the Queen, not the Prime Minister."

"Er, to be fair, I think they'll be looking to both," Aaron intervened. "They certainly looked to Winston Churchill during the Second World War."

"It's irrational to think that we should keep the monarchy merely for the sake of tradition," I grumbled to Olivia. "It must serve a practical purpose that will prove more lucrative than other alternatives. Imagine how we could administer the resources that go into maintaining the monarchy. It's also a matter of caution that the head of the nation should only be allowed to sit for so long. We've seen how totalitarian a ruler otherwise can become. Have you learnt nothing from when you studied constitutional law?"

Soon after I'd said it, I leaned back and blinked. I hadn't meant to sound so harsh. Fortunately, Olivia knew me better than most, so she took no offence. She merely shook her head and replied curtly, "We will never agree on this. And the separation of powers guarantees that no such thing can happen, so I actually did pay some attention while we studied constitutional law, thank you very much."

"Biscuits, anyone?" Mary-Anne offered and sent the dish around the table. As soon as I saw them, I recognised them as my favourites. Mary-Anne made the best butter biscuits in the world.

"Oh, Mary-Anne," I cooed. "Butter biscuits."

"Of course, darling. I made them especially for you."

"You shouldn't have."

"Of course I should have."

"That attenuated the intense debate rather quickly," Tyler commented after a chuckle.

"Cara is quite similar to a beast, actually." Olivia laughed. "Feed her her favourite treats, and she'll be placated."

"I'm sorry. I'm too opinionated – I just get so engaged," I apologised.

"Never apologise for that, my dear," Mary-Anne insisted. "You're a delight."

Tyler asked me, "Have you considered going into politics?"

I snorted. "No, thanks. I imagine I'd have to sacrifice my values on several occasions if I hoped to get anywhere."

"The caustic tone." He smiled. "Honest question: did you vote leave or remain?"

"Brexit? Remain, absolutely, for an abundance of reasons."

"Me too."

"Let's not go into that," Olivia complained. "I'm done with politics. It's so boring."

I couldn't have disagreed more. "Right."

"I heard you received an offer to extend your placement at Day & Night this summer," Mary-Anne said to me then.

If the mention hadn't immediately reminded me of William, I would have grinned, but instead, a shy smile was all I could offer. "I did."

"That's something we ought to raise our glasses to," she said and lifted hers.

"Aaron's placement at Dentons deserves the same," I insisted.

"To Aaron and Cara, then," Mary-Anne said with a nod.

"Meanwhile, my marks didn't make the cut," Olivia mumbled, amused.

"Hey," I said after a sip. "Your effort will be recognised soon enough. Don't let this bring you down."

"I won't," she assured me. "I'm honestly overjoyed on your behalf. Knowing how much you and Aaron work, you deserve it. I wish I could say the same, but I'm much lazier than you. Now I'm paying the price."

Mary-Anne reached over to squeeze her hand. "That's the spirit, pet. In the end, perseverance is always rewarded."

"Mary-Anne, you are ever fantastic," she replied fondly.

I said, "On that note, I say we raise our glasses to Mary-Anne."

§ § §

After dinner, I helped Mary-Anne clean the dishes in the kitchen and was thankful for some quietness. The others remained in the living room and watched TV. My brain was exhausted after today's exam, and socialising was something I usually found taxing, so I didn't say much, but that was something I'd always adored about Mary-Anne: just like Aaron, she was extremely comfortable to be around. I never felt the need to say something to break the silence because, around her, I always felt welcome to be entirely myself.

"Aaron told me the exam was tough," she murmured after a while.

"It was."

"And the next one is on Thursday next week?"

"Yes. I'll start revising for it tomorrow. I've required a day off."

"Understandable." She reached over to stroke my arm. "I'm very grateful for you, Cara. Aaron's always been a bit of a loner, but I can tell he's thrilled with his life at UCL, and I suspect I have you to thank for it."

I chuckled. "Hardly. Between the two of us, he's the more likeable person. I've been told I tend to intimidate people. Aaron earns the favour of everyone – especially Cassie."

"Cassie?"

I glanced at her. "He hasn't mentioned her?"

Mary-Anne looked amused. "No."

"Well, she's a girl in our class, and she's got a soft spot for Aaron. He won't agree if you ask him, though."

She laughed. "That's Aaron for you. He's always been clueless about girls."

"Clearly." I laughed as well.

I heard my phone ring in my pocket then, so after drying my hands, I fished it out and saw that Jason was calling.

"Hiya," I answered.

"Hi, love. How did it go?"

"Okay, I think, but it's hard to say. I might have missed the target. Who knows?"

"I'm sure you nailed it. Anyway, just thought I'd say that I'm heading to Will's, so I doubt I'll be home when you get back. We're playing a game of chess, and it tends to last a couple of hours."

"I see. Sounds like fun. Thanks for letting me know. Tell him I said hi, I suppose."

"Will do. Love you."

"Love you too."

As soon as I rang off, I saw that I had a couple of notifications, but one in particular earned my immediate attention because it contained another message from William.

Congratulations on completing the first of your exams! I'm checking in to make sure you're still alive.

Sensing Mary-Anne's eyes on me, I looked up to meet them.

"That's a lovely smile you're wearing," she commented astutely. "Could it be due to a lucky man?"

I feared my blush exposed me, but nevertheless, I shook my head. "No, just a friend – and a funny one at that, hence the smile."

"Mm-hmm," she uttered, evidently not convinced, but instead of probing me, she merely gave me a knowing smile. I wondered for a moment if she would have reacted the same had she known about my arrangement with her son.

Turning my focus back to my phone, I replied with a meme

of a man in seemingly impenetrable armour of the medieval sort, with the caption 'Me: fully prepared for exams'. But in the image straight below, an arrow struck through the slim gap in his helmet, with the text 'question number one' written across its shaft.

After that, I tucked my phone back into my pocket and promised myself I wouldn't look at it again before I left.

§ § §

Since Olivia and I had planned to sleep over at mine, we headed home together shortly before midnight, and by the time we parted ways with Aaron and Tyler, I had grown impatient with wanting to check if I had received any new messages. As soon as we stepped onto the central line Tube that would take us from Wanstead to Notting Hill Gate, I fished my phone out of my pocket and was delighted to see that William had replied.

> Haha I'm sure you nailed it

> Ever the pessimist

Smiling to myself, I liked his last message but decided not to reply until we stepped off the train, because Olivia wanted to talk about Colin. She'd heard he had started seeing Alison now, who was the girl he'd cheated on her with. Naturally, she was rather irate about it, and she had only found out yesterday, so she was worried the news had affected her performance in her exam today. Listening to her was a solid reminder of exactly why I would do best to avoid William. To find myself in her shoes – my attention divided between a man and my ambitions – was a far cry from tempting.

"You need to put that arsehole out of your mind, Livy," I said. "He's not worth your attention. I know it's easier said than done, but if he's really seeing Alison now, you should consider that another reason never to give him a single thought again. He really doesn't deserve even a scrap of your time."

"It just feels so unfair," she complained, upset.

"The world isn't fair."

"Your realism is hardly what I need right now."

"I'm sorry." I pouted. "I wish there were something I could say to make you feel better, but I seriously don't know what. I completely agree that you don't deserve this, but it is what it is. You've spent three years of your life with a man who didn't deserve it, but that can happen to the best of us. You ought to do yourself a favour and learn from it as you move on."

"Yeah, it's just difficult to accept."

"I get it. I'd probably feel the same way."

"Ugh." She tossed her head back. "I can't wait for exams to be over so I can start dating again. The lack of male attention isn't helping me forget about him."

"I'll gladly be your wing-woman again. That's if you would dare to entrust me with that task after it failed last time."

She laughed. "You'll be too busy working anyway."

"Not on the weekends – I hope."

"We'll see. Either way, I'd love that. Speaking of, how's that going? Have you met William since?"

"Not since he helped me assemble my wardrobe and since dinner with his parents, but I've already told you about that."

"He's not made any other advances?"

While I could tell her that he had started messaging me on Instagram, I hesitated, because I worried it would make everything real to me. If I told her, he would inevitably become a recurring subject, and I didn't want that. I was struggling enough as it was with putting him out of my mind, so I couldn't see what good it would do. The constant reminder would only worsen the headache he was giving me.

"No."

"Hm. Well, I'm glad he's respecting your boundaries. I do pity him, though. And I still think you made a mistake."

"Whatever."

As we walked along the pavement towards my flat, Olivia was busy messaging one of her other friends, presumably about Colin, so I took the opportunity to reply to William.

> I wasn't all that frustrated tbh ;)

> Should work out fine (I hope).
> Anyway, how's your Friday?

> Spending it with this knob

He sent a photo of Jason. I chuckled at first, but my amusement subsided when it occurred to me that he was currently hanging out with my very best friend who had no idea at all that we were chatting under his nose. What had my life come to? All this secrecy wasn't something I was used to. I'd always been one to favour transparency in my friendships, but now I had lied to Olivia and continued to withhold information from both her and Jason, not to mention Aaron.

> Yes, he told me you're playing chess.
> Who's winning?

> I am, of course. Always

> But he'd never admit that

> So I can expect to find him licking
> his wounds tmrw?

> Probably

> Have you played chess?

> Only once or twice with my dad.
> Not my forte

> I could teach you

> Imagine his surprise when you suddenly
> defeat him

> Haha that'd be something

> Sold then?

> Enjoy your evening, Will. Glad you're
> having fun. Don't destroy your
> brother completely tho. I like him

Left on read. Again.

12

---•◆•---

LIVERPOOL'S IN THE LEAD

SINCE I NEVER INITIATED, WILLIAM HADN'T SENT ME MUCH since Friday last week. I supposed he had too much integrity, and I supposed the same integrity was also to blame for his continued pattern of always leaving me on read.

He'd sent me a message on Wednesday to wish me luck with my next exam the following Thursday, but I had grown so irritated with his existence by then that I had left him on read without even replying despite the kind gesture. It wasn't really because I was angry with him, but rather because I was angry with how I responded to his attention, or lack thereof. The constant waiting around, the frequent check-ins and the ensuing disappointment in ninety-nine out of a hundred instances was driving me mad. The dopamine rush upon arbitrarily discovering a message no longer compensated for the distress.

The last few days, I'd been thinking about him more than Company Law, and while I was angry about it, it was also truly starting to frighten me. I didn't feel half as prepared for this exam as I had felt for my last one, and I blamed him. Well, I blamed his existence, not his actions. It wasn't his fault that he was the first man ever to have caught my eye this way. It wasn't his fault that he made my heart behave in strange ways while my body ached for his caress. It was neither of our faults. But it was his fault that he kept contacting me, and for that, I was angry.

During a moment of reflection, it had dawned on me that what I was going through now must be similar to what Olivia had gone through on the daily over the past three years, and I had pitied her profusely then. Her relationship with Colin had been a volatile one, so now I was able to empathise with at least a portion of her distress. I also knew she'd had it far worse than I currently did, so I was frankly impressed she had managed to perform decently at university at all, especially when the man had also cheated on her and broke her heart while he was at it.

I'd made a note to myself to treat Olivia with more patience in the future wherever Colin was involved. The poor thing must really have gone through hell, and now I knew from first-hand experience that putting a man out of your mind was indeed easier said than done. And William was kind. Colin was the spawn of the Devil. Poor Olivia, indeed.

Either way, I knew ignoring William's messages was the only sensible course of action at this point, so by Wednesday night, I had sworn to myself that I wouldn't check my social media till next week. Should my attention be required imminently within that timeframe, I could always be reached by more conservative means, like ringing or sending text messages.

§ § §

To celebrate that we had completed our exam in Company Law the next day, Aaron and I headed back to mine to enjoy each other without clothes involved. Since I knew Jason finished work at five o'clock this week, we had hurried home to take advantage of our few moments of privacy. The instant we stepped through the front door, Aaron pinned me to the wall beside the shoe cabinet and removed my clothes with urgency. By the time we approached my bedroom, I'd managed to remove only his shirt, and the garments lay scattered across the floor.

When he grabbed below my bum, I knew he was about to lift me to carry me to bed, but it wasn't what I wanted, so after shutting the door behind me, I dropped to my knees, my attention fixed on undoing his trousers. While gathering my long hair in his hands, he cast me a cheeky and lopsided smile.

"So eager, Cara."

"Well, I love the taste of you, so yes," I lustfully replied as I jerked his trousers down. After helping him out of them, I reached up to trail my fingertips along the band of his grey boxers. His erection strained against the material, and it made me smile. Cupping it in my hand, I gave it a gentle squeeze. All the while, I gazed up at him through my long lashes.

"Fucking hell, you're so damn hot," he stated with a chuckle and brought one of his hands beneath my chin. Using his thumb, he traced the line of my jaw while wonder vibrated in his dark eyes.

A lascivious smile crept across my lips while I hooked my fingers into his boxers and lowered them to liberate his erection. It pointed horizontally, straight to my waiting mouth. Wasting no time, I grabbed around the base and pushed my tongue past my lips to lick around the crest of him. As I focused my point of impact on the back of his head, I looked up at him and saw his chest expand with his deep inhalation.

"Mm," I hummed and slowly wrapped my lips around the tip before I took him deep into my mouth.

Bobbing my head, I heard him groan above me. His hands fisted in my hair, tugging it until tears formed in my eyes. My jaw started aching after a while, but I had no sympathy for it. Determined to send him over the edge, I persisted despite the discomfort.

"Ah, Cara," he warned. "Stop."

Disobeying, I continued obstinately. While my mouth drew in on him, my hand synchronised with my labour, pumping him.

Meanwhile, my tongue swirled around his length within my mouth, just the way I knew he liked it.

"Shit," he cursed and, using his hold of my hair, tugged me harshly away from him. "I don't want to come yet," he growled under his breath and ministered me towards my bed. With a smouldering look in his eyes, he glared at me.

"Still upset about the other day?" I teased, referring to Monday. I'd performed fellatio on him then and had made him come in record time.

When my legs bumped into the frame of my bed, he leaned towards me to force me to recline onto the mattress. As I gazed up, I saw him admire the body he'd undressed.

"A bit," he said. "Won't let that happen again anytime soon," he stated as he climbed over my figure to hover above. "Honestly, love," he said while his eyes wandered across my curves, "it's ridiculous how gorgeous you are." He trailed his right hand up my flat stomach. "Three years of this, and yet I could never grow bored."

"Right back at you." I smiled coquettishly and circled his neck with my arms. Bringing his face to mine, I leaned up to engulf his lips.

Kissing Aaron had never felt wrong, but it had never felt quite right either – merely familiar. By now, I knew the motion of his lips like the back of my hand.

It had been weeks since I'd experienced a kiss as entirely right for the first time, how consuming and intense it could be. Only one set of lips had managed to set my system on fire like that, but they weren't present.

Surprising me, Aaron pulled away from my mouth sooner than I'd expected. Instead, he traced lustful kisses down the slope of my neck until he located my pulse, a spot on my body that he knew was susceptible. Once there, he gently sucked and nibbled on it.

My eyes closed from the pleasure and, subconsciously, my limbs locked around him to welcome the intimacy. After a good minute, he started trailing soft kisses down the valley between my breasts, and then further down to reach the tops of my thighs.

While biting on my lower lip, I smiled as I gauged his intention. Aaron always made a point of returning the favour. We hardly ever had sex without him demanding to go down on me, and I relished it. His skill in that department was his ace in bed. Without fail, his mouth always triggered my climax.

His tongue lapped over my folds, warm and wet. Groaning, my head jerked backwards as I welcomed heaven. Only vaguely did I notice his arms locking around my thighs – he knew me well. In the throes of passion, I tended to shudder away when the pleasure bordered on unbearable, so, in time, he'd learnt to take pre-emptive measures.

"Ah, Aaron," I moaned and ran my palms across his dense hair. He was so damn good at this.

The tension coiled inside my abdomen, spreading out all the way to my fingertips and toes until his expert flicks sent me over the edge. "Ah!" I cried out, my back ascending from the mattress. Responding to impulse, I squeezed my breasts while I savoured the delicious aftermath of my orgasm, a smile ever-present on my face.

"You look well funny after you come, Cara," he teased while his mouth climbed up my stomach. After hungrily sucking my left nipple, he pushed himself up to grin down at me.

"Funny how?"

"You look high."

"Well, that's how I feel."

"Good," he said with a chuckle and dived for my lips. I could taste myself in his mouth, but I'd never minded the flavour. It was faintly salted, was all – neutral and natural.

Reaching between us, I grabbed his member to align it with my entrance, and as I teased myself with the tip of him, I delighted in how wet I was. Starving for more of him, I directed my eyes to his with a lewd smile.

"Don't be mean," he scolded. "You know I lose my head when you smile like that."

"Yeah? Which head?"

Growling, he thrust harshly into me, successfully repressing my sassiness. "Both," he purred and lowered his head to trail ravenous kisses down my pulse. It drummed for him, begging for more of his gratifying treatment. After a gentle retreat, he charged forward again, and he knew exactly where to strike.

"Ah," I groaned and clasped his head to bring his mouth back to mine, but his smile interfered with our kiss.

"Stop smiling, idiot."

Pulling away, he laughed and nuzzled my nose with his. "Sorry, I can't help it. I'm enjoying myself too much, as well as curbing your attitude."

"Attitude?"

"You heard me."

I smirked. "Whatever gets you off, I suppose."

"*You* do," he declared and demanded my mouth again, but all of a sudden, he pulled away. "Would you like to do it with your vibrator this time around? You loved it last time."

Sometimes, I was certain we sounded like a married couple, and in many ways, we often acted like one. We were so familiar and comfortable with each other that questions that might otherwise have seemed odd were now perfectly normal. All that we lacked were romantic feelings. Then again, I reckoned plenty of marriages were guilty of losing their spark a few years down the road, when they inevitably started to take their partner for granted.

"Nah, I'm good with you," I replied with a shrug.

"Alright," he said and pushed into me again, and he reached so fucking deep.

"Oh my God," I wheezed out and smothered him against me. Pushing back against my legs as they pressed him to me, he retreated only to plough into me again, his thrusts slow but hard. I rarely felt so devoured.

A few minutes later, I was moaning nonstop as I closed in on my second peak, but a sudden slam made us both freeze before I could reach it. It had sounded like something had either fallen or broken. For a split second, we stared at each other, stunned.

"What was that?" I whispered, frightened.

Aaron was the first to break out of his paralysis. While hastily withdrawing from within me, he suggested, "Jason?"

"Hello?" I called and heard subtle swearing outside my bedroom door.

"Aaron!" I whispered harshly when I saw he was recklessly approaching the door. "It could be a burglar!" I warned in another whisper. "Did we lock the door?"

Responding to my concern, he proceeded to lock it and eyed me with a furrowed brow. While my heart pumped fresh adrenaline into my bloodstream, I gripped the duvet to cover my nudity.

"Who's there?" Aaron demanded and lingered by the door while I searched for my phone in case I had to call 999. Fear made my heart contract when I recalled that it was in my bag, which was still in the hallway outside. What were we supposed to do now? Open a window and call for the neighbours?

"I...It's Will, Jason's brother."

Even though it was barely audible, I recognised his voice immediately. Air stormed out of my mouth as if I'd just been punched in the gut. How long had he been outside? Had he heard us?

This was the last thing I'd anticipated, so I had no idea at all of how to handle the amount of guilt I instantaneously experienced. What was he doing here?

"Cara?" Aaron prompted, awaiting my verdict.

"William?" I called, but since I was completely shocked at his presence, I was acting on autopilot.

"Sorry," he replied, and his voice was a little louder now, but the tone of it penetrated my heart like a blade. He'd sounded so defeated.

Seeming to realise the absence of danger, Aaron bent to recover his boxers from the floor, and after pulling them on, he reached for the door.

"Aaron!" I cried impulsively because I hadn't been prepared for them to meet, especially not like this. Moreover, I didn't want him to walk out wearing only his boxers when it would essentially mean rubbing our arrangement in William's face.

"What?"

"Get dressed first," I insisted.

He frowned. "My shirt's outside." With that, he unlocked the door and opened it. "Shit," he uttered at once, and I could tell from the look on his face that the view was chaotic.

"Sorry about this. Knocked it over by accident," I heard William murmur.

Seized by panic, I stormed out of bed and grabbed my nightgown from my desk chair. I wrapped myself in the black satin before I stalked towards the door to observe their encounter.

Peeking past Aaron's broad shoulder, I saw that the coat stand had fallen over, and it had brought the shoe cabinet with it. As I continued to assess the damage, I wondered how on earth this was even possible to manage through mere physical laws. The coat stand I could understand, as it could overbalance, but the shoe cabinet? Was the coat stand even heavy enough to tilt it over?

Without concluding my speculations, I bent to help William clean up the mess.

"I wasn't aware you were coming," I said while I tossed Aaron's shirt to him, and I hoped he heard the apology disguised within my statement.

Without looking at me, he grabbed the shoe cabinet to lift it back up. "Arrived just now," he murmured. "Chelsea's playing at half four, and I didn't want to miss it even though Jason won't be here till sometime after five. I sent you a message to warn you, but I suppose you haven't seen it."

"I haven't checked my messages since last night," I replied and struggled to hide my distress. It dawned on me then that I would need to keep tabs on whenever Chelsea was playing so that I could avoid another incident like this in the future.

"So you're Jason's brother," Aaron said then. "Suppose that also makes you Cara's future boss. I'm Aaron, by the way."

My eyes darted to William to observe his reaction, and I could tell from his delayed response that he was reluctant even to acknowledge him. After a moment's hesitation, he directed his attention to him and nodded vaguely. "I didn't mean to interrupt."

Aaron chuckled. "Never mind that. Happens to the best of us. Bit awkward for Cara, though, since you're going to be her boss."

"Thanks for the reminder, Aaron," I muttered. "Awkward hardly covers it."

"It's past half four now," he told William after glancing at his wristwatch. "Don't worry about this. Cara and I can clean up."

"Thanks, but I was taught to clean up my own mess."

"Right. Decent parenting. I'll find the match on the TV for you, then. I'd like to see it too, as it happens. They're playing against Liverpool, and that's my team."

"Thanks."

As soon as he'd disappeared around the corner to enter the living room, I searched for William's eyes, but from his elusive demeanour, I could tell he was deliberately refusing me the satisfaction of finding them.

"I'm sorry," I said, but he didn't reply. Instead, he merely reached for my beige coat, which had fallen to the floor along with the coat stand, and once he lifted it, we both froze for a moment. Underneath it lay the knickers I'd worn today.

"Fuck," I cursed and snatched them off the floor to tuck them into my palm.

"I'm leaving," he said without looking at me and reached for the door. "I'll tell Jason I went home instead."

His decision struck me like a cannonball to the chest. A sharp breath escaped and I stared at him. I'd obviously hurt him, and for a moment, I hated myself for it.

"I thought you wanted to be friends." I murmured it quietly so that Aaron wouldn't hear. "Surely this shouldn't matter if friendship is all you want?"

Finally, he met my eyes, and the crestfallen expression in his

SKIN OF THE NIGHT

clawed viciously at my chest. "I thought I could manage it," he explained. "But as soon as I heard you – as soon as I saw this—" he motioned towards my clothes on the floor—"I realised I can't. It's impossible – I'm sorry."

Without further ado, he opened the door and left.

Trying to process what had just happened, I stared at the door for a while after he'd closed it. He had actually heard us. Immediately, I felt nauseous on his behalf.

"Liverpool's in the lead," Aaron said. "Er, where's he gone?"

After drawing in a composing breath, I turned to face him. "He felt too awkward to stay."

Aaron grimaced. "Shit. Really?"

"Really."

He walked up to tilt my head back. "Are you okay?" he asked worriedly and placed a kiss upon my forehead.

I swallowed. "I'm actually feeling a bit weird. That was very uncomfortable."

He wrapped his arms around me in an attempt to comfort me. "I'm sure he just needs a minute, Cara. I hardly think this will pose a problem once you start work."

While hugging him, I glanced at the shoe cabinet and surmised that it had never fallen by accident. It had been pushed deliberately, and it puzzled me. William wasn't a violent person. He was cunning, however. As I considered it in that light, my eyes widened. He must have done it solely to guarantee an end to our session.

I had to give it to him – his methods were ironically discreet, but his genius hadn't fooled me.

"I'm not really in the mood for sex anymore," I told Aaron as I pulled away. "I'm sorry."

He chuckled. "I'd be surprised if you were. Don't worry about it. Shall we watch the match instead?"

He knew full well that I wasn't one to watch football, but since it was better than the alternative of hanging out in my room with nothing to do but talk, I said, "Sure. I'd like a shower first, though."

"I'll just wait in the living room, then."

Half-time was just over when Jason stormed through the front door to find us in the living room.

"Fuck," he grumbled when he saw the score. "Not again. We can't afford this! What the hell are they doing?" he moaned and gestured towards the screen.

"I'm having a great time," Aaron replied, amused.

"Yeah, fuck you," Jason said with a laugh and folded his arms. "By the way, heard you've had an awkward afternoon."

I stiffened. "Will told you?"

"Yeah."

Aaron sighed and reached over from where he was lying spread across the sofa to squeeze my thigh. "Yeah, it was proper awkward. I tried to pretend like it was nothing, but he left anyway."

"Can't say I blame him," Jason murmured and walked over to claim the spot beside me, which forced Aaron to move his arm. "You've had her all day," he joked. "My turn."

I hadn't thought anyone could manage it, but Jason's comment actually left me grinning.

"Sharing is caring, I suppose," Aaron replied, and when I glimpsed him, I could tell he was equally amused. That was something I'd always been grateful for: Aaron had never felt threatened by my friendship with Jason at all.

"Honestly, women smell so good," Jason said and wrapped his arm around my neck to pull my damp hair under his nose. "So sweet – like dessert."

Aaron burst into laughter, and the sound caught me. "How long has it been since you got laid, Jase?" he asked.

"A millennium," Jason joked back.

"Your right hand must be growing sore by now," Aaron remarked.

"You've no idea."

§ § §

I was grateful that Jason had come home because it was chiefly him who had entertained Aaron after William's abrupt arrival and departure. I hadn't been in the mood for socialising at all since then and had been counting the seconds till Aaron would leave. Shortly before midnight, he did, and the first thing I did afterwards was head into my bedroom to check my Instagram.

When I saw that William had sent me a message like he'd said earlier today, my heart stilled in my chest. Very slowly, I found a seat on my bed and grimaced.

11:09

I'm coming over after work to watch Chelsea play. Hope your exam went well x

Brilliant. A reminder of his kind and decent character was precisely what I needed right now. It might as well have been a slap to the face or a punch in the gut. I knew I'd hurt him, and the more I thought about it, the more it pained me to know. Eventually, tears welled in my eyes, but they never spilled over because I simply would not let them.

I was upset because I had hurt him, not because I felt I'd done something wrong. I owed him no fidelity – we weren't even dating – and I hadn't known he would be here. He could hardly hold it against me that I would enjoy Aaron in my own home the way he probably enjoyed Francesca, Violet and Kate in his. The only difference was that he had a key to my flat, but that came with the risk of walking in on scenes like these.

Either way, he shouldn't have had to witness that. I couldn't imagine how nauseous I would have felt had the roles been reversed – had I walked in on him and Violet, for example. There was something brutal about even just the idea; that sort of intimacy was unique, so to witness a person you had shared it with offer it to someone else, especially enthusiastically, seemed like a defilement.

After taking a composing breath, I focused on what to write to him. He hadn't answered my apology earlier, but since he'd had a few hours to restore his equilibrium, perhaps he would now. Regardless, I wanted to apologise again to show that I had thought about this since so that he would know that it had sincerely bothered me.

> I'm genuinely sorry you had to witness that. I don't really know what else to say

Seen

I hadn't anticipated that he would see it immediately, but he did, so I sat there for quite some time, hoping to be told that he was typing a reply, but it never happened.

DEEP SEA

A PENSIVE MOOD SUMMARISED MY ENTIRE FRIDAY. William had been active on Instagram several times without responding to my message, but I hadn't expected anything else, because what was there to say? That I was forgiven? That would require something to forgive, but I had done nothing wrong, and he knew that as well as I did.

Since I didn't want to be a nuisance, I hadn't sent him anything else either. Nevertheless, remaining focused on my exams was nearly impossible. While I no longer expected to hear from him and was finally free of that anxiety, it hadn't been half as satisfying as I had hoped, because I was left with the feeling that he was keeping his distance for the wrong reason – he was avoiding me not to respect my boundaries but because I'd hurt him. It wasn't impossible that he was staying silent to punish me for the pain I'd caused him. I understood his need for space, but what I didn't understand was his total lack of a reply. A simple thumbs-up would have sufficed.

I had no idea of what was currently running through his mind, but thinking about it got me no further. I sat on all the questions while he sat on all the answers, and since we weren't speaking, I doubted I'd ever know them.

Ultimately, I was unable to appreciate the revelation that he hadn't been able to friend-zone me either. While my ego was restored, it was no victory in the grand scheme of things. I'd hurt a person I had started to care for, and that was nothing to celebrate. Truthfully, I worried he would only despise me from now on.

By Saturday, I'd been able to work through some of my feelings, which had enabled me to revise for most of the day. Still, he disturbed my thoughts more than I appreciated, but at least I was able to be somewhat productive.

It was nearing six o'clock when I heard Stephen and Jonathan enter through the front door. They had been there the first time I had met Jason at the pub three years ago, and I'd grasped early on that they were a trio that had lasted since childhood. Stephen was the one who had lived here with Jason before I'd moved in.

"Hiya," Jason greeted them. "Don't tell me you forgot the sushi."

"I haven't got a death wish," Jon replied. "You ready to get robbed tonight?"

I assumed he was referring to the lads' night they made time for once a month. "Poker night", they always called it. I had been aware of that tradition of theirs for several years, but it wasn't until this morning that I had registered that William was a regular participant. The same applied to his friend Andy from work, and another man named Alexander. Apparently, William, Andy and Alex were also a trio alongside Jason, Stephen and Jon. The six of them often interacted because of that, although Jason was supposedly an uncounted member of William's group as well.

Sensing that there was about to be some activity outside, I reached for my noise-cancelling headset since I required silence to remain focused. They'd been covering my ears for no more than ten minutes when my chair was suddenly pulled back. Next thing I knew, I was dangling from Jon's shoulder while I rushed to save my headset from falling to the floor.

"Oh my God!" I shouted. "Put me down! Immediately! I'm revising!"

All three of them guffawed at the frantic motion of my arms, and it increased in volume when I proceeded to spank Jon's arse.

"Jon! Put me down!"

After three pirouettes, he charged towards my bed and launched us onto it.

Dizzy, I struggled to fix my gaze on anyone at all, but once my vision settled, I stared into Jon's devilish grin. "Hello, pet. Long time no see."

It was impossible not to laugh at the genuine humour in his eyes. "You absolute twat."

Ruffling my hair, he proceeded to lie down beside me while he tucked his hands under his head. "We got sushi for you. Dinner's served."

"Oh. That was kind."

"It was my idea," Jason said proudly. "You've hardly eaten for the last couple of days. Don't think I haven't noticed. You barely touched my scrambled eggs this morning, and that's unusual, to say the least." If only he'd been aware that it was solely because the taste now reminded me of William and the morning in his flat.

"Everyone needs dinner, Cara," Jon said strictly and ran a hand through his short, light-brown hair in an attempt to tidy it.

"How's living with Giselle?" I asked Stephen.

"It's great. I'd forgotten how nice it is to have a female round the place. Everything smells wonderful all the time. Even the bathroom after I've had a shit."

"Same," Jason said and patted his shoulder. "Moving apart wasn't all that bad after all. Cara keeps the place constantly clean. There's hardly a speck of dust anywhere – ever."

Amused, I smiled. "You clean just as much as I do."

"Perhaps."

"That he does," Stephen agreed with a nod. "Then again, he's

been scared of germs since forever. Occupational hazard, I presume."
After a visual sweep of my bedroom, he directed his brown eyes to
mine. "Love what you've done with the place. All I had in here was
that closet, a desk for gaming, and a bed. I hardly recognise it."

"Agreed. It's strangely homey, but fashionably so," Jon remarked
and reached for one of my beige decorative pillows to tuck it under
his head.

"The rug is a nice touch," Stephen added and stepped forward
to rub his foot against it. "Very soft."

I said, "Thanks, I think."

"Anyway, let's eat," Jason proposed. "I'm famished."

§ § §

Poker night was being held at Alexander's place, so the lads left
at half six to be there by seven. Their friendly presence had helped
me forget about William for a couple of hours, so the silence that
ensued after their departure came as a bit of a shock. Suddenly,
it was just me and my thoughts again, and for once, it wasn't
something I enjoyed. In an attempt to drown them out, I played
music so loud that I couldn't process a single word on the page as I
tried to revise. Finally, I abandoned revising altogether and allowed
the music to consume me instead.

In the darkness of my bedroom, I listened until my ears ached.
Only then did I shut it off and decide it was time for bed. It was
nearly midnight when I did, but I didn't expect Jason home anytime
soon, so sleep was my best option in the search for a distraction.
As I closed my eyes, I hoped he would find his way into my bed
instead of his own.

Though scarcely, I'd managed to catch some sleep when I
suddenly woke to the sound of the front door being slammed shut.
Harsh whispers followed, but I couldn't distinguish the words.

Jason, I presumed, but he was evidently not alone. My pulse
spiked when my thoughts settled on William. I hoped desperately
that it was him because, if it was, I could force him to talk to me. Then
again, I hardly dared to hope for it since I considered it highly unlikely

that he would risk re-encountering me at all, especially so soon.

Pushing my duvet aside, I decided to find out. While slipping on my nightgown, I heard the subtle sounds of retching. Jason must have had too much to drink.

As quietly as I possibly could, I opened my bedroom door and saw light streaming out of the bathroom. The door was open, and once the sounds of vomiting settled somewhat, I heard Jason moan, "Shit, the world's spinning so fast. Did I lose? I ought to go home."

"Shush, be quiet. You'll wake Cara." My heart jolted at the sound of William's authoritative voice. My prayers had been heard.

"Cara's not here. She's at home."

"You *are* home, you fucking knobhead," William whispered harshly. Under any other circumstances, that would have made me laugh, but William's presence had made me apprehensive, so not a sound made its way out of my mouth.

"Really?" Jason queried, surprised. "Ah, yes, this is my beloved toilet, isn't it?"

"Yes."

"God, I'm so drunk."

"You really are."

"How come you never get plastered, Will?" Jason asked, his words slurred.

"I don't enjoy being rendered powerless, nor helpless."

"Damn. That's deep. I'm the opposite."

"That's 'cause you're fucking stupid."

"Cunt."

"Come on. Wash your mouth."

Jason released a surge of loud laughter then.

"Why the hell are you laughing? Quiet down," William urged quietly but aggressively.

"You're telling me to wash my mouth 'cause I called you a cunt?" Jason replied.

"No, I'm telling you to wash your mouth because you've just vomited every meal from the past year."

"Oh."

"Fucking hell."

After a deep breath for courage, I stepped out and approached the bathroom. The instant I entered the doorway, William glanced up to catch my reflection in the mirror. As soon as he registered my presence, his eyes frosted as though he'd just come upon an internal ice age, and it occurred to me that his forgiveness was far from my reach.

"Is he alright?" I asked him, but he was spared from having to answer when Jason noticed my arrival.

"Cara, my darling." He smiled affectionately. "There are two of you now, but I love you both equally," he cooed, but I barely managed to understand him. "Double the love."

"Christ," I said. "Is there anything I can do?"

"No, go back to bed. I've got it," William insisted.

"How come you got this drunk, Jason?" I asked.

"I was sabotaged. Stephen and Jon kept pouring and mixing my drink. All of a sudden, I was plastered."

"Christ," I repeated. "I should've anticipated this."

William shoved Jason's toothbrush into his hand while scolding, "When are you going to learn that you shouldn't let them mix your drinks for you? This isn't the first time this has happened, and I'm sick of being your voice of reason and getting completely ignored."

Confused, Jason looked at him, and it was obvious from his expression that he was too intoxicated to comprehend what he was hearing. "You're always so strict."

"Only when you're reckless," William argued. "Cara, go to bed. He needs a shower."

Disobeying, I waited outside the bathroom till they were finished, and William didn't bother hiding his annoyance when he discovered me.

"I told you to go to bed," he said, his irritation scorching, but his focus diverged when Jason proceeded to approach my bedroom.

"That's not your bedroom, Jase," William reminded him while

grabbing his shoulder.

"I know. I want to sleep with Cara."

Wide-eyed, my gaze darted to William's, and the wrath it contained expelled my soul from my body.

"That's not happening," he growled and tugged Jason harshly in the other direction.

"What?" Jason uttered, nonplussed, and writhed his arm out of William's hold. "The hell's your problem, mate?"

"William, it's fine," I said. "He does it all the time – it's only friendly," I continued, as I hoped it would reassure him.

"She's *my* friend," Jason reminded him impudently. "Not yours."

William's chest expanded with his deep breath, although it seemed to have no appeasing effect because antagonism continued to swell in his eyes. "Fine." In the dim light, I saw his jaw clench and unclench repeatedly, and for a moment, it looked like he'd stopped breathing.

Jason gave him a snort before he zig-zagged towards my room, where he went straight to bed. As I went to close the door after him, William charged towards the front door, but I stopped him before he could pass me. I'd just managed to shut the door when I gripped his arm, and I was shocked at the way he thrashed my hand off him. Pure intimidation exploded in my chest when he faced me properly and stepped forward to trap me between his huge body and the door.

My heart was beating at a hundred miles per hour when I looked frightened into his blistering gaze. His breath reeked of alcohol. He had clearly seemed soberer than he actually was.

"You are to stay the fuck away from Jason," he commanded chillingly. "Do you hear me?"

Colour drained from my face as I swallowed. "Of course."

"I won't let you get your claws into him as well," he spat resentfully.

My breath caught at his abominable insinuation. Was that really his impression of me now? "I haven't touched him – not like that. I'd never."

C.K. BENNETT

He arched a brow to convey that he didn't believe me in the slightest. "If you so much as *try* to lay a hand on him, I'll tell him everything, and I'll make sure he won't appreciate you after that."

His brutal threats brought unexpected tears to my eyes. I hadn't thought him capable of such malice. He'd always been so kind.

"Of course, Will," I said, and surprised myself with my calm tone, but I was desperately trying to deescalate the situation. "You have my word. I'll never touch him like that."

He glared at me for another while to assess my sincerity before he suddenly went for the door.

"William, I am sorry to have hurt you," I called after him. He froze at once, hand lingering on the handle. Seeing a chance to speak, I added, "Will, I'm not your girlfriend. I've got to be allowed to do this sort of thing in my own home – and it's not as if you haven't been guilty of the same."

He whirled around with a look of disdain. "What?"

"Yes." I motioned towards him. "Francesca, Violet, Kate? How many are there, really?"

I tensed when he stalked towards me again. Halting only a foot away, he glared down at me. "For your information," he seethed, "Kate is my ex, and I haven't spoken to her in well over a year. As for Violet and Francesca, I haven't seen them like that for weeks and had actually planned to end it with them because of *you*."

My lips parted with shock. Since it was far from what I'd expected, it took me several seconds to conjure a reply. "I…I'm sorry. I didn't know."

He narrowed his eyes. "Of course you didn't. That's precisely my point. Stop assuming you know anything at all."

I gulped. "You're right. I'm sorry." After a brief while, his shoulders sank somewhat. Sensing that he was calming down, I dared say, "I don't expect you to stop seeing them," although I couldn't deny that my greedy ego wished he would. "I don't expect anything from you at all."

Directing his gaze back to mine, he studied me for some time,

200

and the vulnerability in his eyes made my heart contract. "Why are you like this?" he asked then, audibly upset.

I grimaced. "I tried to warn you."

"You're in love with him, aren't you? With Aaron?"

His question beat the air out of my lungs. "What? No!" I asserted. Was that really what he inferred from this? "I've already told you, I—" He cut me off by clasping my head between his hands, and before I knew it, his warm mouth had moulded against my own. Instantly, my chest filled with delight as I rejoiced in the taste of him. Again, that uncanny sensation spread throughout my system to remind me that this was how a kiss was supposed to feel – entirely right.

When his tongue pushed past my lips for a dance with mine, he obliterated what remained of my self-control. Swinging my arms around his neck, I pressed myself against him and returned every ounce of his passion. Responding, he pinned me forcefully against the door to my bedroom, but I was so engaged in the moment that I cast caution to the wind and paid no attention to the fact that we might wake Jason.

Hungry in their movements, his large hands explored my curves, squeezing and stroking, leading lust of a whole new level to override my reason. As his hand moved to grasp my breast, I groaned into his mouth and pushed it deeper within his possession. His remaining hand trailed lower, skimming down my waistline until he gripped my nightgown to lift it. Sliding his hands across my bared flesh, he cupped my lower cheeks and proceeded to hoist me up. Trapped between his body and the door, I wrapped my legs around him and gasped when he suddenly thrust against me. His erection pressed straight against my bare entrance, and the sensation aroused me like no other.

At that moment, I caught myself wishing he wasn't going to be my boss. I wished he wasn't Jason's brother, and for a second, I even wished I didn't care about my ambitions at all.

But it was short-lived. All at once, I realised what I was doing and pulled abruptly away from his mouth.

"Fuck," I uttered and stared at him. I nearly lost myself in his gaze. In the deep sea of his eyes, I was a hundred miles from shore. Though I tried to swim, the powerful waves pulled me further in. The deep beckoned. If I stared for too long, I knew I'd sink.

So I looked away.

Retreating a step, he said, "As I thought."

His words struck me like a knife. "I'm sorry," I whispered, upset, and felt tears prickle my eyes again.

Contempt poured from his. "Spare me," he said and went for the door again.

"No, you misunderstand," I urged. "I pulled away because I don't want to hurt you."

"Don't patronise me," he replied venomously.

"Please, listen to me. I can't give you what you want, Will."

He paused in front of the door, and the silence that elapsed seemed to last for infinities. "You can," he eventually said and glanced at me over his shoulder. "You just won't."

Panicking, I rushed towards him to stall him from leaving. We couldn't part like this. It was absolutely paramount that we settled this once and for all, because it was crucial that we maintained harmony, especially for Jason's sake.

Once I reached him, I stepped in front of the door to prevent him from leaving. "Can we talk? When you're sober?"

He refused to meet my gaze. "Have you got any idea how frustrating it is to feel injured by something when I have no right to feel that way?" he asked vehemently. "There is no satisfaction – just an everlasting state of limbo."

To know that he felt that way led a single tear of mine to well over. "Perhaps if you allowed me to explain, you won't feel that way anymore."

He scoffed. "There's nothing to say, is there?"

"No, there absolutely is. Please. Are you free tomorrow?"

His jaw clenched as he glared away.

"William, please," I entreated.

"Fine," he bit out.

Instant relief released me from my rigidity. "Thank you. I'll message you when and where."

He didn't reply, nor did he give me the satisfaction of looking at me. Instead, he opened the door and forced me to step aside.

"I'm sorry," I repeated before he could shut the door between us. Though briefly, he met my eyes through the gap, and the view burnt into my memory as one of the more painful things I'd experienced.

After his departure, I locked the door and remained immobile for several minutes, trying to calm myself. Now that I had privacy, my tears demanded to flow over, and I didn't fight them. But they were silent tears — not so much as a sob escaped me.

I wasn't sure how long I'd been standing there when I finally mustered the courage to return to my bedroom. For all I knew, Jason could have woken up and heard us. If he had, I'd have a lot of explaining to do, and I dreaded it. However, as soon as I opened the door, I found him comatose in my bed, dead to the world.

I puffed out a sigh of relief.

After snuggling up to his side, I closed my eyes and hoped William wouldn't cancel our plans tomorrow morning. While I dreaded it, we desperately needed to talk. Perhaps then, he would finally understand that he'd do best to abandon the thought of me.

14

---◆ • ◆ • ◆---

BITS AND PIECES

M Y CIRCADIAN RHYTHM ENSURED THAT I WOKE NO later than eight the following morning. I wasn't too happy about that since I doubted William was awake yet, so now I had hours to spend wallowing in anxiety instead. On the bright side, I could use the time to consider what to say in depth. A list of bullet-points was not a bad idea, although I would use it only to memorise what to say so that no stone would be left unturned.

Sneaking carefully out of bed so as not to wake Jason, I grabbed my phone from my nightstand and went straight to the kitchen, where I started jotting down my thoughts in my Notes app. After an hour, my list was complete. The next step was to message William where and when to meet me.

I blew out my cheeks as I opened Instagram to find our message thread. He hadn't been active for sixteen hours, so I reckoned he was still asleep. Nevertheless, I started typing, and I hoped he wouldn't change his mind and decline.

Good morning. I hope you caught some decent rest. Farm Girl at one o'clock?

After pressing Send, I went into the bathroom to get ready for the day. He still hadn't seen it by the time I'd showered, dressed, and applied some makeup, but since it was only ten o'clock, I refrained from jumping to the worst conclusions. His active status informed me that he hadn't checked his Instagram for seventeen hours now, so I doubted he was intentionally ignoring me.

Unsure of what to do with the rest of my time, I returned to the kitchen and thought I might as well cook a full English breakfast for Jason. I spent another hour on the task, so it was eleven o'clock by the time I walked into my bedroom to serve it to him.

"Jase," I called softly and placed the tray on my desk. "It's time to wake up," I said when he groaned and turned. Approaching my black-out drapery, I pushed the curtains apart to let the light of day stream into my room. It was raining cats and dogs outside, so I was glad I'd suggested meeting Will at the café Farm Girl, because a walk in the park was out of the question.

"Oh my God. It smells amazing," Jason remarked when he turned onto his back and proceeded to sit. After settling with his back against the white headboard of my bed, his gaze landed on the breakfast I'd made him. "Cara, you're an angel. I'm starved."

"No wonder. You drank yourself sick last night."

He winced. "I've got a terrible headache."

"I'll fetch you some aspirin," I said and handed the tray over to him.

"I love you," he cooed.

"I love you too."

After locating the aspirin, which I kept in my top drawer in the bathroom, I took the chance to check my phone. I tensed when I saw that William had now seen my message but hadn't responded. His active status had reduced from seventeen hours to seven minutes. He must be contemplating whether to decline or not.

With a sigh, I returned to my bedroom and found Jason slowly devouring my cooking. It was obvious from the way his hand trembled that his blood sugar levels had been running terribly low.

"Thank you," he said when I placed a pill on the tray.

Climbing into bed, I sat next to him and rested my back against the headboard. Comfortable silence passed between us for a couple of minutes until Jason broke it.

"I hardly remember anything from last night."

"I'm not surprised. You were completely off your face. I can't remember the last time I saw you that drunk."

He frowned. "I remember bits and pieces, though."

Apprehension clasped my heart. Had he heard William and me?

"Anything in particular?" I asked.

His frown persisted. "Yeah. Will brought me home, didn't he?"

"He did."

"Is it just me, or was he acting a bit odd?"

"Odd how?"

He was quiet for a beat, thinking. "I don't remember exactly. I've just got this vague memory of him being grumpier than usual."

"Perhaps he was tired. He did tell you he's sick of being your voice of reason only to get ignored."

He rolled his eyes. "Honestly, he was in such a mood all of yesterday. Hardly said a word the entire night. It's not like him."

Since I didn't know what to say, I remained quiet.

"I think it's this Sandra bitch he keeps going on about."

I almost gasped, but thankfully stifled the urge.

"Sandra?" I echoed, feigning obliviousness.

He nodded on a mouthful. After swallowing, he furrowed his brows. "It's this girl he met a while ago. They slept together, and he was gutted that she didn't want to see him again. Then, sometime last week, he told me he'd met her again, and that they've started messaging each other a bit, but that she still doesn't seem interested in anything more. To make it worse, he said he'd seen her on a date with another lad – kissing each other and things like that." He shook his head in blatant disapproval of Sandra. "I think she's doing his head in."

I hadn't been aware that William had been talking to Jason about me using my alias, and the news upset me rather a lot. It was nearly impossible to keep a straight face.

"Poor Will," I said. "I'm sure Sandra has got her reasons, but I totally get why Will would be upset about that."

"Yeah, I get it, but don't lead the poor man on. I mean, come on. How cruel can you be?"

Was that the impression William had given him? That I was stringing him along? That was hardly fair, I thought with annoyance. In the end, I hadn't ever initiated a single conversation.

Since I didn't say anything, Jason continued, "I just feel so bad for him because he's not one to fall for women the way he seems to have fallen for Sandra. I mean, he hardly ever spoke about his ex, Kate. Frankly, I'm not even sure he ever actually loved her since we never got to meet her."

I stopped breathing for a moment. Jason had never met Kate? "When you say 'we'…?"

"The family."

"Well, how long were they together?"

"About two years."

I blinked. That was a substantial piece of information to process. "Shit."

"That's what I'm saying. I've never seen him like this. It's got to be because of her. Nothing else can explain his foul mood as of late – and he insists work's going fine."

"Seems a bit weird, though," I murmured after a while. "They can't have interacted all that much if she's told him she's not interested in anything more. Have they slept together more than once?"

"Not that I'm aware of."

"Then perhaps it's not because of her. I hardly think his feelings would become so profound so quickly, especially if he hardly knows her."

He reached for his glass of orange juice, and after necking

the contents, he put it back with some emphasis. "I don't know all the details, but I seriously think he's infatuated." He shrugged. "I should probably ring him today and ask to come over – try and fish some information out of him. I'm growing worried."

My emotions were in chaos upon hearing Jason's suspicions. I'd realised William wanted to explore more with me, but I hadn't considered that his feelings could be this profound already. I had thought it was chiefly his ego that I had bruised. If Jason were right, what I intended to do would only hurt all the more, because William was a wonderful man, and most women would be lucky to have caught his interest. He had simply picked the wrong target. I wasn't interested in pursuing anything at all with him, let alone a relationship. I was committed to myself and my ambitions, and I planned to keep it that way for at least another couple of years until I'd established a career.

"I'm sure he'd appreciate that," I eventually said. "Anyway, I need the loo." Climbing out of bed, I went to the bathroom to recheck my phone, and as luck would have it, William had answered me with a thumbs-up emoji.

Relieved, I steered my gaze to the mirror, but the fire in my eyes had dimmed. The woman that stared back was less confident than I wanted her to be.

IF YOU DON'T PLAY, YOU'LL NEVER WIN

AT TEN TO ONE, I ARRIVED AT THE CAFÉ. WHILE I DESPISED withholding information from Jason, I'd told him I was meeting Aaron to revise when he had asked me where I was headed. I'd even brought my backpack with me to make my lie more convincing, but there were no books inside. Instead, all it contained was a paper bag in which I had placed William's T-shirt and boxers to return to him. Although I'd washed them, they'd been collecting dust in my wardrobe ever since the morning in his flat.

Since he wasn't here yet, I grabbed a vacant spot by the windows so that I could scout for him after I'd placed my order. I left my jacket on the chair to reserve the spot before I approached the queue. While standing there, I took my phone out of my pocket and messaged him to let him know I had arrived.

> I'll order for you. Black coffee,
> nothing added, right?

Seen

He saw it immediately but didn't reply, and I perceived that as consent. Perhaps he didn't reply because I'd surprised him by remembering his usual order. After all, he'd only told me once, which was during the morning in his flat.

I ordered an avocado sandwich for us both as well, and he still hadn't arrived by the time the order was ready. Carrying it over to the spot I'd chosen, I settled into my seat and scouted the courtyard outside while I sipped my flat white.

Some minutes had elapsed when I caught his figure striding past the windows. With one hand in his grey trousers' pocket, the other held a black umbrella to shield him from the rain. For a moment, all I did was admire his elegance. He walked so confidently, so wilfully. His movements conveyed his strong, self-assured spirit. I caught myself smiling, though faintly, when I compared his graceful deportment to John's. They radiated the same assertive aura that demanded one's unquestioning respect. Truly, he was the spitting image of his father. I wondered if he knew.

While it was evident that he knew where he was going, he didn't search the windows for my presence, and I wondered if it was deliberate. Perhaps he felt too intimidated by the idea of meeting my eyes so soon. He must have sensed that I was looking at him, or perhaps he was too hungover to notice much at all.

My heart raced as he drew nearer. Just before he reached the entrance, he put down his umbrella, shook it, and grabbed the door. He stepped in. Halting in the doorway, he scanned the surroundings to locate me, and once he did, he averted his eyes to close the door after him.

His approach was swift. "Hi," he greeted and pulled out the chair at the other end of the table.

Nervous, I sucked in some air. "Hi."

As he shrugged out of his beige coat, I thought that the man had an excellent sense of style. He looked like he'd walked straight out of a fashion magazine, but then I'd always thought that. I knew he favoured formal attire, so it didn't look like he'd dressed up for the occasion. Frankly, I wondered if he owned a pair of jeans at all.

"Thanks for ordering," he said once he'd settled into his seat. "You didn't have to."

"I wanted to."

He gazed around, and I got the feeling he hadn't been here before. "Have you been here before?"

He shook his head.

"Well, I think you'll find their food most delectable. Their avocado sandwich is the best."

"I wasn't expecting lunch."

"Have you eaten?"

He shook his head again. "No, but I had expected this to be a brief thing."

I rested my elbows on the table and crossed my forearms. "It can be, if you want."

"I'm not sure what I want," he replied, and his honesty took me aback, so I was silent for a beat.

Unsure of how to proceed, I asked, "How's the hangover?"

While reaching for his brew, he arched a brow and kept his eyes on the black liquid. "Manageable." After a sip, he placed his cup back while saying, "Speaking of, I'm sorry about my behaviour last night." When he finally met my eyes, I was unable to detect any emotion at all in his. Getting a read on him was impossible. "I was out of order," he continued. "I didn't mean to frighten you. You caught me at a bad moment – I was neither prepared nor ready to speak to you."

Because I appreciated his apology, I gave him a faint smile. "It's alright. I understand you must have felt cornered."

"Cornered," he echoed with a chuckle, but he didn't look at me. Instead, his eyes were fixed on the counter. "That's one way of putting it. Suppose I did feel a bit 'cornered'."

I had no idea where to start, so I racked my brain for something to say. "Have you spoken to Jason today?"

He nodded. "He rang about a minute ago, just as I was about

to answer your text."

I chewed on my lower lip before I stated, "He remains unaware."

"Alas, he does." William leaned back and turned his profile to me. "I'd hoped we would wake him, but then luck hasn't been on my side for quite some time."

I frowned. "You were trying to wake him?"

He scoffed. "No. But I wouldn't have minded if it were a consequence."

His reply annoyed me. "Don't you think that's a bit imprudent?"

Finally, his gaze struck mine. "That would depend on what the overall goal is."

Leaning back, I folded my arms over my breasts and glared at him. "The overall goal is to keep things civil."

"That's *your* goal," he corrected me. "Mine diverges."

Though I had an inkling, I asked anyway, "And what, precisely, is your goal, Will?"

He looked uncomfortable, eyes fleeting. Finally, he said, "To be more than just a fun night to you."

An instantaneous crack spread and pained the fibres of my heart. What a horrible thing. He couldn't be further from the truth.

Shaken, I replied, "Is that how you think I see you? As a 'fun night'?"

He was silent, gaze maintaining an absence from mine.

Swallowing, I frowned and said, "I don't, Will – not at all."

He moaned and tossed his head back. Despairing, he studied the ceiling. "Then you're being your own worst enemy."

"How am I being that?" I queried, despairing, too. "I'm actually looking out for myself here, and you."

He groaned, and his relaxed behaviour mystified me. "No one's going to care about us. It's all in your head," he insisted.

While I appreciated that he was speaking straight from the heart, I disagreed. "You're basing that on the premise that we'll last a lifetime," I retorted. "You have no guarantee we would. And if things ended badly between us, where do you think that would place Jason? He's my best friend, Will. I don't want to put him in a situation where he might have to choose between us, because I know he'll pick you. I can't afford to lose him. I won't take that risk."

"You are ever pessimistic." He studied me as though I were an enigma. "I sometimes don't understand you at all."

I folded my arms tighter. "Perhaps if you actually cared to listen, you would."

He chuckled. Leaning forward, he held my gaze, and I was rendered helpless against the powerful spell that danced in his light-blue eyes. Ensnared by his beauty, I continued to stare while I sensed myself losing grip on the present.

"I am listening," he told me patiently, "and the more I do, the surer I am that you're making a mistake."

"I'm not," I bit out.

He shrugged. "Honestly, it's your loss."

I sighed. I didn't think I'd ever meet someone as stubborn as myself, but here he sat, embodying everything I desired in a man.

"I wish you'd stop being so difficult," I said. "I'm trying to look after your best interests here. You need to move on. I'm not right for you."

"But you are," he insisted, as though it were obvious.

"No, William, I am not." I leaned forward again to rest my head between my hands. "Listen, I agree our personalities are compatible, but you forget a crucial factor, which is that I am not at a point in my life where relationships are something I want to consider. I'm just not ready for it, and I'm begging you to respect that."

Dropping his gaze to his cup, he traced his thumb along the edge of it, seemingly lost in thought. Hoping he was on the cusp of obliging, I added, "You need to stay away from me, Will. I'm scared you'll end up seriously hurt if you don't. I can't give you what you want – for the last time."

Eventually, he curved a brow and slowly raised his gaze to meet mine. Upon trapping my eyes, he searched through them and tilted his head. "Why are you so scared to be loved? I'm not saying

I do. I just… What's the issue?"

It was apparent that he hadn't grasped "the issue" at all, considering what he had asked. "I'm not scared to be loved," I replied with a questioning tone. "You misunderstand. I'm scared to find my attention divided. I'm scared *to* love."

Scepticism spilled from his features, so while drawing in a deep breath, I folded my arms and considered how to erase it. To make him understand, I would have to be more thorough in my reasoning than I had initially thought necessary. After all, that I wasn't interested in a relationship should have been enough to make him back off. However, it was clear that, to respect my wishes, he required an elaborate explanation, and I would oblige.

"Will, do you remember what I said when we first met?"

He snorted. "Hard to forget."

"Then what did I say?"

He seemed to find my rhetorical approach somewhat offensive, because his eyes were steely when he peered at me. "That you haven't got the capacity for a relationship right now. But you based that on the notion that you can't give your partner enough time. I'm arguing I won't need much of your time. All I need from you is exclusivity."

I nodded. "Right, well, allow me to elaborate."

His thumb stopped tracing the edge of his cup. After a brief pause, he leaned back and folded his arms as if to brace himself. "I'm all ears."

I sucked in another deep breath and looked out the window to gather my thoughts. "Well, to begin with, I'd like to stress my starting point: I am disinclined to date anyone at all. Like I've said, I'm determined to remain focused on my career, and that alone, for another few years."

There was a slight twitch of his brows, but other than that, he remained impassive. "Go on."

"In other words, the primary purpose of my reluctance to date anyone is that I want to pursue and establish strictly my career right now. Let me repeat that. The reason – the whole fucking purpose – I am avoiding dating is that I am determined to make my dreams of having a prospering career a reality."

"Duly noted. Now, explain how dating me would come in the way of that."

Facing him, my eyes narrowed as I analysed his expression, but it was impossible to gauge his thoughts.

"I shall. First of all, this means I would already be difficult when asked to date anyone at all, since it would inevitably mean that I would have to prioritise something other than my ambitions. Entering a relationship – dating in general – requires time, attention and energy that I would much rather invest in establishing my career. This is where you come in, in the role of my fucking *boss*. If things go south between us, and I should find that I'm not interested in pursuing things further with you – that I don't want to continue dating you – work will be an awful place for me to be. It will be awkward at best, and detrimental to my career at worst.

"So, not only are you asking me to push my primary aspiration aside for you, but you are also asking me to do it for my *boss*, which directly contravenes the purpose of the whole thing – to pursue my career and avoid anything that might jeopardise it. Dating you could, in the worst-case scenario, mean career suicide, Will."

He frowned faintly, eyes escaping mine as he pondered over my statement. "I'm not asking you to push anything aside for me. I'm asking you to include me."

"Next," I continued, "if people found out about us, it would ultimately taint their impression of me. All my hard work over the years would be reduced to nothing, as they would think I got the job merely by sleeping my way to it instead. Such a reputation could spread, too. It could impede me from getting promoted at Day & Night, impede me from getting hired by Day & Night – or even by other law firms!"

He grimaced, but he dared not meet my obstinate glare. "No one needs to know," he murmured. "We could keep it under wraps until—"

"Third," I cut him off uncompromisingly, "I have applied for a training contract at Day & Night. I still haven't secured one, but it's well known that you are far more likely to be hired by the firm where you complete a placement than by other law firms. That is especially true if you're applying for a contract at City firms, where the competition is already extremely intense. My goal is absolutely to work for a City firm, Will, and dating you could diminish the chances of that happening. What's worse, if dating shouldn't work out, I might not even *want* to work for Day & Night. Being your colleague might turn out to be difficult, uncomfortable, and-or unendurable. I'll have to look for positions elsewhere then, which can be easily avoided if we just don't date."

Slowly, he raised a hand to scratch his cheek while he, absentmindedly, scanned the guests sitting in the courtyard outside. "I had no idea you were this career driven – to the extent that you would cast aside a chance with a person who might just be the right one."

"The right one will be there at the right time," I argued with a shake of my head.

Hearing that, he fell silent altogether and avoided looking at me for quite some time.

When the tension grew unbearable, I sighed, my shoulders sinking. "It's different for you, Will. You've already established yourself. Your career is stable. I'd hardly want to start mine by sleeping with and dating my boss. It's just setting myself up for a greater risk of failure, and I'd rather avoid that. Dating you – it's too inappropriate, Will. I'm just not comfortable with it. I'm sorry."

He started shaking his head, slowly at first, before each shake became faster and firmer. "It's three months, Cara. We don't have to tell anyone, and it won't turn sour. Besides, colleagues date and marry all the time. Moreover, the hiring process is entirely objective. A potential relationship between us will not affect your chances of getting hired – I promise you. If you're scared about that, I guarantee I'll maintain our secret at least until you've been hired. And if it doesn't work out between us, I promise I'll be able to act civil."

My eyebrow jerked up. "What – like you have up till now? You didn't exactly act civil after you walked in on Aaron and me – ignored me for days, and then threatened to ruin my friendship with Jason last night."

He winced. "I've apologised for that. I was drunk and emotional – it won't happen again. I'll clean up my act – I swear."

I tilted my head. "A moment ago, when I said the overall goal was to keep things civil, you explicitly said that your goal diverges."

He shook his head. "I never said that keeping things civil wasn't within my goals. All I said was that it wasn't my *overall* goal. My overall goal is to change your mind. Keeping things civil is subsidiary, but still a goal. So, should you agree to date me, you won't have to worry about that if things don't work out. What's bothering me right now is that you're not even giving me a chance. You're rejecting tremendous potential without investigating whether it's actually the best course of action."

I expelled a loud breath. "You're not even listening to me, are you? Honestly, Will, I've made myself more than clear, and you need to respect it. I am not comfortable and will not date my boss. It's out of the question. It's just not worth the risk, and that's the end of it."

His Adam's apple ascended and fell while he stared blankly at the staircase leading to the floor above the counter.

"You're also Jason's brother, Will," I reminded him with a pout. "If things turn to shit between you and me, it might cost me not just my career but also my best friend and my home. I live with him. If our friendship is put under pressure because of this, I might have to move out, and I might lose him. You know as well as I do that he'll side with you – you're his brother."

When he reached for his cup, it was without a glance in my direction. After a sip, he asked, "Do you think you'll ever feel ready? For a relationship, I mean?"

Pain stung my chest upon his question, and I froze. Was he considering waiting for me? Could his interest really be that severe? I hoped not. He didn't deserve to have to wait for someone. He deserved a woman who would recognise his worth at once and grab him without hesitation.

"Yes," I replied honestly. "Just not now. In a few years' time, perhaps, so you shouldn't wait for me."

I thought I detected a ghost of a smile on his mouth, but he took another sip before I could be sure. "Because you want to focus on your career," he said as he lowered the cup.

Staring absentmindedly at his plate, I shrugged my shoulders and nodded. "This is my only chance to be selfish, Will," I said and set my eyes on him again. "I want to take advantage of my freedom while I still can. As soon as the time is ripe for finding a man to settle down with, my personal aspirations, like my career goals and things like that, will have to take a backseat. He'll be my main priority then, and I'm not ready for that to happen just yet. I want to chase my dreams and prioritise myself – and only that – for a while longer. I just feel like I can contribute to this world with more than my ovaries – or the role of a girlfriend."

Something I'd said caused a faint smile to bend his lips. "Are you trying to say that finding love isn't really your goal in life?"

I chuckled. "I wouldn't phrase it like that."

"How would you phrase it, then?"

Chewing on my lip, I looked sideways. "It's more precise to say that finding love isn't my *only* goal, and as of now, it's certainly not my *main* goal."

"But it will be later? Your main goal?" His playful tone extracted another chuckle from my mouth.

Meeting his eyes, I smirked. "Perhaps. At least I won't dismiss the idea. But for now, I really love law, and I think I can be good at it. I'd like to practise it for a few years – nurture my passion for it – before I consider other aspects of my future."

His head tilted as he studied me, and he seemed beguiled, if not even besotted. "You are such an anomaly. Do you know that?"

Since I could hear it was intended as a compliment, my lips

formed a small, lopsided smile. "For better or for worse."

"It's fairly ironic, because it might just be the thing I admire the most about you, but at the same time, it's also what's keeping you away from me. I can't quite decide what to make of it. Not sure if I love or hate it."

"Well, I am who I am."

"That, you are." He nodded. "Unapologetically."

I sighed, my hands dropping to the table. Motioning with them, I said, "You see, I just think there's more to this life than chasing love. It's so primitive. Reproduction? Really? Is that all there is?" I shook my head. "It's not – not to me. There is the option to make the world a better place for those already in it, there are intellectual challenges, there's personal growth – really, the meaning of life doesn't have to be reproduction, and certainly not exclusively."

The curve of his brows told me he hadn't anticipated the conversation to take such an existential turn. "No, I agree. Reproduction doesn't have to be the sole meaning of life. But, without it, there'd be no life. So, in the end, without life – without reproduction – there'd be nothing to add meaning to."

I tittered. "Valid point, but still, I said 'exclusively'."

I watched as his familiar crooked smile surfaced on his mouth, and this time, the vulnerability it veiled was clearer than ever. "I'm assuming now that, by reproduction, you also mean love."

I cocked my head. "Well, I suppose that – in this day and age – you can love without reproducing. But, genetically, we're wired to fall in love in order to ensure reproduction – that's my understanding, at least. Anyway, what I'm trying to say is that there's so much I want to explore before I go down that route, so I need things to happen in a specific order. First, I establish my career, and after that, when things have become stable, I'll probably be open to finding a partner."

He had another sip of coffee. "So, it's about self-realisation."

"I guess you could call it that."

The corner of his mouth tugged up briefly. "You're surely at the top of Maslow's hierarchy of needs."

"Yes. I'm privileged that way." My brows furrowed. "So are you, though. It's just that your goal, right now, is to find a partner."

He raised a brow. "My goal wasn't to find a partner until I met you."

I inhaled sharply. It was like something had bolted straight through my chest – the intensity bordered on painful. A second later, my face might as well have caught fire. I hadn't expected such a forthright confession, and I didn't appreciate it either. It only reminded me that I was probably hurting him, which was far from what I wanted.

"I…"

Since I failed to continue, he stared at me for a beat, thinking. "What if I could help you with that – with achieving your goals? In case you've forgotten, I'm already a practising lawyer. I just don't understand why you're adamant that it must happen in a specific order."

I grimaced. "Because, Will, once I find a partner, I won't be able to put my career first anymore." When I reached for my flat white to sip on it, I noticed how my hand trembled. This conversation was challenging me more than I had realised. "If ever I get a boyfriend, if ever I start a family, they'll be my main priority. It's just who I am and, knowing that, I'd like to postpone it until I am ready for it to happen, which I am not right now."

He blew his cheeks out and rubbed the back of his head. "Jesus Christ, Cara. You're overcomplicating things."

"That's easy for you to say, and that's really quite offensive, too. This is my career we're talking about, and that makes it extremely important to me."

He frowned. "I'm sorry. I didn't mean to offend you. However, I can't help that I disagree. I mean, you're completely ignoring that a relationship is all about partnership. You help each other grow. You don't weigh each other down. And it's not like I'd force you to have kids before you're ready – if we even reach that point. As for your career and your goals, I'll be doing everything within my power to help you out."

My body tensed. I'd thought when I'd arrived here that rejecting him would be relatively easy, but the more he opened his mouth, the harder it was. Every single sentence that came out of him was a testament to how intriguing he was, how dedicated he would be if I gave him a chance. And yet, reason forbade me to do it.

There was an abundance of rational reasons for why I should avoid him, and only a single reason why I shouldn't – I liked him. In light of that, it would be absolutely ridiculous – totally imprudent – to explore our romantic potential. I couldn't possibly let my *feelings* be the deciding factor; especially not when it might cost me the future I had strived so hard for my whole life.

"Will, that's just one among the several concerns I have stated." I groaned, despairing. His ability to hear only what he wanted to was seriously getting on my nerves. "Look," I said, "I appreciate your intention – really, I do – but I've assessed my capabilities and this is beyond them. You've no idea how distracted I've been lately, and it's all because of you. Frankly, I've no idea whether I failed or passed my last exam because, ever since you reached out to me on Instagram, I've hardly been able to revise. I've been thinking about you constantly. I'm not inventing this – it's an actual problem. You've become the distraction I knew you would, and it's just not defensible. I can't maintain this. Dating you will impact my career prospects – negatively."

Shocked, his eyebrows shot up his forehead. Disbelief spilled from his face. "Christ. Seriously?"

"Yes," I confessed without a trace of shame. Finally, I sighed.

He directed his gaze to his sandwich and, while grabbing his cutlery, arched a brow again. "Well, it's obvious you've never been in a relationship before."

His comment bewildered me. "Why do you say that?"

"Because you're severely overestimating what's required of you. Relationships don't have to be hard. When two compatible people are together, it usually works out with little effort. Compromises are made, and frankly, it offers a support system that might even help you prosper and reach levels you otherwise would not. I just don't think it's necessary to choose one or the other. It's possible to do both. You can have a relationship without it jeopardising your career, as long as it's with the right person." When his eyes met mine, his gaze was searing. "I'm the right person."

My brain warred against my heart upon his confident statement. The former refused to yield, but the latter put up an admirable fight and would not surrender either. The result was utter havoc.

I swallowed. "You're still going to be my boss, Will."

He snorted. "Yes, for three short months – a quarter of a year, Cara. It'll be over before you know it." While cutting into his sandwich, he continued without looking at me, "Besides, the initial excitement subsides after a while. That's when things really start to get interesting, because that's when you'll know whether it's real or not. Unfortunately for me, my last relationship didn't stand the test."

What he said made me remember Jason's doubt about whether he had ever loved his ex.

"You're shooting yourself in the foot right now," I warned. "Hearing that I might just invest years of my life for naught doesn't exactly tempt me into giving relationships a go right now."

He rolled his eyes. "If you don't play, you'll never win, Cara."

Though it was bold of me, I asked, "What happened with her? With Kate?"

He looked up at me then, and I could tell from his expression that he was carefully considering whether to elaborate or not. "I'd rather not go into it," he eventually decided. "Maybe some other time."

"Alright," I said, respecting his boundaries.

Suddenly, he shook his head, and his expression told me he was unimpressed. "Right, correct me if I'm wrong," he said, "but what I'm hearing right now is that you refuse to give me a chance because you haven't got time to date since you'd rather focus on yourself and your career."

"That's right."

He glared at me. "And yet you still find time for Aaron."

I groaned. "That's different."

"How is it different? Really, how the hell is it different?" He leaned back while frowning at me as though I were the daftest person alive. "Aside from exclusivity, all I'm asking from you is what you're already giving him."

Resting my head between my hands, I let out a frustrated breath. "First of all, Aaron isn't my boss or my flatmate's brother. Second, what I've got with him is perfect, Will. He's exactly what I need. He doesn't demand anything from me. I can just keep on doing what I'm doing, and I don't need to consider much, if at all. My choices are entirely mine to make. And he's my best friend. We've got three entire years of friendship behind us. It's all so peaceful and predictable, so I'm determined to keep things as they are. He doesn't pose a threat to my career the same way you do."

William shook his head but said nothing.

"On another note," I murmured to change the subject, "I'd appreciate it if you stopped speaking to Jason about me. I'm aware you've been referring to me as Sandra, but please avoid it. If he suddenly learns the truth somehow, I imagine he'll be very cross with me. He's not exactly fond of 'Sandra' as it is."

After swallowing his mouthful, he pointed at me with his knife. "Cara, I owe you absolutely nothing," he reminded me tersely. "I've agreed to keep it secret only because you begged me to and because I intend to respect your feelings, but I need to be able to talk to my own brother about things that are affecting my private life. He's my best friend – and he knows something's wrong. I can't hide things like that from him, and even if I could, I won't. This is the only compromise I'm willing to make on that. I'm doing it as a favour to you, nothing else. Personally, I couldn't give a monkey's about whether he found out. On the contrary, I'd prefer it. Remember that."

I pouted. "Please spare me at least some of the wrath."

Impatience clouded his features. "No. I refuse to be anyone but myself with him. What you're asking for is enough as it is."

Realising that I'd lost this battle, I looked sideways for a moment. "Right, well, you'll relent your advances, then?"

He nodded.

Somehow, I hadn't expected him ever to agree, so the surprise made me gape. "Really?"

"Well, it's not like you're giving me any other option, is it?" He gave me a scowl before he focused on cutting his sandwich again. "And, if it's true that you've had a hard time focusing on your exams because of me, I'm genuinely sorry. I hardly want to get in the way of your education."

"William, thank you," I breathed, relieved, and stared gratefully into his eyes. "You're doing us both a favour."

He laughed, but it was a humourless sound. "I'm really not. Giving me a chance won't stunt your career, Cara. On the contrary, it will boost it. I can't believe you don't see that. You're denser than I thought – definitely too stubborn for your own good."

Offended, I glowered at him. "Look who's talking. And there's no need to be rude."

"Well, pardon my manners," he replied nonchalantly. "You were right about one thing, though: these really are delicious." While giving me a wink, he filled his mouth with another bite. I couldn't fathom how he managed it, but his playful tone and laidback behaviour left a smile on my mouth.

"My dad makes similar ones," I murmured. "He's an excellent chef."

"What's his name?"

"Jamie."

"And what does Jamie do?" he queried, and I sensed his interest was sincere.

"He's a sixth form philosophy teacher."

"Ah." He smirked. "No wonder you're so confused."

I tittered. "Twat. I'm not confused."

Regardless of how much I tried to deny it, his winsome grin made my heart throb. "And your mum?" he asked. "What's her name? Are they married?"

"Her name's Lillian, and yes, they are. Going on twenty-one years."

"So, they had you before they married, then?"

"Yeah."

"What a bastard you are," he joked, and I was amazed at his ability to extract genuine laughter from me under these circumstances. "What does Lillian do, then? She a teacher like your father?"

I shook my head. "She's an economist. Inspired my sister, actually."

Evidently surprised, he looked up and paused chewing. "You've got a sister?" he asked after swallowing.

I raised a brow. "She's lesbian, Will, so you may abandon that mission at once."

The sound of his ensuing laughter was music to my ears. "I honestly wasn't thinking along those lines."

"Sure you weren't."

"Is she younger or older?"

"Younger. She studies business at Columbia in New York."

He seemed impressed. "Your parents have birthed clever children, I hear."

I smiled. "I could say the same to you."

"I've always suspected you of being an elder sister."

"Really? Why?"

He shrugged. "Don't know. Might be your independence, not to mention your drive."

"Hm."

Never in my wildest dreams would I have expected this interaction to unfold the way it did, but we remained in the café for another two hours, talking about everything and nothing. He shared heart-warming stories from his childhood with Jason, and I adored hearing about it. The strength of their bond was something I truly admired, because it was even deeper than the one I had with Phoebe.

Tales from his days as a student had been particularly riveting, because his inexorable drive had been clear between the lines. We'd dived into politics, too, and I had been amazed when I'd learnt we shared the same view on almost everything. From there, the conversation had travelled to music and art, films and literature – I'd told him *Alice's Adventures in Wonderland* was one of my favourite classics from childhood, and I was pleasantly surprised to learn that he had read and enjoyed it, too. We'd even discussed celebrity gossip, although neither of us boasted much knowledge on that.

The whole experience was so intense that when we were about to part ways, I caught myself wondering whether I was actually making the right decision. Our chemistry was more apparent now than ever, and I wasn't blind to it. If there existed such a thing as soulmates, I thought he might be the closest I'd ever come.

"Here," I murmured as we stood outside, about to head in different directions once and for all. Withdrawing the paper bag from my backpack, which contained his clothes, I handed it over to him.

"What's this?" Frowning, he unfolded it to have a peek inside. Upon recognising the contents, he froze, and for some reason, seeing him react like that upset me rather a lot.

"Thanks for the loan," I murmured.

Unexpectedly, he handed it back to me immediately. "Keep it."

"I've no need for it."

"Neither have I. Please, keep it." As I looked into his eyes, it occurred to me that he wasn't offering it as a token of kindness. He was begging me to hold onto it because he couldn't bear the memory, much less the finality which the return entailed.

"Okay," I said, because I wanted to spare him from any more pain. As soon as my hand closed around it, his gaze fled mine.

"Thanks," he mumbled. "I...I'll see you around, I suppose."

"Yeah."

I watched as he turned to leave, and my heart felt heavier now than ever before.

16

---◆·◆·◆---

SMOOTH, BUT POWERFUL, JUST LIKE YOU

INALLY, IT WAS MONDAY THE 10TH OF JUNE, WHICH MEANT my exams had come to a close and that I was about to start work. I'd partied all of Friday night with my fellow students as we celebrated completing our bachelor's degree. It was odd how having a degree to my name suddenly made me feel much older than I was. I had surely become an adult, hadn't I? Milestone accomplished. Wherever had my teens gone? I missed them. They'd been such carefree days. All I could think of now was overcoming the next obstacle in my career. For the moment, that was showing up for my first day at one of the top City firms, being Day & Night LLP, for my work experience placement.

I'd woken up at six to prepare for it. Knowing I would be shadowing and assisting none other than William for the span of the next three months, I'd been trepidatious while I'd completed my morning rituals and cooked breakfast for Jason and myself.

I had encountered William several times since our conversation at Farm Girl, but we'd always made it brief. Every time he'd been over to visit Jason or watch a match with him, I had stuck around for ten minutes to be polite before I had retired to my bedroom. Similarly, he had avoided prolonging interactions with me as well, and he hadn't sent me a single message since that fateful Sunday in May.

I had frequently questioned whether I had made the right choice, but upon receiving my exam scores back, I had been reassured. The exam that had suffered the most was Company Law, which was when my trouble with William had been at its peak. After we had settled our dispute, I'd been able to ace my remaining two exams.

To be as prepared as possible for my first day, I had decided what to wear the day before – a beige pencil skirt with a white silk blouse to go with it. Low, white heels completed the outfit as I made my way through the revolving entrance door of the huge Day & Night building on Cannon Street. At the reception sat a lady, brown hair tied into a bun atop her head. Nervous, I approached to let her know I'd arrived, and struggled to keep my rising pulse under control.

Halting before her marble desk, which was decorated with beautiful flower arrangements, I met her dark eyes. There wasn't a trace of a wrinkle on her face, though I suspected she was in her early forties from the experienced gleam in her eye.

"Hello, Miss," she greeted. "How may I help you?" She smiled up at me, baring white teeth behind rosy red lips.

Dazzled by her smile, I swallowed. "I'm a new trainee. Cara Jane Darby is the name."

Nodding, she typed on her computer. After confirming my name with a virtual list, she pressed the hands-free device attached to her small ear. A silver earring flattered the lobe of it. She had an excellent taste in jewellery, I noted; she presented herself as positively elegant.

"Yes, hello, Ellie. It's Debbie. Miss Cara Darby just arrived." She paused and then nodded. "I'll let her know. Thank you." Hanging up, she directed her attention back to me, and smiled again.

"Elisabeth will be down in a moment, Miss Darby. May I offer you any refreshments while you wait? A cup of tea, or perhaps some coffee?"

I paled. Did I look like I needed coffee? Or refreshments? At once, I stifled my self-conscious thoughts. What was I thinking? She was only being accommodating, which I was certain was part of her job. Hold it together, I told myself, but I was extremely nervous about seeing William again. Even though I had no plans of dating him, I wanted him to think me beautiful – not tired.

"I'm alright, thank you." I motioned towards a group of white chairs at the far end of the lobby. "I'll wait over there." I headed towards them.

I'd hardly grabbed a seat by the time Elisabeth's round figure exited the lift and approached the security gates. While swiping her card, she gave me that ensnaring smile of hers, and I was amused that I still remembered the beauty of it.

"Hi, Cara," she greeted excitedly. "How are you?"

"Hi, Ellie." I stood to approach. "I'm alright, thanks. How are you?"

"Excited to start your first day?"

"I am."

"Good. Will usually arrives at eight, so we'll have some time to get you settled before then."

"Great."

§ § §

Elisabeth had left my side for a minute while I was setting up the computer I would be using for work. Of course, that was when I saw him from the corner of my eye, and the way my heart responded made me cease breathing for a moment. It lashed out against my rib cage, beating so aggressively that I could feel my pulse thumping in my throat. Inwardly, I begged him not to notice me immediately, as I could have used a few seconds to regain my composure, but judging from the direction of his travel, he already had.

The sight of him made me want to sob. It wasn't fair that anyone should look so appealing fresh out of bed. How did he do it? My memory did him no justice at all. Every time I saw him, I was equally astounded by his beauty. I hoped I would be able to keep from blushing, but as soon as I thought it, heat crept into my cheeks and all the way to my scalp.

With a winsome smile on his face, he halted in front of my desk. "Morning, Cara."

"Morning, Will."

"Glad to see you're already familiarising yourself with everything."

I smiled. "Ellie thought you might appreciate the efficiency, so she asked me to arrive at half seven."

"She knows me well."

Lowering my gaze from his handsome face, I noticed he was carrying two cups of Starbucks coffee.

"This one's for you," he said and placed the smallest on my desk. Perplexed, I studied it for a brief second.

He'd bought me a coffee on his way to work? He'd thought of me this morning? How often did I cross his mind? Part of me wished it were often. Since he persisted in plaguing my mind, I wanted it to at least be mutual.

"That was kind." I looked up at him. He shrugged his broad shoulders and sipped on his own cup. After swallowing, he exhaled and grinned.

"Flat white is your favourite, right? Smooth, but powerful, just like you."

Surprised he remembered, I stared at him for some time, gathering myself.

"It is. Aren't I supposed to be fetching coffees for you, though?"

He chuckled. "As if I'd ever trust you to fetch my coffee for me. It'd be laced with poison, I'm sure. I haven't got a death wish."

His banter made me laugh.

"You've got an adorable laugh," he commented and gave me a bashful smile. His compliment made me stop. Instead, my blush increased in intensity.

I cleared my throat. "Don't you have work to do, Mr Night?"

"Right now, I'm working on you."

It was far too early for this. "Well, you know it's futile, so you might as well stop."

He grinned. "How did your exams go?"

"Really well, actually. Well, apart from Company Law, where I could've done better."

He nodded and tucked his hand into his pocket. "Glad to hear leaving you alone served its intended purpose."

"Yes." I smiled. "Thanks." Behind him, I saw Elisabeth reappear.

"Morning, Will," she greeted.

He turned. "Morning, Ellie. Thanks for being here earlier than usual to help Cara get started."

She smiled. "Least I could do."

"Still, I appreciate it."

"I thought you might."

"Anyway," he said, his eyes straying to the door to his office, "I'll leave you to it."

Hopelessly intrigued, I stared after him with a smitten expression on my face.

"No," Elisabeth suddenly said. "Trust me, Cara, you do not want to dig into that."

It felt like somebody had just punched me in the gut. Had she seen me ogle him just now? She must have. Breathless, I responded, "What?"

She sent me a stern look. "Trust me."

While clearing my throat again, I focused on my new computer. "Dig into what? I wasn't—"

"You were."

I pouted. "Well, I'm sorry. I was only admiring the view. He's a good-looking man."

She chuckled. "He is, but don't fall for it. He's a complete workaholic and has absolutely no interest whatsoever in relationships. Trust me. I've asked him several times, and it's always the same ambiguous answer: 'I'm single, but I'm not available.' So, don't fall for his charms, alright? I'd hate to see you mess this up."

I didn't blame her for having that impression. However, in

this particular respect, I suspected I knew him better than she did. Nevertheless, her statement did make me wonder. What did he mean when he said he was single, but not available? Had he abandoned the idea of relationships since our talk? The possibility intrigued me.

I sent her a warm smile. "Ellie, I'm committed to my studies. Don't worry. Besides, I've already got a man of my own to serve that purpose, but it's nothing serious."

"Really?" She beamed at me. "What's his name?"

I chuckled at her childlike display of enthusiasm. "Aaron."

"Aaron," she echoed. "Did he study law as well?"

"Yeah. We were in the same year. He's shockingly clever. I owe him several of my A's actually, seeing as he was also my study partner."

"Good for you," she said with a smirk. I nodded as I reached for the coffee William had given me. While lifting it to my mouth, I noticed the black ink of a marker on the side. The instant I turned it, my eyebrows arched in dread.

Viva la Sandra, it read. What the hell was that supposed to mean?

"Long live Sandra my arse," I muttered under my breath.

§ § §

William had remained in his office while Elisabeth and I covered some basics. She'd shown me how to fill in timesheets, which time codes to apply depending on the tasks I completed, as well as the difference between non-chargeable time and chargeable time. She'd also taught me the basics of 'WIP', which was short for 'Work in Progress'. Essentially, it translated to the total amount of chargeable time a team had recorded against a time code on a specific client code. After that, she had taught me the basics of billing, and had brought me to the finance team at Day & Night to show me how to send an invoice to a client. Once we returned, she taught me the firm's IT system, how to accept calls, where to store notes on clients, and how to set up appointments and meetings in the solicitors' calendars.

We were just about to head for lunch when an associate exited her office and proceeded to approach Elisabeth and me. Glancing up from my computer, I stared at her, entranced. I remembered her vividly because she was one of those women you simply did not forget. Her eyes captured mine almost immediately, and below them, a slow smile made its way across her lips.

Violet.

I thought as I watched her that it was no wonder William had wanted her as a sexual partner. Her beauty was remarkable, and there was an assertive aura about her that reminded me of William's. They had to be kindred spirits, so of course they would take a liking to each other. I wondered if she was still sleeping with him.

"Hello," she greeted once she reached my desk. Now that I had the chance to look at her more closely, I assumed she was in her early thirties. "I haven't had the chance to introduce myself yet, but I'm Violet." She extended a hand to me, and I admired her manicured nails before I took it. Her grip was firm, and her smile bright.

"Hello," I greeted enthusiastically. "I'm Cara."

She released my hand to fold her arms. "I'm aware. Will's told me a lot about you." Her eyes gleamed in a way that made me question whether he had told her more than I'd be comfortable with.

"Has he? Only kind things, I hope."

She chuckled. "Absolutely. Your dedication to your ambitions has been particularly emphasised."

I swallowed. Was she insinuating something? I struggled to understand whether she knew about us or not.

"He knows me well, I suppose."

"Hearing it reminded me of myself," she said with a smile. Tilting her head, she continued, "So, I'm sure you'll manage brilliantly during your time with us."

"I hope you're right."

Her eyes narrowed faintly, and I got the feeling she was trying to get a read on me. "Just be careful you don't sacrifice too much for them – your ambitions, I mean. I've been there and done that, and if I could go back, I might have proceeded differently."

Her words confirmed my suspicions. William must have told her about us. Nevertheless, I was shocked by her advice. Was she insinuating that I ought to have given William a chance back in May? If she were, it was the last thing I'd expected. She clearly wasn't a possessive type, and the reality of that made me realise that their arrangement was indeed only casual, if it even existed anymore.

"Consider me warned," I murmured with a nod.

Just then, William exited his office, and as soon as my head whipped around to acknowledge him, Violet followed my gaze. Upon seeing us, he hesitated for a second, but I was unable to guess his thoughts from the blank expression on his face. Seeming to recover, he approached with determination.

"Violet," he greeted.

"Hi, Will," she replied fondly. "I was just introducing myself to our new paralegal."

His gaze shifted from her to me. "I hope she didn't scare you. She can be a bit intimidating, but she always means well."

"I'm still here," she replied, amused.

"She didn't scare me at all," I assured him with a frown. "She was merely offering some words of wisdom to an aspiring solicitor."

Sceptical, William knitted his brow and turned to regard her again. A message I couldn't decode passed between their eyes before she said, "Anyway, lunch?"

"Yes." He nodded.

§ § §

Lunch had been an awkward event. Andy had joined us for it, and re-encountering him had been a strange experience because I didn't recall him being so aloof. While he had been polite in his greeting, he hadn't said much to me, and I suspected it was because William had told him about us. However, I frequently sensed his eyes on me, but whenever I looked over, he'd averted them. Even so, I could tell he was scrutinising me, and it made me feel slightly uncomfortable.

Elisabeth, who I was seated across from, had initiated most of the conversation while Andy traded regular glances with William across the table. Neither Violet nor Elisabeth paid them any attention, so I assumed that they probably behaved like this on a regular basis. In the end, they were best friends, so it was to be expected that they would have secret and silent conversations that no one else would understand.

Things had taken a turn for the worse when John Night had arrived by our table, along with his fellow partners. I'd met Mr Philip Day, for instance, who was John's first partner in establishing their empire. He was a nice man of short build, with a beer-belly that strained against his expensive suit.

While asking how my day had been thus far, John had grabbed his son's shoulder. "Brilliant," I'd said. It wasn't entirely a lie. The professional aspect of the firm had kept me on my toes all day, even if my boss had kept me on my toes for another reason entirely.

Looking John in the eye, while knowing I'd slept with his son, was an unpleasant experience. Even though I had endured it before, it still unnerved me. I should not have been sitting on the knowledge of how William performed in bed, but I was.

I worried my gaze had been a tad too fleeting, but I hadn't been able to help it. What I'd done was unbecoming, and I was scared he would catch on to it somehow. Underestimating his perceptiveness was not something I intended to make a habit of.

So, when it was time for William's meeting with our client Clifford Paints, I was relieved. Finally, I'd be provided with intellectual distraction.

Elisabeth was unlinking her MacBook Pro from her desktop computer when Violet caught my eye. She was walking beside Frederick Silverstone – a senior associate who was leading the team on the potential merger between Clifford Paints and Craft Interior.

The sexual prowess she wielded was outstanding. It was noticeable from her confident strut, which I paid keen attention to as she guided Mr Clifford and his son, as well as their company's financial advisor, towards a conference room. Instead of watching the floor in front of their feet, the three men kept their eyes glued to her firm bottom.

"Ready, then?" Elisabeth asked and sent me an encouraging smile.

"Yes," I confirmed and closed my computer to bring it with me.

"Good. Might you fetch Will for me? I'll get set in the meantime."

A lump gathered in my throat as I nodded. After a deep breath for courage, I turned for his office and scraped together what little strength I had left, but just as I was about to knock on his door, he ripped it open and nearly crashed into me. In my rush to dodge him, I tripped on my heel. As I was about to tilt backwards, his hand shot forward to grab my arm, and then he yanked me towards him again with such force that I knocked face-first into his chest.

The irony of the situation was not lost on me. By trying to evade him, I'd only ensured bumping into him. However, since his intoxicating scent hit me before his muscles did, it successfully distracted me from the pain. Good grief, he smelled amazing, but his scent instantly provoked the memory of our sensual night together.

"Careful, there," he scolded when I tilted my head back to regard him. Hyperaware of his proximity, I felt the thumb of his hand – around my arm – gently rub me. Delicious electricity derived from his action, making my skin tingle beneath his touch. No man had ever made me feel this way, where merely a touch could send my heart into overdrive.

Blushing scarlet, I cleared my throat and struggled to suppress the erotic memories his scent had triggered. Clutching my MacBook to my chest, I tried to ignore how hard my heart pounded against it.

"Your client is here," I murmured. "Ellie told me to fetch you."

"Violet's already notified me."

"I see." I nodded. "Do you always charge out of your office as though you're late for a flight?"

At the corners of his mouth, a smile threatened, but it never made it to full bloom. "As a matter of fact, I'm nearly late for a meeting."

"Right. Am I insured under the firm's policy if I end up seriously injured next time you stampede out of your office like a bull? Because I didn't find that clause in my contract. 'If your boss happens to run over you, you are entitled to compensation depending on the extent of your injuries'," I joked.

"I'll personally make amends if that happens," he assured me, and his tone was loaded with insinuation I couldn't quite decipher. "Though, for next time, try not to be such a slow turtle."

My nostrils flared. "Why don't you try walking next time, instead of bolting out like you're trying to outrun The Flash?"

"DC Comics?" His head tilted as he caught my reference. "That was unexpected. Anyway, it's not every day that I've got a slow turtle lurking outside my door. You know, if you want to touch me, you don't need to risk your health to have an excuse. Just do it. I won't mind."

I glowered up at him. How he was able to angle everything as though I were incurably smitten with him was beyond me. It must be a talent, and it made me grit my teeth. Eventually, I retorted, "Weren't you running late?"

I detected a flicker of intrigue in his light-blue eyes as he stared down at me. Slowly, he released my arm to journey his hand to my back instead.

"After you." He ushered me down the aisle. Acutely aware of his hand on my back, I heard my pulse drum behind my ears while my heart appeared to have relocated to my throat. I was tempted to ask him to remove it, but at the same time, I never wanted him to.

We exchanged no words during our swift journey to the conference room, for which I was grateful, because I wasn't sure I'd be able to string together any coherent sentences. His touch was far too distracting. However, that didn't prevent me from wondering about the reason for his preference for silence. Perhaps he was mentally preparing for the meeting. Even so, a small part of me hoped it was because I'd rattled him equally.

When we reached the door, I was about to open it for him seeing as I considered my role here similar to that of a servant, but he beat me to it. Pushing it open, he ushered me in first.

"Mr Night," Mr Clifford greeted immediately, rising from his seat.

"Mr Clifford," William replied. "This is Ms Cara Darby, a new trainee of ours. She'll be helping Ms Tallis with the report." As he introduced me, his head cocked in Elisabeth's direction at the end of the table.

Violet studied me from head to toe from where she stood beside Mr Clifford, but her expression made me no wiser.

"Hello," I greeted and walked over to shake hands with them. As I escaped William's touch, I was struck by how cold my back felt without it. Odd. I'd never noticed escaping someone's hold quite so consciously.

Once I had greeted Gerard Clifford, I moved to greet his son, Tom Clifford, and then finally their financial advisor, Bo Zhang. Afterwards, I grabbed my seat beside Elisabeth, placed my computer on the table, and puffed out an anxious breath.

The meeting was intense. While Frederick was present, it was clear he had left William in charge. Was it normal for a junior associate to lead a meeting like this, or was it a testament to William's competence?

Overcome with admiration, I observed as William led Mr Clifford and his son through the process of the congeneric merger and what it would entail in terms of legal aspects. They discussed which information Day & Night would require to proceed, the specific technologies and sensitive information Clifford Paints had which required added security and would be included in the mutual non-disclosure agreement, as well as how soon we could pass said agreement to Craft Interior for signing. In the event that Craft Interior would sign, Clifford Paints would return to us with more information regarding the financial details for how they wanted to complete the transaction, as well as material for the legal due diligence process.

I didn't dare to question the state of my underwear while I watched William. He was in his element, and it was awe-inspiring to witness. I had never been this desperate for a man's sexual attention before – never been so aroused. I could almost hear my ovaries call his name. Clever as he was, he was tantalising to a fault.

I could hardly fathom that I had managed to find my way into this astounding man's bed. How lucky was I? His brain nearly gave me an orgasm in and of itself, and yet I was adamant about casting the idea of him aside. For a brief moment, I hated myself for it, but in the next, I didn't.

This was precisely why I couldn't have anything to do with him in that sense. I'd been seated here for an hour by now, and I had hardly written a word. To make matters worse, I hadn't had the mind to watch Elisabeth's work, either. All I had done was ogle, admire and drool over William. He was much too distracting, far too arousing.

This wouldn't do. He was going to ruin both my career and me.

Tormented, I sat there till the meeting finally concluded. When it did, I remained paralysed in my chair, flabbergasted. My face had been constantly flushed. I felt out of breath, for crying out loud. Under the table, I squeezed my thighs together, desperate for some friction, and I shocked myself when I did. My fluids had not only drenched my knickers, but they'd also lubricated the better part of my inner thighs. My skin was moist and sticky.

"Cara?" Elisabeth called after the solicitors had escorted our client out of the room. My head jerked up, and when I met her eyes, I found her frowning at me. Only then did I realise that this was the second time she was calling my name.

"You okay?" she asked, concerned.

"Yeah." I swallowed. "Just a bit overwhelmed."

She smiled knowingly. "Yeah, well, you'll get used to it soon enough. It's a fast-paced environment, but you shouldn't feel intimidated. It's always like that in the beginning. Everyone's been there."

All I could offer was a nod.

"Well," she said, "now that I've written down the first draft of the report, I'll have to do some polishing. We should probably do it together. Will, Fred and Violet are likely to want it on their desk by the end of the day."

"Sounds good. May I use the loo before then?" My voice had a pleading tone because I was anxious to clean up the mess that William had unwittingly made. Would I have to bring spare underwear to work from now on?

"Of course."

§ § §

Later, she read through my polished version of the report, and I was extremely relieved when she said, "This is actually really good work, Cara. Well done."

While we had initially planned to do it together, she had been called to attend another meeting with Frederick, so she'd told me to attempt it by myself using her notes. I had appreciated that. I always learnt faster when I was simply thrown into a situation and forced to sort it out on my own. Being guided was one thing, being micromanaged was another, and I was not a friend of micromanagement.

Her remark made my day. It truly did. After all the chaos I'd endured with regards to William Night being my boss, I was in dire need of positive feedback. During the meeting earlier, I'd been genuinely concerned about my performance, seeing as I hadn't had the mind to admire anything other than him. Thankfully, it would seem I'd managed to compensate for what I'd lost by completing this report.

"Thank you." My shoulders relaxed, and so did my heart. Not even my final exams had left me as battered as my first day here, but to my relief, I had reached the end of it.

"Why don't you print it and hand it over to Will?" Elisabeth suggested. "After that, I'm sure he'll let you leave for the day."

"Okay."

Nervous hardly covered how I felt when I stood outside William's door some minutes later, mustering the courage to knock. In fact, my hand was trembling when I raised it towards the dark brown wood.

"Yes?"

I sucked in a sharp breath and opened the door. Poking my

head through the gap, I said, "I've finished the report."

Ripping his gaze from the screen of his desktop computer, he offered me his undivided attention. "Have you? Well done. Let's have a look, then."

Stepping in, I closed the door after myself and approached him with some vigilance. Because I desperately wanted to impress him, I hoped he would approve of the report.

An amused frown crossed his face when I proceeded to extend the report to him.

"Your hand is shaking," he remarked, and I hated that he noticed.

"Caffeine overdose," I lied.

He raised a brow. "Perhaps you should consider reducing your intake."

"I'm an addict."

"Typical law student," he murmured before his eyes locked on the document. When his eyebrows eventually furrowed, my heart clenched in panic. Had he spotted something? Taking his sweet time, he turned the page as he read through before he slowly began nodding to himself.

"This is excellent. Great job, Cara."

Air stormed out of my lungs, and I didn't bother about him noticing. "Really?"

He studied me with some surprise. "Really. Are you alright?"

"I'm just a bit anxious. I want to get this right."

His gaze softened. "Cara, calm down. You'll do fine. I'll make sure of it."

His calm demeanour was strangely contagious. Before I knew it, his soothing statement had reassured me somewhat. "Thank you."

After dropping the document on his desk, he said, "You're free to go. I'll see you tomorrow."

"Right. Thanks. How long do you plan to stay? Just curious."

He chuckled and turned his attention to his computer screen. "I usually leave at eight or nine – unless Chelsea's playing. But the season's over, so work has got my full attention now."

I laughed. "You are such a football nerd."

"I really am."

"I'll see you tomorrow, then."

"Yes. Tell Jason you did wonderful on your first day, or else I will."

"Alright," I replied with a grin, and I was still wearing it when I exited the lift and stepped onto the street. Perhaps shadowing him wouldn't be as bad as I had feared after all. Thus far, we'd managed to maintain a professional relationship impeccably, I thought.

CURIOSITY KILLED THE CAT

NEITHER WILLIAM NOR ELISABETH WAS HERE YET, WHICH I was glad to see. To make a good impression, I had meant to arrive before them. It was Wednesday now, and my first two days here had gone rather well. In particular, I had William to thank for that. Before I'd started, I had feared he would return to his old ways and have difficulty treating me as a colleague, but his behaviour had exceeded my expectations. He hadn't sexualised me so much as once, much less forced me to remember our one-night stand. Instead, he had been perfectly professional and had taken me under his wing precisely the way he had promised he would when I first signed my contract some months ago.

Grabbing my seat, I booted up my computer and opened William's virtual calendar to get an idea of his day. I knew I had to visit Clifford Paints this afternoon to collect some documents on William's behalf, so I was trying to figure out when to complete the task. Shortly after lunch, he had a meeting with Violet, so I gathered I should do it then.

At five to eight, I heard the gates to the lift slide apart. Turning my head, a smile caught my lips and radiated from my eyes. Approaching me with two coffees in his hands was William. It amused me that he continued to bring me coffee every morning. He'd done it yesterday as well. While I appreciated it, I wondered if it were special treatment because I was new and he wanted me to feel welcome, or whether he had been in the habit of doing this for Charlotte – the paralegal who had taken maternity leave – as well.

"Morning, love," he greeted. "You're here early," he continued but surprised me when he proceeded past my desk. "I thought you could work in my office today," he said with a grin when he noticed my bewildered facial expression.

"Your office?"

"Yes. We've got plenty of material to go over today, so I thought it might be more efficient. Bring your stuff."

Heeding his command, I charged up from my seat and began to gather my things. Once I'd collected everything, I headed towards his office, where he stood waiting by the door.

The closer I drew, the more intense his gaze seemed, so a faint blush had smeared my cheeks by the time I reached him. Too shy to look up at him, I walked in while mumbling, "Thanks." My own shyness unsettled me somewhat. I couldn't recall having felt this way around a man – ever. Too shy to look him in the eye? What on earth was going on with me?

As I dropped my things on one side of his desk, my eyes investigated the surrounding chaos for a second. Myriad files covered nearly the entire surface of it, and it made me swallow. So this was what I had in store? How did he keep track of all this? Then again, he did strike me as an organised man.

Recalling his flat, I remembered how tidy it had been. I hadn't noticed a speck of dust anywhere, but perhaps he had someone to do his cleaning for him – a maid, for example. With his schedule, I couldn't imagine he had time to spare for chores like dusting.

He shut the door. A heartbeat later, I heard his graceful footsteps approach. "I'll get this out of the way," he said as he rounded his desk. "Here." He extended a cup of coffee to me. Although shyness still dominated my feelings, I was able to meet his gaze and offer a smile of gratitude.

"You don't need to do this every day, Will. I appreciate it, but you know I'd be happy to do it instead, right?"

He chuckled as he dumped his brown leather bag in his desk chair. "I don't expect you to bring me coffee, Cara. The shop's in the same building as mine. It's part of my routine to stop by every morning."

"Expensive habit," I commented.

He raised a brow at me. "I can afford it," he said, and from his tone, I was reminded that he didn't enjoy drawing attention to his wealth.

"Time-wise, too?"

Amusement swam in the corners of his tempting mouth. "It hardly takes a minute."

"If you insist."

"I do."

"Did you bring coffee for Charlotte every morning as well?"

He shook his head. "Never occurred to me."

My ego appreciated hearing that, as it made me feel special to him.

"Suppose I should start doing it once she returns," he added then, which punctured the boost my ego had just enjoyed.

Scared he'd notice, I avoided his eyes as I focused on setting up my computer while he cleared his desk. "I'm sure she'll appreciate that."

He might as well have said "enough small talk" when he proceeded to change the subject. "Anyway, we've got quite a lot of work to do. As you know, you've got to fetch the files from Clifford Paints later. For now, I've got to continue my work on the DD for the deal between Porter BioScience and Elixerion Pharmaceuticals. I've got a meeting with Violet shortly after lunch to go over it.

"While I work on that, I thought you could have a go at drafting up the mutual non-disclosure agreement for the merger transaction between Clifford Paints and Craft Interior. I've got a few templates you can use to help you get started. I'll of course look over your work, but if you have any questions, don't be shy. Please ask, and I'll be happy to help you out."

While nodding, I pulled a chair over so that I'd be working across from him. "Right, to summarise – and correct me if I misunderstood anything," I said as I descended into my seat. "First, you want me to get started on drawing up a draft for the non-disclosure agreement. While you're meeting with Violet after lunch, I'll head over to Clifford Paints to collect the files, and I suppose you'll want photocopies of those. Then, whether it's today, tomorrow or next week, you'll go over the draft of the NDA I've written?"

He stared at me for a second, but I couldn't gauge the look in his eyes. "Yes," he said then, and a slow smile climbed to his mouth.

"Okay." I nodded. "Why don't you email me the templates and I'll get started at once."

"Brilliant."

§ § §

One of several things which I appreciated about shadowing William was that we worked exceptionally well together. In that regard, he reminded me of Aaron. We hardly ever spoke while we worked, and if we did, it was always with a razor-sharp focus that intensified my excitement about getting things done. We seemed to speak the exact same language, perfectly synchronised. Neither of us was prone to beating around the bush. Instead, we were direct and efficient in our communication, and since neither of us were sensitive people, we never had to fear that our clipped tone would offend the other party. William was also remarkably pedagogical, so whenever I'd voiced any concerns as I worked on the NDA, his explanations had been easy to grasp.

Overall, working with him was an exhilarating experience. I hadn't thought we would be so compatible in areas relevant to work, but we obviously were. To be perfectly fair, I couldn't recall having had such a good partner in anything before.

It was nearing time for lunch when I received a call from the reception. Adjusting the hands-free device attached to my ear, I answered, "William Night's office, Cara speaking."

"Hello, Cara, it's Debbie. Would you please inform Mr Night that Francesca Strafford is here to see him?"

The world crashed down on me all at once, and I froze. Suddenly, I lost every train of thought I'd had today and stared blankly at the document I was working on. Francesca? He was still seeing her?

For some reason, I hadn't expected this, and the news struck me like a bucket of cold water. Suddenly, my whole body tensed. Breathing hurt.

Seeming to notice my sudden rigidity, I sensed William's eyes on my profile.

"Cara?" Debbie prompted.

Her voice dragged me back to the present. "Of course."

As soon as I'd hung up, I drew in a long breath to steady myself. The idea that he was still seeing Francesca was more painful than I'd anticipated. Then again, why was I surprised? I'd rejected him. Of course he'd moved on since then. I had no right to be upset about this – he wasn't mine. This pain was entirely self-inflicted.

"Are you alright?" William asked me then. The sound of his alluring voice only intensified the sting of my loss.

"Yes." My voice nearly cracked, so I cleared my throat. Without looking at him, I continued professionally, "Francesca is here to see you. She's in the lobby."

"Is she?" He sounded surprised, but I wasn't sure it was genuine. I could sense his eyes on me, inspecting, and it perturbed me. To be put under his microscope was the last thing I wanted right now, because I was experiencing feelings that I hadn't seen coming. Now more than ever, I wished he'd look away, and I also wished he would order me to call Debbie back and say to her that Francesca wasn't welcome. But instead, he asked, "Collect her for me, please, would you?"

Exerting every ounce of my self-discipline, I nodded and refrained from exhaling the ton of air that I desperately wanted to.

"Of course." I stood.

"You might want to bring your computer out," he warned, and I thought I detected a hidden message. Had he tried to say, "I intend to fuck her, so you might want to step out for that bit"?

I frowned at the thought. He wouldn't go that far, would he? Surely, he was above that sort of behaviour. No, I refused to believe he would do such a thing. He couldn't be that unprofessional.

Though I avoided his gaze, I could sense that he was still scrutinising my reaction. However, I denied him the satisfaction of correctly identifying my conflicted state by feigning nonchalance.

With my heart in my throat, I collected my computer to bring it with me, and I didn't so much as look at him while I exited. It felt like I was in a trance when I approached the available desk beside Elisabeth. After leaving my computer on it, I gave her a vague nod of acknowledgement before I went to the lifts. While I waited for one to arrive, I tapped my foot, my arms crossed as if to protect myself from harm.

Francesca. Francesca Strafford, William Night's what? His girlfriend? His plaything? What was she to him? Were things getting serious between them?

I knew they had been seeing each other for months by now. While I was curious to meet her, I also dreaded it. It wasn't jealousy, but it felt wrong to look her in the eye while knowing that she was completely unaware of the fact that I'd also seen him naked once – that I'd also been on the receiving end of his divine sensual care. Like her, I knew what his vulgar mouth could do. Like her, I knew how delicious it felt to have him buried within. But she had no idea I'd experienced that side of him, did she? I couldn't imagine he would have mentioned me to her. Sure, he'd clearly told Violet, but I suspected their friendship was to blame for that. William's conduct with Francesca didn't strike me as friendly in nature. Then again, what did I know?

My thoughts continued their unpleasant voyage while I travelled down to the lobby to collect her. Once the doors slid apart, my heart skipped a beat. Beyond the security gates stood a tall Black woman with a slender frame. Drawn back into a high ponytail was caramel coloured and wavy hair. Her skin was light brown with a golden shimmer to it, and she was immaculately dressed into a bright yellow and elegant summer dress of expensive fabric. It was undoubtedly a designer dress, but I'd never cared for brands.

When she turned towards me, my breath caught. She was nothing short of stunning.

At the centre of her face was a small, round nose, and her hazel eyes – set slightly wide apart – glanced curiously in my direction. Somehow, the distance between her eyes made her look all the more attractive. She was an intriguing beauty. Not the type you saw in makeup commercials, but rather that of Vogue.

Was she a model? She could be, I thought, if she wanted. She had the height and build for it.

"Hello," I called and forced forth a smile as I exited through the security gates to greet her. "I'm Cara, a new trainee. Mr Night's assistant, of sorts," I explained and extended my hand to her. "I'm here to collect you on his behalf."

Not a trace of a smile was present on her face when her limp hand reluctantly reached for mine. "I see. How's his mood?" she asked, startling me.

Did he tend to be in a bad mood around her?

"He's...William?" I gave her a lopsided smile, but she was not amused.

"Shit." She sighed and folded her arms.

"Something the matter?" I tilted my head.

"Well, he's not expecting me, so I'd hoped to find him in a good mood. Suppose luck's not on my side today. It's just..." She waved a hand in the air. "I'm headed for a job in Spain, so I wanted to say goodbye."

It was tempting to ask if she were his girlfriend but, of course, I refrained. It wasn't my place, regardless of how badly I wanted to know. "Right. Well, he sounded happy when he asked me to collect you," I said, hoping to reassure her.

Hope ignited in her eyes. The same moment I saw it, I knew she was in love with him. Was he in love with her, too?

"Really?" she asked, and finally, a small smile flirted with her lips.

I nodded. "If you'll come with me?" I proposed and ushered her towards the security gates.

Her mesmerising legs moved with such elegance that I was further convinced she must be a model.

"Spain's lovely," I said to create small talk while I scanned my card to let her past the gates.

"It really is, but it's sweltering during summer. Third time I'm there this year."

My eyebrows climbed higher. "Travel a lot, do you? I'm jealous."

A smug smile decorated her mouth. "Yeah. Occupational hazard, you might call it."

"What's your occupation?"

She shrugged. "I'm a model." And I was correct.

"To be honest, I suspected," I replied, amused. "You're absolutely gorgeous."

Her smile transitioned into a full-blown grin upon my compliment. "Thanks, but you should have a look in the mirror."

I chuckled. "Oh, I do that every morning. Don't you?"

She laughed. "You know what I meant."

I grinned. "I do. Anyway, so you get to travel for work. I'd have loved that, I think."

She cocked her head from side to side while we headed for the lifts. "It gets a bit tiresome. I sleep in hotels more often than I sleep in my own bed."

"Really?"

She nodded. "Makes it hard to maintain relationships – and friendships," she murmured, and I found myself wondering whether she was alluding to some sort of difficulty with establishing a relationship with William.

Once we were in the cage, I sensed her do a visual sweep of my body. "So, how long have you been on the job, Cara?"

"Two days." I turned to smile at her. "This is my third."

"How do you like it?"

"I love it. It's hectic and demanding, but definitely riveting."

"I bet. How's having Will as a boss?"

"He's brilliant. I'm very lucky to be shadowing him."

"I can imagine. He fits the role, doesn't he?"

I chuckled again. "That he does."

We continued to chat about William, and it was an odd experience because whenever I tried to change the subject, she continued to make him the centre of our conversation. I therefore got the impression she was a bit obsessed with him. If she were, I could hardly blame her. He was certainly a beguiling man, after all.

Though, I did wonder whether she persisted in talking about him because she felt possessive of him and perceived me as a threat. If she did, I pitied her. I had no plans to pursue him, so it saddened me to think that she might be worried about it. Even so, I thought she was a sweet girl, so I could understand the appeal. We were quite different, however, but perhaps that was why William had chosen to stick with her.

"I suppose you know the way?" I said once we exited the lift.

She glanced in the direction of William's office, and suddenly, I thought she looked a bit nervous. "I do."

"Well then. It was lovely meeting you, Francesca." I offered my hand, and when she took it this time, her grip was firmer. "I hope you'll have a wonderful time in Spain and that you won't melt in the hot weather."

Her wide smile revealed her bright white teeth. "Thanks, Cara. Best of luck to you."

"Thanks. I'll need it."

When I'd found my seat, Elisabeth murmured, "She stops by every Wednesday she's in town. She won't be leaving for at least half an hour," and I could hear she was amused.

My brows knitted as I turned to regard her. Quietly, I said,

"You sound like you think they'll have sex."

She tittered and looked rather charmed, which bewildered me. "Oh, you are *so* new to this."

"New to what?"

"An actual workplace."

"What do you mean?"

Her smile was patient. "Love, I hate to burst your bubble, but do you really think people don't do questionable things at work? People cheat on their spouse left, right and centre. Not everyone, of course, but definitely some. Sometimes, people have sex here, too. This is the real world, Cara. Your naivety is charming, but this really shouldn't surprise you. I'm not saying what they're doing is acceptable, but it's absolutely to be expected. Humans are stupid, and we like to pretend we're above animals, but the truth is, several of us are not."

I shook my head. "It's not that I don't expect it. I just don't expect it from Will. It's not my impression of him."

The curve of her brow disclosed her disagreement. "Well, what do you think they'll do? Talk? They don't need to meet up in person for that, especially not during work hours. Besides, had you seen what I have – the state of her when she's left his office in the past – you'd suspect the same. It's clear as day they've had sex."

Hearing that, I found myself quite appalled by his lack of work ethics. What sort of professional would have sex in their office in the middle of the day when they had work to tend to? "Just seems a bit unprofessional. I hadn't thought Will was like that."

"Hey," she frowned, "don't be so sanctimonious. Cut the man some slack. Honestly, he deserves it. He practically lives in his office. I'm sure that's the only reason. I've often wondered why he won't just invest in a bed. That way, he'd never have to leave. Though, upon second thought, that's probably why he hasn't. If he did, he'd actually never leave. This way, he's got to."

I didn't want to talk about this anymore, so I got back to work without further ado. Gossip was definitely not my thing, but it was clearly Elisabeth's. Still, she hadn't lied. Francesca departed half an hour later, and the whole time she'd been in there, I'd struggled to remain focused. I had so many questions.

My eyes dashed to her figure the moment she exited William's office. Her long, wavy hair cascaded down to her shoulders now. He'd obviously made a mess out of her ponytail.

Amused by William's lascivious behaviour, Elisabeth struggled to stifle a giggle and shook her head. I didn't share her amusement. I was disappointed in him. To add to it, I was slightly gutted that he'd moved on. However, this was what I had intended for, so I tried my hardest to quell my unruly emotions.

Some minutes later, William rang. My heart bolted to my throat. After a moment's hesitation, I accepted the call. "Yes?"

"You can come back now." He sounded a bit strange, but I wasn't sure why I thought that. He didn't seem stressed, but he didn't seem calm either.

I swallowed. "Alright."

He hung up.

At that moment in time, I couldn't think of anything less tempting than returning to his office. I was certain I'd imagine the two of them naked, the scene awakening in my mind as though it were my present circumstance. Had he fucked her on his desk, for instance? Where I was supposed to work? Despite how nauseous I suddenly felt, I closed my laptop to heed his command.

Since he was expecting me, I didn't bother to knock. Opening the door, I found him in front of one of the windows. It was open, probably to ventilate the room so that I wouldn't smell the sex that had been in the air.

Immediately, he turned towards me, eyes darting. His lips were slightly swollen and redder than usual, no doubt due to the things he'd been using them for. The more I investigated, the surer I was that Elisabeth had been right. They must have had sex.

Unsure of what to make of the situation, I shut the door and approached his desk without a word. I was appalled he would fuck someone while at work, essentially right in front of me, and then order me to work in here straight afterwards. It was incredibly inconsiderate of him, not to forget insensitive. To have to work here now was wildly uncomfortable.

First and foremost, I was upset at his lack of work ethics, but I felt too intimidated to speak up since it was only my third day here. I also didn't want him to think that I was only complaining because I was jealous. While it was true that part of me was hurt that he had moved on, I wasn't jealous. I was upset only because it had been that easy for him to move on. By contrast, I wasn't over him at all. When he focused on me, I heard only him. When he walked into the room, I saw only him. And yet, despite that, I thought to myself that if he were actually happy with Francesca, he deserved to be. Indeed, he deserved to be happy, and he deserved to have his feelings returned by someone worthy of him – someone who wasn't me – because he was a wonderful man.

"Sorry about that," he murmured.

Lifting my gaze, I stared blankly out of the windows. For the first time since I'd started here, a moment of sadness gripped me. The traffic of London hummed in the background, reminding me of why I had never really fancied cities. Above the pulsating metropolis, I saw the clear blue sky on this serene summer day. The breeze flirted with the white curtains, and I closed my eyes to savour its dance across my cheeks. On the face of it, losing William seemed trivial, and yet I couldn't ignore the way my heart ached.

"No worries," I eventually murmured and, somewhat reluctantly, planted my computer back on his desk. "Do I need to clean this surface?"

He blinked at my bold question. "No, that's not necessary."

At least they hadn't fucked on his desk.

Giving him a vague nod, I found my seat again, and I sensed him watching me the entire while it took for him to return to his own and focus on work.

One question kept bothering me while I tried to concentrate

on my screen, and after a while, I realised that I might as well ask to get rid of it. Besides, it wasn't unusual for colleagues to discuss this sort of thing, was it? In the end, it was rather obvious what he had done. Even Elisabeth suspected, so would I be speaking out of turn if I asked?

Since I considered it my best option to end my urgent and gross level of curiosity, I decided to bite the bullet and asked, "So, are you two seeing each other now, or...?"

When I glanced up, I caught him regarding me with an arched brow that revealed his scepticism. "With all due respect, Cara, I'm not inclined to discuss my romantic affairs with you." Since he immediately focused on his computer again, it was apparent that trying to dig further would get me nowhere.

"I'm sorry I asked," I mumbled, embarrassed. While I felt robbed of the satisfaction of knowing the answer, I returned my attention to my computer screen to respect his boundaries, so I was surprised when he suddenly asked, "Why do you care?"

It was an excellent question. Why did I care? I had no right to. However, the fact remained, which was that I did care. Was it because of my supermassive ego? Was I so narcissistic that I couldn't accept his moving on? Did I want him to yearn for me eternally, despite my continuous rejections?

No, it was really quite simple. I cared because he remained the only man who had ever captured my interest this severely. He was the only man I had ever experienced butterflies in the presence of, the only man I'd ever lusted after without end, the only man I had ever felt so connected with, and he was the only man it had ever felt right to kiss. So, it hurt me to know that it wasn't mutual.

While I had myself to thank for his moving on, it wounded me to know that it had been that easy for him, as I was nowhere near the same point. I still fancied him.

But that didn't change anything. I was adamant about remaining strictly professional, so I had no claim. My feelings were simply not justified.

"I was just curious," I murmured.

He scoffed. "Haven't you heard? Curiosity killed the cat."

I looked away from him. "No, I've heard. It's just…"

"Just what?" he prompted, and I sensed him study me.

I sighed. "It's not my place, but I think she might be in love with you." I had said it because I wanted him to refute it. Nothing would have satisfied me more than to hear him ridicule me for even thinking such a thing. But instead, he replied, "You're right. It's not your place," and he didn't look remotely impressed with me.

Since I had no right to be doing it, I felt ashamed of myself for prying into his romantic life, so I got back to work and counted the minutes till the clock would strike half eleven. As soon as it did, I stood. "Lunch?"

"In a minute. I've got a few more things to look over before my meeting with Violet."

"I'll join Elisabeth, then."

He merely waved his hand in the air to indicate I was free to go.

§ § §

Over lunch, Elisabeth and I had exchanged some small talk, and I was grateful for the distraction. We had spoken about where we lived, what sort of party-scenes we were into, what interests we had in common – we were both avid readers – as well as romantic statuses. Elisabeth was engaged to a man named Brian, whom she had met four years ago. He was an economist, and their encounter hadn't been particularly unique, according to her. They'd both been drunk at the same pub, when Brian had decided to chat her up.

She had been sharing stories about their relationship when I'd noticed William's arrival, but instead of joining us, he'd taken a seat at Andy and Violet's table. While I'd been disappointed, I had also been thankful for his avoidance. My mood was still unstable after Francesca's visit today, so I appreciated some mental room to sort out my thoughts – especially my feelings.

"But you're determined to remain single?" Elisabeth asked, with a tone of surprise, as we waited for the lift after lunch. The doors opened, and I was just about to elaborate when a large hand landed on my back to usher me in gently. As I tilted my head back, a spellbinding pair of eyes instantly hypnotised me.

"Please, don't let me interrupt," said William and continued to hold my gaze. Speechless, I stared back.

Elisabeth demanded his attention when she teased him with, "Mind your own business, Will. Nosy." She wasn't one to talk, but I refrained from commenting on that.

Instead, I said, "No, it's okay. I was only going to say that I'm committed to my career. That's the only thing I've got the capacity to maintain at the moment." To emphasise my point, I stepped away from William's touch and propped my back against the wall.

"She sounds like you," Elisabeth remarked and peered up at William. His lips twisted as he tried to restrain a smile.

"She does, actually."

Mystified, I frowned. What was that supposed to mean? Wasn't he seeing Francesca now?

Hearing my thoughts, I nearly groaned. I couldn't continue doing this. It would do me no good to keep wondering.

To distract myself, I changed the subject by saying to William, "I'll be leaving to collect the files from Clifford Paints."

"Good. You might get back while I'm meeting with Violet. If you do, just continue your work on the NDA."

I nodded.

§ § §

It was nearing three o'clock when I returned to the office, and it took me another hour to make copies of all the files, seeing as there was a horrendous amount. Scurrying back to William's office with the stack of paper in my arms, I opened the door with my elbow, but he was nowhere in sight. Glancing at his desk, I was inevitably reminded of Francesca's visit. With a sigh, I walked in to drop the documents on the black surface of it.

Standing there, I wondered what to do if William was currently seeing her with the aim of building something lasting. I would need to move on as well, that was for sure, but I was already trying and had been ever since our conversation at Farm Girl, and it hadn't brought me far. However, given enough time, perhaps I would consider this a blessing in disguise. If he and Francesca were getting serious, perhaps I would come to realise that it was the best thing that could have happened. Nothing would get in my way then. Perhaps I would finally be able to view him solely in a professional light.

As for his male beauty? Well, I would admire that in silence until it became like furniture – familiar and something I didn't give a thought.

Sinking into my chair, I decided to get back to work. I'd been sitting there for a few minutes when my phone received a message, and it was from the single person I appreciated hearing from most right now.

Aaron.

> You available tonight? I'm curious to hear how your vacation scheme is going. Mine's chaotic, but amazing x

> Yes! Mine? I finish at five x

Just after I'd pressed Send, William stepped in, and his arrival jolted me. For some reason, the fact that I'd just texted Aaron made me feel like I'd been caught committing a crime. With haste, I placed my phone next to my computer and focused on the NDA again.

"You're allowed to look at your phone," he said with a tone of amusement.

"Sorry. First time I've looked at it today. How was the meeting?"

"Efficient. Violet's not one to waste anyone's time." He reclined into his seat.

I was just about to respond when the screen of my phone lit up to notify me that Aaron had replied. The instant after I'd read his name, I saw that William had stolen a glance as well, and what happened next was extremely awkward. It was obvious that we'd both seen it, but we refused to look at each other. It felt like an elephant had jumped into the room, but neither of us was willing to acknowledge it.

"I'll need you to stay for a while longer today," he suddenly said. When I looked over, he seemed completely unfazed. Deciphering his thoughts was impossible, and I hated it. "Would that be alright, or have you got plans?"

A vague frown crossed my face. While we certainly had plenty of work to finish, I considered the timing of his question somewhat conspicuous. "No, I can stay, but for how long?"

He shrugged. "I'm not sure. We've got a lot to do."

"Okay." Suspicious, I wondered whether he had asked me to stay solely to impede my plans with Aaron. Then again, it seemed unlikely when taking his affair with Francesca into account.

A few more minutes elapsed before he said, "By the way, on Fridays, the office tends to grab a few drinks at Disrepute – the cocktail bar where we first met. You should come. We'll celebrate your first week with us."

Elisabeth had already mentioned it during lunch, but after today's events, alcohol and William didn't strike me as company worth seeking out. It seemed like the recipe for a devastating night out. Under the influence, I didn't trust myself not to do something stupid, like act on my lust for him. Alcohol severely reduced my inhibitions, and I was struggling enough already. If I made a pass at him, I'd never be able to live it down. He was my boss, and I had just been preaching to Elisabeth about maintaining professionalism. It would make me a hypocrite, to say the least.

To make it worse, William was likely to reject my advances now, due to Francesca. Acting on my lust for him would also mean contradicting myself, and I wasn't about to allow that. I had chosen my career, and I intended to stand by my decision. In fact, I owed it to William to stand by it. I respected him too much to do anything else. Regardless of how much I liked him, I simply refused to get in the way of him and Francesca.

"I can't. I've got plans," I lied. "Maybe next week."

"Next week it is, then."

§ § §

William had made me stay till eight. Since I was exhausted after having spent more than twelve hours at work, Aaron and I had agreed to postpone meeting till tomorrow. After a shower, I'd settled on the sofa to watch TV with Jason where he had taken it upon himself to massage my feet.

"I'm knackered," I declared with a groan. "Your brother is a force to be reckoned with. Fucking hell. I can't believe he works such long hours every single day. How does he stay so fit?"

"He trains before work."

"Christ."

Jason nodded. "He's a machine. Always has been."

During a momentary lapse of judgment, I muttered, "Well, that machine also has a sex drive."

He stiffened. "Pardon?"

I blinked when I realised how that must have sounded. "No, no, I didn't mean it like that. Sorry. This woman stopped by today – Francesca. I think he fucked her in his office, but I'm not sure."

Mouth agape, he stared disbelievingly at me. "What?"

"Yeah, and he made me work there afterwards. It was all quite uncomfortable." I wrinkled my nose.

"I can't believe he did that. Are you sure?"

I shook my head. "No, but Ellie – another paralegal – told me Francesca tends to stop by on Wednesdays, and she's under the impression it's to have sex. Still, I didn't hear nor see them, so I'm not sure it's what happened, but the evidence is certainly compelling."

He leaned back. "What sort of evidence? Other than Ellie's impression?"

I regretted that I had said anything at all then, but at the same time, perhaps Jason sat on the answer that William refused to provide: was he serious about Francesca?

"Well, when Francesca walked out afterwards, her hair was down, and it had been in a ponytail when she walked in. Then, when I entered his office, his lips were slightly red and somewhat swollen, probably from kissing, and the window was open as well, to ventilate the room. She was there for at least half an hour, too. Plus, he told me to bring my computer out with me, and there was something about the way he said it that I found conspicuous."

Jason continued to blink, visibly appalled. "Bloody hell, that's bang out of order. What's he thinking?"

I shrugged. "Probably wasn't thinking – or at least not with the right head." My joke earned a chuckle from him before I continued, "Are they seeing each other? Like dating?"

He frowned. "I'm not sure. He's been seeing her a lot lately, though."

The information made me swallow. If William had been seeing her a lot, perhaps things really were moving in the direction of a relationship. As I considered it, I was tempted to ask something else, but did I have the nerve? It seemed fake of me. Alas, my curiosity drove me to do it. "I thought he was interested in that girl named Sandra or something?"

Eyes set on the TV, Jason shrugged. "Yeah, he's not mentioned her lately."

"Hm."

I steered my gaze to the screen, but I paid no attention to what was happening on it. My thoughts entertained me instead. Jason had confirmed my suspicions, and while this was what I'd wanted from the start, I experienced no relief. William was finally leaving me alone and, now that he had Francesca, he would continue to do that for the remainder of my work experience placement. I should have been overjoyed about this, but I wasn't. Part of me – the rational part – certainly was, but my heart felt terribly heavy – dense with an emotion entirely foreign to me and which I had no experience dealing with.

Heartache?

"Has he said anything at all? About Sandra?" I probed carefully. "I remember you were quite worried about him when it came to her."

"Only that it's a shame she never realised their potential. I think he's accepted it now, though." Suddenly, he shuddered. "Honestly, good riddance. I don't think I would have liked her much."

I pressed my lips together and stole a glance at him. What he had said made me wonder if he would change his opinion of me if he ever learnt the truth. I feared he would, and because of that, I became all the more determined to keep him in the dark.

"Thanks for the massage, Jason, but I think I'll go to bed," I said.

"Anytime. Though, before you do, did you talk to Will about it? Did you tell him it made you uncomfortable?"

"Well, I'm not even sure they had sex, and it didn't strike me as appropriate to ask."

He frowned. "Yeah, I get that. I'll have a word with him, then. If he actually did that, he needs to be reminded it's unacceptable."

I froze. "What will you say?"

"I'll ask him whether he did it."

I grimaced. "But then he's going to realise I told you."

"Well, would you rather ask him yourself?"

"I'd rather not ask at all."

He frowned. "But then he might repeat it. Would you prefer that?"

What a conundrum. Wearing a pout, I shook my head.

"There you go. I'll call him this week, yeah?"

"Thanks, Jason."

"I'm here for you, love."

"You always are. Will you tell me what he says?" I swung my legs off his lap and stood.

"Of course."

"Thanks."

"Always, Cara. Sleep well."

But I didn't sleep well. I spent hours chasing slumber, and when I finally caught it, I tossed and turned like my worst nightmare was coming to life.

HAVE YOU EVER

AFTER WORK THE NEXT DAY, AARON AND I WERE watching a documentary about white-collar crime in the living room when we heard a key being inserted into the lock of the front door. Sprawled across Aaron's body on the sofa, I lifted my head to welcome Jason's arriving figure.

"Hello," I cooed. "Did you have a nice day?"

Completely ignoring me, he flashed Aaron a fond grin. "Aaron. Good to see you."

"You too," Aaron replied, enthused.

"How's Dentons?" Jason queried as he approached.

"It's brilliant."

When he reached us, he didn't hesitate to smother us with his weight. Squeezed into a sandwich consisting of two unfairly sexy men, I could hardly breathe.

"Jason," I choked. "Can't breathe."

In response, he squeezed me harder.

"Oh my God," I mouthed as I lost my breath.

Laughing, he reclined towards the other end of the sofa.

"How's summer holiday?" Aaron asked him and reached for the remote to pause the documentary.

"It's great. When the sun came out after three, Stephen and I headed to the park with Livy and Giselle to work on our tans. Played some volleyball, messed about."

"I saw that on your Instagram story," I remarked with a pout. I'd been envious at that point.

"Yeah. We missed you guys," he replied affectionately. "Responsible twats that you are."

Aaron shook beneath me as he laughed.

"You spending the night, Aaron?" Jason asked.

Turning his deep brown eyes towards me, Aaron said, "I think so."

Hugging his warm body beneath my own, I smiled up at him. "Of course you are. Why else would I tell you to bring a change of clothes?"

Grinning, he planted a kiss on my head and brought both arms around me to squeeze me against him.

"Sweet," Jason commented. "Fancy a beer, then?"

"Suppose the one won't do any harm."

Nodding, Jason headed for the kitchen. "How was your day, love?" he asked me on his way there.

"It was good. Much better than yesterday," I said, which was the truth. William and I had hardly spoken, and whenever we had, it had been strictly professional. Moreover, he hadn't fucked anyone in his office, which was where I'd set the standard since yesterday. So, whenever William didn't shove his cock into somebody else in my presence, I was having a good day.

"William treat you well?" Jason queried.

"Brought me coffee, actually, so yes."

Aaron tensed beneath me, which perplexed me.

Gobsmacked, Jason halted and turned around. "What?" he asked disbelievingly. "Isn't he your boss?"

"Yes?"

He looked stumped. "Then aren't you supposed to bring coffees for *him*?"

"Oh, don't be so conventional, Jason." I rolled my eyes.

He chuckled. "Sorry. It's just, I've known that man all my life, and I don't think he's even brought our mother coffee."

Aaron studied Jason with a contemplative expression on his face. It bothered me somewhat. What was he thinking? Was he catching on to something? I feared he was, as he was no fool, nor was he gullible. In the end, Jason had essentially declared that I was receiving special treatment. Will's behaviour might not slip past Aaron.

However, I knew better than to ask. Aaron was extremely reserved. If he wanted to talk about something, he would. If he didn't, I would never hear about it.

I argued, "Well, I think he was only trying to make me feel welcome, or perhaps he meant to apologise for yesterday."

"Yeah, you're probably right," Jason said as he disappeared into the kitchen.

"What happened yesterday?" Aaron enquired.

"I'd rather not talk about it," I murmured with a pout.

He hesitated. "Is it related to him walking in on us that time?"

I shook my head. "No. Of course not. Why would it be?"

He glanced sideways, and it roused some alarm in me. I wished I could hear his thoughts. Was he suspicious of William? Had he sensed something that awful day? Sensed my past with William?

"I was just making sure," he finally said. "I've been worried that incident would make things awkward for you once you started work."

Touched by his concern, I smiled fondly at him. "You're very sweet for worrying about that, but you don't need to. I've seen him several times since then, and it's clear he's acting like it never happened."

"Alright. Good." He nodded and rubbed my back. "I'm here if you want to talk about it, though – whatever it is."

I hugged him tightly and drew his soothing scent deep into my lungs. "Thanks, but it's really nothing. He just did something a bit insensitive, but it wasn't on purpose."

"Was he too hard on you?"

"Aaron."

He chuckled. "Sorry, I'll stop."

"Thanks."

§ § §

When I woke the next morning, it was to the feeling of being tilted to the side. Once my eyelids fluttered apart, the sight of Aaron's tender smile welcomed me. Infectious in its nature, I smiled back at him before I rubbed my waking face.

"Morning," he said gently and reached over to brush my hair behind my ear.

"Morning. What time is it?" Since my voice was rather hoarse, I tried to clear it. Then, after rolling onto my back, I spread my arms apart and relished how replete I felt. Sex last night had been exactly what I needed, and it had been *good*.

"Half six. I woke half an hour ago. Made you breakfast."

"Aw, Aaron." I surprised him when I lunged forward to hug his naked back. "Thank you," I cooed and planted a soft kiss on his neck.

"Why don't you have a shower while I set the table for us?"

"Sounds wonderful," I agreed and crawled out of bed. As I paraded completely naked towards the door, I felt his eyes burn into my back, so with a cheeky smile on my face, I turned my head to catch him in his ogling.

"We've got time for a quickie," he said.

I laughed. "Have you showered yet?"

"No." His usually patient voice was filled with eagerness.

"Then let's spare the environment and do it together," I proposed and stepped out. Resembling a young boy in his excitement, I heard him charge after me without a moment's hesitation.

§ § §

Placing a mug of coffee in front of me on the table, Aaron resembled husband material. With a grateful look in my eye, I gripped the black porcelain and raised it to my mouth.

"How long are your days?" he asked, grabbing the seat opposite.

"Eight to five, but they may differ depending on the workload.

You?"

Unlocking his iPad, he opened a newspaper app on it. "Same as you," he murmured, dragging his own mug of coffee to his mouth. "By the way, you busy next Saturday? Not this one, but the next."

I frowned in thought. "I don't think so. Why?"

"Tyler is celebrating his birthday. He said to invite you."

I stiffened. "Shit, when's his birthday?" I asked, worried that I'd forgotten to congratulate him.

He chuckled. "Next Saturday. Don't worry. Can you make it?"

"Yes, of course. Any ideas for a present?"

"Boxers. He's in dire need of them, he said."

I giggled. Student life in a nutshell, that was. "Sorted."

We'd been sitting there for a few minutes when I suddenly started comparing him to William. They were so different, and yet somehow, so similar. Their drive and intelligence were certainly alike, but Aaron was much gentler. It bothered me to realise that, because it made me question why I hadn't ever developed feelings for Aaron when he was obviously a much better influence on me. As opposed to William, he didn't exhaust me, divide my focus or anything like that. Instead, he had always been a positive contribution to my life. Without him, I doubted I would have reached as far as I had within the field of law. So, why couldn't this be love? Why had I always been determined to avoid pursuing a relationship with him?

Because he didn't give me butterflies? Because kissing him had never felt entirely right? It annoyed me. Why should feelings be necessary for the pursuit of love? A relationship with Aaron would have made complete sense. It would have been a logical and rational course of action, as he brought out the best in me. Meanwhile, William possessed the power to turn my world upside down in a heartbeat.

As my thoughts continued to delve into the subject, I caught myself wondering whether Aaron had ever been in my place, where a girl he was attracted to had made advances. Had he rejected her to maintain a strict focus on his career? Had he given it a go, but later discovered that they were incompatible? Or perhaps the opposite had happened. Perhaps he'd fancied a girl and had pursued her, but she had rejected him instead.

I was curious to hear his perspective on this. Was he with me because he had no other option? And would he have considered ending our arrangement if he did?

We had never had this conversation before, but before I knew it, I asked him, "Have you ever considered dating someone while we've been together like this? Cassie, for example?"

Freezing, his cup of coffee remained by his full lips for several seconds. While staring into my eyes, he lowered it slowly. "What's brought this on?" he asked suspiciously, eyes narrowing faintly.

I shrugged. "Only curious. I know we're not supposed to talk about others to each other, but it's been three years, and I'm curious to know if it's ever happened during that time. If it has, I obviously won't get mad."

His frown intensified. "No, it hasn't."

"You've never considered it?"

He shook his head. "Not at all."

"Why not?"

He scoffed. "You know why."

"Do I?"

"Yes. It's because, like you, I'm not interested in anything romantic right now. I prefer just sticking to what you and I have got going on." His eyes narrowed again. "Why? Have you?"

I tucked my cheek into the palm of my hand. "No, not really."

He knitted his brows. "That's not quite the answer I was expecting. What do you mean 'not really'?"

I looked away and folded my arms. "Well, there was one guy who wanted me to give him a chance, but I rejected him, so I was only curious about whether you've ever been in the same boat."

"When was this?"

"Some months ago. Anyway, it's history, so you don't need to worry. I was just curious to hear your perspective – that's all."

"Well, Cassie has asked me out, but I rejected her point-blank. So, the answer is still the same – I've never considered it."

I gasped. "I knew it. When?"

He rubbed his neck. "During the party after our last exam."

"See? I knew she had feelings for you."

"Well, it doesn't change anything."

As soon as the satisfaction of being proven right subsided, I pouted. "Poor Cassie. Was she upset?"

Wrinkles formed across the straight bridge of his nose while he avoided my gaze. "Of course. I don't think anyone enjoys being rejected."

I sighed and reached for my cup of coffee. "I expect she hates me now."

"I wouldn't be surprised, but it would be misplaced. In the end, I'm the issue, not you."

"Good morning!" Jason exclaimed when he suddenly burst through the door, and I was grateful to discover that he was wearing boxers to show Aaron some consideration. Aaron looked entirely unaffected, but I nearly fell off my chair.

"It's a beautiful day!" he sang, quoting U2.

"Bloody hell, Jason! Did you fire crack up your arse this morning?" I scolded, annoyed.

He sent me a smile to die for, complemented by a wink, before he moseyed over to grab Aaron's shoulders. After squeezing them, he leaned over him to steal a piece of bacon from his plate.

"Haven't you made me breakfast, Cara?" he asked and feigned a wounded tone.

"Sorry," Aaron chuckled. "I made it this morning. I wasn't aware you'd be up this early when you're on holiday."

Jason scoffed. "Med student. Hello?"

"Right. Serious as they come."

"Precisely."

"His earlier show says otherwise," I muttered. "But you can

have the rest of mine. He made far too much." I pushed my plate towards him.

"Thanks, darling," Jason crooned and headed over to the kitchen counter to toast some bread.

"Did you wake by yourself today? I was going to wake you in a minute." I turned in my chair to watch his gloriously naked back. Like his brother, he was athletically built and very tall, with defined muscles that beckoned straight women and gay men to drool over him.

"No. I was woken by the sound of your sexual moans arriving from the shower," he replied without looking at me.

My face paled. "Oh," I squeaked. "Sorry."

"Was weirdly erotic. I almost got a boner, but then I remembered that you're basically my sister, so it's all flaccid."

Aaron guffawed while I sagged into my seat, mortified. Sometimes, Jason was much like his brother – vulgar and blunt. For a moment, I wondered who their inspiration was, but soon enough, it occurred to me that it could only be John.

§ § §

Aaron left before I did, seeing as his workplace was further away. As I was seeing him out, he wrapped his arms around my waist and pulled me close. Descending onto my mouth, I felt him smile against my lips. It was a sweet kiss, and it was likely to assist me through the day.

Once he'd pulled away, he rested his forehead against mine and said with affection, "Have a nice day at work, love."

Grinning to show him how charmed I was, I replied, "Yeah. You too."

Leaning back, he called out to my flatmate, "Bye, Jason. Have a great day, yeah?"

"You too, Aaron!" Jason shouted back from a closer distance than I had expected, and sure enough, once I'd shut the door after Aaron, I turned to discover that he'd been peeking at us from around the corner.

"Pervert," I accused.

Laughing, he walked into full view. "Honestly, I'm only fascinated. How the hell have you managed to keep your feelings in check for three bloody years? You look like a couple! If I hadn't seen it for myself, I would never have believed it."

I shrugged. "Well, aside from you and Livy, he's my best friend. I don't know how to explain it. It just…is."

"I'm honestly amazed. Where do I get one?"

I giggled and shook my head at him. "I'd start by breaking up with your hand, perhaps."

"Noted."

19

---•◆•◆•---

IN MISERY

WILLIAM

I N MISERY, WE FEEL MOST ALIVE, OR SO I HAD ALWAYS BELIEVED. I was no melancholic, but the pain of sadness reminds us we are still drawing breath because, if we were not, we would not have felt anything at all. There is still an option to end the pain, to seek relief, which comes only with life. In death, only nothingness awaits us. Pain is, the way I see it, the clearest expression of life. It's an acute experience. One feels it closely. Where pain is a solid blade, delight is an obscure cloud. In happiness, we lose identity. It evaporates into the dizzy elation that comes with joy. After all, happiness is only real when shared. The same cannot be said for misery. Misery feasts on loneliness – thrives on it.

Since Cara, my misery had enjoyed prime conditions. She had abandoned me in May, and in the wake of it, I had tried time and again to pursue other women, desperately searching for her replacement – a woman capable of making me forget about her. But, as time dragged on, I'd realised it wasn't possible. I'd sleep with Violet and wish she were Cara. I'd look at Francesca's naked body beneath my own and hate her for not being Cara.

In my desperate search for her replacement, I had even brought Andy out on the prowl with me, but it had always been a pathetic endeavour, since neither of us had been able to cast aside the thought of the woman we loved. Instead, we had drowned our sorrows in our drinks and had ignored every woman casting a glance in our direction. The few who'd dared approach us I'd intentionally offended and chased away, because they didn't meet my requirements – they weren't Cara.

Now more than ever, I was grateful for Andy. His broken relationship couldn't have happened at a better time. It was selfish of me to think it, but then if he and Chloe had to suffer, I wanted it to be now, because if I hadn't been able to enjoy his solidarity, it was perfectly possible that I would have lost my mind.

For tactical purposes, I had abstained from informing Jason of anything at all, and it had come at a price. I could no longer seek solace in his friendship, but then it had also been a price I was willing to pay if it meant I could ultimately have *her*. Instead of revealing the truth to him, I had created the illusion that I still kept Francesca and Violet as my lovers because I had hoped that the information would somehow find its way to Cara and set the wrong impression. I wanted her to think I had moved on, because if she did, perhaps it would inspire her to miss my attention.

Suddenly, lies had become my closest friends. Deception had seemed the only way. It was a gamble, but then I had nothing to lose. *He* – whose name I refused to mention out of spite – had the luxury of owning her fond laughter, her gentle kiss of good morning, her loving touch after lovemaking and her mysterious thoughts as she confided in him before sleep. I had no claim on such luxuries at all. I felt poorer now than I ever had because her affection wasn't mine to keep.

She'd left behind a vacancy in me that could only be filled by her. Upon realising that, I had made it my quest to win her over once she started work, but I knew I'd have to change my strategy. The weeks leading up to June, I had spent cogitating on how to proceed.

Although I had been satisfied with the discovery, my pursuit of friendship had failed. She had confessed she couldn't stop herself from thinking of me, that I had distracted her so profoundly that her focus had shifted from her ambitions and onto me, and I had inferred from it that she harboured at least some interest that I could nurture. However, I knew I had to be careful about it.

To spare her education, she had begged me to abandon her, and while I had agreed at the time, I hadn't told her it would only be temporary. I'd respected her wish solely because I knew how important her education was to her. In light of her relationship with *him*, it had been a difficult decision, but for her, there were few things I wouldn't do. Alas, it had enabled my jealousy over their bond to fester beyond measure. After dark, I'd lie in my bed and imagine her beside him, on top of him, the melody of her moans ringing in my ears like a customised means of torture.

I could still hear her so clearly – sometimes so plainly that her voice might as well have been drifting through my current surroundings. The sound of her pleasure haunted me even in my sleep. There had been pure ecstasy present in her moans, and I hadn't been the one to deliver it. *He* had.

To end my agony that day, I had pushed over the shoe cabinet and the coat stand in the hope of ending their session. It had been an impulsive action, but I had feared that calling her name would only have made them quiet down – pause, at best. It had occurred to me to leave without making my presence known, but the part of me that resented her for her actions had forced me to remain. Instead of leaving, it had urged me to draw her out only so that I could force her to face what she had done. I'd wanted her to know I was there, and that I had heard her. In fact, I had experienced it as a compulsion. I had hoped it would stir some remorse in her, perhaps even inspire her to change her mind and pick me over him, but instead, all she had offered were rational apologies, and I hated them all, for reason had deserted me in favour of love.

I'd felt so hollow in the wake of it that I still hadn't recovered the parts of me that the sound had carved out. It had wounded me more than anything else ever had. What made it especially unbearable was knowing I was not entitled to my feelings. Rationally, she had done nothing wrong. She wasn't mine, and she owed me no loyalty.

I sometimes projected my hate for that fact onto her. Indeed, I frequently hated her as though she had committed the worst imaginable crime a lover could. It repulsed me to know that she would allow him to touch her the way I was supposed to, and it made me feel sick to know that she furthermore enjoyed it. He wasn't right for her, and it drove me mad that she couldn't see it.

I'd taken it as an insult that she favoured him over me. It made me feel inferior. I hated the idea that she preferred his company to mine in bed, because it could only mean he was able to offer her pleasures where I had failed. I'd been an inadequate lover. Despite my ardent efforts, I hadn't been able to love her body sufficiently. Why else would she have chosen him? My touch hadn't been addictive. The pleasure I had meant to provide had been deficient.

"The right one will be there at the right time," she had told me during that awful day in May. All I had heard was that *he* might still be there, just waiting for her to reach the point when a relationship would be something she'd want. She'd been with him for three years already. In light of that, I was confident he was in love with her, too. The only reason he hadn't made romantic advances yet was that he knew how she worked. Like me, he knew how formidable the strength of her convictions was. In all likelihood, he had settled upon strategic patience because of that. Then, the instant they weakened, he would strike.

What made matters worse was that, from her perspective, he didn't carry the same risks as I did. She'd made it clear that my role as her boss prevented her from considering me in a romantic light. Being her best friend's brother didn't aid my case, either. *He* had none of those titles. Instead, he owned the title of being her lover. The advantage that gave him in the battle for her affections made me ill with jealousy and fear. Considering her threshold, the likelihood that she would date him was far higher than the likelihood that she would date me.

They'd been sleeping together for three entire years. That could easily advance into a relationship. I had no guarantee that her feelings towards him wouldn't evolve soon. It was evident she already harboured some version of love for him, or else she wouldn't have been so attached. And I was scared that love could grow. What if, in a few months, she realised she'd like to keep him around for years to come? She'd told me what a comfort he was, how simple he made her life, that he was "exactly" what she needed. What if that inspired her to make their situation permanent?

I couldn't bear the thought.

At first, I had considered whether to wait for her – at least suspend my pursuit until her vacation scheme was over – but her relationship with *him* had convinced me I could not. Waiting could cost me my only chance with her. I couldn't afford to take that risk. I had to act now – when there might still be some trace of affection for me left in her. And, most importantly, I had to be there before *him*.

While biding my time until she felt ready to settle down with someone, I would try to warm her up to the idea of being with me. I'd show her that, rather than take from her, I meant to give to her – everything within my power to help her reach her goals. She was convinced she could manage it on her own, and while I was sure she could, too, my presence in her life would make it even easier, not harder. I meant to prove that to her – that I'd be a convenience, not a burden.

"Spare me the brooding, Will," Violet said, and I was instantly jolted out of my thoughts and into my current situation. I'd been here several times since that fateful night and several times before then. Still, Disrepute now reminded me only of Cara. It was strange how empty it seemed without her presence.

"Who's brooding?" I said and looked over to acknowledge Violet by my side.

"You are."

"I was enjoying a moment of thought."

She curved a neatly plucked brow and raised her gin and tonic to her mouth. "You're horrible company."

"Where's Andy gone?" I queried when I noticed his absence. He'd been here just a minute ago, entertaining her. Had he left me with the task instead?

"The gents'," she explained with a shrug. "Anyway, what's eating you?"

"Nothing."

"Don't offend me, Will. I can tell when you're lying."

Sometimes, her ability to read me irritated me rather a lot. Then again, it was precisely her ability to do that which had summoned me into her bed that first time, now a year ago. In Violet, I had discovered a kindred spirit. While our bodies were composed of different genes, I could easily have mistaken her for a long-lost twin. She was almost as calculating as I was, and she was undoubtedly one of the more perceptive people I'd met. I'd learnt with time that it was her ability to perceive people's true intentions that had led her to dislike people in general. We had bonded over her view on that, as I frequently found myself guilty of the same. It was arrogant of us to presume we were above others, but then people often did such silly things it was difficult not to. If only people would care to think, so much could have been avoided.

"What do you want me to say?" I replied with irritation.

"I want you to admit that Cara's absence tonight is bothering you."

Rolling my eyes, I reached for my glass of lager and looked away from her.

Since Violet and I had always confided in each other about almost everything, she'd been one of the first to know that I had fallen in love. Though I hadn't expected anything else, she'd been supportive. When I had confessed that Cara was the target of my affections and that she would start working with us, she had immediately suggested that we should end our arrangement so that we might avoid unnecessary trouble. I'd been surprised at that point, as I hadn't expected her to be on my wavelength quite so perfectly. While I had brought it up with the intention of ending things, she had beaten me to it, and I doubted I could ever tell her enough how much I appreciated that.

After a sip, I answered, "What's the point in telling you something you already seem to know?"

"Well, I was mainly looking to introduce the subject," she replied, and her sly method left a faint smile on my mouth. I wished she played chess. I would have loved having her as an opponent.

"Why is that?"

"Ellie told me something curious today, which you've failed to mention."

"Which is?"

"I heard Francesca paid you a visit on Wednesday."

I sighed. Elisabeth and her never-ending blabbering. After a slow nod, I turned to face Violet "She did."

"What's that all about? I thought you ended things with her last week."

"I did," I said. "She showed up unannounced to beg me for a second chance."

The news surprised her. "Christ. Where's her pride? I never understood what you saw in her."

"I saw nothing. That was in fact the problem," I reminded her curtly.

She frowned. "Did Cara see her?"

"She did."

She grimaced. "How did she react?"

Her question prompted the scene to awaken in my mind as though it were my present reality. I vividly remembered how Cara had frozen in her chair when Deborah had called, and even clearer did I remember how consciously she had avoided meeting my eyes.

Her reaction had inspired me to hope that, despite her pretence, she would actually care if I gave my attention to other women. I had been both desperate and eager to find evidence to support it, so I had told her to collect Francesca. It had occurred to me to collect her myself, but upon recalling my encounter with *him*, I hadn't been able to resist the opportunity to retaliate and give Cara a taste of her own medicine. Since I'd been forced to interact with and acknowledge *his* existence, I had wanted her to experience what it was like, hoping it would humble her, or at least enable her to empathise with at least a portion of my misery.

It was like a vengeful demon had reigned my brain when I'd told her to bring her computer with her. The insinuation had been rather obvious, and I had seen from her reaction that my deceit had fooled her.

To substantiate my deception, I had intentionally prolonged Francesca's visit. While it was cruel of me, I had at first listened to her pleas while giving a false impression that she could, perhaps, sway my mind, but I had done it solely to drag out the time. Patience and interest had emitted from my demeanour while she had tried to explain why we were compatible and that she would work harder to ensure my satisfaction with her.

When she had reached that point, my conscience had finally suffered, so I had decided to put her out of her misery because I knew better than most how much it could hurt. I'd broken her heart and told her never to contact me again, and she had wept and wept in the wake of it. The sick demon in me had appreciated that, because it had further prolonged our interaction while we waited for her tears to run dry.

It would be a lie if I said I didn't wish Francesca all the best, and that I had intended to use her solely for my personal gain, but I simply hadn't seen the harm in taking some advantage of the situation.

It was absolutely immoral, but then, for Cara, there were few things I wouldn't sacrifice. I'd already cast aside my honour and my pride. All that remained was my virtue, and at that moment, I'd decided to throw that to the wind as well.

Francesca had been about to leave when I had reached for her ponytail. "You look so lovely when you let your hair down," I had said as I'd freed her hair of its confinement. While I'd meant it, it was also a deliberate action to give Cara the wrong impression. What I hadn't seen coming was Francesca's response. She'd launched herself onto me, lips locking on mine as though she thought it could somehow change my mind. The shock had paralysed me at first, before pity had driven me to kiss her back for a moment.

Eventually, guilt had demanded that I should pull away. I had kissed the wrong woman, and the thought of the right one being just outside had made me feel instantly nauseous. To calm my upset stomach, I'd opened a window for some fresh air, but as soon as I'd turned back, Francesca had gone.

At first, I'd been angry that I had pulled away. I'd been angry that I had felt nauseous about kissing someone else, and I'd been angry that I couldn't reciprocate her affections. She was a sweet girl, and I was confident she would have gone far to ensure my happiness. That sort of dedication was what I hoped to discover in Cara. Nevertheless, the reason for my anger was simple: Cara didn't deserve my loyalty, and yet no matter how hard I tried, my body refused to agree and would not cooperate with my notion. It would accept Cara, and only her.

"How did she react?" I echoed as I returned to the present. "She asked whether she would need to clean my desk."

A titter poured out of Violet. "Wow. That's brilliant. I love her already, and I don't even know her. What did you say?"

I'd known even before Cara started that Violet would come to adore her. Had she been mine, I would have appreciated it, but for now, it served only as a sore reminder of how intriguing the target of my affections was. "I told her it wasn't necessary."

Violet necked the remains of her drink before she turned towards me. "Given her question, I think it's safe to say she assumed you had sex."

All I offered was a nod.

"Did you correct her impression?"

Behind her, I saw Andy exit the men's room, and I was grateful when I saw him approach. After meeting his eyes, I returned my attention to Violet.

"Not plainly."

She gave me a look that made it obvious she thought I was making a mistake. "You ought to."

I disagreed. If not love, I hoped my deceit would awaken at least a sentiment in her that I could work on. "If she jumps to any conclusions, that's her mistake, and I'll be happy to correct it when the time is right."

Because I found it patronising, I didn't appreciate the way Violet reached for my hand. "Will, this stunt might cost you."

I removed my hand from her hold. "I disagree," I asserted. "You don't know her like I do. She's too stubborn for her own good. Reverse psychology really seems to be doing the trick. If she learns prematurely that I intend to wait for her, she'll probably leave me on a bed of nails for an eternity while I wait for her to make up her mind. This way, I'm forcing her to act. We'll just have to wait and see."

She tutted, and I hated the condescending sound. "After hearing this, I'm not surprised she declined to show up here today. She's probably upset with you."

"Everyone's always upset with Will," Andy interrupted when he reached us. "Though, in this particular instance, who is?"

"Cara," Violet said, because she knew I wouldn't mind. After all, Andy already knew everything.

"Ah, Cara," he echoed with a nod. "The headfuck."

"That's putting it mildly," I muttered. "I was just telling Violet about the incident with Francesca on Wednesday."

"Were you?" he asked and turned his attention to our mutual friend. "What do you make of it? I thought it was brilliant. True Will-style."

"I think he's insane."

"All is fair in love and war," Andy joked.

"As an able lawyer, you know that's not true," Violet contested. "It might not work out."

I said, "Let's just wait and see. She's been quite reserved ever since it happened, and I'm hoping it's because she's miserable." Like me.

"You can lead her to the water, Will," Violet said, "but you can't make her drink."

"Nor do I mean to." I frowned. "I'd never force her to be with me, and it's not like I could, either. She's not one to get pushed around. My intention is simply to scare her a bit – make her doubt my interest. If that doesn't work, I'll think of something else. One way or another, I'll let her know the truth when the time calls for it, but until then, I see no harm in letting her mind run wild with ideas. All I'm trying to do is find out whether or not she's got feelings for me. I'm aware I can't force her to feel anything. But, if she harbours some portion of interest in me, I'm hoping this incident might serve as a catalyst."

"Have you told Jason about this?" Violet queried then.

I shook my head. "I haven't told him anything at all. Seeing as they're best friends, I'm worried it could jeopardise things."

"Do you think he'll be cross?" she continued to question, and her sincere concern charmed me.

"Not with me. Perhaps with her, but I'm absolutely certain he'll side with me when he eventually learns the truth. He'll understand where I'm coming from without a doubt. In the end, she's the one who begged me to keep it secret from him."

Andy cocked his head from side to side. "Have you considered the implications of that? If he gets angry with her?"

I nodded. "Yeah. Depending on the outcome, I'll tell him to back off. I can't imagine he'd hold a grudge against her if she decides to give me a chance."

"And if she doesn't give you a chance?" Violet probed dubiously.

"I haven't decided yet. On the one hand, I'll be bitter if she doesn't, and that will ultimately make it tempting to tell him the truth and let her handle it on her own. On the other hand, I sincerely care for her, and she's already voiced concerns about losing him as a friend, so there's that to consider. I'm not sure I'll have the heart to let her suffer like that, but then I also can't stand keeping Jason in the dark. To clear my conscience, I'll have to tell him someday, but when I do, I might let him decide for himself what to do about it. In that case, I'll assure him I'll have no problem with it if he remains friends with her."

"But you'll definitely have a problem with it," Andy remarked sceptically. "If they remain friends, she'll always be around, Will."

"Doesn't mean I'll have to see her."

"But you'll be curious to hear about her."

I frowned, annoyed, and impatience rang from my voice when I retorted, "I'll worry about that bridge when I cross it, alright?"

"Sounds fair," Violet agreed.

Just then, my phone vibrated in my pocket. Reaching for it, I saw that Jason was calling.

"Speak of the Devil," I murmured. "Excuse me for a minute."

To escape the music, I headed into the men's room before answering.

"Evening, J."

"Evening. Are you busy?"

His clipped tone made me frown. Something was clearly on his mind. "I'm having drinks with my colleagues. Why?"

"Have you got a minute?"

"Yeah, sure. What's the problem?"

While Jason hesitated to continue, I wondered if Cara was there or whether she was with *him*. She'd told me she had plans today, and I'd hoped all week that they were plans with Jason or her friend Olivia – not *him*.

"I've meant to ring you about something. Cara came home from work the other day, saying you'd fucked Francesca in your office and that you had made her work there afterwards. Is this true?"

```

To calm my nerves, I closed my eyes and pinched the bridge of my nose. I had anticipated that she would tell him this, but I hadn't expected Jason to be the one to confront me about it. For that reason, I required a moment to consider my next steps. The facts were simple. I didn't want to enlighten her just yet. At the same time, I had to reassure Jason somehow, but how to do it would depend on my overall goal.

As soon as the solution occurred to me, I opened my eyes and was welcomed by my reflection in the mirror. "No, Jason, that's not true."

"Thank god. I honestly almost believed it for a second."

"Did you? Why?"

"Well, she said you'd opened a window, that Francesca's hair was down, that your lips were red... Honestly, the list goes on." The details he included satisfied me immensely. I hadn't thought of the window till now, but what a happy coincidence that had been. She had noticed even more than I had, and it could only mean one thing – she had cared, and she had cared profusely.

I watched as a smirk made its way across my mouth. Finally, my method was showing results.

"Apparently," Jason continued, "another paralegal – I think her name is Ellie – is under the impression you tend to fuck Francesca in there, too."

Even though Elisabeth had unwittingly aided me in deceiving Cara, I grimaced when I heard that. Her tongue was far too loose for my liking. Still, I wondered if her taste for gossip had been exploited by Cara. Had she probed Elisabeth about my love life? That would surprise me. She didn't strike me as the type to dig into someone's private affairs, but if she had, I took it as a compliment, because it could only mean she still harboured some remnants of feelings for me.

"God. Fucking Elisabeth," I muttered, annoyed.

"Yeah, you should have a word with her. Sounds like she's spreading false rumours about you."

"Well, in her defence, I've fucked Francesca in my office before,
```

but I didn't on Wednesday. Still, I absolutely need to have a word with her."

"Will, what the hell? That's really unprofessional."

I rolled my eyes. "Spare me, Jason."

"No, I mean it. You can't keep doing that. Cara's been dreading going to work all week because of this incident. What you did made her feel seriously uncomfortable."

To hear that she had been dreading going to work ever since Francesca's visit inspired hope in me that her supposed discomfort was in fact jealousy in disguise. If I played my cards right, perhaps I could trick her into confessing it.

"Jason, listen. It won't happen again. Truth is, I ended things with Francesca on Wednesday, so you don't need to worry about that."

"You did?"

"Yeah, and she took me aback with a kiss. That should explain why my lips were a bit red."

"But I thought things were stable between you."

"A lot's happened lately. Anyway, regarding Cara, I ought to be the one to tell her, so I'd appreciate it if you refrained from saying anything. As her boss, I consider it my responsibility. I'm not happy to hear she's been feeling so uncomfortable about this, so I should be the one to explain things to her. After all, I'm best suited to answer any questions she may have."

"Yeah, you're probably right. Do it on Monday, though. As I said, she's been dreading going to work ever since it happened."

"Of course," I said, but now that the conversation had reached its end, I realised that one question remained, and the potential answer made me feel sick. "Is she with you right now?"

"No, she's with Livy, a friend of hers." Relieved, I exhaled a pent-up breath.

"Probably complaining about me," I murmured.

"I'd say that's a safe bet."

"Well then. Was that all?"

"Yeah."

"Why not come over and join us for a drink, Jase?" From his hesitation, I could tell he was on the fence. "Come on," I urged. "It'll be fun. Just don't get hammered again."

He chuckled. "Course I won't. Stephen and Jon won't be there to make sure of it."

"True. So you'll come, then?"

"Is Andy there?"

"He is."

"Alright. I don't see why not? I'll come for a pint."

"Great. I'll see you soon."

"Yeah."

After he rang off, I placed my phone back in my pocket and washed my hands. As I did, I gazed at my reflection and smirked.

In misery, we feel most alive, but also most alone. Fortunately, Cara seemed about to put me out of mine.

ALL THE BEST ONES ARE

CARA

"I'M GOING TO TAKE YOU NOW," HE WARNED, BREATH spreading across my face and my kiss-swollen lips. "And I assure you, love, you'll be feeling me for a week." A lecherous smile emerged on his mouth before he claimed mine. Untamed and powerful, he dominated me completely through a mere kiss.

I could hardly breathe. My heart threatened to burst with suspense. Finally, I would feel him enter me again, his perfect shaft thrusting in to reach a depth no other man had. I had longed to feel him buried inside me for months now, and for each day that had gone by, my lust for him had grown more extreme.

He pushed in, his gaze searing while he extracted a long moan of pleasure from my mouth. Clawing into his muscular back, my face contorted at the unmistakable sensation. *God,* he felt good, and he stretched me so far. Closing my eyes, I relished how complete I felt.

Never had I met a man more irritating, challenging, and yet so seductive. Against his allure, I was powerless, and he was finally claiming me as his own for the night. Caged beneath his strong, naked body, I marvelled. How had I ended up here again?

The same moment I thought it, I realised I was dreaming. Gasping awake, my eyes sprang wide. Glimpsing my alarm in the dark, I saw that it was six in the morning – too early to wake up, but too late to go back to sleep.

Groaning, I noticed how soaked I was. My juices covered the better part of my inner thighs, deriving from the cleft above which throbbed and tingled from the illusion of his touch. Clearly, they were called 'wet dreams' for a reason. However, waking up from one about none other than my boss was not an ideal way to start my day. What made it worse was that it was easily one of the most fantastic sex dreams I'd ever had, and he hadn't even made me orgasm. Though, last week, he had managed to on several occasions, albeit in my dreams and fantasies of him.

This was getting out of hand. Not even during sleep did he give me any space. He was driving me insane. Ever since Wednesday last week, his presence in my dreams had escalated in frequency, and I despised it. My subconscious clearly refused to let him go, despite how much I wanted it to.

In an attempt to exorcise him from my mind, I'd even gone so far as to masturbate to the thought of him a few times, but it hadn't helped at all. Time had shown that all it had done was reinforce my lust for him instead. Sleeping with Aaron on Saturday hadn't helped either. I'd been distracted under his touch, comparing it to my memory of William's, which had ultimately led Aaron's to lose its impact. I hadn't even been able to reach orgasm – I'd had to fake it – which was surely a first for me. In the three years I'd slept with Aaron, I had never been unable to climax – until now.

It infuriated me. William had clearly moved on, so why couldn't I? Why had my body latched onto the memory of him like this?

A few tearless sobs escaped me while I rubbed my face. Pushing my duvet aside, I stepped out of bed to prepare for another intense day under his smouldering glare. Trapped in the consequent daze of my erotic dream, I showered for longer than usual, as if the hot stream of water would cleanse my mind, too, and wash away my lust for William.

When I eventually finished, I walked dispiritedly out of the glass cage to wipe a line of condensation off the bathroom mirror. Leaning towards my reflection, I saw how discouraged I looked. My freckles were fainter than they tended to be, and purple bags had gathered under my eyes.

I watched as a frown surfaced. "Stop thinking of him, Cara. He's your goddamned boss," I scolded and opened my second drawer to fetch my makeup kit.

I started by moisturising my face, hoping it would treat the symptoms of my exhaustion. Then, I grabbed my corrector to apply it under my eyes before I covered the deep pinkish tint with my concealer. Soon enough, I'd managed to hide away any sign of sleep deprivation. Since I preferred a natural look, I didn't apply anything else to my skin. As I got started on my eyes, on a whim I decided to add a very faint smoky eye to the mixture. I would look fiercer like this. Ready to attack the day. Ready to fend off any daydreams about my tantalising boss.

§ § §

As intended, I arrived before him. Since he had wanted me to work from his office all of last week, I headed straight into it at ten to eight to clear his desk and organise the files on it for him. While he would likely assume that I had done it as a favour to him, I was in fact determined to do it solely because I couldn't stand untidiness. Mum had always said, "Order around you, order within you", and that statement of hers had stayed with me. Unlike Dad, she and I had always shared a passion for cleaning, and I was about to put it to good use.

At two minutes to eight, my gaze dashed to the door and I saw the handle turn. In stepped William, and the grin he presented nearly made me sob. The fact that he looked even better in reality than in my dreams was hardly fair. Looking him in the eye now, especially after I'd just had a vivid and erotic dream about him, was not something I desired. To keep from blushing was impossible, and I was certain he noticed the new colour of my face because his grin suddenly broadened.

"Morning, Cara. Blushing merely at the sight of me, are you? I'm flattered."

"Don't point it out," I muttered and looked back to the files. "And don't flatter yourself. I'm blushing only because you caught me tidying up your mess, and I don't want you thinking it's to suck up to you."

He shut the door and approached. "Someone got out of bed on the wrong side."

My heart plummeted when he placed a Starbucks cup in front of me. He had to stop doing this. I couldn't stand his kindness. All it did was remind me of how irresistible he was. If he kept this up, I might as well wave my sanity goodbye.

"Perhaps this will help," he said.

I couldn't bring myself to look at him. "You need to stop bringing me coffees, Will."

"Er, why? I swear I'm not poisoning them."

Though I hated it, his joke managed to leave a brief, faint smile on my mouth. Keeping my eyes on his desk, I tried to hide it. "Because it's unnecessary. I've got a machine at home."

"So? I thought it could be a nice custom. Besides, you can't make flat whites at home, can you?"

I let out a loud breath. "I don't need flat whites."

"Well, I've got to stop by the shop anyway. Might as well—"

"Fine."

My hostile attitude made him pause. "Are you alright?"

"Yes, I'm fine. Sorry."

What he did next nearly made me smile again. Very slowly, he proceeded to push the coffee towards me, as though I were a wild animal that would chew off his hand if he did anything too abrupt.

To get this moment out of the way, I grabbed it with a sigh

and raised it to read the black ink. *True grit*, it said, and my heart skipped a beat.

I swallowed. Was it a reference to our conversation the night we'd met? What else could it mean? Was it merely a coincidence? Or was he implying perseverance? Then, regarding what? Me? Was this his way of telling me that he wasn't giving up? Or was he trying to tell *me* not to give up – on him?

No, he wouldn't do that. He couldn't possibly be trying to flirt with me – not when he had Francesca.

None the wiser, I turned my attention to him. "What's this supposed to mean?"

He shrugged. "Just some innocent inspirational words for our new trainee. You've done an excellent job so far, and I wanted to motivate you to continue with it."

My eyes narrowed suspiciously. "Hm. 'True grit' sounds familiar, though."

I was certain the same memory I was thinking of flared through his eyes then. "Does it?"

"Never mind," I mumbled, because I didn't feel like giving him the satisfaction of knowing my thoughts. Pretending I didn't remember anything from our first encounter at all was much more tempting. "Thanks."

"I'll help you out," he said after he'd rounded his desk to leave his bag on the floor, and his immediate proximity made me freeze. Delicious electricity seemed to charge between our bodies when his beautiful hands reached out to organise a stack of paper, and mercy was nowhere to be found when I caught his seductive scent.

"I can do it," I said, because his closeness was clouding my thoughts.

"I know you can, but four hands will get the job done quicker."

I grew quiet.

"That's a lovely perfume you're wearing," he murmured after a while, and my blush intensified. Could he stop being so goddamned charming? I had to move on, but he was making it impossible.

"What's it called?"

"It's called none of your business," I replied impassively.

He chuckled. "Christ. It was only a compliment. What's got your knickers in such a twist?"

You.

"Sorry. Time of the month," I lied.

"Ah. I'll tread gently."

"Do you ever?" I had said it under my breath, but when his hands froze, it was apparent he'd heard me.

After a brief pause, he leaned forwards to lock eyes with me, and his glowed with a strictness that I found oddly arousing. "I do not appreciate your passive-aggressive behaviour right now. If there's something you'd like to say, be direct about it."

Ripping my gaze from his, I glared away and wondered for a moment whether to tell him that I hadn't remotely appreciated his conduct last week with regards to Francesca's visit. At the same time, I was reluctant to enlighten him, as it could inspire him to think that I was only jealous, which I wasn't. If he got that impression, I feared it could make things awkward between us.

"Sorry," I eventually mumbled. "You're right. You didn't deserve that. I'll remedy my mood pronto."

"Thanks."

A period of silence elapsed, and I spent it dreading the rest of my day here. I hoped Francesca or another lover wouldn't make an appearance, but if it were to happen, I hoped he'd retain the decency not to ask me to work in his office straight afterwards, like he had on Wednesday.

We spent another five minutes on the task before we got started on actual work, and we hardly exchanged a word until lunch. Even so, I caught him stealing glances at me so often that my irritation with him continued to increase. I hated being placed under his microscope, so I didn't want to work in here. I wanted to work next to Elisabeth. His presence was bothering me immensely – his whole existence was.

He was my boss, and I was madly attracted to him. Watching him sit there in his light grey suit with that olive green tie around his neck – a neck which I had ravished with kisses some months ago – was beyond frustrating. Though I'd never been religious, I could relate to Eve's time in Eden. Though, in my case, Eden was my job – my personal paradise. The serpent was my lust for William, always whispering in the back of my mind, trying to tempt me into tasting the forbidden fruit that was my boss – William fucking Night. Truly, the more we interacted, the harder it was to resist him, and it pissed me off.

I'd have to think of something to rectify this situation. Being in his audience was far too distracting – it was difficult to maintain a strict focus on work. So easily, my thoughts ventured into erotic fantasies about him. I could hardly look into his eyes without seeing the sizzling gaze he'd once trapped me with, when I'd been spread flat across his dining table.

Groaning to myself, I decided I'd hit the gym straight after work. Perhaps blowing off some steam would quell my lust for him, at least for a while. Indeed, to tackle this, I would make the gym my go-to place for therapy in order to cure my anger and frustration with myself. I'd exhaust myself completely, to the point where I wouldn't have energy left to spare for anything other than breathing.

§ § §

Over lunch, I hardly shared a word with anyone. Violet tried to strike up a conversation with me, but I was dismissive in my replies because I was preoccupied with my thoughts. She didn't seem offended, though, for which I was grateful, but then she didn't strike me as the sensitive type either. Besides, while she was trying to talk to me, all I could think was that she might be trying to play me for a fool. I knew perfectly well that she had been, and perhaps still was, William's regular partner, so I was suspicious of her friendliness. It was perfectly possible that her interest was innocent, but part of me wondered whether her curiosity was based solely on the fact that we had shared a man.

Regardless, I decided to give her the benefit of the doubt, because there was something about her character that I found rather agreeable. Perhaps it was her assertiveness, or perhaps it was her intelligence. Either way, she had acquired my respect, so while I was dismissive, I was also polite about it.

When Andy tried to get a word out of me, asking how things were going for me thus far, I had enough. So, after replying, I stood from my chair to declare that I wanted to get back to work.

Dropping his fork, William nodded his head without looking at me. "I'll come with."

"No, I'll be fine," I rushed to say, because I was eager for some space from him. "Please, enjoy the rest of your lunch."

He pushed his seat out. "I'm finished."

I cursed inwardly.

§ § §

At half three, I attended the meeting that William had with our client Clifford Paints to go over the draft version of the NDA. Elisabeth had joined us for it to write the report, so I looked over her shoulder a lot while William discussed the specifics of the NDA. Fortunately, I managed to resist admiring him this time around and instead remained focused on what was being said. Once it concluded, it was nearly five o'clock, and I caught myself hoping that William wouldn't ask me to stay longer to complete the report or polish the NDA. If he did, I considered whether to ask him if I could do it from home instead, as I was all too eager to depart from his presence and hit the gym.

Shortly after William had seen our client out, he returned to the meeting room and answered my prayers by ordering Elisabeth to stay longer instead, but his strict tone surprised me. However, Elisabeth seemed unfazed, so I got the impression he frequently spoke to her that way.

Curious, I decided to ask him, "How come Ellie puts up with your barking?" as we journeyed back to his office.

Towering beside me, he scoffed. "I do not bark."

"You did just now."

"The appropriate thing to call it is delegating responsibilities."

I nodded. "While barking." When I looked at him, I thought I detected a ghost of a smile on his mouth.

He shook his head and opened the door to his office for me. "Call it what you want. She puts up with it because she knows I actually respect her. I've grown on her. Perhaps I'll grow on you too."

Hearing that was the last straw. I did not want him to grow on me at all. Frankly, I wanted him as far away from me as possible. Losing my patience, I tactlessly replied, "I'd prefer cancer," just as I passed him.

I had not expected him to react the way he did, so a loud gasp stormed out of my mouth when he suddenly gripped my wrist to yank me back harshly. Colliding into him, I staggered back a step until the fury in his eyes rendered me paralysed.

To reduce the distance between us, he lowered his head, and his glare contained such heat that my eyes were scorched.

"Right," he growled and slammed the door shut. "That's enough. Talk to me. *Now.*" It was a command.

Instantly nervous, my body turned rigid while a faint, "What?" poured out of my mouth. He stepped closer, eyes narrowing accusingly, and my heart responded by drumming the beats of a dramatic orchestra inside my chest.

"Something's clearly wrong," he said. "You avoided me all of last week, and today you've hardly said a word – and when you do, you're grumpy and rude."

His audacity extracted another gasp from my mouth. "Rude?" I echoed disbelievingly and twisted my wrist out of his grip. "*I'm* rude?" I'd reached the end of my tether. "Says the man who fucks a girl in his office and makes his colleague work there straight afterwards."

His reaction bewildered me. Not a single flicker of emotion crossed his face, and it made him impossible to understand. "There it is," he said and folded his arms.

"What is?" I bit out.

"The reason. Why didn't you tell me immediately?"

My eyebrows arched. This conversation wasn't heading in the direction I had anticipated at all. Nonplussed, I struggled to make sense of what to think. Since I had no idea how to respond, I was quiet for a moment, and he spent it patiently observing me.

"Why didn't I tell you?" I repeated his question to buy myself more time. "Well, if you would use the right head for once, perhaps you'd understand why."

He pressed his lips together upon my phrasing, and I suspected it was to hide a smile. "Enlighten me, then."

Agitated, I motioned towards him. "Are you being serious? Have you got any brain cells to speak of?" Or was it all just sperm?

He shrugged. "Treat me like I don't."

I gnashed my teeth. He was clearly determined to drag the words from my mouth. "I didn't think it was my place to say anything, and I was worried you'd get the wrong impression if I did. Moreover, you're my boss. In case you need your memory jogged, I'm brand new at this job, and I'm still trying to find my footing round here. Scolding my superior for his lack of work ethics isn't exactly a tempting thing to do on my third day."

He nodded. "I'll agree on one count, which is your remark about my lack of work ethics. But I'll need you to elaborate on why you were worried that it would give me the wrong impression."

My cheeks boiled. Frowning, I broke contact with his eyes and clutched my computer to my chest to hide my unruly heart. "I didn't want you to think that I was jealous because you're seeing someone else, because I am not."

Since he didn't immediately respond, I couldn't resist glancing at him. When I did, I discovered him regarding me with a raised brow. His scepticism was obvious, and I hated it.

"You're lying," he dared accuse.

"I'm not," I retorted defensively.

He sighed. "You are. I wish you'd admit it. This is becoming ridiculous, Cara."

Appalled by his claim, I replied fiercely, "You're utterly conceited. There's nothing to admit." Turning on my heel, I was about to approach his desk when he once again locked my wrist in his grip to make me face him.

"Admit you were upset about it," he demanded. "Not because you had to sit there but because you thought I was with someone else."

At first, my instinct was to refute it, but as I processed his phrasing, a single question left me stunned. "What?" I queried instead. "What do you mean when you say 'thought'?"

Releasing my wrist, he folded his arms and glared at me. "I mean exactly that – you assumed."

My lips parted. "You didn't have sex with her?" I questioned in my disbelief. I'd been so sure. Nothing else made sense. What else had they been doing? Even Elisabeth had thought they'd had sex.

He shook his head. "No. I didn't."

Several seconds elapsed while I tried to make sense of the facts. "But her hair," I probed in my confusion. "The window, your lips…."

He remained silent. The bright light of day reflected against the sharpness of his jaw, and I watched as it clenched and unclenched several times.

The more I remembered the scene, the more severe my confusion became. "You even asked me to bring my computer with me, and the way you said it…"

"You jumped to conclusions."

Mortified, blood drained from my face. "I…I'm so sorry." Grimacing, I averted my eyes and scolded myself for having been so quick to assume the worst. I couldn't believe I'd just accused my boss of something like this without any firm evidence whatsoever. What had got into me? "Please, forgive me. I don't know what came over me. I…" I pressed my computer to my chest. "It won't happen again."

We were quiet for some time. Eventually, a loud sigh travelled out of his mouth. "Please, don't apologise. I'm the one who's truly in the wrong here."

Nonplussed, I looked at him. "How?"

Nervous, he unfolded his arms to run a hand through his hair. While avoiding my eyes, he said, "It was intentional."

Unsure of what he meant, I frowned. "I'm not sure I understand," I said, but the instant after the words had left my mouth, the unlikely truth dawned on me. My eyes widened. "You did this on purpose?" I asked, shocked.

"I…" His face contorted. "Sort of."

He didn't dare so much as a glance in my direction while I stared at him, speechless. I'd always known he was cunning, but this was beyond anything I'd imagined. Frankly, to think he was capable of something so calculated and callous intimidated me immensely. If he were truly capable of orchestrating schemes like these, I would need to keep a much keener eye on him in the future.

Still, while his method had been morally dubious, I harboured no doubt that he had done it solely to provoke a reaction in me. He'd been trying to trigger a sign of my affection. To a certain extent, the end could justify the means because of that. Ultimately, some part of me found it flattering. However, the larger part of me was distraught that he would allow himself to hurt me like that, especially deliberately. The idea that he was willing to manipulate me was completely abhorrent.

"I'm sorry," he said after a while, and I could both hear from his tone and see from his behaviour that he was upset at what he'd done.

"You're sorry?" I asked while my heart slowed. "What exactly are you sorry for, Will?"

He grimaced, and his obvious shame prevented him from meeting my gaze. "For making you believe I was with someone else," he mumbled, upset. "For letting you believe I did to her what I should only be doing to you."

I was far too appalled by what he had done to fall victim to his incidental declaration of devotion. Indeed, sympathy was miles from his reach right now. Instead, anger erupted in my chest. "You manipulated me," I accused.

He winced. "I know. I'm sorry."

"This is outrageous!"

"Cara, I'm sorry. Please, forgive me. I've meant to correct your impression all day."

"All day!" I echoed, astounded. "You shouldn't have had to in the first place!"

He lost his bearings. "You gave me no choice!"

My lips parted at his attempt to turn the tables. "You're doing it again! How dare you? I won't tolerate being manipulated like this! 'Gave you no choice' my fucking arse, Will! Piss off!" Furious, I stormed to his desk to pack my things. I didn't want to spend another second in here.

"Please, can we talk about this?" he entreated.

My tone was saturated with venom when I caustically replied, "What – so you can try to manipulate me again?"

He exhaled loudly. "Cara, please. I swear I won't do something like that ever again."

Whipping my head around, I glowered at him. "Why the hell should I believe a word you're saying?"

When our eyes collided, a lump gathered in my throat, as I could see that his were shinier than usual. Tears were threatening. It was clearly a genuine reaction, and it stirred my sympathy somewhat, so I calmed.

"Cara, I made a mistake – I know I did. I won't repeat it. Please." He grimaced. "What I did – it wasn't premeditated. I just saw a chance and I took it. I was desperate to find out where you stand. It's been a whole month since…"

"I've told you a million times where I stand," I replied impatiently.

He looked so broken where he stood, eyes wide while he struggled to find a safe place to rest them. Quietly, he asked, "I just need to know – can you honestly say you haven't got any feelings for me at all?"

Since I hadn't expected his question, my heart jumped to my throat. Quickly, I looked away to think. It was paramount that I considered my reply carefully. Pressing my lips together, I closed my bag and turned to face him. "William, it doesn't matter whether I do or not. I'm not inclined to pursue a relationship with you – with anyone! I want to be single. As I've told you, I want to focus on my career and myself, at least for another couple of years."

He blew his cheeks out, and he looked about to explode with exasperation. "You don't deny it, then."

I released a moan of despair. "William, you're not listening to me. You're focusing on the wrong thing. I'm not available. Yes, if I had been interested in a relationship, and if you hadn't been Jason's brother, and my boss, you'd be the man I'd want to try it with, but that's not the case, and I'm begging you to acknowledge that."

He nodded repeatedly, but I could tell he was struggling to remain composed. Considerable stress radiated from his demeanour. With fleeting eyes, he asked, "So, you weren't upset about Francesca?"

Realising he required full transparency, I sighed to myself. It was obvious he wouldn't let this go unless I explained the dissonance between my feelings and my convictions in depth. Grabbing my bag, I approached his figure by the door. Pain and panic poured from his eyes, and the sight cut into my chest like knives. A foot away from him, I halted, and it took me a moment before I decided to bite the bullet.

"No, I was upset about Francesca," I confessed. "I wasn't jealous, but it hurt to think that you had moved on. However, that's just my feelings, and I don't intend to act on them. They'll pass. They always do. Knowing that, I've been determined not to get in the way of you two. I've relinquished my claim on you, and I plan to respect that. So, if you mean to keep seeing her – and Violet, for that matter – you shouldn't consider my feelings. I've no right to them, and I know that, so I wouldn't dream of behaving as though I do. That said, I'd appreciate if you didn't fuck them here, but aside from that, I won't stand in your way. I've got no right to."

He sighed, and from his wandering gaze, I could tell he was despairing.

"I want you to be happy, Will. You deserve a woman who recognises your worth and who wants to give you everything – someone who's got space for you and who will put you first – someone who isn't me."

Fixing his eyes on me, he looked at me as if I were the dawn when all he'd ever known was the dark of night. "But I don't want anyone else."

My breath caught. I tried to swallow, but my throat was aching so terribly that it did little to ease the pain. "Perhaps if you actually gave Violet or Francesca a real chance, you would."

I didn't think I'd heard him right when he disclosed, "I've already ended things with them both."

"What?" I breathed out. "Why? When?"

He waved his hand in the air. "Violet about a month ago. Francesca a bit less. As it happens, Francesca showed up on Wednesday to beg me for a second chance."

Pity swam in my eyes when I tried to make contact with his, but from his behaviour, I got the feeling he couldn't bear the sight of me. "You should have given it."

He shook his head. "No."

"You're not mine, Will."

I stopped breathing when he suddenly raised his hand towards my face. Curling his index finger beneath my chin, he tilted my head back and captured my gaze completely. "But I am," he asserted. His face didn't even twitch. Unyielding, he stared fixedly at me.

Disbelieving of what he had just said, my body started to tremble. Intense heat engulfed my cheeks, and when he saw it, a faint smile crowded his mouth, but there was sadness in it – wistfulness. His eyes travelled across my face to savour the pinkness, and after a while, his smile transitioned into the unsullied and crooked version that I often saw in my dreams.

"I am open to something more only with you," he professed, and hearing it expelled all air from my lungs. After everything I had just said, I struggled to fathom that he remained loyal to me.

"Are you actually mad?" I asked, entirely overwhelmed.

The sound of his miserable chuckle made my heart throb, but the emotion in his eyes nearly made it explode. "All the best ones are," he replied, and the reference to one of my favourite classics from childhood left a coy smile on my mouth. I'd told him that *Alice's Adventures in Wonderland* had a special place in my heart during our lunch at Farm Girl in May, and I was charmed he still remembered.

"I should go," I said.

He brushed his thumb across my cheek before withdrawing his hand, and the absence of his touch had never felt more noticeable. "Before you do, will you forgive me?"

I sighed. Of course I forgave him. "I'm not one to stay angry. However, you can be sure I'll be keeping a keen eye on you from here on out."

He grinned, and it was exhilarating to see him so relieved. It was evident that his conscience had truly weighed him down, and I appreciated seeing that, as it assured me he had one at all.

"I won't fuck up like that again," he promised.

"Please don't."

"I won't," he stressed. "I swear."

I nodded. "Friends, then?"

Wrinkles formed across his nose, and I could understand why, because the term didn't suit us in the slightest. It was too poor a label to do our bond and chemistry justice.

"Let's just be *us*," he proposed instead.

I gave him a lopsided smile. "*Us*, then."

Without another word, he stepped aside to open the door for me. "I'll see you tomorrow."

"Yeah. No schemes then, Will," I reminded him strictly.

"No schemes."

As I walked out, everything seemed bizarre. My body felt like a gooey mess, all because of his amorous declarations.

Had he truly meant what he'd said?

21

JUST GIVE IT A THOUGHT

B
ECAUSE I'D HAD NO IDEA OF WHAT TO WEAR, I'D SETTLED
for a maroon-coloured Bardot dress that hugged my curves.
In it, I felt opulent – ready to seduce the night.

It was Friday now, and Elisabeth had begged me all week
to join her to meet her fiancé Brian at a club after we'd had a
few drinks with our colleagues at Disrepute. That was why I had
struggled to decide what to wear tonight. It wasn't easy to find a
dress that would be suitable for a posh cocktail bar, as well as on
the dance floor, but I was pleased with my choice.

However, since Disrepute also happened to be the place where
I had first met William, returning there wasn't something I had
particularly looked forward to. I was certain the surroundings would
evoke the memory of his skilful hands sliding across my body while
he thrust powerfully into me – again, and again, and again.

And I'd been right. Aroused, I inhaled sharply, eyes searching
for his presence, but it was nowhere to be found. Nevertheless,
I could have sworn I felt him within me then, hard and forceful

while he reached deeper than any other man had, elevating me to a delirious state of pleasure.

I had just arrived and was sitting with Elisabeth when Lawrence came through the doors. Because I hoped that every person who entered would be William, I had refused to look, and I had because I didn't want to give him the satisfaction of discovering my foolish expectation. However, I had no guarantee he'd show up at all. Sometime after lunch, he'd asked whether I was coming today, and once I'd confirmed that Elisabeth had persuaded me, he'd fallen silent. I'd asked whether he would come as well, but his reply hadn't been definitive. All he'd said was, "I'm not sure yet."

Since it was only Lawrence who had arrived, my heart sank with disappointment, but at least I could dare to look properly in his direction.

He wasn't the tallest man. I'd noted the first time we'd met that we were around the same height – five-foot-eight. Despite that, there was something about his general demeanour that made him easy to notice in a crowd anyway.

I'd barely spoken to him, but I liked him so far. He was a quiet type, always brooding, with eyes that were such a dark brown that they bordered on black, and his skin was paler than even mine. The dark circles around his eyes made him look constantly sleep-deprived, and yet somehow, it suited him. He seemed more mysterious that way – and he was mysterious. He'd hardly said a word to me since I started. It was Elisabeth who had informed me that he was thirty-five years old and married to a male nurse with whom he had two young children.

Elisabeth called him over while I considered my situation.

It was weird to be back. Last time I'd been here, I'd been swept away by William's unconventional charm. My heart tingled at the memory. I'd wanted to strangle and praise him at the same time. That hadn't changed. Odd how he managed to divide me like that. I liked to think I was a collected person, but William severed that notion apart. That night, he'd nearly ruined my defences, and I was still working on returning them to their original strength.

Lately, he had made that job much easier for me, because after I'd confronted him about his inappropriate behaviour, he'd actually left me alone. Though he had continued to bring a cup of coffee for me in the mornings, it no longer carried inappropriate or cryptic messages. All that was written on it was my name. He had also made a point ever since of avoiding having lunch with Elisabeth and me. Even today, when Andy had decided to join us, he had kept his distance and had instead lunched with John. And whenever he talked to me, he kept it professional and discussed solely work.

It was like night and day. Finally, he was respecting my boundaries, like I'd demanded – like I was merely a colleague to him and nothing more. Judging from his recent behaviour, he had at last decided to stow our sensual night together into oblivion – our past forgotten. Staying true to his word, it was apparent that he intended to respect my wishes, and while I mainly appreciated it, a small part of me did wonder now and then whether rejecting him had been the right choice. After all, I couldn't deny that I was attracted to him, but this seemed like the best – if not only – solution.

However, when he walked through the door half an hour later, my beliefs were put on trial. Powerful and magnetic, he exuded a will that petrified those contesting it. He was unbearably elegant and alluringly self-assured. I could see it in his strides. He carried himself with pride and grace, as if nothing could shake him.

While he put the whole place to shame on his way to the bar, his magnificent eyes scanned the room – browsing, browsing, and then they met mine.

My breath abandoned me as I pressed my thighs together beneath the table. Merely with a glance, he had soaked my underwear. Damn it. What was my body doing, getting all hot and bothered under his attention? It wasn't being particularly cooperative.

Trapped under his seemingly unbreakable spell, I blatantly ogled him from where I sat. He was wearing a shirt that matched the colour of my dress, and it made his eyes sparkle. A grey waistcoat encased his powerful chest and torso, and the sight made me wet my lips. Below the red material, grey trousers matched his vest.

He was quite the vision. It wasn't fair that he should be so well endowed when he was both my boss and my flatmate's brother. I didn't deserve to suffer like this.

Suddenly, fingers snapped in front of my face, breaking me out of my trance. Blinking, I turned my head to find Elisabeth's frown.

"Shit!" I squeezed my eyes shut, wildly embarrassed. She'd caught me again.

"You're hopeless," she scolded me, albeit amusedly.

"Sorry. Thank you for—" I paused—"helping me out," I continued with a pout and dragged my espresso martini back to my mouth.

She tossed her head back as she laughed. "That's what I'm here for, love. And I don't blame you. He's been keeping a keen eye on you ever since you started. Honestly, I feel bad for you. Had I not been happily in love with Brian, I would have drooled after him all day long, too – especially if he handed me that sort of attention."

Her words held comfort. Then again, I could always count on Elisabeth to offer a sympathetic shoulder.

"Ladies," Andy greeted from our side then. "You look dashing," he continued and chose the seat next to mine. With a playful gleam in his kind brown eyes, he turned towards me. "*Cara*," he emphasised. "You look like you frequent this place." My eyes widened at his unexpected insinuation. What impeccably slick humour. "That colour on you should be illegal," he continued to flatter to conceal his surreptitious poke.

I arched my brow at him and proceeded to study his own choice of colours. Wearing white, grey and beige, he looked positively edible.

"You look rather good yourself, Andy," Elisabeth pointed out and tilted her head. "Still single? Or has that changed since last?"

"Semi-single." What was that supposed to mean?

"Elaborate," Elisabeth requested.

He sighed and leaned his back against the chair he'd grabbed. "Chloe's difficult. She wants children. I'm not ready for that yet. Because we're not on the same wavelength, she's told me to make up my mind. Either I have to let her go or go all the way with her. So, while I make up my mind, we're on a version of a break."

Sympathising with his distress, I gaped. What an ultimatum.

"You've been together for a decade, Andy," Elisabeth murmured. "It's not surprising she's reached that point."

He looked displeased as he stared at her for a beat. "Well, when she puts it like that, I feel like my only purpose is to impregnate her. It's not romantic. I don't feel seen. I just feel like a bag of sperm she desperately wants. And I've always been scared of babies. I'm not ready to change nappies and clean up spew, and I am definitely not ready to sleep three hours a night. I'm building my career, Ellie. Children will have to wait until I've reached a stable point in it."

I was surprised to learn I had so much in common with Andy. Suddenly, I liked him much more, because he was finally starting to make sense to me. We were similar. I was certain I would have reacted precisely the same way if my partner had demanded we conceive.

Elisabeth rested her cheek in her hand while patience emitted from her eyes. "Well, do you think she'll change her mind?"

A sigh left Andy's mouth, and I could hear that it had come from his heart. "I'm negotiating it with her. I'm trying to make her give me a few more years. I started with five, but she drives a hard bargain, so I'm down to three at the moment. She keeps going on about female fertility depreciation, and saying that our children are more likely to have biological problems the longer we wait, things like that."

I pursed my lips because I found this information somewhat hilarious. True to his title as a solicitor, he was treating it like a case.

"But do you love her?" Elisabeth brought herself to ask.

He stiffened, and from his frown, I could tell her question had offended him. "Of course I love her. I can't imagine my life without her in it. We've been together for ten years, Ellie. I've forgotten what it feels like not to love her."

"Well, at least you're certain about that," she responded, visibly charmed.

From behind, William's voice rang through me. "Give her the bloody baby, Andy. Hire an au pair if time's becoming a problem. You've got the money."

I froze when I felt the heat of his body radiate against my own. How close was he?

I had my answer when he leaned across my shoulder to place a gin and tonic in front of me. Afterwards, he relocated his hand to my naked shoulder. His touch burnt like wildfire and sent delicious electricity throughout my body. Hyperaware of his hand on me, I didn't dare to face him. I was much too overwhelmed.

Andy bent his neck to look up at him as he stood behind us. "I've already heard your opinion, Will – ten thousand times. Give it a rest already. It won't be your baby to deal with."

William sent him a smirk. "No. But if I were in your shoes, I'd give her the baby. Andy, last time you and Chloe hit a bump in the road, you lost the plot. You can't manage without her. If you let her go, you'll regret it for the rest of your life."

"I'm with Will on this one," Elisabeth chimed in.

I remained completely silent, pretending not to exist. This was not a discussion I wanted to get involved in. I knew too little to be able to form an opinion, but from the little I knew, I was honestly inclined to support Andy.

"What about you, Cara? Are you with me?" William asked and successfully ruined my efforts to evade the topic. Bending my neck slightly backwards, I met his smouldering eyes. I wanted to submerge myself in them, swim in the sensual pleasures they whispered of. Bewitched, I watched him – and forgot all about his question.

"I think you've dazzled her," Andy laughed softly when I failed to respond. His comment dragged me back. Whipping my head forward again, I looked towards the toilets. I had to escape William's attention somehow. He looked nothing short of devastating, and I was clearly still susceptible to his allures.

"I'm not dazzled," I lied. "I'd just rather not comment on something that is absolutely none of my business. I think we should let Andy decide for himself. Anyway, excuse me," I said and pushed my seat out.

"Thanks, Cara," Andy replied, and the affection in his voice made me give him a smile.

As I approached the ladies' room, I sensed William's stare burning into my back the entire time.

Though it hadn't been urgent, I decided that I might as well relieve my bladder. I required a minute to muster my strength before I could dare go outside again. Being in the presence of William was like high-intensity interval training: quick breaks to regain my strength before I'd push myself to the limit again, and with each interval, my overall strength declined.

"Fuck," I muttered and was shaking my head to myself when I eventually headed out of the stall to wash my hands. That was when Violet's presence startled me. She was leaning over the basins, drawing on a thin layer of nude lipstick while she studied her plump lips in the mirror. In the reflection, I saw her brown eyes swivel sideways when she heard my exit.

"Cara," she greeted me with a smile. "You look lovely."

I batted my lashes before I studied her from head to toe. She was wearing a beautiful black dress that clung to her curvaceous figure. She had such a beautiful bum, full and perky, and it was pointing straight at me. Between her incredible body and keen intellect, Phoebe would have lost her mind over Violet, and frankly, my bi-curious side was, too.

"Thank you, Violet. So do you," I finally replied and approached the basin by her side.

"How have you found your first weeks with us?" she queried while she searched through her purse for her blush.

"Exciting," I answered as I collected soap in my hand.

"Good. I've come across some of your work. The NDA you drafted for Clifford Paints was excellent. I was impressed." A sweet smile presented itself on her lips.

She intrigued me. Did she like me, or did she not? I couldn't be sure. Then again, she didn't strike me as the sort of woman who bothered much about men. My impression of her was that she was not the type to grow bitter and petty solely because I often interacted with her past plaything. On the contrary, I found her integrity rather apparent.

"Well, you've impressed me during every meeting," I replied as I cleaned my hands under the tap.

"Have I?" She smirked. "Has Will impressed you as well? I think he wants to."

Startled by her insinuation, I froze beside her. Was she jealous? When I looked over, she sent me a knowing look.

"Listen," she murmured and brushed a few strands of her hair away. "He told me you know about us."

My face paled. Why had he done that? "It's not my business," I squeaked and avoided her eyes.

She reached forward to grab my arm. "Cara, don't worry. I'm not angry with you at all. I know you didn't ask him to end things – he's told me that. I just need you to listen for a second."

To assess her sincerity, I met her eyes, and when convinced, my shoulders relaxed.

She sighed and shook her head to herself while muttering under her breath, "I can't believe I'm doing this."

Doing what? I was about to ask when she raised her finger at me.

"Though he's easily misunderstood, Will is in fact a remarkably good man, and he's an outstanding solicitor – one of the best of his generation. In many ways, he's the spitting image of John." Well, I could agree with that. "They have this unique assertiveness about them. They don't waste time getting things done, and they don't stop until they've reached their goals. But unfortunately, Will's brilliance doesn't always extend to women. Because of his assertive character, he can come across as a tad too calculating and aggressive."

A gap formed between my lips. He'd told her? How close

were they?

"But just—" she sighed—"please, cut him some slack. He's trying very hard with you. I can tell. Aside from Andy and his father, I know him better than anyone else in this firm. I truly wish for him to see his efforts pay off. I've never seen him like this."

Well, I surely hadn't foreseen that. "I...I appreciate the sentiment, Violet, but Will and I have already talked about this."

She gave me an embarrassed smile. "I know, and I'm sorry for meddling. I just can't help but think you're making a mistake. If you've actually got feelings for him, giving him a chance is the best thing you can do. I swear you'll be rewarded tenfold."

Unsure of how to react, a titter escaped me. "I hadn't expected you to be so supportive."

She chuckled. "Did you think I'd be bitter?"

"Perhaps slightly more bitter than this, but not much," I admitted.

"Well, I'm not at all. He's all yours. I've never had feelings for him – only respect and a friendly fondness." Was William to her what Aaron was to me? "And perhaps a little lust, but honestly, he's a bloody gorgeous man, so who could blame me? Anyway, I'll stay away from now on. I hope you're not angry with me for sleeping with him."

I looked to the heavens for aid, utterly despairing. Why did everybody seem to think that William was mine? "Violet, I'm not remotely angry with you. He's not...mine, for lack of a better word. I don't understand where all of this is coming from."

"He could be, if you wanted," she countered with a shrewd smile. "Give it a thought, Cara. You're just a trainee. You can reciprocate his flirting. It won't get in the way of you getting hired later. People marry their colleagues all the time. As long as you conduct your affair appropriately, no one's going to care. Besides, I'm sure John would be delighted to have you on board, regardless of you and Will. You're a clever girl. You'd be an asset without a doubt." She folded her arms before she continued, "And I'd love to see you make him happy. I've had a few cocktails already, so excuse me for speaking out of turn about all this, but you know as well as I do that he is exceptional in bed. Why settle for any less when you can have him?" She sounded baffled. "So yes, he's a bit of a challenge on certain fronts, but overall, he compensates for that with his intellect and personality. Honestly, he'll make you feel like a goddess if you just give him a chance."

Shocked by how blunt she was with me, I blushed crimson. I hardly knew her, and yet, I did appreciate it. She was authentic, real – and clearly a bit drunk, but then at least her heart was in the right place.

"Just give it a thought," she repeated and sent me a wink before she headed towards the door. When she opened it, she eyed me over her shoulder. "Oh, and this conversation never happened. He'd break my neck."

I swallowed the massive lump that had gathered in my throat and nodded. As soon as the door shut after her, I propped my hip against the counter and felt my pent-up breath leave me. She and William really were eerily similar. Perhaps that was why I found myself slightly attracted to her as well.

Turning towards the mirror, I studied my reflection. I'd gone for smokier eye makeup than usual, but it looked good. I hadn't overdone it. According to Jason, it didn't look like somebody had tried to punch me to death, which he had said as he drooled after my figure sauntering down the hall. Like his brother, Jason was terrific at offering compliments. His body language even more so. I'd felt like a million quid when I'd left our flat today, confident in my strut.

When another lady walked into the room, I was dragged back to reality. It was time to step outside again. I was quite confident that a certain someone had been counting the seconds I'd spent in here, and for each one that had ticked by, I imagined his overbearing character becoming increasingly impatient and concerned. So, with my chin raised, I returned to the bar, where I saw that a group of men had replaced William and Andy, and they were all chatting with Elisabeth.

Scouting the room, I eventually located William and Andy by the bar. A herd of girls surrounded them now, circling the two lads like vultures. There were six of them, and they looked slightly older than me.

William's eyes caught mine across the room, so with haste, I averted my gaze and decided to be Elisabeth's moral support. Surrounded by three strangers, she was visibly uncomfortable. I was certain she'd already informed them she was engaged, but not everyone respected boundaries.

"Hi," I said when one of the men looked over. He wasn't particularly handsome. He had a pointed nose and mouse eyes, with thin lips and a narrow head, but his gawk made up for it because it boosted my ego.

Turning my attention to Elisabeth's desperate eyes, I gave her a fond smile. "Gorgeous girls only, or am I allowed?" I asked and gestured towards the only vacant seat.

The lad that had noticed me first immediately stood to grab the chair for me. "Please," he said and cocked his ginger head towards the seat. While smiling at him, I allowed him to help me into it.

"I'm Lewis," he introduced himself. "Those things over there are James and Francis, but you shouldn't mind them," he continued as he sat.

"What the hell, mate?" James complained. "Killing the competition already, are you?"

"Like a true capitalist."

"Christ," Francis moaned.

I giggled.

"Can I buy you a drink?" Lewis asked me, brown eyes intense, like he wanted to suck out my soul.

"She's already got one," Elisabeth interrupted and pushed a gin and tonic towards me, which I recognised as the one William had placed on the table earlier. He'd bought it for me?

"Alright, then. I'll still be here for the refill, hopefully," Lewis responded, amused.

I sent him a wry look while I raised the refreshing beverage to my lips.

"So, what's your name?" he queried.

"Jessica," I lied. It was just so amusing. I couldn't shake off the habit. From the corner of my eye, I saw Elisabeth struggle to repress a smile.

"And how was work, Jessica? Do you work?"

"Does it look like I don't?"

"You look like luxury, so no, it doesn't."

Slick.

"Got a taste for the finer things in life, have you?" I teased back.

His thin lips tucked up into a smug smile while a ravenous gleam entered his brown eyes. "There's not a doubt in my mind."

I soon realised that I had become Elisabeth's entertainment for the night. She laughed nonstop while I teased the men accompanying us, and as though my attention was in short supply, they fought for it until they nearly surrendered their dignity. For a good two hours, I kept them on their toes while they ordered round after round for Elisabeth and myself.

In fact, I had forgotten all about William by the time he demanded my attention, so when he suddenly placed his large hands on my bare shoulders, I nearly spurted my latest sip. Only one touch could make me feel this way, so I didn't need to turn around to know who it was. Besides, after a shy glance at his handsome hands, I had enough proof to be certain. Those beautiful long fingers had once caressed my skin, and they had done it so well that I couldn't ever forget their appearance, much less the pleasure they had provided.

Nevertheless, I tilted my head back to look up at him, but he didn't meet my gaze. Instead, his eyes resembled two blue flames as he glared at the men around me.

"Gentlemen, I'm afraid I'll have to steal this one away from you. Considering how many drinks you've bought her, I doubt she can walk in a straight line anymore," he said, voice composed, and squeezed my shoulders.

He did have a point. I felt positively drunk by now, but I wasn't completely off my face, either. Although I doubted that I'd be able to walk in a straight line, I could probably make some fancy zigzag pattern for him.

Lewis frowned up at him. "I wasn't aware she had a boyfriend."

"You don't strike me as being aware in general," William brought himself to reply before he dragged my seat out with surprising force. I gasped at his insolent comment, shocked.

Meanwhile, Elisabeth pursed her lips so as not to laugh, but when James and Francis started guffawing, she lost control. Her laughter rumbled out of her until she snorted, and it made me giggle to hear it, so much so that I barely noticed William's hand around mine while he dragged me away.

He didn't stop until we'd reached the bar where Andy stood waiting. Once we did, he released my hand to glower down at me, but he said nothing.

Drunk as I was, I swayed a little under his glare. "What?"

"Cara, not in front of me. Please," he begged.

Beside us, Andy sighed and shook his head while William's jaw clenched rather hard. Was he suppressing his anger? It looked like it.

My heart squeezed upon hearing his fears. Was that why he'd been unsure about whether to show up tonight? Had he been afraid that he might witness me go home with a stranger? "What? I wasn't even thinking of it. I was only trying to help Ellie out."

After summoning the bartender's attention, Andy asked, "Sorry, could I have a bottle of still water, please?"

"What happened to all the girls?" I asked and looked around. Had they left?

William merely continued to stare at me. Why wasn't he taking his eyes off me? It unnerved me. Folding my arms, I leaned against the counter and turned my side to him.

"Thank you," I heard Andy say before he walked to stand between William and me. After undoing the cap, he handed me the bottle. "Drink. You've had more than a barrel of gin by now. It's going to hit you any moment," he ordered.

I scoffed. "Christ, Andy. I'm not a child. I can manage my intake. But thanks anyway," I muttered and raised the bottle to my mouth. He gave me a fond smile. Then, looking towards his best friend, he sighed and raised his hand to pat his shoulder.

"Calm down, Will. She's fine."

William shot him a glare. Meanwhile, I saw his Adam's apple ascend and fall. The same moment I did, it dawned on me that I'd read him wrong. He wasn't angry. He was anxious, perhaps even worried – for me. But why? Because I was intoxicated?

"Cara!" Elisabeth called then, having left the table. When I looked over, I found her waving me forward. Right. The club.

I had hardly moved a step when William clasped my arm to drag me back, and he did it with such force that I nearly dropped the bottle I was holding when I crashed into his chest.

"Where do you think you're going?" he questioned, annoyed.

Awfully confused, I frowned into his chest. Why was he so overbearing?

"Ellie and I are meeting Brian at a club. I've got to go," I explained, slurring my words.

His eyes flickered in Elisabeth's direction before they landed on mine again, and they were searing. "Given the state you're in, there's not even a slim chance I'll let you head to a club. When the drinks kick in, you'll be up for grabs."

"Excuse me? You are *not* my boss!" I fired back. "Fuck," I mumbled as soon as I heard what I'd said.

His eyebrows arched, and his head tilted while slight amusement swirled in his eyes. "Actually, Cara, I am."

"That's not what I meant. I meant you don't get to decide that."

His chest expanded against me with his deep inhalation. "Fine," he snapped. "Then I'm coming with you. Andy?"

With his hands tucked into his pockets, Andy shrugged. "Sure. But we aren't appropriately dressed for that."

"I'm sure they've got a cloakroom," William countered and proceeded to tug me towards Elisabeth.

She blinked confusedly once we reached her, and it made me sigh. She wasn't an idiot. If William didn't change his ways, it was only a matter of time before she would realise the true nature of our relationship.

"Mind if we join you, Ellie?" Andy asked affably.

A grin took over her mouth. "Of course not!" Always so cheerful. I wished she'd said no. Then again, I doubted that William would have listened.

22

---•◆•◆•---

CATCH ME IF YOU CAN

AMATORY IN ITS BEATS, THE PULSATING MUSIC OF THE club pounded against my eardrums – the sort of music that would transform even the most sensible person into a lustful animal. The place resembled a strobe light illuminated jungle, where the wild creatures unleashed their primal core. Still, there was a level of class to it. The guests weren't casually dressed. However, what they had in common was the lack of much clothing to cover their glistening skin. Spread over three floors, the whole area was quite impressive.

William and Andy had left their waistcoats and ties with the cloakroom staff. While they still looked somewhat out of place, they weren't a lost cause. Looking at William, I saw that he had already rolled up his sleeves, which was a nice touch of casualness. All that was required was a little tweak. I put theory into practice by raising my hands towards his collar, but when my fingers gripped it, he clasped my wrists. My breath hitched upon the contact of our skin and the ensuing current that charged through my bloodstream. For a moment, I wondered whether the same electricity was the reason for his defensive response. Had he felt it, too?

As he glared at me, his grip tightened around my wrists. "What are you doing?"

From his tone, I was almost sure that the same current was bolting through him as well.

"Damn." I smiled. "Who let you out of your cage today?" I asked as my hands reached to undo his top button.

Hearing me, charming laughter spilled out of Andy's mouth. "I didn't," he said. "I'd rather he stayed in it all the time."

"That makes two of us," I joked back.

William was not amused, and I could tell because his glare shifted onto Andy instead. After undoing a second button, I retreated a step to judge my artistry, and I immediately regretted it. Like this, he looked edible. Unexpectedly, the sight of him even made my vagina throb, and when I felt it, I nearly sobbed. How on earth did I manage to resist him? I deserved an award.

"Decent," Andy commented and moved to copy my work.

"Thanks, love," William murmured to me as he tucked his hands into his pockets, and his casual stance only made him more appealing. Still, something prevented him from looking at me.

"That colour really suits you," I told him sincerely.

He scoffed. "Hardly as much as you do." Taken off guard, I gaped and stole a glance at Elisabeth to see if she'd heard him, but her face was buried in her phone. Relief closed my mouth again.

"Cheeky, Will," Andy remarked approvingly with a crooked smile.

I was about to reply when Elisabeth exclaimed, "He's texted me. He's in there, far end!" She pointed into the crowd. A heartbeat later, she'd caught my hand and was guiding me into it.

Countless bodies ground against each other, and mine. Numerous eyes glanced in my direction, and most of them looked faded, drugs lifting them high above the clouds. Going in had been like sinking into quicksand – the more I shifted, the deeper I got. Andy and William had charged after us, but the moving crowd had swallowed us up until they were no longer in my view.

"Fuck," I said to myself. William was not going to like this. "Hey, Ellie!" I called and jerked her hand. "We lost the others!"

"They've got my number, and they know where we're headed! We'll be fine!" she yelled back and continued warring through the crowd.

Suddenly, a pair of arms hooked around my waist. Tugging me into a warm embrace, they successfully broke my hold of Elisabeth's hand. Whirling around, I stared up at a face I had never seen before, so I pushed him away somewhat harshly before turning towards Elisabeth again so that I wouldn't lose her, too. Glimpsing the twists of her mane, I charged after her. To my relief, she had stopped, eyes searching for me.

"Cara!" she yelled as soon as she spotted me, and when she extended her hand, I grabbed it firmly.

"Don't let go!" she ordered and turned around again to guide me through the crowd until we reached a bar at the far end. Among the people around it stood a group of five men. One of them met my gaze before his eyes darted to Elisabeth's person, and then to the man in front of him. As he cocked his head towards us, all five of them looked over.

The smile of one of them caught my immediate attention because it mirrored the warmth of Elisabeth's. Beaming over at us, he spread his arms apart to welcome Elisabeth's arriving figure, and once she reached him, she swung her arms around him and planted a firm kiss on his waiting mouth.

I couldn't hear what they said to each other, but while they embraced, his friends blatantly ogled me from head to toe. Feeling out of place, I gave them a wave. Elisabeth pulled out of Brian's arms and motioned towards me. Eventually, he yelled, "Nice to meet you, Cara! I've heard lovely things!"

Since there wasn't much room for conversation above the pounding music, introductions were swift, but I was too drunk to remember the names of Brian's friends. When one of them dragged me towards the dance floor, I glanced at the bar, hoping to locate William, but I couldn't see him anywhere. I faced a dilemma, because while I wanted to find him and Andy, I didn't want to be a spoilsport, especially since the initial plan had been to spend time with Elisabeth tonight. So, with some reluctance, I allowed myself to get dragged away.

Like William and Andy had warned, the drinks suddenly kicked in. The room spiralled around me while I danced against this good-looking stranger. We danced until we were glistening with fresh sweat. Even though we were out of breath, the music hypnotised us into continuing.

I had to give it to him: he was a remarkable dancer. Did he have a single stiff bone in his body? I could feel a stiff muscle, but it contained no bones.

We'd danced for some time when I sensed his mouth beginning to search for mine, clearly hoping for some action. Three months ago, I wouldn't have minded a random snog, but something prevented me now, and the reason wasn't present. I'd lost him some time ago, and he still hadn't found us.

It was quite bizarre, but ever since I'd met William, random one-night stands had lost their spark. The idea of them didn't ensnare me. I was too preoccupied with Will, and Aaron already satisfied the little of my libido that was left for anyone else. Besides, I felt terrible for being the reason that William had come here in the first place, and then I had just abandoned him. Though I hadn't asked him to join us, I still felt partially at fault. I knew he had his best friend by his side, but it didn't relieve my conscience much. So, the last thing on my mind was to kiss a random stranger.

I continued to avoid Brian's friend's lips until my bladder became an imminent concern.

"Sorry, I need the loo!" I shouted to him and escaped out of his hold. Staggering towards the edge of the crowd, I searched desperately for the toilets. I could barely hold it in. When I found them, I rushed to join the queue and begged myself to last until it was my turn.

Once I saw my chance to pee, I reeled in a deep breath, determined to breathe only through my mouth to avoid the stench of the place. I hurried to finish because I despised toilets in clubs and pubs. Thankfully, there was still a little soap left that I could wash my hands with.

Returning outside, I leaned against the wall. I was so drunk, and the thought of having to find Elisabeth again made me want to go home. It seemed so impossible a quest. While standing there, I got the eerie feeling that I was being watched, so I scouted the crowd for a presence, but I didn't register any familiar gazes.

I'd been standing there for about a minute when I glimpsed Brian's friend – the one I'd been dancing with – and his arrival was like a light at the end of the tunnel. He was just making his way out of the men's room. Perhaps he had a better idea of where the others were currently located.

Our eyes locked, and the smile that caught his mouth was infectious. The music was quieter here, so when he said, "Hey, there. Cara, was it?" I could actually hear him.

I nodded and watched his approach with a friendly smile on my mouth. Once he reached me, he placed his hands against the wall on either side of my face. His action made my smile fade at once. Instead, I felt somewhat intimidated.

"Well then, Cara. How are you?"

"Quite drunk," I confessed as I gazed into his dark eyes. His brown hair was longer than that of the average male, with a side parting, and, like Will, he had symmetrical features and neatly groomed stubble.

"Well, you're not alone." Smirking, he lowered his head. He drew closer and closer to my lips, but just before he reached them, I turned my head. My gut twisted with discomfort. This didn't feel right. I didn't want this.

"Oh, come on, love. Just a peck. I swear you won't regret it." He clasped my jaw to turn my face towards him. Grabbing his shoulders, I wriggled my jaw against his grip.

"N-no." I tried to push him away and was just about to thrust my knee into his balls when a large and familiar hand gripped his shoulder. A moment later, Brian's friend was ripped away from me with violent force. Upon the removal of his body, I was presented with a seething William. His eyes were ablaze as he glowered at Brian's friend.

"Touch her again and I swear I'll rearrange your fucking face," he growled and moved to stand in front of me, protective. "She's made it abundantly clear she doesn't want you."

Peeking past his strong right arm, I saw Brian's friend leap into the crowd, clearly intimidated. William continued to glare after him for another second until he finally turned towards me. Immediately, his eyes softened.

"Are you alright?"

Overcome with lust, I swallowed. This wouldn't do. I wanted him so badly.

The waves of his hair cradled his ears, and the bigger wave above his forehead made me raise my hands to run my fingers through it. My breath hitched at the feel of it. It was exactly how I remembered – thick, but velvety soft. With wonder in my eyes, I gazed up at him, hypnotised by his male beauty. Day or night, he was a sight to behold.

"I'm sorry we lost you," I murmured and dragged my hands to the nape of his neck to play with the strands there. Reuniting with him made me realise that I had actually missed his company – immensely. It was amazing to be able to look into his eyes again – to admire him.

"That's not what I asked," he reminded me and lowered his head somewhat. From his dilated pupils, I could tell he was intoxicated as well, and the smell of alcohol on his breath confirmed it.

He stared into my eyes, intensely, and it made my heart wreak havoc within my chest. Merely by looking at me, he made me feel more alive than I ever had. What was this mysterious creature? What magic did he wield? Caught under his influence, I bucked my hips forward, wanting to be closer to him.

His lips formed a brooding line as he snuck his arms around my waist to press me flat against him. "Cara, say something. Tell me you're alright." His voice was intolerably sensual when he used that tone. I'd never heard a voice more inviting in my life. I knew he was merely speaking to me, but I could have sworn he was singing, luring me to my doom.

"I'm fine." It was almost a whisper, but at least it was a reply.

He grimaced. "I'm sorry I didn't intervene sooner. At first, I thought…"

"You were watching me?"

He nodded vaguely. "I thought you wanted him at first. I saw you dancing earlier."

"You did?" I asked, surprised. "Why didn't you come over?"

"I wanted to, but…I wasn't sure you'd appreciate it."

I frowned. "That didn't stop you earlier tonight."

He sighed. "I know, but that wasn't right of me. I didn't want to repeat my mistake, so I left you alone. I have no right to interfere like that, and you looked like you were enjoying yourself." Furrowing his brows, he averted his eyes. "Frankly, I…I gave up for a moment."

Had I not been so intoxicated, I would have told him he'd be wise to give up on me. However, ruled by the alcohol in my blood, no such thing occurred to me. Instead, I told him honestly, "I wouldn't have minded if you came over, just as I didn't mind when you came over at Disrepute earlier. On the contrary, I would have preferred it. I've been looking for you, but since I was supposed to spend time with Ellie tonight, I didn't want to leave her side."

Fixing his gaze on me, something bright shone from his eyes, and I knew at once that he could tell I was slowly submitting to his power. "I'll bear that in mind for next time."

After smiling at each other for a beat, he glanced over his shoulder. When he faced me again, he had knitted his brows. "I've got to say, though – I'm a bit disappointed. Of all women, I'd expect at least you to escape predators like that."

I chuckled. "Well, I was just about to kick him in the balls when you arrived."

His lips stretched into a smile. "Really?"

I nodded.

He looked proud. "Good. I'm almost sorry I intervened, then. A kick in the balls is what he deserves, and even that would be merciful."

Nodding my agreement, I looked at the crowd. I wanted to dance again, but with William – only him. Biting on my lower lip, I glanced back at him with a cheeky smile. His brows twitched faintly, revealing some bewilderment as he tried to gauge the thoughts behind my expression, but before he could ask, I pushed him away. As I strode past him, heading for the dance floor, I vaguely wondered where Andy had gone.

"What are you doing?" William called after me, confused.

Eyeing him over my shoulder, I offered a lascivious smile. "Escaping a predator," I teased with a wink.

His eyes grew darker as he stalked after me. I had barely managed to pass a few dancing bodies when he reached out to clasp my hand. Enchanting electricity bolted through my body at his touch. When he moved to entwine our fingers, I took a deep breath to steady my rising pulse.

"I'm not letting you out of my sight," he declared behind me. Good. I didn't want him to, and I let him know by squeezing his hand.

Once we had moved far enough, I turned to face him. "Can you dance?" I asked above the music, genuinely curious.

He chuckled. "With you, I'll do just about anything."

His statement roused a blush in my cheeks, but the dim light prevented him from seeing it. When he brought his arms around my waist to pull me closer, my high colour intensified.

I had never felt so anxious before – not over a man. Because of it, I had to swallow a lump in my throat when I circled his neck with my arms. My blood simmered in my veins. He was so fucking hot. Thankfully, the fact that he was my boss, as well as Jason's brother, didn't cross my drunken mind. For now, all I wanted was to submerge myself in his seeming divinity.

Lowering his head, he paused by my ear. "Stay close," he said and began to move along with the carnal music. With my heart in my throat, I followed his movements and felt arousal drench both my mind and my underwear. All I could think of was my intense yearning for his flesh, how much I wanted him – all of him.

I hadn't thought a man like William could dance, but he was indeed proving me wrong. Then again, considering his skills in the bedroom, it shouldn't have surprised me. He practised perfect control over his body, and right now, it seemed determined to make mine come undone.

And it was working. My hands were all over him, exploring and caressing.

We'd danced for a while when he gripped my hips and whirled me around so that my back was facing him. Smoothing his hands down my arms, he didn't stop until they covered the back of mine. There, he entwined our fingers before bringing our arms around me to form an embrace. My heart jolted when he hugged me tightly. Our new position was powerfully intimate, and it made me catch my breath. When he moved along with my body now, I felt his erection straining against my bum.

Oh my God. I was going insane.

Resting my head on his shoulder, I closed my eyes and surrendered to the euphoric moment. He was seduction in the flesh. The longer he held me, the more unbearable my lust for him became. Eventually, my desire for him grew so heavy that I knew I would be crushed under its weight if I didn't act on it.

All at once, lust capsized my good sense. I needed to kiss him – it felt as vital to my existence as oxygen did.

Opening my eyes, I saw a shadowed area at the far end of the space, and it became my quest to bring him there. As I pushed against him with my bum, his arms fell from around me. Immediately, I rushed forward, but not before I had cast a lewd smile at him over my shoulder.

"Cara," he called, though it sounded more like an order. He charged after me. Sniggering, I snuck through the crowd, always just barely escaping his grasp. Like a man determined to redeem himself, he followed me, eyes resolute.

"Cara!"

Twirling, I gave him another wink. "Catch me if you can, Will!" I shouted back. Still giggling like an infatuated young girl, I manoeuvred past the dancing bodies towards my desired spot. It was just below the staircase leading to the second floor, and it was shrouded in beckoning darkness.

I'd nearly reached it when I turned to wait for him. About three feet away from me, he stopped, eyes flickering between my mischievous smile and the dark spot behind me. As soon as he gauged my intentions, his chest expanded with his deep inhalation, and in the faint light, I saw his jaw clench.

With a lustful gleam in my eye, I extended my hand to him as a silent invitation. I couldn't quite detect the emotion that danced in the depths of his eyes. All I could tell was that it was intense.

Without wasting another second, he gripped my hand and pulled me forcefully towards him. Somewhat startled by his urgency, I slammed into his muscular chest, and before I could recover, he was moving forward, hands on my hips as he guided me backwards into the darkness.

Now veiled by shadows, he didn't stop until I met the wall behind me. Once I did, he lowered his head in search of my ear.

"You are such a tease."

I wetted my lips while my arms circled his neck. "Am I?"

"I swear to god, Cara, you'll be my undoing," he growled.

"What, you can't handle me?" I teased and ran my fingers through his hair. Placing my leg between his, I proceeded to grind against his thigh.

"Oh, I'll fucking handle you," he asserted and thrust his hips against me to pin me to the wall. Air exploded out of my lungs at his lustful action. A heartbeat later, his mouth found mine, and my chest ignited with a passion I'd only felt twice before.

Truly, he was the best kisser I'd ever encountered. How I had managed to resist him before was beyond my comprehension. I must have been an idiot. The mesmerising motion of his mouth obliterated all my defences. Tender, and yet simultaneously forceful, it ravished my own. His tongue didn't plough my mouth. It merely teased it, and it aroused me to an extent nobody but him had ever managed.

However, his kiss was somewhat different this time around. It held such resolve that I was rendered powerless.

Dopamine raged through my system when the delectable taste of him detonated in my mouth. I had missed it more than I'd been aware of. He tasted so good, and he kissed even better.

My heart ached while he continued to possess my mouth. Pleasure feasted on the very fibres of it. When William kissed me, I felt ecstatic. It was as though nothing else mattered anymore. Everything faded – everything but him.

It just felt uncannily right. Whenever his lips blessed my own, I felt complete, as though a vacancy I hadn't known I harboured had been occupied, as though our lips had been designed for each other, and as though we had been fated to combine all along.

It was entirely liberating to finally allow myself the sin – to touch him, to taste him. I wanted the moment to last forever. There would be no consequences then. Just him and I, marvelling endlessly at our overwhelming chemistry, in a moment locked away in infinity.

"Mm," he groaned into my mouth and cupped my cheeks in his hands. Pulling away, he rested his forehead against mine and heaved for air to stabilise himself. "Shit, Cara. What you do to me."

"Less talk, more kissing," I replied on a ragged breath and brought his mouth back to mine. His stubble scraped my palms when I grabbed hold of his strong jaw, and I felt him smile against my lips. God, he was enticing. I wanted to devour the entirety of him.

Adhering to my wish, he kept kissing me for minutes on end,

and I never wanted him to stop. He was so bloody good at it. I was addicted to his mouth, and all the things it could do.

My heart seemed to have caught fire, and his lustful hands on my body were adding fuel to it. Again, a most uncanny feeling poured into it, nibbling on the fibres. I hadn't felt it quite so intensely since the last time I'd found myself in his sensual care.

What was it? It was so alien to me. So sweet, and yet so achingly vulnerable. Delicate yet profound. I frowned while I struggled to identify it, but when his right hand trailed down my thigh, I forgot all about it.

Groaning into his mouth, I invited his touch to progress. Seeming to understand, he hooked his arm around my thigh to bring my leg around him. After securing it in place, his fingertips travelled as light as a feather up my thigh again, and then inward towards my aching sex. He was barely touching me, and yet a touch had never felt more powerful.

"Will," I moaned and pulled away from his enchanting kiss.

Chuckling, he reclaimed my mouth as his fingers drew closer and closer to my soaked folds, and once they flirted with the wet part of my thong, he broke our kiss to rest his lips by my ear. Meanwhile, I found myself preoccupied with recovering from the shocking tingling he'd left behind between my legs.

Suddenly, he cupped my sex with his hand, and I instantly gasped.

"Always ready for me, Cara."

"Yes," I whined. "You drive me insane!" I confessed and gripped his collar to tug him back to my mouth, but he refused me the satisfaction. Halting mere inches from my trembling lips, his breath breezed across them while his eyes assessed the desperation in mine.

"Good."

A smirk found his tempting mouth before he gently rubbed me. At once, I shuddered against him, caught by the delicious friction he provided. Hooking his fingers into my thong, he pushed it aside to reveal my wetness. One finger lapped over me once before he dipped it into me, although barely.

Again, I shuddered, wanting him to continue.

"More?" he purred into my ear.

"Mm, yes," I replied, high-pitched, and curled my fingers into his hair to drag his amazing mouth back to mine, and this time, he allowed it. He pushed his finger deep into me then, making me groan into his mouth. It felt *so* good.

Using the thumb of his other hand, he rubbed across my clit. The sensation rippled up my spine and made my head jerk backwards, knocking into the wall. He seemed determined to make me come using only his hands, and I marvelled at the idea of it. No man had ever managed to make me come this way before, but William was well on his way to becoming the first.

Adding another finger, he was thrusting two in and out of me now, and he focused his point of impact on my front wall. Meanwhile, the thumb of his other hand continued to rub me. My lips parted, and my eyes grew wide. *Whoa.* This was nothing short of delicious.

The tension rallied in the pit of my stomach. Growing larger and larger, it expanded until every muscle of my body tensed.

"Shit," I breathed. All the while, he watched me intensely in the faint light, assessing the efficiency of his methods.

My brows furrowed as I chewed into my lower lip, my grimace revealing how much pleasure he was giving me. Heat spread across my skin, burning. Everything was so *hot*. My heart accelerated with the speed of his fingers, my breathing growing louder, harder, ragged. The background faded. All I noticed was him.

His thumb struck my clit with perfect precision then. "Ah!" I moaned, my eyes squeezing shut. Applying more pressure, he continued to rub my throbbing bud, making my thoughts scatter into dizzy elation. Inside of me, his strong fingers continued to stroke that susceptible spot.

"Will," I panted. Responding, he thrust his fingers harder into me. I gasped. At once, my walls clenched around his digits. Shivers bolted through my system while my toes curled in my heels.

Oh no.

"Fuck!" I cried as I climaxed. To my relief, the pounding music drowned out my voice. There were plenty of other couples around us, but they were too busy with each other to mind Will and me. Besides, he was positioned in a way that looked relatively discreet.

Trapped by William's arresting eyes, I felt myself drift away as a blissful orgasm raged through my body. As I convulsed away from the wall, he rushed to cage me in his arms. Whether he remembered my tendencies or not was lost on me, but it was entirely plausible. I always quivered when I came, and he had experienced that first-hand before.

His intoxicating scent filled my nose while I recovered against him. Once I lifted my head again, he followed the motion of mine. A coquettish smile flickered across my lips when he nuzzled his nose against mine.

No words were required. Simply the look in his eyes was enough of a statement. He was happy, and I was the reason.

Holding my gaze captive, he leaned away and raised his hand to his mouth. Then, he sucked on each of the fingers that had been inside of me, savouring the taste of his masterful creation. My mouth dropped open while intense heat restored in my cheeks. God, he was erotic.

Seeing my expression, his lips curved into a ravenous grin. "What an appetiser, Cara."

Lost for words, I merely looked at him. Following a chuckle, he folded his hand around mine and entwined our fingers. Moving next to my ear, he said, "About time we leave this place, don't you think?"

I nodded.

He leaned away to scour the crowd. When he looked back, he said, "I've got to find Andy first, though."

"Mm."

23

SWEET DREAMS

WHILE SEARCHING FOR ANDY, I HAD STARTED TO sober up somewhat, after which the gravity of what I had done with William slowly began to dawn on me. The ensuing remorse was something I'd tried to drown in three shots of tequila, much to William's distaste. We'd argued like an old married couple when I had placed the order, and his eyes had been spitting fire when I'd necked them.

"You're going to black out, Cara," he had berated.

"That's the point," I'd fired back. At that point, he had looked rather hurt, which had upset me, too. It was evident that he had understood my intention as well as the reason behind it, and – justifiably so – he resented me for it. However, I wasn't ready to face up to what I had done. It had been a drunken mistake, and now that some of my lust had receded, I regretted it intensely.

Consequently, I was drunk out of my senses when we located Andy among a group of women. Previously, I'd thought William was the womaniser between the two, but I'd been misguided. Andy was apparently the more promiscuous man, although I doubted he'd been with anyone following his trouble with Chloe. Either way, he was clearly out of touch with himself in the wake of it, and I pitied him for it. Some part of me could also empathise to a certain extent. In the end, I could hardly recognise myself when it came to the management of my attraction to William.

Either way, it was a good thing William persisted in supervising him, because he desperately needed someone to guide him away from trouble.

"Andy!" William shouted over, and his body trembled against mine. He was seething, I could tell, but I wasn't the cause at this moment – at least not chiefly. "Put your dick away and get the hell over here!" he continued and tightened his embrace of me.

Like a scared dog, Andy walked over with his tail between his legs. Pouting, he avoided William's glare and instead looked at me.

"Christ, is she alright?" he queried once he reached us.

"She's completely off her face," William groused and jerked me towards him since I nearly collapsed. "I need to bring her home, but I'm not leaving you here, you absolute knobhead. I leave you alone for two minutes, and this is what happens. Have you got no self-restraint? If Chloe had seen this…"

"Chloe, Chloe, Chloe. I swear, sometimes, you'd think *you* were her boyfriend," Andy muttered.

William inhaled deeply. "Well, sometimes, I think she'd be better off with a man like me," he retorted mercilessly.

"Careful, Will," Andy hissed and gave him a vicious glare.

"Sorry. Tough love," William replied and sighed long and loud.

My stomach turned, its contents rising to my throat. It demanded all my remaining strength to swallow it back down.

"Will," I moaned. "I feel sick."

"You – oh, for fuck's sake, Cara. What am I supposed to do with you? You never listen."

"That's why you fancy her," Andy twitted and tucked his hands into his pockets.

Digging into his own, William withdrew his ticket for the cloakroom and handed it to Andy. "Fetch our things. I'll meet you outside."

By the time William managed to get me into a taxi, I had nearly passed out. So, when he slid in next to me, I rested my head on his shoulder and surrendered to the darkness.

I woke not much later to the sound of Jason's voice. "Bloody hell, is she alright?"

"She's completely off her face. I tried to steer her away from those last three shots of tequila, but you know how she is," William's voice replied with exasperation.

"Still, I seldom see her this plastered," Jason murmured.

Batting my lashes apart, I saw a white ceiling above William's jaw and realised he was carrying me across his chest. Where were we?

This angle made me feel sick again. It looked like the ceiling was spinning. I wouldn't be able to hold it down for much longer. "Will," I whimpered. "Toilet."

"Ah, fuck me," he moaned and turned towards it.

The second he released me onto the floor, I lifted the lid of the toilet and vomited.

"Cara," he groaned as he gathered my hair to hold it for me, "you're a bloody idiot."

I couldn't reply. I retched and retched until nothing came out. Tears welled in my eyes from vomiting so hard. Once I finished, I leaned away, exhausted, and rested my head against the cold glass of the shower.

"I can't believe she allowed herself to get that drunk in front of her boss," Jason muttered from the doorway. "You might be my brother, but for heaven's sake."

"We've hardly been together all night," William defended me. "She was meant to go out with just Ellie, but Andy and I asked to come along. We lost each other in the club. Suppose she didn't expect to find me again."

He was sort of lying, but I appreciated it, nevertheless. I was certain I'd wake up to proper angst tomorrow.

"You asked to come along? Wearing that?" I heard Jason respond, sounding flummoxed. "And since when do you go clubbing?"

"Jason, that's enough," William growled, sounding like a parental figure.

"Are you drunk as well?"

"A bit."

"Well, you can sleep here if you're too tired to go home. I'm sorry you had to babysit Cara, man. I'm embarrassed on her behalf."

"It's alright. It's not the first time I've had to babysit a drunk idiot," William said and shot him a look. "But yeah, I'll sleep over."

"Can I get you anything?" Jason murmured and rubbed the back of his head.

"I think Cara could use some water. She's completely emptied her stomach. While you're at it, bring some for me as well."

"On it." Jason turned to depart.

Sighing, William reached over to flush the toilet after me. Upon his retreat, his hand skimmed my cheek to brush my hair away. "Come on, darling," he soothed. "You need to brush your teeth." He grabbed my arms to lift me. Tearless sobs escaped me while I grimaced in protest. Although I felt better after puking, all I wanted was my bed. Nevertheless, he managed to make me stand, although his arm remained firmly wrapped around my waist.

"William, I'm sorry," I said, but I slurred the words and struggled to keep a steady gaze on him in the mirror. "You deserve better."

Pain clouded his features before he averted his eyes. "We'll talk in the morning. Which one's yours?" he enquired, indicating the two toothbrushes.

"Green," I mumbled just before Jason returned to toss William a bottle of water. Afterwards, he came towards me and undid the cap of another.

"Cara," he sighed. "This isn't like you. You're worrying me."

"Well, I've had a rough week," I mumbled and wrapped my feeble hand around the bottle.

"Clearly." Leaning forward, he planted a firm kiss on my forehead while he rubbed my arms. "I'll make you a full English for breakfast tomorrow, yeah?"

"I love you," I cooed and attacked him with a hug.

He chuckled and pressed me against him. "Love you too, idiot." He didn't release me as he turned towards his brother. "Poker night still on tomorrow?" he queried while I raised my bottle to my lips.

"Of course," William replied after a mouthful from his own. "Have you got a spare toothbrush around?"

"Yeah. Bottom left drawer."

After Jason and William had forced me to brush my teeth and rinse my mouth with Listerine Total Care to get rid of my bad breath, they guided me to my bedroom where I changed into my pink silk nightie. While Jason tucked me into bed, William leaned against the doorpost with a brooding expression on his face.

When my eyes closed, Jason said, "She's going to pass out any moment now. You know where my bedroom is."

"You're sleeping here again? With her?" William asked, and his voice lacked any trace of emotion.

"Yeah."

"Jason, is there something you haven't told me?"

"What?"

"Why do you always insist on sleeping with her?"

Baffled, Jason replied, "We do it all the time."

"But you haven't had sex with her, right?"

"What the fuck? What the hell have you been drinking tonight, Will?" Jason questioned, astounded.

"Fair question," Will argued.

"No, of course I haven't."

"Ever wanted to?"

"Get out, Will." I could hear that Jason was losing his patience. I'd called it. If there was one person in this world whom I had thought capable of stirring Jason's temper, it was William, and I was currently hearing it live.

"Don't," William demanded.

"Don't what?" Jason snapped.

"Don't fuck her. I have."

Complete silence filled the room for seconds that felt like hours. I'd been close to drifting off, but now I was only pretending to be asleep. Although I was drunk, I wasn't so drunk that this didn't send my heart racing in panic, and vomiting had made me feel much soberer.

When Jason finally found his voice, it was low and cold. "Are you taking the piss?"

"No," William replied. "It was a happy accident at first, but I've every intention of doing it again, so I thought you should know." His voice was devoid of emotion. He might as well have been reading a sheet of instructions.

"What the hell, Will? That's my fucking flatmate! She also happens to be my best friend!"

"I'm aware. I would say I'm sorry, but I'm not."

Jason whirled around in my bed to grab my shoulders, and he shook them so hard that I'd have been an idiot to pretend I was asleep. "Cara! Tell me he's joking!"

"He's joking," I said.

"Are you lying?"

"Yes," I squeaked.

He was quick to release me. "What the actual fuck, Cara? And you haven't told me?" He was fuming. "Did you even plan to?"

Tears welled in my eyes. I was far too drunk to handle this right now. "I'm sorry. I didn't mean to have sex with him." My voice was light and feeble and broke at several points. "I wasn't aware he was your brother at the time. Had I known, I would never have done it."

"For fuck's sake, you guys. This is honestly unbelievable." Jason groaned and dropped his head between his hands while he tried to comprehend the truth.

"Jason, I'm really sorry." My tears ran over. "I didn't want to tell you because it was an accident, and it had only happened once. I thought it'd be best to just leave it at that, especially since it isn't going to happen again."

"Isn't it?" William chimed in and tilted his head. "That wasn't my impression when I fingered you at the club earlier."

Colour drained from my face. It felt like he had stabbed me straight through the chest, even though he hadn't told a single lie. However, he had broken his promise, and the betrayal was considerable. I couldn't recall having seen Jason so beside himself before.

Blatantly despairing, Jason shook his head. "I honestly can't believe this has happened," he murmured to himself, before he turned to glower at his brother. "You really are an absolute prick, Will."

"Really?" William countered aloofly. "And how is that, exactly? It's not like my intention here is to make your life any harder. I can't help that she's... Well, that she's her." He gestured towards my figure in the bed. "It's not like I want to feel this way about her. I mean, she's a right pain in the arse sometimes – even most of the time. Honestly."

"Well—" my tone was saturated with sarcasm—"at least we've got that in common. You swore you wouldn't tell, Will! You could at least have warned me before you decided to drop the damned bomb! The fuck's wrong with you?"

Jason gaped at me. "You made him promise not to tell?"

"I've wanted to tell you for months, Jase," William declared, and resentment poured from his eyes when he glanced at me. "Cara begged me not to."

"Because I was scared of how you would react!" I defended myself while looking at Jason. "Jason, I was scared you'd be angry with me – that you'd stop being friends with me!" My tears formed relentless rivers along my cheeks.

Struggling to comprehend the situation, Jason queried, "Does Dad know about this?"

William responded by arching his brow at him. The entire time, he'd remained wholly composed. It was astounding how he managed that. "Of course he doesn't, and I wouldn't tell him either if I were you."

"When?" Jason continued.

Perplexed, William frowned. "When what?"

"When did it happen?"

After a shrug, William rubbed the back of his head. "April."

Jason gasped. "April!"

"Yeah. She was at Disrepute, with Olivia. Remember I told you I'd met a girl named Sandra there one evening?"

Jason was quiet for several seconds, seemingly struck by shock. "Oh, my God," he eventually gasped. "Sandra? That girl you just wouldn't shut up about? That was *Cara*?"

"Yeah."

"Jesus Christ," he whispered to himself. "It all makes sense. It was Cara you saw that time, wasn't it? With Aaron?"

"Unfortunately," William confirmed through grinding teeth and gave me a scowl.

I stilled on the bed at the awful memory.

"Ah, shit. Fuck. I should never have recommended that bar to her. If I hadn't, we could all have avoided this," Jason thought aloud and ran his hands through his dirty blonde mane.

"Jason, we're brothers. It was only a matter of time before I'd meet her. You'd only be postponing the inevitable. We would have ended up fucking one way or another. Calm down."

"Calm down? You're telling me to calm down when you've fucked and fingered my best friend behind my back, and she turns out to be the girl you've been hung up on for months? And *you*!" He turned towards me, and the anger in his eyes made me sob. "You've lied to me for months!"

"I didn't lie," I said, but my voice broke again. "I omitted, Jason."

"The result is the same," he seethed. "Cara, I am so disappointed in you right now."

"Jason, please." I reached for him, but he writhed away from my touch. "I didn't know what to do," I explained desperately. "I was scared you'd pick him."

"I don't want to hear it. I need to think. You've had some fucking cheek, probing me about 'Sandra' this entire time."

"Has she?" William queried, surprised.

Jason ignored him. "How could you do something like that, Cara? How could you play me for a fool like that?"

I sobbed again. "Jason, I'm so sorry. I was only trying to find out what was going on. I never meant to hurt him. I really didn't. And I was scared to tell you because I didn't want to put you in a situation where you'd have to choose between us. I thought it would be best if Will and I kept it strictly between us and sorted it out like *adults*." I glared at William upon my last statement.

He rolled his eyes and raised his bottle of water to his mouth. After an extended mouthful, he swallowed and exhaled loudly. Was he trying to be even more agitating than he normally was?

"Adults," he echoed mockingly. "Spare me, Cara. You can't even face your feelings. You're the immature party between us."

Furious, I retorted, "Says the man who devises a scheme to try and make me jealous!"

He winced.

"What?" Jason was stunned. "What's she on about, Will?"

"Nothing," he murmured and looked away. "Silly mistake is all."

"Your brother made me believe he fucked Francesca in his office on purpose," I revealed without a hint of mercy.

Jason's jaw looked about to unhook. "No fucking way. Will, is that true?"

"I'd rather not talk about it. It was an error in judgment on my part."

"You guys..." Jason shook his head to himself, appalled. "You need to clean up your shit. This isn't it. What the hell are you doing to each other?"

"Toxic things," William murmured. "Lots of them."

"It needs to end," Jason decreed.

"I agree," I uttered with a sniff.

William blew his cheeks out and stared blankly at the floor.

Meanwhile, Jason turned towards me again, and after staring at me for some time, his eyes finally softened. "What about Aaron, Cara? Is he aware of any of this?"

I wiped my cheeks as I shook my head. "No. Really, Jason, what happened tonight between Will and me wasn't supposed to happen. I was just very drunk, and—"

"I'll stop you right there," William snapped at me, and his eyes glowed with anger. "Don't you dare try to blame that on your intake. We both know it was bound to happen sooner or later, Cara, and you're lying if you say anything else. I did *not* take advantage of you. Hell, you were the one initiating everything. If anyone took advantage of someone here, it was *you* who took advantage of *me*. I might not be as plastered as you are right now, but I haven't exactly been sober tonight, either."

"I wasn't going to accuse you of that!" I yelled back. "I was going to say that it was a drunken mistake that should never have happened!" Turning to Jason again, I insisted, "Jason, I'm not going to sleep with him again. Tonight was a mistake. Please, forgive me."

He threw his hand up in the air. "Oh, that's brilliant, just brilliant. Does he share your feelings on that?"

"Absolutely not," William murmured.

"That's what I thought." Jason sighed before he yelled, thoroughly exasperated, "Cara!" He took a deep breath. "Do you realise the clusterfuck you've made? Not just for you, but for me? I'll be torn between loyalties here! There's Will on one end, and then there's you on the other! If things end badly between you, where do you think that'll place me? I don't want to choose between you! The man's got serious feelings for you! What the hell are you doing? Seriously? He's not a toy!"

"Yes, make up your mind, Cara," William joined in.

"I'm sorry! I'm so fucking sorry!" I sobbed and shielded my face with my hands as I surrendered to crying, loudly. "I've tried to tell him, Jason – several times – but he just won't listen."

"That's because you're contradicting yourself, Cara," William defended himself. "You tell me you don't want me, but then you act as if you do. I seriously don't understand what your problem is – this fear of commitment, it's so extreme – it can't be about just your career. Have you been hurt once? Jason, do you know?"

"No," Jason quietly replied, "but she's not interested in a relationship, Will. I know that much." He crawled over to hug me. "Oh, Cara. I'm sorry. I know you didn't mean for this to happen," he murmured and squeezed me against him. "I'm sorry I shouted at you like that. I'm just a bit shocked, and I'm worried about how this will turn out."

His sweet words only made me cry harder. I felt so terrible for the position I'd put him in.

"Good god – look at you two," William grumbled. "This is ridiculous. There shouldn't be a problem to cry over. I want her, she wants me. It really is that simple. I don't understand her need to overcomplicate things."

"Will, sometimes, I seriously think Mum dropped you when you were a child," Jason chided. "She's upset. You don't always have to agree with the reason."

"I clearly picked the wrong brother," I managed to say through a few sniffs.

William's eyes turned steely. "Oh, come on, love. What do you want me to do, then?" he retorted.

"I want you to leave me alone," I answered sassily.

He looked to the heavens for aid. "Why her?" he asked. "Just...why her?"

When Jason saw it, he actually smiled.

Lowering his head again, William sighed. "Alright. Get out then, Jase. I'll deal with her."

"No! I don't want you near me," I growled like a ferocious animal.

He shook his head and approached nevertheless. "Yes, you do."

"You broke my trust!" I accused.

"Like you haven't broken shit yourself, Cara," he alleged bitterly, and I gasped. "I've had it with you tonight."

"Jason," I called, for help.

"See, this is what I mean. Don't drag me into this. This is your mess. I'm not taking any sides in this," he muttered, annoyed.

"Jason," William said as he reached the bed, "we can either sleep here all three, or you can get out. One way or another, I'm not leaving her side until we've reconciled."

"I'll see you in the morning," Jason mumbled as he released me to climb out of my bed. "Try not to kill each other."

"No promises," I said and folded my arms. Irritated, I watched him leave and close the door after himself. He didn't so much as look at me, and it was likely because the expression on my face would have changed his mind.

"Well then," William said once the door had been shut. Turning towards me, he proceeded to undo the buttons of his waistcoat. "Remind me how little you actually wanted me tonight."

I turned my back on him and glared holes into the wall beside my bed. "You're insufferable."

"How am I insufferable? I haven't done anything wrong. You're the one that's fucking everything up with your indecisiveness." He sounded baffled.

"Could you sleep on the sofa, please?"

"No."

"Then don't touch me," I warned. "I will bite off your fingers."

He chuckled. "And here I thought you preferred them inside of you."

My cheeks boiled at his witty remark. "William!"

"Cara."

"Ugh!" I shuddered. I could tear him to shreds.

He sighed behind me. "You'll feel better in the morning. Jason deserved to know. You'll see that, eventually."

"You could at least have warned me that you meant to tell him! Instead, you made me look like the most deceitful wench on the planet!"

"Cara, I'll take care of it. I'll explain things to him in the morning, and I'll make sure he'll forgive you."

Unexpected tears returned to my eyes. "He was so hurt, Will. I really hurt him – my best friend."

"He doesn't like being deceived. Who does, really?"

"But I didn't mean to. I just didn't want to—"

"I know, Cara, and I'll tell him that. Don't worry. I'll have your back."

I closed my eyes and turned mute on him. Meanwhile, he merely undressed, killed the lights, and then climbed into my bed.

"Give me at least a portion of your duvet, Cara."

"No. You don't deserve it. I'm hoping you'll die of cold during the night."

He sighed. "It's summer. It would prove difficult."

"Well, I feel like a glacier, so perhaps that might help."

"More like a volcano, I think."

"If that's the case, then I hope the pyroclastic flow of my eruption will kill you off," I fired back and frowned to myself, horribly annoyed.

"You are such a nerd, and I fucking love that about you," he countered, but he sounded profoundly charmed. "Pyroclastic flow," he echoed to himself. "Honestly, I am amazed by your flair for comebacks. You're fucking sharp. Really, you're going to make an exceptional solicitor one day."

My heart was acting weird, all tingly and light, when I was supposed to be pissed off. He'd told Jason about us without consulting me first, and I was furious about it. He could at least have warned me that he intended to enlighten him so that I could have prepared a proper defence.

And yet, the fact that he took each of my blows the way that he did only reminded me why I fancied him so much. He wasn't intimidated by me – at all. He stood up to me, and it turned me on like nothing else. Being the fierce woman that I was, I required a man like him to keep me on my toes. Otherwise, I'd grow bored within the span of a mere breath.

He gripped my duvet then and, with brutal force, dragged it off me completely. After rolling himself into the entirety of it, he exhaled, satisfied.

"William!"

"Yes, darling?" he replied with a tone of infuriating contentment.

"I swear I'll kill you one of these days!" I whirled to face him.

"You'd regret it," he replied self-assuredly. God, he really knew how to stir my temper. "If you give me a kiss, I'll share," he then brought himself to say.

"That's blackmail."

He snorted. "It isn't. It's bargaining."

I folded my arms and realised at once that I didn't have to be here? I could sleep with Jason if I wanted, or on the sofa. Relief found me at the same moment.

I had crawled halfway over William's large body when he suddenly freed his arms to wrap them around me. "Where do you think you're going?"

"Out!"

He scoffed. "Don't be ridiculous. Here," he said and rearranged the duvet to cover us both. Hooking his strong arms around me, he pulled me towards his warm, naked chest. Divided, I lay rigid against him, paralysed by my confusion. Part of me wanted to leave, another wanted to remain in precisely the same spot. "Cara," he cooed and nuzzled his face in the crook of my neck. "Just sleep. You can kill me in the morning."

"I intend to."

"Make good use of my heat while you still can," he replied smugly and wrapped his leg over mine.

How had it come to this? This was not how I had anticipated my night would end.

"You're a bloody headache, but I do adore you," he mumbled and kissed the slope of my neck.

"If I'm a headache, you're a tumour."

I felt him shake against me, clearly amused. "That's an original way of saying you can't take your mind off me. I'm flattered, Cara. I can assure you it's mutual."

I moaned in his embrace. He had an unmatched ability to twist my words.

"Suppose I've finally grown on you after all." While squeezing me against him, he continued, "Drunk out of your mind, and still, you maintain your bravado. I take my hat off to you."

"I'd prefer if you kept as many clothes on as possible."

He shook against me, evidently trying to stifle his laughter. Silence ensued afterwards, and I was nearly asleep when he propped himself on his elbow beside me and leaned over my figure. As light as a feather, his fingers brushed my hair behind my ear before he lowered his lips to my cheek. He left a prolonged kiss there before he softly said, "I'm not going to hurt you, Cara. You've nothing to be afraid of. If you give me a chance, I'll take good care of you – I promise."

Affection set my blood aflame while I pressed my lips together in the dark, and it took some time before I'd calmed enough to reply. "I don't want you to take care of me, Will. I want to take care of myself."

He hesitated. "Has anyone hurt you? Is that why you're like this? Please, be honest."

I sighed. "No. You know I've never been in a relationship before. They scare me."

"Why?"

"The ownership," I murmured. "I can't stand the idea of it. I want to be free. I want to be free to do exactly what I want, when I want, without having to show consideration to anyone else. At least for now."

He fell silent.

"You were right when you called me immature, Will," I eventually added. "I am immature, and I'm certainly too immature for a relationship. There is so much I want to do. I'm not ready to focus on anyone other than myself. There's just not enough space in my life for anyone other than me right now.

"I shouldn't have kissed you tonight. It was cruel of me, and I would understand if you hate me for it. As I said, you really deserve better, Will. I don't expect – nor do I want – you to wait for me. I mean it."

He exhaled loudly and collapsed. "Like I've any choice."

Tears of sympathy prickled my eyes. Turning to face him, I stared through the dark and raised my hand to stroke his cheek. "You're a wonderful man. This will pass before you know it. Feelings are fleeting. Soon enough, you'll meet another woman who can give you what you want, and who will be ten times better than I ever could be."

"You're wrong. There's only one you."

I snuggled closer and stopped only when our noses touched. "You're such a romantic."

"About you, yeah. You've driven me mad."

"Well, you drive me mad, too, but I'm sorry either way," I mumbled, upset.

"Me too."

"I didn't mean to."

"I know you didn't."

"Perhaps we should see if I can work for Violet instead," I suggested.

"No. I'll be fine."

"But—"

"You'll always be around anyway. As long as you and Jason remain friends, I'll never be rid of you."

My lips protruded as I pouted, which made them tickle against his. He must have thought I was searching for a kiss because, as I was about to pull back, his hand caught my neck to hold me in place. Before I knew it, his mouth was on mine again. The beats of my heart had never been louder. My pulse drummed behind my ears, attenuating the sound of our lips moving passionately against each other. When he rolled onto me, sudden, intense feelings overwhelmed my chest. For a moment, I couldn't breathe. It was like my lungs had ceased functioning to create space for that foreign emotion.

"Will," I said on my remaining breath, "we shouldn't."

His hands felt like fire on my skin, resolutely amorous and awakening the desire to sin again.

"We absolutely shouldn't," he agreed while his hand slid down my waist. Using his knee, he pushed my legs apart to place himself between them, and once there, he descended onto me. On either side of me, his arms supported the weight of his upper body, and I'd never felt so safe.

His mouth dived for mine again, and I was instantly lost in its sensual dance. I knew I ought to pull away, but I couldn't. His magnetism was too powerful to resist, and our bodies communicated too well. They wanted each other desperately, and it seemed impossible to deny it.

"Just one chance," he whispered between lustful kisses. "Say you'll consider it. Just one chance, Cara."

Turning my head, I heaved for air to steady myself. My thoughts were scattering into utter disorder, and my feelings didn't aid me in sorting them. I wanted him so badly. My body was begging me to surrender, begging me to leap into sin.

When his mouth landed on my throat to trace the vein that revealed how hard my heart was beating solely for him, I was reminded of how irresistible he was. "Oh," I groaned and ran my fingers through his hair. An aching commenced between my legs, begging for his intrusion. I wanted to feel him within me again. If I didn't, I thought I'd lose my mind.

"Will, we need to stop."

"We do," he agreed again and returned to my mouth. Meanwhile, his hands travelled hungrily across my body, and he knew exactly where to squeeze, where to stroke and where to pinch. "But I can't," he eventually professed. "You'll have to push me away."

Instead, I closed my legs around him and pressed him tighter against me. Extreme arousal flooded my system when I felt his hard member between us, pressing against my entrance. Letting my lips land on the crook of his neck, I inhaled his scent deep into my lungs and felt myself fade ever so slightly. His embrace was the closest I'd ever come to experiencing heaven. I was sure.

"Say you'll consider it, Cara," he urged and folded his hand over my breast to squeeze the aching mass, and the action made me moan against his skin. "Let me pleasure you like this—" he purred and lowered his lips to my ear, where he gently whispered— "over, and over, and over."

His words unlocked an emotion in me that refused to be ignored. In the wake of it, I found myself questioning whether avoiding him was really the right course of action. If he left me now, I knew I might regret it in the future. However, there was still his impact on my focus to consider. I'd hardly been able to think of anything other than him since April. Then again, would rejecting him really make a difference? Perhaps in the long run, but then he'd also promised me once that the initial excitement that comes with infatuation would subside after a while. So, did I really have anything to lose? One way or another, I'd remain preoccupied with him for quite some time.

Considering Jason's reaction earlier, it was probable that he would prefer if I gave Will a chance. When it came to the question of work, both Violet and Will had provided strong arguments for ignoring our role as colleagues. However, I had to consider those arguments more thoroughly – when I was sober – before making up my mind. It was true that I was only going to work under William for three months, and that I could always get someone else to write my reference – Violet, for example. And if we kept our affair a secret, it wouldn't harm my chances of getting hired. However, if things didn't work out between William and me, working at Day & Night might turn out to be difficult.

There was also Aaron to consider. I'd need to end things with him, and I wasn't looking forward to it. While I'd never been in love with him, I was certainly attached to him as a person. He'd become a habit, and it was a habit I loved in my own way, because it offered freedoms that a relationship with William would not.

It was like my heart switched off my brain and took control of my tongue instead when I said, "Okay." After pulling in a deep breath, I repeated, "Okay, I'll consider it."

All at once, he stopped. "Really?"

"Yes," I panted. "I'll *consider* it."

Surprising me, he rolled off me immediately and proceeded to pull me into a spooning position instead. His erection pressed against my bum, but since he made no further advances, I found myself confused.

"What are you doing?" I queried, and I couldn't hide my disappointment.

"I don't fuck drunk women unless they're my girlfriend."

An abundance of heat claimed my face. "Seriously?"

"Yes."

"Will, you have my utter consent."

"Not happening. Matter of principle."

"But you'll take my word regarding whether I'll consider dating you or not?" I replied disbelievingly.

"I'll take what I can in that regard."

"But you fingered me in the club!"

"That's different. If you want drunk sex, you'll need to be my girlfriend. This is a boyfriend level request you've made. If you'd like to upgrade your subscription, you'll have to go on a date with me."

Awfully frustrated, I moaned loudly. "You bastard. Have you got any idea how aroused I am right now?"

Smug laughter spilled out of him. "Don't worry. I'll make it up to you as soon as you agree to go on a date with me."

Disbelieving, I asked, "Are you saying you won't fuck me again unless I agree to go on a date with you? Even if I'm sober?"

"Yes."

I sighed. He surely drove a hard bargain. Then again, in light of his feelings, I could understand why he was unwilling to sleep with me unless I committed to him – he was looking out for himself. Really, he was being wise. "I respect that."

"Until then, you can dream about us having sex instead. I do it all the time."

I blushed. "Oh my God, Will."

"Not even slightly ashamed of admitting that."

"You're not right in the head. Then again, I'm guilty of the same."

He stiffened against me. "Have you dreamt about me, too? Actually?"

"Night, Will."

Complacent, he replied, "Sweet dreams, then."

WEAPON

AN EMPTY BED WELCOMED ME AS SOON AS I OPENED MY eyes the following morning. Though I couldn't recall much of the previous night, bits and pieces were forming a horrid notion of it in my head. The club. William. The spot under the stairs. Kissing. His fingers inside of me. Tequila. Vomiting.

Jason.

"Jason," I whimpered and pushed my duvet aside to search for him, whereupon the sight of my nightie reminded me that William and Jason had tucked me into bed last night.

I was suffering from a tremendous hangover, but Jason and I needed to talk, and it couldn't wait. I was desperate to clear the air and make amends. I felt terrible, and it only added to my headache.

When I opened my bedroom door, the smell of bacon filled my nose, and it was sent directly from heaven. Was Jason making me breakfast? He couldn't be too angry with me, then – I hoped.

Nevertheless, I wanted to face him cleaned of any evidence from last night, so I decided I'd have a shower first. Striding across the hall, I gripped the handle of the bathroom door and turned it. As I opened it, a sight I had not expected welcomed me.

There stood William, naked in all his glory and drying his hair with a towel. What a beautiful backside he had. Slabs of prominent muscle hugged his long spine, and dimples carved into the flesh right above his enticingly taut bum. His biceps and deltoids, as well as the muscles of his hairless, broad back, rippled with his motions. Saliva amassed in my mouth. What a bomb of testosterone. He was strikingly masculine. I wasn't even remotely prepared for the captivating sight of him.

With haste, I looked away and stood perfectly still. As my eyes flickered around the humid room, I saw that his clothes from last night were dumped on the toilet seat.

His head turned towards me, and when our eyes locked, a wicked smile claimed his mouth. He looked elated. His eyes glowed with a joy I hadn't seen in them before. Although he'd had a long night yesterday, he still looked dangerously appealing. Why? I moaned inwardly.

"Morning, love. I'm flattered you wanted to shower with me, but I'm afraid you're a few minutes too late. Better luck next time."

Blushing crimson, I felt about to combust. "Are you quite finished?"

"Oh, don't be that way." He chuckled. "Nothing you haven't seen before. Last time you caught me naked, you were rather excited about it. Quit pretending."

Since I was far too exhausted to tolerate his banter, I trembled where I stood, and my hands formed fists – the audacity of this man. What made matters worse was the fact that he was absolutely right. Naked, he was a breath-taking vision. Still, how could he discern my thoughts so effortlessly?

"Care for a look of the front? It's all yours," he continued to tease and turned towards me, but I'd whirled around before I could see anything.

"Cover up, you wanker, and get the fuck out! Bloody exhibitionist."

"Sorry, that was inconsiderate of me. The view would of course only increase your current sexual frustration since I refused to fuck you last night."

"That's not it, you conceited twat!" But it was.

He laughed, and I heard him turn on the tap. Assuming it was safe, I turned to peek at him. To my relief, he'd wrapped the towel around himself. Amused, he watched me in the mirror.

A pout formed on my face. "Could you hurry up, please? I need to shower as well."

"Then do. I don't mind. At all." He gestured towards the glass door.

"Without you here!"

He rolled his eyes and raised his toothbrush to his mouth. "Then you'll have to wait."

Fuming, I folded my arms and tapped my foot, but he took his time.

"William!" I growled when I'd counted to a minute.

With white foam around his delicious mouth, he grinned at me in the mirror. "Are you always this cranky when you're hungover?"

"I'm cranky whenever *you're* involved."

"Good thing I'm weak for your bitch attitude," he playfully responded before he spat into the basin. I gaped. After rinsing his mouth, he stretched up to his full height and turned towards me. "It turns me on."

Frustrated beyond belief, I raised my hands to my hair and pulled it – this man. Regardless of what I did, he twisted and turned it in his favour, and it was infuriating. No wonder he was so good at his job.

His lips spread into a grin, and a playful twinkle danced in his eyes. "So much frustration, Cara. You look in dire need of another orgasm. Lucky for you, all you need to do is agree to go on a date with me, and I'll be happy to oblige."

"Stop using sex as a weapon against me!"

His grin was devilish. "Why? It's clearly working." Indeed, it was. I couldn't recall ever having been so sexually frustrated.

"Out!" I barked and pointed to the door.

Still grinning to himself, he nodded and finally approached the door, but when he was about to pass me, he paused to curl his hand around my neck. Bringing me close, he planted a firm kiss on the top of my head. "Enjoy your shower," he purred as he pulled away. "I'll see you in a bit."

Paralysed, I heard him close the door. My body was complete chaos. I couldn't make sense of a single thought or emotion. Everything lacked sense. But there was one thing I knew.

He fuelled the fire of my soul and gave the beats to my heart. In his presence, I felt capable of glowing in the dark.

I stepped into the shower and adjusted the temperature. After a dreadful night, my body was feeble, so I sat on the beige tiles under the stream of cold water, reviving. I'd obviously had too much to drink. Those last three shots of tequila hadn't helped anything at all apart from offering a temporary relief from the remorse I'd experienced.

After dragging myself out of the shower, I decided not to blow-dry my hair since I didn't have the strength. I required food and water to recharge myself. So, after drying myself with my towel, I pulled on my white satin bathrobe and headed out to confront reality.

William and Jason were talking in the dining room, so I paused to eavesdrop.

"I can't believe you eavesdropped," William said, and my heart leapt to my throat. At first, I thought he was speaking to me, but soon enough, I realised he was speaking to his brother. Jason had eavesdropped on us last night?

"Of course I had to eavesdrop," Jason replied, irritated.

"What if I had fucked her?" William countered. "It's weird, J. You should have that looked at by a professional."

"Then I would have left, you tit."

"So you heard her moaning, then?"

"I nearly left at that point. Then again, it's not the first time I've heard her moaning."

"Don't remind me," William replied vehemently.

"Sorry."

"Either way, it's still an odd thing to do."

"Excuse you, Will, it really isn't. You were arguing like the apocalypse was arriving and you disagreed on how to avoid it. It was intense."

"Interesting comparison."

"Seriously."

"Cara and I have always bickered. It's just who we are together. Really, it's just how we flirt."

"I can see why you like each other – bloody hotheads, both of you."

"Yes, we're quite compatible," William agreed.

"I should've known you'd fall for her. You're so similar it's honestly ridiculous. Now that I think about it, I can't believe I didn't try to set you up with her."

"You should've."

"But then neither of you were interested in a relationship."

"Not until I met her," William clarified.

"Suppose that's what happens when you find the right one."

"Suppose so. Though, you sort of did set me up with her by sending her to Disrepute, which you know I frequent, on a Friday."

"True," Jason chuckled. "But since you're not one to have one-night stands, and since you already had Violet and Francesca, it never occurred to me that you might end up interacting, much less actually sleeping together. Honestly, when she came home the next day, I was sure it had to be someone else – perhaps a colleague of yours or something. I definitely didn't think it could be you, all things considered. Though, in hindsight, she did say you were really rude and forthright, so perhaps I should have suspected at that point."

"Very funny."

"I'm actually not joking. Anyway, sounded like you made up last night."

"I'm not sure. She was rather drunk, even at the end. And she just scolded my ear off in the bathroom."

"She's probably hungover, and you can be proper annoying."

"True. Anyway, don't give her a hard time when she comes out," I heard William command. "Please, Jason. You'll only be making my life much harder. She's enough trouble as it is."

"I won't. I can see why she would hide it from me. I'm only a bit upset because I really despised Sandra on your behalf. Safe to say I'm shocked it's been Cara all along," Jason murmured. "It's been an eye-opening experience on so many levels. Not just because of Cara, but in general, too. I fell victim to bias and prejudice, and now that I know it was actually Cara, my whole perspective has changed."

"Understandable. I tried telling her you wouldn't care, but she was seriously scared of losing you, Jase. Kept mentioning she knew you'd pick me and things like that. And, to be fair, I get it. I mean, my intentions with her haven't changed at all, and she knows that. Naturally, that would make her hesitant about telling you anything, because she'd hardly enjoy being the reason for your brother's broken heart. So, I suppose she was scared that my feelings for her would potentially force you to choose between us."

Jason sighed. "Yeah. It makes sense. Either way, I was livid at first. I couldn't believe she would keep me in the dark about something like that, but after further thought, I realised that's exactly why she did it. It's typical of her. She never wants to drag anyone else into her mess. She absolutely hates drama, so I'm sure she did it only to protect me. Her heart was in the right place. However, if she ever does something like that again, I won't be as merciful. She fucked up, and I mean to let her know."

Slight relief had found me by the time I dared to make my way into the dining room. William had kept his word and had supported me, and I appreciated it immensely because, without his intervention, I was confident that Jason would have stayed angry with me for much longer.

They sat at the dining table, and the view made my heart jolt. Orange juice, coffee, and a full English breakfast. I could've kissed

Jason. This was exactly what I needed.

William appeared to have borrowed a pair of sweats from Jason, but both brothers had neglected a shirt this morning. Had I not been so hungover, I might have appreciated the view more than I did. They were a strikingly attractive pair of brothers. Their gene pool was clearly a winner.

When they noticed my arrival, they simultaneously turned their heads to acknowledge me. In that brief moment, I seriously wondered how I hadn't realised that William was Jason's brother when I'd first met him. While their hair colours were different, they had nearly identical eyes, although William's were slightly more piercing and somehow darker, even if their irises were exactly the same colour. However, William's eyebrows always formed a slight frown, as if he was sharply judging and examining everything he looked at. Jason gazed around with an innate desire to appreciate everything he saw for what it was.

Aside from their eyes, William's jaw was a little sharper, but even their noses and full lips were eerily similar. I was such an idiot.

"Morning," I mumbled and completely ignored William's grin to meet Jason's patient gaze instead.

"Morning, love. How are you feeling?" Jason responded affectionately while he pulled out the chair beside him. My heart throbbed at his tone. I didn't deserve him. I hated that I'd betrayed and disappointed him.

"I've got an awful headache," I murmured as I descended into my seat. My eyes zoomed in on an aspirin beside the glass of orange juice then, and my heart melted. He would make a girl the luckiest in the world someday.

He smirked at my reply and pointed towards the pill. "I'm miles ahead of you, dear."

Nodding, I necked it with a mouthful of orange juice. Afterwards, I faced him with a pout.

"Jason, I'm seriously sorry about everything. I hate myself for betraying you like that. I—"

"I know, Cara. I heard you last night. But we'll talk about it later," he cut me off, but his tone was forgiving. "I'd prefer if Will wasn't here."

Glancing over at William, I saw that his eyebrows were arched in surprise, and surprise caught me too when he didn't object. Instead, he recovered his composure rather quickly and focused on his breakfast.

"Okay. Me too," I said and grabbed my knife to smear a thick layer of butter onto my toast. William's eyes looked about to fall out of his skull when he saw it.

"Damn. Would you like some more bread with your butter?" he joked.

I glared at him. "I like butter."

Beside me, Jason laughed. "Correction, she loves butter."

William's lips slid into a charming grin. "Yes, I can see that. Duly noted," he murmured and nodded to himself.

I rolled my eyes and proceeded to top my slice of toast with a layer of scrambled eggs, but as soon as I did, I sensed William's eyes on me.

"Weak for his scrambled eggs, are you, love?" he asked. "Familiar recipe, perhaps?"

I tensed. Seeming to catch on to William's surreptitious comment, Jason frowned. "Right, what's going on?" he demanded.

I sighed. "Will made me scrambled eggs the morning after we first met. I thought they tasted familiar, but I... It just didn't strike me."

"Oh my God," Jason laughed. "This is ridiculous."

William's grin endured while he sought my gaze. As soon as he caught it, he told me with a gleam in his eyes, "When you eventually accept your feelings for me, you may consider it a bonus. I'd be happy to make it for you anytime you like."

I wasn't sure if it was because I was angry with his continued persistence and flirtatious behaviour, or because I felt exposed, but I turned bright red at once. "Are you actually socially inept? I can't catch a fucking break with you ever, can I?"

Jason reached for his iPad beside me, clearly determined to sign out.

Meanwhile, William argued, "To be fair, I choose to be. Either way, it doesn't make your feelings for me any less true," he muttered and reached for his cup of coffee. "We could have dinner today, if you like."

Utterly despairing, I looked at Jason. "Jason, seriously. Can you tell this utter knob to give me a break, at least for a day? I'm fucking exhausted."

Jason sighed and scrolled on his screen, refusing to meet my desperate gaze. "Cara, if there's one thing I know about my brother, it's the fact that he doesn't stop until he gets his way. I'm sorry, but I've had to live with it all my life, and now you do, too – especially when he knows you're attracted to him. At least we can rejoice in our solidarity. For next time, don't let him finger you when you're out drinking together – that's about as counterproductive as it can get."

"Can we please kick him out?" I begged over a tearless sob.

Jason remained mute.

"So?" William prompted. "What's it going to be, Cara? Dinner?"

I frowned. "If it wasn't clear enough already, no! I've got plans, anyway."

His handsome head tilted. "What sort of plans?"

"I've got a birthday to attend." I abated all mention that I was going with Aaron, as I was sure that would only lead him to detonate. A caveman version of William was not something I had the strength to handle right now. I'd had enough drama – enough for a lifetime. Besides, his objection wouldn't get him anywhere. I wasn't about to cancel my plans with Aaron last minute for a man I wasn't even certain I wanted to date. It was also Tyler's birthday, and he was my friend, too. I had to show up. To add to it, who I was going with was none of William's business. I hadn't made up my mind about whether to date him yet, so for now, I had no obligation to him whatsoever. Besides, by not mentioning Aaron, I was sure I was sparing William from unnecessary anxiety.

"Who with?" William asked.

"Lad named Tyler," I said, and I sensed Jason stiffening beside me. Meanwhile, William's features hardened.

"He a friend, or…?"

I groaned. "Yes, William, I haven't sat on his cock, alright?"

Sharply focused, he scrutinised me. "Will Aaron be there?"

My heart stilled, and it required all my strength to seem unaffected. "No."

He narrowed his eyes for a beat, suspicious. "Well, I've got poker night. We can make it an early dinner."

Groaning, I reached for my own cup of coffee. "No," I replied after a sip. "Besides, do you really think I'm in any shape to have dinner with you today? You're more exhausting than a bloody marathon, Will."

He chuckled, and so did Jason. "How about tomorrow, then? If you last the entire dinner, I'll make sure to give you both a medal and a reward."

I lost my patience. "William, I said I'd *consider* it! It was absolutely not a 'yes'. What you're asking of me is considerable! I need time to think it through. I won't make this decision lightly, or on an emotional whim. Dating you could cause irreparable injury to my career. I need to be certain that I can bear the consequences of the worst-case scenario – that if things don't work out, or if my career is somehow jeopardised, I won't look back and regret my decision."

Caught by my anger, he leaned back and frowned. "I'm not going to get in the way of your dreams and ambitions, Cara. All I want is to be by your side while you chase them – cheer you on and help you out whenever you need it."

"So you've said, Will, but you can't control the outcome of this. I wish you'd understand that."

Jason cleared his throat. "Should I leave you alone?"

"No," I replied with a shake of my head. Returning my attention to William, I said, "Give me a week to make up my mind, yeah?"

His nods started slowly before they picked up the pace. "Okay, yeah. A week. I can do that."

"Thank you," I said with relief.

25

———◆•◆•◆———

NAIL IN THE COFFIN

At five o'clock, William and Jason were about to head out to shop for groceries and spirits for poker night, which Stephen would be hosting this time around. However, just before they left, Jason stalked into my room where I was lying on my bed, listening to music. As I observed the urgency of his movements and how carefully he shut the door, apprehension unfolded in my veins, so I took my headset off at once and watched him approach my bed.

"You lied to him," he whispered accusingly.

I gulped. "Where is he?" I whispered back.

"In the bathroom."

"Jason, I'm not his girlfriend," I replied defensively. "He hasn't got a right to know, and he would probably lose his head. It's just unnecessary to tell him."

"Cara, I can't stand this." He was visibly upset. "Please, you need to make up your mind."

Caught by his misery, I inhaled deeply. "Jason, I don't know what to do. Please, don't make it any harder for me. I'm not going to cancel my plans with Aaron last minute for a man I'm not even sure I want to date, and it's really none of William's concern whether I see him or not. We're not exclusive, and Tyler is my friend, too!"

This aggressive whispering was really challenging my throat.

His jaw clenched while his brows drew together with worry. "This isn't going to end well. I can feel it."

"Just don't say anything."

"But this secrecy. Doesn't it tell you something? That it's immoral, for instance?"

"But it's not immoral!" I replied, flustered. "How is it immoral, Jason? I've told your brother a million times that I'm not ready for that sort of commitment, and last night, I agreed to *consider* going on a date with him. The only reason you think it's immoral is because you know he'd be upset at the truth, but just because his feelings would get hurt, it doesn't mean I've no right to take such actions. I'm still single, Jason, and I'm honestly looking forward to seeing Aaron and Tyler. In fact, I *need* to see Aaron to make up my mind! Just don't tell Will, and you'll save us all any trouble."

"I hate this," he declared.

"How do you think I feel? It's ridiculous that I should feel bad for wanting to see my best friend when I'm not even in a committed relationship with your brother. It's emotional manipulation, Jason. I owe him no further consideration at this point."

He glanced away.

"Jase?" William called from outside, puzzled.

"Yeah, I'll be right out. Just having a word with Cara."

"Have fun at Stephen's," I murmured, and I was no longer whispering. "Tell him I said hi."

Jason pointed at me. "If you don't come clean about this now, promise me you will if you start seeing him. Immediately."

"I promise," I said, and I meant it.

"Good." He turned to the door.

"Jason?"

"Yes?" He paused to face me.

"I really am sorry. I love you. Please don't think I don't, because you really are the most precious thing in my world."

He blew his cheeks out and gripped his hips. "I love you too, Cara. Always. I know what you're like, so I get that this is inconvenient, to say the least. One way or another, we're both in it now, but at least we've got each other."

His empathic character really was remarkable, and it wasn't something I took for granted. "Thank you. There's no one I'd rather be stuck with."

His smile was tender. "I know, Cara. You and me both."

"Have fun tonight."

"You too."

A few seconds after he'd opened the door, William popped his head in. "I'll see you on Monday, Cara."

Looking into his eyes, it felt like my heart was being ripped in different directions. I really had no idea whatsoever of how to proceed, and it was driving me mad. This had to end sometime, or I would surely lose the plot once and for all.

"Yeah. Have fun tonight."

"You too. Call me if you need anything."

I frowned. "Like what?"

He shrugged. "I don't know – like if you get plastered again, for instance."

"I'd rather die than do that again anytime soon."

His nose wrinkled somewhat. "I'd prefer it if you got plastered rather than died."

Despite my anxiety, I managed a chuckle. "Alright, I'll call you if I am considering dying."

"Good. Thanks." With that, he closed the door between us and left with Jason.

§ § §

Earlier that day, I had been suffering a tremendous hangover, which William's presence had amplified. I hadn't thought anything would be capable of plastering a genuine smile onto my face today, but somehow, Aaron managed it. Tyler's birthday had been a great success, and I'd appreciated the few moments of forgetfulness regarding my troubled heart and how to proceed with William.

Holding hands, Aaron and I strolled along the pavement towards my flat. It was nearly two o'clock, so it wasn't very late taking English party hours into account, but I was exhausted after going out two days in a row and after facing all the drama with William. Aaron had noticed when my enthusiasm over shuffleboard had diminished.

Though by a slim margin, Tyler's girlfriend and I had beat Tyler and Aaron. After the match, Aaron had proposed to take me home. I'd expressed concern about ruining his night, but he had convinced me that I wouldn't. "I've never been much of a party-person," he'd reminded me.

Aaron was a peaceful man. Around him, I felt calm and serene, and sometimes even static. Letting go of my hand, he wrapped his arm around shoulders and tugged me closer to his side, and the sensation made me smile up at him. He felt so familiar. I truly adored his embrace because it soothed me the same way Jason's did. In a moment of weakness, I compared it to William's. Unlike Aaron's, William's embrace didn't soothe me in the slightest. On the contrary, it made me tense, because it triggered such extreme emotion, which ultimately exhausted me.

The three years I'd spent with Aaron had always been so placid, although I would never mistake them for boring. Since William, I'd savoured his calming effect on me more than ever. However, with his arm wrapped around my shoulders, I couldn't help but remember that I still had a choice to make. I'd hoped that spending time with Aaron tonight would aid me out of my confusion, but it had only exacerbated it. I was more confused now than I'd been earlier, because I loved my lifestyle as it was, and Aaron's presence was a firm reminder of that.

I didn't know any other way of life. In Aaron's arms, I felt like myself. In William's, I felt like I was turning into a person I couldn't recognise, and it frightened me. The unknown frightened me, and it did because I feared it would take away my happiness and my freedom.

So, there we walked, embodying idyllic joy while remaining completely oblivious to the drunk Londoners we passed on our way.

"You've been rather quiet tonight," Aaron remarked when we neared the building. "Something wrong?"

"I'm just drained. I had such a rough night last night."

"I can't believe you got that drunk. So unlike you."

"I know."

"Work stressing you out?"

"You could say that."

I sensed his eyes on my profile. "You know I'm here if you'd like to talk to someone, right?"

Wrapping my arm around his waist, I hugged him tightly. "I know. I'll be fine, though."

§ § §

I had just unlocked the front door when I heard music coming from the living room. Since I hadn't expected it, I paused in the doorway, confused. Was Jason home already?

"Hello?" I called and stepped aside to let Aaron in. That was when I noticed five pairs of shoes on the floor that did not belong to Jason or myself, and one pair looked particularly familiar. They were formal brown leather shoes, and if I had to guess, precisely the size *he* wore. An alarm went off in my head.

"Home already?" Jason yelled back.

"Hi, Cara!" I heard Stephen greet.

My heart faltered. Immobile, I stood next to Aaron while he kicked off his shoes. Panic swallowed me whole as I feared the worst: had their plans changed? Had poker night been moved to our flat instead? The likelihood made me gulp in horror. I had Aaron with me, and if poker night was being hosted here, it would mean William was here as well.

I looked back at the brown leather shoes. They had to be his. *Shit!*

Colour drained from my face as I turned my head to see Aaron tuck his hands into his pockets. When he was about to move forward, my hand acted of its own accord and reached out to stop him.

What was I supposed to do now? I couldn't just kick him out. I'd invited him, for crying out loud, and he would certainly gauge that there was something off if I suddenly told him to leave. However, I didn't want to enlighten him about my past with William, either.

First of all, William was my boss, and that was surely not going to impress Aaron. On the contrary, he'd probably judge me for it. Secondly, we weren't supposed to tell each other about people we had slept with on the side.

To top it all, there was William to consider. In light of last night, how would he react to this, especially when actually facing the man?

Fuck, I thought to myself. Another clusterfuck. I wanted to hide in my room and never come out.

"What's the matter?" Aaron enquired, puzzled.

Within me, my heart sprinted. How would I handle this?

"I…" I couldn't bring myself to say anything coherent. I was too shocked. Why hadn't Jason informed me? Had he thought I'd be home later than this?

"Cara, you're acting strange."

"Sorry. I'm only surprised. I didn't think we'd have company. Jason wasn't supposed to be here." My voice sounded anxious even to my own ears.

Aaron's eyebrows furrowed. "So what if he is?" he replied, bewildered, and jerked his arm out of my hold to approach the living room.

Oh no. This was not going to end well. I could feel it in my bones. Acting out of pure desperation to avoid any chaos, I rushed after him and grabbed his arm again to stall him.

"Actually, could we grab a bite somewhere first? I'm starved, and I'd love a kebab." I hoped to the god I didn't believe in that he'd agree. If he did, I could buy myself more time to think out a solution to prevent them from meeting. The few seconds he considered my plea I spent conjuring a plan. When out on the street, I would phone Jason and tell him to read my texts, in which I would order him to throw his guests out before I returned.

"Honestly, Cara, I'd rather not. Can't we get something delivered instead? My treat."

I nearly surrendered to despair, but quickly lied, "The place I had in mind doesn't offer delivery."

I could see he was on the fence when he pressed his lips together and stared at me for a few breaths. Just when he was about to share his verdict, my worst nightmare came to life. Exiting the bathroom, a tall figure entered my peripheral vision, and I vaguely saw it pause after only a single stride. Slowly, I turned my head to acknowledge the person.

Halfway out the door stood William, and with eyes wide, he stared disbelievingly at Aaron.

I could barely hear the music above my own heartbeat anymore. This was real intimidation.

I wanted to cry. William was not going to handle this well, possessive as he was, and Aaron would be completely blindsided. And, in all honesty, I didn't want to hurt William like this. He didn't deserve it.

While I hadn't decided whether to continue my arrangement with Aaron, there was no need to rub it in William's face. However, I hadn't meant for this, and that was the sole reason I didn't immediately seek shelter in my room. I was desperate to defend my actions against William's wrath.

"Hi," Aaron greeted with a faint nod.

It took William several seconds to break out of his thoughts and nod back, but not a word escaped his lips. When his eyes suddenly flickered in my direction, my heart skipped a beat. With haste, I fixed my gaze on the floor. The alcohol in my blood made it particularly difficult to think clearly, so I hadn't the faintest idea of how to proceed from here.

Since William failed to respond, Aaron continued, "Been a while since last time, but it's Will, right?"

I sensed William's subsequent glare upon my figure before I saw it. Thoroughly intimidated, I barely managed to steal a glimpse at him, and from the way his jaw clenched, I could tell he was fuming.

"Cara, a word," his powerful voice demanded.

I'd never been so close to pissing myself as a grown woman. Unsure of how to respond, I peeked up at Aaron. His kind brown eyes stared back at me, full of confusion.

After swallowing the lump in my throat, I tried to say without revealing too much, "Aaron, could you excuse us for a sec?"

Evidently suspicious, his eyes narrowed when he glanced at William again. Without a word, he merely nodded and headed down the corridor, past William's rigid figure. Just as they overlapped, I saw them exchange a vigilant glare.

William watched him the entire time it took him to round the corner and reach the living area, and only after he was out of sight did he turn his head to acknowledge me again. After five strides, he stopped in front of me. With a slight bow of his head, he glowered down at me while I stared nervously into his chest. Meanwhile, the stench of alcohol filled my nose. He was just as drunk, if not drunker, than I was.

"What the fuck do you think you're doing?" he demanded. He nearly spat every word.

"I wasn't aware you'd be here," I excused myself. "Had I known, I wouldn't have invited him."

He was silent for such a long time that I dared to glance at him again, and I found him watching me in wounded disbelief. "You lied to me."

I searched frantically for air, but my lungs weren't receptive. "Because I knew you'd react like this."

"Of course I'd fucking react like this!"

Extremely intimidated, I retreated a step and continued to avoid his eyes. "Will, I said I'd consider it. Until I make up my mind, I'm free to do whatever I want," I reminded him, distraught.

Livid, he stepped after me. "Are you trying to say that you intend to keep fucking him until you have? Despite what happened between us last night?"

I had no idea what to say. My thoughts collided with my feelings, and the result was chaos of an incredible scale. Trying to buy some time, I looked anywhere but at him until he gripped my jaw and forced me to meet his gaze. In his eyes resided a thick layer of resentment, but it was the unmistakable vulnerability shining through that made my heart ache. He looked completely shattered.

Calmly, I said, "Take your hand off me, Will."

Swallowing, he released my jaw at once, and he had the decency to look ashamed of himself.

After a deep breath, I said, "What I'm saying is that, until I've decided whether or not to date you, I have no obligation to you. Besides, I was going to tell you after I'd met him." Retreating another step, I folded my arms and evaded his eyes, as if I could hide from the blatant plea in them.

"You are unbelievable," he claimed. "Have some fucking respect."

Spreading my arms apart, I waved them in frustration. "Respect?" I echoed. "You're one to talk. You haven't respected my boundaries at all."

"I have respected them plenty, Cara. Meanwhile, you've contradicted yourself and acted like you don't want me to anymore," he argued and stepped closer again. Retreating another step, my back collided with the wall behind me. Now trapped between his body and the wall, I froze in panic.

"For fuck's sake, Cara. Have you even changed your bedding? Or have you already forgotten that you spent last night sleeping in my arms after begging me to have sex with you?" he reminded me harshly.

When he put it that way, he made my actions sound so much

worse. A grimace covered my face while I shook my head. "N-no. I haven't forgotten."

"Then what the hell are you thinking?" he hissed impatiently as he scrutinised me. "I won't let this happen," he told me, and his tone remained calm and resolute. "I won't let you do this to us."

Us. His phrasing tore the fibres of my heart in a way I hadn't expected. Biting into my lower lip, I folded my arms even tighter.

When I failed to respond, he continued fiercely, "If you sleep with him tonight, or on any other night from now on, that will be the nail in the coffin, Cara. I won't be able to overlook that. I won't forgive you."

The ultimatum made me suck in a deep breath while my heart hammered in my chest. He'd just made it crystal clear that if I went through with this, it would seal our fate, once and for all. He'd move on, and I would permanently lose the option to explore our chemistry. Up until now, I had thought I could recover from that, but now that he had actually placed the gun in my hand, I was hesitant to pull the trigger. Suddenly, what was at stake became much more real to me.

Sensing how conflicted I was, he reached forward to entwine my fingers with his, and the intimacy of his gesture set my feelings ablaze. I didn't quite know how he did it, but he always managed to pull me back every time I was about to stray. Now, when I stared into the sea of his eyes, denying my lust for him seemed completely absurd. It was thick and dense as it coursed through my veins. Had he proceeded to kiss me right then, I knew I would have returned it.

It crossed my mind that he must have realised as much from the expression on my face, because he soon lowered his head to trail the tip of his nose across mine. Meanwhile, he raised his free hand to brush the back of his fingers across my cheek.

His mouth rested dangerously close to my own, and the warm breeze of his breath teased my lips, beckoning.

"Don't fuck this up, darling," he urged, fingers moving into my hair to clasp the back of my neck. Using his thumb, he pushed my jaw to tilt my head back so that I would meet his eyes.

Flustered, I – perhaps too loudly – answered, "What am I supposed to do, Will? Kick him out?"

"Yes."

He was just about to kiss me when someone I had not anticipated interrupted us. "Am I missing something here?"

I ripped my hand out of William's hold and turned my head to acknowledge Aaron's presence. Immediately, guilt flooded my system. Leaning against the wall at the end of the corridor, he stood watching us with his arms folded.

Without stepping away from me, William turned his head to regard him as well. The silence that ensued was deafening. Lost for words, and at a loss about what to do, I covered my face and shook my head to myself.

Since neither of us answered him, Aaron continued, "I was under the impression he was your boss, Cara. Nothing more."

After a loud sigh, I lowered my trembling hands and met his eyes. What I found in them struck my chest like a bullet.

"Please don't tell me you've slept together," he murmured, and his voice was achingly quiet. Pushing himself away from the wall, he tucked his hands into his pockets, and I saw them form fists there.

"Aaron, I… It's complicated," I said, flustered, and stepped away from William. When I looked into Aaron's eyes, they were etched with disappointment. I had never seen him like this, and it gnawed at my chest like vicious poison. He looked not only disappointed, but also hurt.

"Aaron," I prompted when he didn't respond. Instead, he steered his gaze to William's hostile expression with a grimace on his face.

"More than once?" he queried, but it was directed at William.

After a glance in my direction, William replied, "Last night wasn't exactly innocent."

I studied Aaron with wide eyes, desperate to soothe him, desperate to make amends, but I knew that if I reached for him, he'd only shudder away. He always did when he was upset about something, and this time, he was upset about something *I* had done.

"That's strikingly unprofessional. Aren't you supposed to be her boss?" Aaron retorted.

William raised a brow at him. "It's not as simple as that."

"Humour me," Aaron demanded with a snort.

Revealing his uncertainty, William furrowed his eyebrows. "You're sure you want to know this?"

Aaron gritted his teeth. "Yes."

"Your call, I suppose," William responded with a shrug. "We slept together before her vacation scheme started. As for last night, I suppose we realised that three months was too long a wait." After a beat, he continued, "You should leave her alone, Aaron. I don't intend to stop pursuing her, and you won't win."

Cringing, I moaned, "William, please stop talking."

His head whipped around to regard me, and I was struck by how his eyes frosted. "No, I will not. I've had quite enough of your disrespectful behaviour, Cara. You're clearly incapable of handling the situation," he said venomously. "I will not stand for being treated like this. I'm going to settle this once and for all." His eyes narrowed accusingly before he continued, "After what happened between us last night, did you really think I was just going to sit idly by while you fuck another bloke? Honestly, what do you take me for?"

"Last I checked, Cara's single," Aaron defended me. "Stop speaking as if you're in a relationship, you entitled prick."

William turned to glower at him. "That's rich, coming from you. You've just interrogated both of us."

"She may fuck whomever she wants."

Seemingly amused, William gave him a lopsided smile. "Then why do you look so upset?"

"William, that's enough!" I intervened and walked to stand between them.

"Do you know," William continued, regardless, "when she first mentioned you to me, she compared you to air and said she hardly ever pays you a thought? I just thought you deserved to know of the insignificant light she views you in."

I gasped. That lawyer in him was bloody ruthless. He was deliberately angling this all wrong just to provoke Aaron. I didn't care whether he was drunk and acting on emotion. He was crossing the line by miles, and Aaron was an innocent target of his malice. I was the only one deserving of it here.

"That's bogus!" I rebuked. "You know that's not how I meant it!" Scared of how Aaron would interpret it, I turned to him. "Aaron, he's completely twisting my words. When I said that, I was referring to how comfortable you are to be around."

"Right." Aaron gnashed his teeth and glowered at William. "I'm not falling for your bullshit. You're deliberately trying to stir an argument between Cara and me, just to get what you want, and I'm not having it."

William's eyes darkened while his jaw clenched and unclenched. Meanwhile, hope filled my chest. Aaron was clearly too clever to fall for William's manipulative ways.

He scoffed before he continued, "Do you honestly believe that you know her better than I do? We've been sleeping together for three years, and there's a reason for that. We're best friends. It's going to take a lot more than a mere fuck-up to ruin that. Besides, we're not exclusive, so if you think this is going to chase me away, you're sorely mistaken. And I can tell you one thing for certain – being a dick to her isn't going to make her warm up to you."

William reeled in a deep breath before his gaze slid in my direction. His light-blue eyes resembled glaciers as they studied me. He looked intensely scary. Without a doubt, Aaron's immunity to his ways was adding fuel to the fire.

Looking back at Aaron, he said, "I'm not a dick to her. I've said nothing but the truth. It's not my fault she can't take responsibility for her actions. Frankly, she's the one being a dick in all this." He directed his gaze to mine. "Please, just tell him to leave, Cara. I'm begging you," he implored, seemingly changing his methods. Instead of trying to stir Aaron's temper, he was now trying to stir my sympathy and guilty conscience, and it was working. I felt despicable.

What I'd done with him last night had obviously triggered his hope, and by having brought Aaron home with me, I was now brutally murdering it. He must have felt led on, and I loathed myself for it. He didn't deserve it.

Neither of them deserved this.

However, I hadn't thought my actions would result in this dreadful scenario – this pissing contest between them. Rationally, I knew I hadn't done anything wrong, as I was perfectly entitled to sleep with whomever I saw fit. I was not William's girlfriend, and I had told him time and again that I was not inclined to pursue any sort of relationship with him. He had obviously decided to ignore that fact after last night's events, as if I'd had a change of heart – as if I'd told him I'd had a change of heart. But I hadn't said that. He had simply read it that way. All I'd told him was that I would consider it, and that was not the same as concurring with his desires.

To top it all off, exclusivity was not part of the arrangement I had with Aaron. So, at the end of the day, I truly hadn't done anything wrong, but William felt wronged. He had set expectations of me that weren't justified, rational or realistic – expectations I hadn't concurred with. Ultimately, emotions I hadn't predicted were getting involved now. Due to my limited experience with relationships, I hadn't fully considered the irrational aspect of this. Just because his feelings weren't justified did not mean they did not exist, and now I was paying the price for my obliviousness, regardless of how unwarranted I might find it to be.

Either way, I found myself both confused and frustrated. I didn't belong to either of them, but they clearly harboured the strange notion that I did. I was my own, first and foremost, but that didn't mean that I was not responsible for managing their expectations.

What an utter mess. I dreaded the cleaning job already. This simply could not continue. If I intended to maintain my arrangement with Aaron, I would have to leave William alone altogether, physically speaking. It didn't matter if he was a grown man and should be considered capable of making the best decisions for himself. If I acted on my lust for him again, he would dive in headfirst, only to guilt-trip me afterwards, just like he was doing now, and I refused to allow that to repeat itself. I was obviously hurting him, and that was not a matter I took lightly. He did not deserve to have his feelings toyed with, even if it hadn't been my intention.

It was glaringly apparent that I would have to reconsider how I went about things, though I would postpone those contemplations for tomorrow – when I was sober.

"Ever considered that she might be a dick to you because she simply doesn't like you?" Aaron countered and tilted his head.

That pushed William to the end of his tether. "If that were true, how do you explain the scene you just walked in on?" Aaron's face contorted upon the hurtful reminder, but William didn't seem to be finished just yet. "Unlike you, I'm not willing to surrender my integrity to get between her legs. Like you don't mind her sleeping with others." His tone was laced with heavy sarcasm. "It's clear as day that you're in love with her. The only reason you're not asking for exclusivity is that you know you won't get the answer you want. You *know* that will be the end of you two."

My jaw nearly unhooked as I processed his preposterous allegation. "William, think before you speak, yeah? You're well out of order. You've got no idea how crazy you sound," I admonished.

"Hey!" Jason suddenly called. "Everything alright out there?" he continued, and I heard the music quiet down. "Get a move on, Will. We're growing old waiting for you!" I could hear he was anxious. Aaron's presence must have unsettled him, too.

"I'll be there in a moment!" William yelled back and turned his focus on me, clearly awaiting some sort of decision. Meanwhile, I heard the music start again, and it was louder now than before.

"It's no bother," Aaron said to William and removed his hands from his pockets. "You can keep playing. Cara and I will just retire to bed." William shot him a deadly glare at once. Meeting it, Aaron retaliated, "If you're lucky, you might get to hear her moans again." My heart faltered at the awful memory he'd deliberately triggered. I didn't think it could get any worse, but that was before he added, "Although, you won't be the one causing them this time, either."

Hearing him, I wished I could have fainted, but instead, I remained conscious to endure the excruciating aftermath. He couldn't have said anything viler. The painful memory raged in my mind, and I dared not imagine what it was doing to William.

As I continued to process his statement, I found myself utterly appalled by his contemptible insinuation, so I stared disbelievingly at him. How dared he speak of me that way, as if I were an object made to be fucked whenever it suited him. The more I watched him, the angrier I got. "Aaron, how bloody dare you? That was beyond insulting."

Suddenly, William whirled around and rushed towards the front door. Acting on impulse, I stormed to step in front of him, but he continued to push against me, eyes resolutely set on the exit.

The fear of losing him was made real to me then. He was leaving, and this time, I really thought it might be for good. I regretted everything then. If I had been able to rewind time, I'd have gone back to last night, and I would have told him I'd go on a date with him. I'd have cancelled my plans with Aaron, and I would have embraced the unknown.

Seeing him like this was absolutely devastating. The consequences of my actions were finally catching up with me, and I couldn't bear them. While I had treasured what I had with Aaron, it had run its course. My future was with William. He was the only one I was meant to be with, and now that he was about to leave my side, it was made abundantly clear to me.

"William, please stay," I pleaded, but he pushed me aside.

"I can't," he growled through his teeth. "I'm *this* close to striking him, Cara." He spoke with a voice so cold that the hair rose on my arms. I hadn't ever heard him speak like that. The threat of violence dripped from his tone.

"Please, don't leave. I made a mistake. I realise that now. I'm an utter fuck-up, but I swear I'll fix it. Please," I begged. "Stay."

Ignoring me completely, he put on his shoes and ripped the door open. Without another word or so much as a glance at me, he stepped out and slammed the door shut after himself. I jumped at the sound and stared broken-hearted after him, out of touch with reality.

What had I done?

My eyes brimmed with tears. Had I really lost him now? Struggling to collect the broken pieces of myself, it took me quite a while to return to the present, and when I did, I glared at Aaron over my shoulder. "Aaron, leave."

"I'm sorry," he hurried to say, as if it would undo what he had just done. "I didn't mean to insult you. He pissed me off."

"Get out!"

"Cara, you know I didn't mean it like that. I was aiming at him, not you."

"Well, you fucking missed!" I snarled and spun around to pick his shoes up from the floor. After tossing them over to him, I stalked towards my bedroom door and tore it open.

"This is unbelievable," he said bitterly from the corridor. "I hope you'll be very happy together," I heard him continue. Without replying, I went straight to bed to hide under my duvet. A breath later, I heard the main door slam shut, and the sound made me tense under the soft fabric.

From the utter silence that ensued, I realised Jason had switched off the music entirely.

"Cara?" I heard him call for me. I couldn't reply. My chest started to shake as I dissolved into quiet sobs. I was just so shocked – at everything.

"What the hell's going on?" Jason questioned from the doorway.

I allowed my sobs to stream out of my mouth then. William had left, and I doubted he'd ever come back. On top of that, Aaron and I had never had a fight even remotely close to this one in the three years we'd known each other, and it was all because of my obliviousness.

I hated myself intensely. This was all my fault.

If only they would have allowed me to handle it myself instead of acting on my behalf and speaking out of turn. Unlike them, I wouldn't have gone for anyone's throat. I'd have tried to explain things calmly and constructively. Instead, the two of them had created a bloody warzone.

"Where's Will?" Jason asked.

"He left," I cried.

"Aaron?"

"I kicked him out!"

He walked over to climb into my bed. "Oh, come here, love," he cooed when he found my trembling figure under the duvet.

"They were so nasty to each other, Jason!" I complained through stifled sobs and attacked his neck with an embrace. His mollifying scent was precisely what I needed right now.

"Tell me what happened."

"My stupid decisions!"

"Cara, you'll need to be more specific."

"I shouldn't have brought Aaron home with me," I tried to explain. "Why didn't you warn me that poker night had been moved here? I could have avoided all this. Not that I'm blaming you, I just…"

He tucked my head under his chin and squeezed me tightly. "I'm sorry. I wasn't aware you'd be home so soon, and I honestly thought you'd be spending the night at Aaron's since the bash was being held there."

"Well, you were wrong," I croaked back.

"I know, and I'm so sorry. Had I known you'd be bringing him home with you, I obviously wouldn't have agreed to host it here."

"I thought you were meant to be at Stephen's?"

"We were, but Giselle had to take an early shift at the café in the morning. A barista called in sick, so we thought we'd show some consideration and do it here instead."

I sighed long and loud. "Fuck."

"You'll be alright, Cara. You know Aaron. He's not one to stay angry," he soothed.

When I opened my eyes, I grimaced up at him. "It's not Aaron I'm worried about, Jason. It's Will."

He pressed his lips together. "Would you like me to call him?"

"He'll never want to look at me again," I cried dramatically.

"Cara, I understand you're emotional, but you're underestimating his feelings for you. Allow the man some room. He's probably devastated you brought Aaron home with you after everything that happened between you last night. Lying about it can't have helped, either."

"I'm so fucking sorry."

"I know. You haven't really done anything wrong, but he's definitely hurt either way."

"I didn't mean to hurt him. I never meant for any of this. Jason, I've been so lost."

"Oh, darling, I know." He squeezed me tightly again. "Cara, it will all be fine. Just let him simmer down. You know he's got an awful temper."

Sniffing, I wiped my cheeks. "Do you think he'll ever forgive me?"

"He might. Depends on your next move."

His statement inspired some hope in me. "Please call him. I'm worried about him."

"I'll do it straight away," he said and left a peck on my head before he crawled out of bed. "Shall I kill the lights?" he asked on his way out.

"No. I've got to get ready for bed, remove my makeup and all that. I just need a moment to gather myself first."

"Right."

I'd only meant to rest my eyes for a bit after he'd closed the door, but instead – exhausted as I was – I accidentally fell asleep. Then, a few hours into slumber, an obscure reality entered my dreams. Whether it was due to my imploration before he'd left or Jason's call, I didn't know, but I sensed the presence of the person

I most longed to see, in my room and climbing into my bed. After wrapping his arms around me, he kissed the crook of my neck and pressed me against him.

Softly, he said, "I'm sorry, Cara. I didn't mean for it to turn out like that. I know I have neither the right nor claim. But you have to understand that I'll get jealous when you're about to sleep with another man, especially after what happened between us last night. I don't like that I react that way, but I can't always help it. You drive me insane. You're so liberal and modern and I – well, I'm not all the way there with you, but I'm trying to understand."

I recognised the voice, but I barely stirred. I was far too exhausted to latch onto reality properly.

"I just wish you'd give me a chance. Every time you let me in you look...euphoric, and that's all I want to give you."

"Mm," I uttered and snuggled deeper into his embrace. Vaguely, I heard him sigh.

"Sweet dreams, darling," he whispered. Warm lips that made my heart skip a beat lingered on my temple. They felt to burn a mark in my skin, but instead, they'd burnt a mark in my soul.

26

GUILTY AS CHARGED

A FAMILIAR SCENT WAS THE FIRST THING I NOTICED THE following morning. It whispered his name in the air around me, tempting me to wake to a reality that was even stranger than my dreams. Slowly, I opened my eyes. Darkness shrouded his figure, and I spent some time trying to grasp the truth of his presence. While I did, I noticed the surrounding silence. The guests must have left, but he had returned. Instant relief brought tears to my eyes.

My heart threatened to explode at the sight of him. My instinct was to wake him, to thank him for coming back, and to apologise for the mistakes I'd made, but when I saw the calm motion of his bare chest expanding and deflating with his quiet breaths, I could tell he was fast asleep. Since I had no idea of exactly when he had arrived, I didn't have the heart to wake him. He couldn't have caught much sleep by now, and it was all because of me.

Nevertheless, I couldn't resist snuggling closer. Tracing my lips across the soft skin on the side of his chest, I left a trail of feather-light kisses. I hoped he would forgive my wrongdoings the way I had forgiven his. We'd both lied to each other, deceived and manipulated, and it had to end.

I wondered for a moment if it was fate that had become so angry with us for not combining yet that it had decided to punish us both until we would. But I wasn't sure I believed in fate. What I did believe in, however, was chance, and – if he'd still have me – I was going to take it.

I smiled in the dark upon finally realising what his presence could mean. Hopefully, he'd returned because he sought to reconcile. Either way, I would insist on waving the white flag.

When he stirred, I jerked away, fearful I'd woken him. Turning onto his side, he continued to sleep peacefully, and I owed him a moment of it – of peace. After leaving a last tender kiss of good morning on his back, I climbed carefully out of bed to head for the bathroom.

After a shower, I sauntered into the kitchen, and I was grateful to see that Jason had cleaned up after himself last night. I was also grateful to see that nobody had decided to crash here because, after last night's events, I was not in the mood to entertain any guests other than William. In fact, I was mortified. The thought of last night's drama made me cringe to myself.

Unlike William, I didn't have a jealous bone in my body, so I struggled to understand him. What made it particularly difficult was the fact that I wasn't yet his to be jealous over. Then again, jealousy often didn't abide by reason, I reminded myself. It adhered only to desire. So long as there existed desire for something or someone, jealousy could bloom.

So, I supposed that if a desire had established itself, jealousy required only one more thing in order to arise: something or someone had to be standing in the way of the fulfilment of that desire.

With that in mind, I conceived a possible explanation for William's hostile behaviour towards Aaron last night. It was likely that he considered Aaron an obstacle, standing in the way of him acquiring what he wanted – me. Ergo, his jealousy had been triggered. His notion was erroneous, however, because Aaron wasn't the one standing in his way.

I was.

When it came to Aaron, I was mainly extremely disappointed in him because I had expected better of him. Never in the three years I'd known him had I ever seen him sink so low. His attack on William, where he had also insulted me, had been the last straw.

I'd been totally shocked when he'd said that because it was a huge deviation from his general character. I'd never heard him utter such a foul thing about anyone before, and certainly not where I was concerned. I supposed that was why it had hurt me so much – to such a degree that I'd kicked him out.

I still hadn't heard from him, but I hadn't expected anything else. He would reach out to me when he was ready, and I wouldn't initiate any contact before then. After last night, I was reluctant to do anything that might trigger further annoyance. He needed to simmer down first, so until he was ready to reconcile, I would leave him alone.

For three solid years, we'd managed to avoid drama like this. Then came William, wreaking havoc on our harmony. Part of me regretted kicking Aaron out last night, but another didn't. Considering how terribly things had escalated, the last thing I had wanted was to be in his company.

While fetching myself a bowl of cereal, I sighed. A week ago, I hadn't thought my clusterfuck of a situation could get any worse, but clearly, I'd been mistaken. Since then, William had managed to remove one of the obstacles standing in his way, which was my concern for Jason's place in all this. Now he was trying to obliterate the next – Aaron.

But Aaron wasn't standing in his way, and it irritated me that he was under that impression because, as a result, my dear friend was now getting caught in the crossfire.

The only thing standing in his way was my reluctance to pursue anything romantic at this point in my life. Up until now, I'd been intent on focusing solely on my career. However, I had to admit that I was on the cusp of changing my mind, because my interest in him wasn't showing any signs of wavering. No matter how hard I tried, I couldn't seem to repress my growing feelings for him. It was becoming increasingly apparent that they were here to stay, and the more I ignored them, the more chaos they created.

What made it all worse was that I knew for certain that he could tell as much. He knew as well as I did that I was slowly but surely warming up to the idea of being with him. I could deny it all I wanted with my words, but my actions exposed me. Had my interest in him truly been absent, it would not have presented itself this past Friday. I wouldn't have kissed him in that club, and I wouldn't have given him a single thought when Brian's friend had tried to kiss me, either.

But I had.

Before then, he had actually relented in his efforts. Ever since I'd confronted him about his behaviour in his office, he'd left me alone. He hadn't made any inappropriate comments, and he hadn't tried to flirt with me for the rest of the week. It had been obvious that he had seriously intended to respect my wishes.

Then came Friday. Throwing caution to the wind, I had proved to him that my interest in him was far from dead. Of course that would trigger and reinforce his hope that there could eventually be an 'us'. To top it all, I had been the one to initiate intimacy between us. There on the dance floor, I had intended to seduce him. Had I not done that, he would not have reacted the way he did last night. In all likelihood, he would have left without a single objection.

Of course he could deduce from that behaviour that I was feverishly trying to keep feelings that already existed in check. He wasn't an idiot. On the contrary, he was one of the most perceptive men I'd ever met – if not *the* most.

Regardless, I was profoundly unimpressed with the behaviour of both men last night. They should have acted their age and allowed me to sort things out. Instead, they had gone for each other's throats like they were still living in the BC's.

"Bloody cavemen," I muttered to myself with a shake of my head.

But I knew William had only done it because he'd wagered his chances were higher if he terminated those around me. One by one, he would eliminate each obstacle until only I was left standing. He was treating this like a legal case. As the solicitor that he was, he was slowly but surely shredding my arguments apart.

'I've already got Aaron to satisfy my libido.' Will had proved several times that he was more than capable of satisfying my libido, so there was no need for Aaron to do it instead.

'I want to be single because I am too immature to focus on a relationship.' I was certainly still immature, but whether I still wanted to be single was another question entirely. That argument was weakening by the second.

'I can't be with you because of Jason.' He'd already eliminated that argument.

'I can't be with you because you're my boss.' According to him, we wouldn't have to worry about that, and especially not when he was only going to be my superior for the span of three months. He insisted that, rather than stunt my career, he would accelerate it, and I was starting to believe him. After all, the man was a practising lawyer. He had connections, and he boasted an incredibly impressive set of skills, too. I'd already seen how much he could teach me, how great a mentor he was. I harboured no doubt that, if I let him, he would mould me into a successful lawyer, too. And, if we kept things under wraps until my placement was over, it was unlikely that dating him would diminish my chances of getting hired.

I sighed as I pondered over it. Which choice would I regret the least? Rejecting William or risking my career? Frankly, things had reached a point where, if I risked my career, I would probably regret it less. Besides, being with him might not even dent my career.

But what if things didn't work out between us? A shudder ran through me. Hopefully, he'd stay true to his word and act civil. However, the more I thought about it, the more I doubted that we'd end up going separate ways. Like he'd told Jason yesterday, we were quite compatible.

Another important factor to consider was my feelings for him. Ever since April, all they had done was continue to develop. I had tried to move on for months, but it hadn't gotten me anywhere. Time had shown that regardless of how hard I tried, my feelings for him could not be controlled – and ignoring them had done more harm than good. I might as well stop trying to fight them. In light of that, I was now willing to overlook the fact that he was my boss.

Truly, I felt like I was being put on trial, and he drove a ferocious prosecution. Now that he had managed to shred my entire defence apart, I could imagine him looking at me and saying something along the lines of, "Nothing is holding you back now. Accept that you're guilty of wanting me."

Guilty as charged.

"Morning," Jason murmured when he sauntered into the kitchen, and I noted with some amusement that he was wearing boxers.

"Morning," I quietly replied and stared at the miniature whole-grain doughnuts that floated around in the milk. "Wearing clothes, Jason?"

"Well, it seems a bit wrong to walk around naked now that you and William are in…whatever you are. Thought I'd show him some consideration." Vigilant in his demeanour, he approached the kitchen counter, which I stood leaning against with my bowl of cereal between my hands.

"How considerate indeed."

"Is he still asleep?"

"Yeah. Thanks for ringing him, Jason. I honestly can't tell you how relieved I was to find him in my bed when I woke up."

"Took some convincing. He was livid."

I could only imagine. "What did you tell him?"

"That you kicked Aaron out after he'd left and that you were very upset, and that you wanted him to come back."

"I appreciate that."

While pouring himself a glass of water, he shook his head to himself. "I'm seriously sorry about last night, Cara. Had I expected that to happen, I would have refused to host poker night. Will was very drunk. I doubt he would have acted the same if he were sober. Plus, he's a bit obsessed with you, I think. That can't have helped much, either."

"No shit," I muttered and glimpsed his figure from the corner of my eye.

"Either way, you're going to have to make up your mind about him."

"I have."

Surprised, he turned towards me. "Really?"

"Yes." I nodded. "Now that we're on the subject, what's your take on the matter, anyhow?"

"Honest opinion?"

"No, I want you to lie." I frowned. "Come on, Jason."

He folded his arms and gazed into the living room, and I could tell from the look on his face that he was considering various scenarios quite seriously. When he eventually faced me again, he resembled a parental figure, and it occurred to me that he was about to lecture me. "Well, what I'm most concerned about in all this is that if you choose to end things now, you'll need to stick with your decision. And from what Will's told me about your behaviour, I honestly doubt your ability to do that. No offence."

My face contorted with shame. "When did you talk about this?"

He shrugged. "Last night, after he'd come back, and everyone had left."

"And what's he told you, exactly?"

"Nothing you're not aware of yourself. But it wasn't Will who pursued you on Friday, was it? From what I've gathered, it was the other way round, Cara. And he's told me he meant to leave you alone before then."

I pursed my lips. Eventually, I nodded to acknowledge that the truth had been spoken.

He sighed, but his expression was patient. "You can't be doing things like that if you don't mean to give him a chance. Poor man's mad about you. And he's told me he's been unequivocal with you on that. It's disrespectful, Cara. You need to respect his boundaries. I've already said it, but he's not a toy. You can't be playing with his feelings like that."

He didn't need to remind me that I wasn't the only victim in this situation. After all, last night had made it crystal clear to me. Even so, I hadn't expected to be hurt by the reminder, but I was. Regardless, I knew I deserved every last drop of it. While William wasn't without fault, I despised myself for how I'd treated him, and I knew I ought to be held accountable for it. In the end, we were both to blame for how things had turned out between us, because neither of us had handled it well. "It takes two to tango," Mum whispered in my head.

Upset, I faced away from Jason and pouted. "I'm sorry. I didn't mean to play with his feelings. I was just too confused to think clearly."

"I get that, but it's not me you should apologise to."

I groaned. "You don't find it even slightly odd that I've got to apologise to him for having a fuck-friend when we're not even in a relationship?"

Jason shook his head. "That's not what you need to apologise for, though, is it? You're missing the point, love. It's the mixed signals, Cara. That's what you need to apologise for. You're perfectly entitled to keep Aaron around. Will has no say in that matter. But he has a say in how you get to treat him."

My pout intensified. "Yeah, suppose you're right."

"I'll say this – he had no business dragging Aaron into the mess between you, but in Will's defence, Aaron did put him on the spot from what I heard."

"He did," I confirmed, "but Will wasn't exactly reluctant to take the witness box either."

"Sounds like Will," he said in sympathy. "Anyway, what's the plan, then? Are you going to end things once and for all?"

I shook my head. "No. I'd like to give it a try with him. That's if he still wants to." Stealing a glance at him, I discovered him grinning from ear to ear.

"You should," he encouraged. "Let him take you out. I think you'll do really well together if I'm honest."

I eyed him sceptically. "You're sure you truly won't mind, Jason? If I start seeing your brother?"

He chuckled. "No. Seems to me that all I can do at this point is cross my fingers that you'll last a lifetime."

"If we end up not working out, I promise I'll be able to act civil around him. You won't be torn between loyalties."

When he suddenly blew his cheeks out and looked away from me, I realised how much he sincerely dreaded such an outcome. "Yeah, it's not you I'm worried about if it comes to that."

"You don't think William would be capable of the same?" Trepidation unfurled in my chest.

He grimaced. "Considering how things ended with Kate, I doubt it."

I blinked. I would need to probe William about her sometime soon. "Oh. What happened there?"

"Nothing terrible. They ended things on a relatively good note, according to him. However, he prefers to leave exes in the past rather absolutely. I think they've only spoken once or twice since."

"But Kate isn't your friend, so that situation can't be compared to ours."

"I hope you're right. I'll be keeping you around either way, so he'll have to manage."

I gulped. "I'm having second thoughts hearing this, Jason."

"No, don't," he insisted resolutely. "Never mind what I said. I'm just preparing for the worst here, while hoping for the best. Besides, I actually think you'll work out. You're sort of similar in quite a lot of ways – only he's a bigger dick than you are."

I chortled at the way he tried to sell me this. "I'm not a dick."

He gave me a playful smile. "But while he can be a bit of a dick, he generally isn't. He's got very firm principles laid out for himself. He's just very assertive about reaching his goals. Always has been. And I'm sorry to say it, but right now, you're his goal. To make matters worse, he knows you're attracted to him, and since you said you'll consider giving him a chance, he's seeing light at the end of the tunnel. So, unless you make it crystal clear to him that you don't want anything else, and act accordingly, he's unlikely to stop chasing you anytime soon. That means you can't make a move on him on a drunken whim, Cara, much less flirt with him, unless you're serious about this."

I shoved another spoonful of cereal into my mouth. "Tell me about it. I'm starting to realise that I'm causing more damage by not being with him, which is completely counterintuitive. You'd think dating my boss, and my flatmate's brother, would be enough of a clusterfuck. But he makes that look like paradise compared to this mayhem. Anyway, there's no need to worry, because I am serious about this. I know I've been fickle, but once I make up my mind, it's final. I'm in this for the long haul now." After swallowing, I added, "And I am sorry about the mixed signals. I really am. But in my defence, I've been terribly confused about all this. I've never been romantically involved with anyone before, and I was determined to keep it that way at first, because I'm scared that he'll mess with my priorities and that I'll be unhappy in a relationship."

He sent me a shrewd smile. "Cara, if anything, Will is going to be a positive contribution to your life. He's as career driven as you are. He'll be cheering you on more than anyone, and you can be sure he'll go out of his way to help you reach your goals. You don't need to worry about that. I speak from experience. He's cheered me on ever since I can remember. Besides, you're in the same field!" He motioned towards me. "In case you need your memory jogged, the man's already a solicitor. I'm sure he'll offer you invaluable guidance anytime you need it."

I couldn't help smiling at the idea of that. "I see your father and brother have been rubbing off on you. You're arguing like a lawyer, Jase. Picked the wrong course of study, perhaps?"

His laughter was music to my ears, and the sound of it brightened my mood.

"No way," he said. "I'm only damaged by environment."

When silence ensued between us, it dawned on me that I had finally reached a conclusion, so while staring into my nearly empty bowl of cereal, I smiled to myself. "I've got to say – I'm impressed with Will for managing to sway my mind. I seriously hadn't thought anyone could make me even consider dating." After a quick pause, I shrugged to myself and resumed, "Not for another couple of years, at least."

"Yeah, well, you might as well get used to it. I'm afraid that's why he's such a talented solicitor. He can turn any situation around. It made growing up with him a living hell. Fortunately for me, Dad has the same mind, so he sees straight through it. Provided some justice for my less cunning personality."

"He really is remarkably cunning," I agreed with a nod. "That's a perfect word to describe him."

"Yeah."

"It's a gift," I murmured. I had to give it to him: if I were to overlook all the ruckus he caused, he was one hell of a natural talent. Frankly, I was so impressed that I felt slightly intimidated. A relationship with William Night? I imagined myself feeling constantly walked over, and that wasn't something I wanted. But as Jason had said, he deserved a chance. And I already knew I wanted him. So, what did I have to lose?

Perhaps my mind, I thought to myself. And my heart, I continued. I worried he'd launch me into insanity with his overbearing character. But these were mere assumptions and based on very little evidence, and I usually wasn't one to act on mere assumptions. I preferred to keep an open mind.

"I'll need to tell Aaron about this," I eventually said and shoved another spoonful into my mouth.

"Do you reckon he'll be angry?" Jason queried, somewhat concerned.

I grimaced. "After last night? Yeah, definitely. If William hadn't provoked him, then perhaps not, but we'll never know now."

"I'm sure he'll get over it soon enough," he consoled me. "Aaron doesn't strike me as the type to stay angry."

"Yeah, I reckon he'll be more disappointed than anything else, because he'll need to find a new bed partner now. I just hope William won't mind us remaining friends."

Jason cocked his head from side to side. "That's entirely up to you. Fundamentally, Will isn't an insecure person. At all. If you reassure him well enough, it's likely that he won't have a problem with you and Aaron being just mates. But I might be wrong. I mean, I'm seeing totally new sides of him right now, and I think he is, too. You're changing him. But I gather he's only insecure now because you're not actually his."

"His," I echoed. "Sounds so…primitive."

"You know what I mean."

I sighed. "Yeah."

I dreaded Aaron's reaction to this, and honestly, I knew I'd be grieving when I lost him. We were so familiar with each other. Even if there had never been romantic love present between us, there was certainly a platonic version of love. So, while I might not have been attached to him romantically, I was still attached to him as a person, and severing that tie wasn't going to be comfortable. Moreover, the thought of building something new with someone else was somewhat taxing because, if at all, it would take years before Will and I reached the point where Aaron and I were now.

But William made me feel electric, as though my blood tingled in my veins. He set my heart on fire and made me feel more alive than I ever had. He made me not only want him but actually crave him. So, perhaps my concern was ill-founded.

"Cara, can you honestly say that you're not even remotely

infatuated with William?" Jason queried then, bringing me out of my thoughts. I stiffened and glared at him slightly.

"Well, I haven't felt anything remotely similar before."

He folded his arms and arched his left eyebrow. "Thought so. Do you remember how smitten you were when you came back from his after the first time you met? Because I do. And you were like a puppy on MDMA."

My nose wrinkled. "Interesting simile."

"Accurate, though."

I sighed again. "I don't know what I'm feeling yet, Jason. This is all so new to me. But there's no denying that I'm more interested than I've ever been in a man before. Is that not enough?"

"No, it's enough. I'm not entirely convinced, though. I think you're a bit infatuated, even if you won't admit or realise it. And I say that because I've never seen you behave like this."

"Like what?"

"Incapable of keeping your hands off a man."

I blushed profusely. "You haven't actually seen that. You've only heard what Will has told you."

"But was he lying?"

I scowled. "No."

He presented a devilish grin. "And there's my point."

I responded only with a roll of my eyes.

"Will you tell him when he wakes?" He looked so hopeful that I had to grin.

"That's the plan. Do you think he's still interested?"

He curved a brow. "Er, yes."

My heart tensed with panic. "I hope so."

Jason scratched his cheek. "One more thing – and this is going to sound very wrong, but I'm just so curious."

"What?"

"Is he really that good in bed?" he asked, a little intimidated. "I remember you said he was the best you'd ever been with."

I burst out laughing. I wouldn't have seen that one coming in a million years. "Sibling rivalry, Jason?"

"I'm just a bit impressed."

"Well, it's been months since I last slept with him, but if he's maintained his skills, then yes, he is outstanding."

He nodded to himself. "Any tips?"

"Why don't you ask him yourself?" I giggled and opened the dishwasher to stow my bowl away.

"You know, I think I might."

"Do. Men like William should spread their knowledge. It's not fair that such a small number of women get to experience sex like that. What I can tell you is that the woman's pleasure is his only focus. I've never met a man more attuned to the female body during sex in my life. Aaron's great, but William's another level."

"Hm." Jason hummed to himself while I sauntered towards the living room to get settled on the sofa.

"I'm spending the day in today. Have you got any plans, or shall we find a TV show to binge until William wakes?"

"I'm in."

"Can we still cuddle, or is that off—"

"Hey, I've agreed to share you with him, not give you to him."

Charmed, I smiled to myself.

27

SKIN OF THE NIGHT

IT WAS NEARLY ONE O'CLOCK WHEN I WOKE FROM AN accidental nap. Sprawled across Jason on the sofa, I turned my head to see that he was fast asleep as well. Alarm spread through my mind upon realising I'd spent time unconscious. Had William gone in the meantime? I had to find out.

To show consideration, I released Jason from my hold as gently as possible and proceeded to approach my bedroom. As quietly as I could manage, I opened the door to peek inside, and sure enough, William was still sleeping soundly in my bed. The view left a tender smile on my mouth. Closing the door again, I decided to make him breakfast.

Unbeknownst to me, I had been wearing the same smile when I suddenly sensed a presence behind me sometime later. Turning away from the omelette I was making, I nearly squealed at the sight of William standing so close, but knowing Jason was asleep prevented it from streaming out of my mouth. Instead, I recoiled towards the stove while my hand rushed to cover my mouth.

Realising I'd been about to make a harsh sound, William raised his index finger to his lips to command silence before he cocked his head in Jason's direction. Understanding, I nodded. Recovering from the jolt, I straightened myself and did a visual sweep of his body, which towered only a couple of feet away from me. His hair was damp, and a white towel was wrapped around his hips. Yet again, I was blinded by his beauty. Blood painted my face a bright shade of red while my eyes traced the line of hair climbing up from his towel towards his navel. I knew where the strands began, and the thought aroused me.

Breaking out of my trance, I faced the stove again, but I froze with tension when he arrived right behind me. The heat of his body radiated against my own. Gulping, I glanced at him from the corner of my eye. He leaned over my shoulder, eyes shifting between the frying pan and my profile. Very gently, he rested his hand on my hip.

I ceased breathing.

"Have you got a minute?" he whispered.

"Um, is it urgent? I'm cooking you breakfast," I whispered back.

His lips drew nearer to my ear. My heart thundered.

"You're very sweet, but my appetite is non-existent at the moment. Talking might solve it, as well as a lot of other things."

Since I saw no reason to refuse his request, I switched off the stove and left the spatula resting on the edge of the frying pan. When I turned, he reached for my hand and entwined our fingers. Then, he led the way to my bedroom. Knowing how serious our imminent conversation was bound to be, I squeezed his hand and swallowed. My nervous heart was beating at a hundred miles per hour when he opened the door to my bedroom and walked in.

A small gap between the curtains allowed some light of day to illuminate my room, and through it, I saw heavy rain cascading from the sky. The sound of it tapping against the windows soothed my heart somewhat, as it mollified my impression of the moment's urgency. Instead, it summoned a sense of intimacy.

I shut the door after us.

"Did you sleep well?" It was the first thing I could think to say.

Without letting go of my hand, he resumed walking and dragged me towards my bed. Finding a seat on it, he avoided my eyes and kept his gaze upon my bedroom door.

His hesitation was obvious. To allow him room to sort out his thoughts, I patiently took a seat beside him. All the while, I kept my hand within his.

"Cara, I can't do this anymore," he eventually said, and I thought I heard the sound of my heart's last breaths.

Tears of pain and misery surfaced in my eyes, so I looked away from his profile and set my gaze on the rug beneath my feet. Knowing I had failed to appreciate him the way he deserved, I couldn't bear the sight of his beauty anymore. Panic raged through my veins, stopping me from stringing together a reply.

Had he returned only to end things once and for all?

"This back and forth, this waiting around," he continued when I failed to respond, "it's turned me into a man I no longer recognise, and I can't stand him."

Fear made my grip tighten around his hand. "William, I made a mistake."

"You lied to me."

The reminder extracted a whimper from my mouth. "I'm sorry. I was going to tell you after I'd met him."

His gaze remained fixed on the door. "Why did you lie?"

Agony revealed itself in my expression. "I...I didn't think it was any of your business, and I knew you'd react strongly. I just didn't have the strength to handle it yesterday. And I wanted to spare you the anxiety. It was my friend's birthday, Will. I wanted to be there, so your objection wouldn't have mattered. I just thought it would be easier for us both if I lied about it."

Not a sound escaped him.

"William, I'm sorry." I looked at him with desperation. "It was a mistake. I swear I won't repeat it. I learnt my lesson last night. I won't ever abuse your trust like that again."

His jaw clenched. "You're so inexperienced."

"I know." My voice broke. "I'm sorry you've had to endure it."

With some effort, he withdrew his hand from my hold, and it only increased my misery. He was pulling away in more ways than one.

"I still don't understand why you would go so far as to bring him home with you, especially after what happened between us the night before. Lying about him being there is one thing, but then you actually intended to sleep with him as well. Why is that? Is it because you've actually got feelings for him?"

His question sucked the air out of me. "What – no. Of course not."

"Then why? Why did you do it?"

Tears prickled my eyes. Tensing, my face contorted. "I didn't think it was a big deal. It was just sex. I've been sleeping with Aaron for a long time, Will. To me, it would just have been one more time out of many – nothing else. Just casual, meaningless sex."

He pressed his lips together, but he said nothing, and his silence triggered a tear of mine to fall over. He was shutting me out, and I hated it.

"Really, Will – sleeping with him wasn't something I had planned to do. The evening just progressed, and he proposed to take me home. I accepted on a whim because we were having a good time and I was enjoying his company. It wasn't like I woke up yesterday and thought, 'I should invite Aaron over to have sex tonight.' Really, it just…happened. I was drunk, and I didn't see what harm it could do."

His eyebrows furrowed.

Upset, my gaze slid back to the rug beneath my feet. Wiping my cheeks, I said, "I'll admit that part of the reason I wanted to see him last night was that I hoped it would help me sort out my thoughts. He's so familiar to me, Will. I wasn't sure I was willing to sacrifice that for you, but it was stupid. I realise that now."

Processing my rationale, he remained quiet. Since he hadn't said anything in a while, I wasn't sure whether I'd been elaborate enough. So, hoping to enlighten him further, I continued, "In my head, we're not exclusive, Will. We're not in a relationship, so I didn't think I owed you any loyalty yet. However, I realise now that I've treated the situation too rationally – my perspective was too black and white. It was wrong of me, and I know that now. We've been in the grey area, so my actions were tactless. I should have made up my mind before I saw him again."

His cheeks expanded with air. After releasing it, he leaned forward to rest his elbows on his knees. While rubbing his face, he said, "You're so out of touch with your emotions. You give your head too much esteem. You need to listen to your heart more."

Because it was true, I sobbed. "I know. I'm sorry. I'm trying to get better at it."

A sigh escaped him, but when he reached for my hand again, I saw hope for reviving my heart.

"You're not the only one owing an apology here," he murmured and, finally, his gaze blessed mine with its attention. "I was rather drunk last night – drunker than I can remember being in quite some time. Had I not been, I would have handled it better. I wasn't prepared to meet him, and I'm very sorry for how I behaved. Truly, you'll never know how sorry I am.

"After I left last night, I sat in my living room for ages. When Jason called for the nth time, I had started to sober up somewhat." He shook his head. "Cara, my heart was in my throat the whole time. I felt like vomiting. I couldn't think of anything else. I felt despicable. I was angry with you, but I was also angry at myself. I hate that I hurt you like that. What I did, what I said – it wasn't right."

"Apology accepted," I assured him.

His eyes widened with surprise. "Really?"

Tears trickled down my cheeks as I nodded. "I'm not one for wallowing in the past, Will. I prefer to move on. There's very little I can do about what happened, and I believe in second chances. We've both done awful things to each other. I'm no more innocent than you are. However, it needs to end. We can't keep treating each other like this, so if you mess up again, I won't be as merciful."

While nodding his agreement, he dropped his gaze to our hands.

After a loud exhalation, I continued, "Let's get to the hard part, shall we?"

His eyes dashed to meet mine again. Alarmed, he stared at me. "Hard part?" he breathed nervously. "I thought apologising was the hard part."

I rolled my eyes. "Coming from you, that doesn't surprise me."

"Then enlighten me."

I raised a brow. "What are you going to do to mend your ways?" I was trying to gauge his current stance regarding Aaron. Perhaps I could keep them both if I played my cards right. Obviously, I would still want Aaron in my life, even if we couldn't have sex anymore. He was one of my dearest friends.

"Mend my ways?" William echoed. "You mean if I meet him again?" His relief transitioned into frustration in the span of a mere breath.

"Yes."

"I won't punch him, but I won't be nice, either," he muttered like an impudent child.

Wondering where to go from here, I reclined onto the mattress and studied the ceiling for a while.

He sighed, but it didn't make me look at him. "Cara, I know he's your best friend, which is why I'm sorry. I have no right to be interfering with your life like that, and I know it. But you have to understand that when you're about to sleep with another man, I'm not going to like it – especially not after what happened between us on Friday, when you said you'd consider giving me a chance. Frankly, I found it disrespectful. I feel used."

His statement prompted me to look at him again, and I studied him in silence while I tried to weave my thoughts together.

Once I'd figured out where to begin, I sighed to myself before saying, "I understand why you would feel that way, Will, but it wasn't my intention to disrespect you when I decided to invite him home with me. I had no idea you would be here. Had I known, I obviously wouldn't have invited him."

"Yes, but—"

I raised my finger to cut him off. "I wasn't finished."

"Sorry," he mumbled and averted his eyes, and I thought he resembled an adorable puppy in that instant.

"However, William, I entirely agree that it was disrespectful of me to send you such mixed signals. You made yourself abundantly clear on Monday about where you stand. And, since I told you I'd consider dating you, I completely understand why you would assume it was mutually understood that I would refrain from sleeping with anyone else until I had made up my mind.

"In the end, I knew you wanted more, so it was truly ugly of me to disregard your feelings like that, even if it wasn't my intention. Either way, my negligence is unacceptable, and I truly am sorry about that. You didn't deserve it. I was simply too confused to think clearly."

From the intensity of his subsequent frown, I could tell he was growing increasingly confused. "Cara, honestly, you're doing my head in. One moment you're with me, and in the next, you're running for the hills. I don't understand what I'm supposed to do. All I know is that I want to be yours, and I'm not ashamed of it."

Again, that sweet but foreign feeling crowded my heart, making it clench. A moment later, it expanded until it occupied my entire chest, making it difficult to breathe normally. It tickled, too – delicious, profound, and yet somehow so delicate.

In that brief moment in time, I felt entirely alive. Dynamic and full of life. I could feel my blood course through my veins while the sound of my heart drummed in my ears. All my senses sharpened.

Suddenly, life wasn't just something that I had been tossed into and emotionlessly endured. It was vibrant, it was vigorous, and it was magical. The present had never felt more real to me than in that moment.

I hadn't noticed my blush until he pointed it out. My entire body felt hot, so I hadn't given a thought to the fact that my face would be, too.

"You're blushing, Cara," he said, and it was with a beautiful, unsullied smile.

"You're very blunt." I mumbled my explanation.

"Just," he sighed, "give me a chance. That's all I ask – just one chance. I swear you won't regret it. I'll make your time worthwhile. I guarantee it."

"You sound very confident, William," I replied with a grin, and the relief I experienced stowed my tears away. "Why do I feel like I'm interviewing you for employment?"

"Hire me, please." He groaned and collapsed next to me to stare intensely into my eyes. "Please, just fucking hire me. I'll be the best partner you've ever had, and I will work day and night to ensure that your needs are met."

Before he could continue, I chimed in, "Is that a pun?"

An involuntary laugh slipped out of him. "Cara, don't make light of this. I'm being serious."

"Sorry. Please continue."

When his amusement subsided, he raised my hand to his mouth and kissed the back of it repeatedly. "If you hire me, I will make you the happiest you've ever been. I swear it to you."

My grin widened until my cheeks hurt. "Heavy promises."

"I don't make promises I can't keep." He was resolute, eyes glowing like never before. He must be seeing the light at the end of the tunnel.

I pursed my lips at him. So self-assured. Tantalising and alluring, he was, and despite my mistakes, he still wanted to be mine.

To end our misery, I said, "Fine." A giggle escaped me. "You can take me on a date."

Launching onto me, he rolled until his large body covered the entirety of mine. As I stared susceptibly into the splendour of his eyes, my heart raced at our intimate position and our new reality.

"Really?" he asked disbelievingly.

I gave him a shy smile. "Yes."

SKIN OF THE NIGHT

"Oh my God. I can't believe this." He sounded overwhelmed.

"That makes two of us," I mumbled, amused.

"You're – Cara – fuck," he uttered in his disbelief and shook his head. "I thought I'd completely fucked my chance last night."

I shrugged. "No. I understand why you behaved like that, so I forgive it. And you drive a hard bargain, Will. Trial won. Your methods are a wee bit controversial, but they worked."

"I'm honestly speechless." His voice was almost a whisper.

"I should warn you, though," I murmured while wrinkles formed across my nose. "I'm not familiar with dating. I've never really done it before, so you'll have to cut me some slack. You'll need to be patient with me."

His eyes softened. "I'll do my best. Friday?" he suggested. I giggled at his eagerness. He resembled a young boy on Christmas morning.

"Sure. Friday works. If you stand me up, that's it," I warned.

"I wouldn't dream of doing that," he replied, baffled. "I'm not self-destructive."

"Last night begs to differ," I twitted.

He smiled in defeat and nodded. "I'll take care of planning our date."

"No cinemas. I'd like to be able to talk," I pointed out.

"I'm not ten, Cara," he retorted sarcastically.

"You act like it, sometimes, so excuse me for having low expectations."

Instead of replying, he offered another unsullied smile while his right hand travelled to my cheek. While he dried the traces of my tears, the tenderness that shone from his features set my body alight.

I longed to feel him again, both within and without. I wanted him to consume me the way the skin of the night consumed the light of day to reveal infinity. Like the night sky, I hoped his devotion would be infinite. There in the dark, I could strip to my core without fear of judgment, for eternity.

Hesitation emitted from him when he gauged the desire in my eyes. Slowly, he lowered his head to invite my lips, and I met him with full force. A sense of liberation celebrated in my blood when his sensuous mouth moulded against my own, and the ensuing passion it despatched vanquished my self-control. Wrapping my limbs around his strong frame, I hugged him tightly and returned his amorous kiss with vigour.

I'd been so blind up until now, but he had pierced the darkness like a star upon the endless sky. While I was frightened of what awaited me, I trusted him completely to be my guiding light. There was no other man I would follow into the unknown – only him.

Capsized by the lust that I ravished him with, his hands began exploring my body, running down my white satin robe to worship what I had now devoted to him exclusively. His caresses set my system aflame with libidinous urges. I couldn't restrain myself. My aching for his flesh was overpowering.

Smoothing my hands along his back muscles, I didn't stop until I reached the towel wrapped around his hips. There, I slid my fingers beneath it and clawed into his taut cheeks. As he felt it, his smile interfered with our kiss.

Pulling away, he grabbed my jaw to arrest my eyes. I retracted my claws immediately.

"Aroused, Cara?"

Blood flooded my cheeks. Was he going to refuse me again? "Yes," I complained.

"How aroused?" he asked sensually, hand releasing my jaw to trace down my throat. Speechless, I remained captivated by his eyes while his finger travelled lower. Reaching the valley between my breasts, he journeyed left to circle my erect nipple. The tantalising feeling of it led raw arousal to centre between my legs, lubricating me further.

"Please, Will," I begged in a whisper.

His familiar crooked smile emerged on his mouth, and his eyes contained not a trace of mercy. "Please what, Cara?" He dragged his finger across my chest to circle my right nipple. When he suddenly flicked his finger across its erectness, I inhaled sharply. "These are begging for my attention, aren't they?" he purred and continued to circle it.

"Yes," I moaned.

A smug chuckle leapt out of his mouth before he propped himself on all fours to hover above me. Abandoning my breasts completely, he trailed his finger towards the sash of the robe instead. When he proceeded to pass it, my body tensed with suspense.

He lowered his head again, and not even an inch separated our mouths. The mint of his breath spread across my lips, beckoning. "Show me how aroused you are, Cara."

Reaching between us, I responded boldly by gripping his hand to guide it further down. Spreading my legs, I pushed my underwear aside with my free hand and dipped his fingers in my arousal.

A hungry grin spread his lips apart while sore desire awakened in his eyes. "Show me where it feels best," he ordered. Fresh heat painted my face while I raised his hand a little higher and slightly to the left. When his finger rested upon my most sensitive area, I released his hand.

"There," I said vulnerably.

He applied pressure. Pleasure bolted through me at once, and my lips parted.

"Ah."

Suddenly, he pulled away to retreat out of bed. At first, his action inspired dread, but it ceased when he proceeded to reach for his towel. Unfastening it, he revealed his erection to me, and the sight aroused me like nothing else. By now, I had nearly forgotten how well-endowed he was, but the view reminded me at once.

Unashamed, I gawked while my eyes scanned his state of undress. The view made my heart jolt. My memory did his true beauty no justice. He was nothing short of stunning, and he was about to bless me with his carnal attention. I could hardly contain my excitement.

Like an aggressive drum, my heart hammered rapidly when he approached my figure again. Meanwhile, his gaze was sizzling. I was burning up under its heat when he gripped firmly around my ankles to remove my socks, one by one. All the while, I stared at him, transfixed by both his allure and aesthetic perfection.

My breathing grew louder and faster. Behind it, the magnitude of my feelings was entirely overwhelming, and they seemed to have manifested in my chest, embedded to remain forever. Suddenly, my lungs were sharing the space with something entirely new.

One after the other, he tossed my socks away before kneeling beside the bed to trail sensuous kisses up my calves. Under the tingling sensation of his lips on my skin, my body shuddered while the hair rose on my arms.

Teasing electricity charged between our bodies, intensifying my lust for him. At his touch, I felt powerful enough to shake the whole world, as though I'd become divine.

He kissed his way upwards, large hands grazing their way up my thighs until they snuck under the skirt of my robe to hook into my underwear. His shoulders and back muscles rippled with his movements, and I savoured the vision of him. He was exquisitely masculine. I'd never met a man more appealing in my life. Compared with his robust physique, I was fragile, but it was something I relished. He resembled a human fortress – impenetrable and a source of safety.

Ruled by impatience, he tugged my knickers down my legs. Only when the cold air touched my folds did I realise just how ready I was – completely drenched and just waiting to be claimed by none other than him.

When his generous kisses reached my knee, I swallowed my heart back down and tossed my head back. With closed eyes, I surrendered to the blissful feeling of his mouth drawing closer and closer to my sex.

His breath fanned across my thighs. "You have the softest skin, darling." Fastening his arms around them, he yanked me towards him.

I gasped. His swift action resulted in his mouth being much closer to my folds, so I whipped my head forward again and watched him with wide eyes.

A smirk dwelled on his sinful mouth when he glanced back at me through his long, dark lashes. "The taste of you has been haunting me for months, so forgive me, but I demand my share."

Since I'd – for the moment – forgotten his proclivity for verbal expressions when it came to sex, I blushed profusely. Nevertheless, it turned me on to an extent only he could manage, and it rendered me speechless. Immersed in suspense and untameable lust, I ran my fingers through his hair and gently tugged it.

The unbreakable spell that his eyes conjured maintained my imprisonment, so I could only watch as he leaned closer to press a gentle kiss directly on my bundle of nerves. Like a most powerful strike of electricity, the delicious friction rippled throughout my body, making me quiver in my desire for more. Cool air spread across my wetness as he chuckled at my reaction, and then his warm tongue lapped over my folds to sample my taste.

Ah, that felt so good.

"Mm, Cara," he crooned and strengthened his hold of my thighs. "I want you to touch yourself while I make you come with my mouth." Erotic William Night. The thrill of experiencing his verbal ways of delivering carnal pleasure again was wildly refreshing.

Yielding to his command, I caressed myself while he drew slow circles around my clit, sensitising me and preparing me for direct impact. If he'd learnt this technique during his time with Kate, I felt incredibly grateful towards her, because I was the one taking pleasure from it now.

"Ah," I groaned and untied my robe to bare my breasts. Meanwhile, his expert tongue switched patterns, going round and round and then up and down along the sides of my throbbing clit.

This teasing was driving me mad. He was even better than Aaron, and it was nothing short of tormenting. I was desperate for his direct attention. More aroused than I'd ever been, I knew what I had waiting, and I wanted it all. Now.

"Will," I pleaded and gathered my fingers around my erect nipples. "Please, you're driving me mad."

He chuckled against me and gave my clit a single direct flick with his tongue. At once, intense pleasure charged through me, making me stiffen.

"I can't help myself," he claimed and gently pushed the tip of his middle finger into me, but it only flirted with my entrance. "There's nothing I enjoy more than watching your body respond to me."

"But I want you now," I whined and abandoned my breasts to reach for his jaw. I tried to lift his head away, but he refused. Wrapping his hands around my wrists, he locked them by my sides and smiled mischievously at me.

"Trust me, Cara, you've got me. Utterly," he assured me and kissed my clit again. While groaning with pleasure, I collapsed and closed my eyes. There was little use in protesting. Knowing him, he wouldn't stop until he had his way. He was easily the most stubborn man I'd ever met, but I commended his self-restraint. Truly, he was remarkable in that he wasn't one to surrender to impulse. Delayed gratification was clearly something he practised religiously.

To my relief, he increased the pressure of his licks, and when his tongue swept over my left side – precisely where I'd shown him – my back arched compulsively. "Ah," I moaned, brows furrowing. *Shit*, that felt fantastic.

Knowing that I was particularly sensitive there, he continued, and I sensed him watching me as I writhed against his strong hold of my thighs and wrists. Slowly but surely, the tension amassed in my lower abdomen. *God*, he was so bloody skilled with his tongue. He wasn't even hitting my clit directly, and yet I was tensing all over.

"Will," I whined and shook my head before I started to move my hips against him. Responding to my plea, he flicked his tongue directly across my clit.

"Ah." The sound of my pleasure led him to hand it his full attention.

I failed to breathe. *Oh my God.*

At a rapid speed, he licked back and forth, up and down, fuelling the agonising tension. My eyes sprang wide with shock.

Holy shit. This was fucking intense.

"Ah!" I cried out, and again, my back arched off the mattress. Only vaguely did I notice that his hold of my wrists strengthened.

The tension reached a new peak within me. Above it, I couldn't locate my lungs. The pleasure he provided was of such intensity and acuteness that I had to dedicate every single brain cell to withstand it, and so I temporarily forgot how to breathe.

As I convulsed and writhed, he released my left wrist to push his middle finger deep into me, and once inside, he curled it to rub directly across my front wall.

"Oh my God!" I wailed on my remaining breath and fisted my bed sheets with my liberated hand. I thought I would explode.

I climbed higher and higher, desperate for release. Determined to drive me over the edge, he persisted. When my shudders started and my toes curled, he increased the pace of his finger penetrating me.

Fuck! This was sensational.

Overwhelmed, I nearly shuddered away from him, but he was quick to prevent my escape. At once, he withdrew his finger to lock his arm around my thigh again, and his hold was so strong that I couldn't move even an inch away. Grimacing, I struggled to contain the unbearable pleasure. Searing heat burnt my cheeks. I felt so *hot*. Flushed, I panted his name. I would never recover from his impact. He owned me completely.

Suddenly, his tongue hit me with clinical precision, causing the tension to unlock with extreme force. "Ah, fuck!" I uttered, though barely a sound came out since I'd had no air in my lungs.

Bliss flooded my entire body as I underwent my powerful climax, and the sheer magnitude of it left me shocked. I couldn't believe the level of pleasure he could generate in my body, and I was further amazed I'd been able to endure it. The second I collapsed onto the mattress again, euphoria stole me away. To savour it, I closed my eyes. My heart pounded against my ribs while I heaved for air. I hadn't felt this alive yet simultaneously so faded since the last time I'd been with him like this.

"Mm, I love making you come, Cara," his sensual voice affirmed before his mouth trailed enamoured kisses up across my torso.

Subconsciously, my hands found their way to his lovely hair where they lazily massaged his scalp. But, since I was robbed of all strength, they fell away once he lifted his head to loom over mine.

His chuckle drifted to my ears just before he grabbed my waist to flip me around. Sliding his hands down along my curves to my hips, he then gripped them to hoist me onto all fours in front of him.

"You're soaked, love," he said, and suddenly, he kissed my folds again. I jerked forward, overly sensitive now, but his strong hands prevented me from reaching far. After yanking me back to kneel in front of him, he dragged off my robe to reveal the bare skin of my back.

It landed on the floor soon after, and he didn't hesitate to return his attention to my skin. His warm hands roamed across it, nails drawing lanes of red down my back before they travelled to my front, where he paused on my breasts. After squeezing them hungrily, he tugged my nipples.

"Mm," I hummed appreciatively and felt him rest his grinning mouth on my shoulder blade. When his hands continued their exploration, repeatedly sliding along my curves, I smiled as well.

"You have the most beautiful shape," he claimed and dropped his mouth to the spot just below my ear.

As I closed my eyes, I leaned my head on his naked shoulder and circled his neck with my arm. "You're rather stunning yourself, Will."

Suddenly, music blasted from the living room, causing us both to freeze.

"Oh my God," I whispered, embarrassed. Jason had evidently woken up.

"Wise man," William stated with a laugh before his mouth ravished my neck with kisses.

His hands burnt wherever they caressed me, smooth, hot and appreciative. I loved his hands on me. They awakened parts of me that I hadn't even known I harboured until him. Upon acknowledging it, I considered myself either incredibly strong, or remarkably stupid, for having stayed away from him for as long as I had. In the end, it was clear as day that this was what we were meant to be doing.

Yearning for more of him, I reached behind me to trace my hand along his thigh towards his crotch. His erection was hard as concrete within my palm, and the feel of it left a lewd smile on my mouth. As I gave it a gentle squeeze, he groaned into my ear and tightened his embrace of me.

My action must have triggered him because, suddenly, he grabbed my shoulders and pushed me harshly onto the mattress, following my descent. To ensure that I was pinned to the bed, he maintained his firm grip of my shoulders when he proceeded to trail hungry kisses down along my spine. Upon reaching the dimples on my back, he gave each of them extended kisses, and when he finally released my shoulders, he proceeded to claw down my back till he settled on my bum.

"Where do you keep your condoms?" he asked, fingers clawing into my lower cheeks.

The suspense had never been more palpable. I could hardly wait to feel his merciless penetration again.

"Nightstand."

His hands abandoned me entirely. To prepare myself, I inhaled sharply. From the corner of my eye, I saw him lean over to open the drawer and withdraw a foil packet. Upon his return, my heart skipped a beat, and once it resumed, I heard him tear apart the foil.

Now filled with thrilling anticipation, I stared at the white headboard of my bed.

At last, I would feel him within me again. I had never wanted anything as much as I wanted him right now. It was imminent, and it was intense, so when I heard him sheathe himself in the latex, I bit my lower lip and toyed with my bed sheets while I mentally begged for his intrusion.

At first, his hands smoothed over my lower cheeks, but then he spanked me – fucking *hard*.

"Ah!" I was certain the sting of his palm had left a mark on my skin.

"That's for lying to me when we met," he growled. After lifting only my bum away from the bed, he spanked me again, just as hard. Whimpering into the mattress, I fisted the sheets to counter the pain.

"That's for fucking with my head ever since," he berated before he struck me again. "And that's for lying to me yet again, you unruly woman," he continued to scold and then thrust into me without a single warning.

The fulfilment shocked me. He was so fucking big. I'd forgotten how deep he reached. Gasping, I clawed the bed sheets again until my knuckles grew numb.

"Ah, Cara. You feel so fucking good," he groaned and leaned forward to twirl my long, brown hair around his wrist. "The way you're gripping me, just barely letting me in…" His sharp inhalation echoed in my ears as he pushed all the way into me, slow and steady. Using his hold of my hair, he tugged me backwards to pull himself even deeper, and effectively lifted my upper body away from the bed till I was on all fours again. At this point, he was buried so deep within that it was on the verge of being painful.

"Shit," I mouthed, out of breath, and shook my head to myself. This was overwhelming. He felt so good, stretching me to my limit. It bordered on unbearable.

Upon his gentle retreat, he released my hair to grab my hips instead. Then, he started a most staggering rhythm, shocking me again. I'd never experienced more sensual thrusts in my life, and I'd slept with my fair share of men. Each one was slow at first but picked up the pace the deeper he got. As he went, he focused his point of impact on my front wall.

I wished I could have seen him move like that, like a fly on the wall. I was confident it would have been the most erotic thing I ever saw. How he bucked towards me, while his big hands held onto my hips, was devastating. If he kept this up, I'd be coming in no time.

Although, ironically, it was obvious that he was in no rush to see this finished. He wasn't looking to blow his load. On the contrary, he was looking to make me come undone for him, time and again, as though it was his sole purpose in this.

He was looking to experience me.

What a man. From the way he praised and tended to the female anatomy, keenly attuned to our every response, he did indeed make his lovers feel like goddesses. In bed, he behaved like his main objective was to provide divine pleasure, despite his proclivity for dominance. However, it became apparent that he had a taste for dominance because he trusted himself to deliver heavenly gratification. It stemmed from his profound confidence, and with good reason.

"Fuck," I breathed and frowned to myself while I savoured his shaft sliding back and forth across my front wall, which he repeatedly struck just perfectly. In and out – so fucking delicious. My fluids trickled down my thighs while the pounding sound of our flesh meeting, again and again, drove me wild with desire. I couldn't recall having been so wet before.

My vaginal walls began quivering around him, and when he noticed, he crouched over me and gathered my breasts in his hands. Struck by the intimacy of our new position, I moaned his name and thrust against him, aching for more of him. I just couldn't seem to get close enough. I wanted him to consume me – the entirety of me.

Across my upper back, he planted starving kisses. "Enjoying me, Cara?" he asked, and there was a smile present in his voice.

"Mm, yes. Don't ever stop," I answered breathily and turned my head in search of his lips. Realising what I wanted, he carefully folded his large hand over my throat and guided my mouth to his. Dopamine flooded my brain upon the enchanting motion of his kiss. I never wanted him to stop. I loved kissing him. It was one of my favourite things to do in this world, as well as enduring his sensational lovemaking.

He continued to kiss me while the tension rebuilt within me, dense and heavy. My shudders started again, a warning of my looming climax. Immediately, he tightened his embrace to smother me against him.

Responding to my impending orgasm, his thrusts accelerated, hitting me faster, deeper, harder. *Fuck!*

He held me tightly, trapping me in his embrace – trapping me in a state of complete pleasure. In and out. Back and forth. I would detonate like never before.

"Oh!" I moaned against his mouth and reached for something to hold onto. I was desperate to release at least a portion of this wicked tension that rallied within me, so I gripped onto the arm of his hand around my throat, and I didn't mind the fact that I was clawing harshly into his skin. I was much too preoccupied with enduring my internal torment.

"I…coming," I warned breathlessly.

"Yes. Let yourself go for me, Cara," he demanded and ploughed powerfully into me, successfully knocking the air out of my lungs. I tried to pull away from his kiss, but he refused to let me. Like a famished man, he continued to kiss me while I trembled in his hold – so close to the edge that I was only seconds away from coming. Another thrust and I would reel straight into bliss again.

He fucked me so hard then that I promptly fell victim to yet another orgasm.

"Ah!" I collapsed in his embrace, held up solely by his arms around me. My walls clenched around his shaft, quivering and overly sensitive, but he continued to pull in and out of me, slowly, allowing me to ride my orgasm for longer. Meanwhile, his mouth remained on mine, kissing me while I surrendered to oblivion, lost to the world and lost in the feeling of him.

Eventually, his smile interfered. I was heaving for air when I finally opened my eyes to gauge his thoughts. The sight melted my heart, as bottomless affection exuded from his blue eyes. While nuzzling my nose with his, he chuckled to himself and closed them.

"Sorry," he quietly murmured and pecked my lips again. "I just can't believe we're doing this again. Feels like I've waited for an eternity."

Nose to nose, a coy smile teased my mouth while I chuckled, too.

"I'm glad you swayed my mind, Will," I hoarsely replied, but moaned when he pushed deeply into me again.

"I've sincerely missed the sound of your moans. Most beautiful thing I'll ever hear."

I blushed at his carnal declaration. "Well, you're the one extracting them."

My response prompted him to open his eyes again, and his stare was piercing. "Indeed, and I intend to keep it that way."

Using his careful grip of my throat, he lifted my upper body until I was kneeling in front of him. Then, he closed his arms around me, and he held me so intimately that my heart thundered. Meanwhile, he continued to thrust slowly but powerfully into me.

Marvelling, I closed my eyes again and rested my head on his shoulder while I wished to myself that we could do this forever. Nothing would ever feel as good as this, as right as this. I was certain.

I LIKE THIS

S INFULLY LATER, HE WAS FINALLY REACHING HIS PEAK. Merciless as he was, he had withdrawn every time he had been close to coming to proceed with giving me oral attention instead. By now, I'd lost count of the number of orgasms I'd had.

This was reclaiming, and it was fucking intense.

No man came close to William's divine lovemaking. He was out of this world. It was as though he'd been created to do this – pleasure women into the celestial. It was a remarkable talent and, blessed as I was, I was on the receiving end of it.

In our current position, I'd been hoisted up against the headboard of my bed, essentially seated against it. With his hands under my thighs, he secured my legs in place around his waist. Between them, he was kneeling, charging savagely in and out of me now.

A thorough layer of sweat covered both our bodies while I crouched over his broad shoulder, close to fainting. I couldn't make so much as a sound anymore. I was completely battered after my streak of countless, mind-blowing orgasms. All I wanted now was for him to finally allow himself to come.

"Ah," he groaned and buried his hand in my hair to tug my head back. Through hooded eyes, I watched him, saw how his square jaw clenched while his eyes drizzled of animalistic pleasures. His pupils were dilated as he ground his teeth and stared intensely at me.

He was close.

Just as he performed his hardest and deepest thrust yet, he placed his mouth back on mine and passionately kissed me. Shocked by the fulfilment of such a powerful shove, I whimpered against his mouth and clawed down his back.

"Please," I begged, out of breath.

His crooked smile crossed his lips when he slowed his thrusts but increased his strength. "Nearly there," he consoled before he kissed me again.

One hard thrust. Another. Another again.

"Ah," I sobbed.

"Fuck, Cara," he groaned and suddenly flipped us around. Now beneath him, I stared up at his hypnotising beauty and gulped, momentarily overwhelmed by the sheer view of him. His eyes softened when they locked with mine, and a gentle smile took over his mouth. Letting go of my thighs, his hands moved to my flushed cheeks and cupped them instead before he kissed me like I'd never been kissed – soft, tender, and yet so formidable.

Gently, he withdrew from within me only to push forward again, but fast this time. He groaned against my lips. From the sound of it, I knew he was reaching it.

Now.

Retreating again, he pushed a little harder into me, sliding further and further until he reached the very end of me. *Fuck*, he reached deep. He lingered there, his kiss growing harder against my mouth before he groaned again and repeated the process one more time.

Finally, he stilled, and a smile formed on his mouth while he continued to kiss me. I followed the motion of his lips lazily, and we'd kissed for quite a while when he eventually withdrew and pulled away to look at me.

"You okay?" he queried hoarsely.

I huffed out a loud breath and shielded my eyes with my forearm, utterly destroyed. "I'm dead," I whispered in response. It was all I could manage. My sore vagina was pulsating as though my heart had relocated to it.

He chuckled above me and lowered his head to suck each of my nipples. "Sorry. You've got yourself to blame. You're irresistible, and I love watching you come."

I shook my head to myself and wondered if this was what it was going to be like – crazy sessions every time we got down to business. Would I survive a relationship like that?

"You're inhuman," I alleged.

His lips trailed down my stomach. When he reached the apex of my thighs, I tensed completely. A sadistic laugh escaped his mouth right before he planted a firm kiss on my throbbing bud. Hissing, I jerked away and lowered my arm to glare at him.

Complacent, he grinned back. "I said I'd fuck you if you agreed to go on a date with me. I don't make promises I can't keep."

I chortled. "Evidently."

"I need another shower, and so do you. We're drenched in sweat."

Gazing down the length of my body beneath his beautiful one, I sighed to myself. He was right. It looked like we'd been in a steam room.

"You go first. I can't move yet," I replied, exhausted, and closed my eyes again.

I was going to be terribly sore tomorrow. He was abnormally large, and he'd been at me for ages. Already, I dreaded having to sit. As if I required a reminder of him. Lately, he was all I thought about – and now I wouldn't be able to sit anywhere without feeling his phantom cock within me.

"Why are you blushing?" he asked curiously. Had he been studying my complexion? I was confident I was flushed from before, so how had he noticed my blush that easily?

"Because I'm not looking forward to sitting tomorrow," I moaned and opened my eyes to look away. He laughed wholeheartedly, lips spreading wide apart to reveal his straight teeth, and his eyes sparkled. For a moment, he looked years younger than he was.

"Might as well get used to it," he teased and descended to plant a soft, extended kiss on the slope of my neck. Afterwards, he pushed himself away to climb out of bed.

"By the way," he murmured while approaching the door. Once he reached it, he turned to study me in the bed amidst the tousled duvet. Appearing to appreciate the view, he bit his lower lip while he smiled lopsidedly to himself. At least the admiration was mutual. He was unfairly sexy, and he wasn't even trying. "Are you on contraceptives?" he finally continued.

I smiled, amused. Eager to drop the rubber already, was he? "Yeah. I've had an IUD inserted. Why?"

"Are you clean?" He narrowed his eyes at me. In turn, I raised my brow at him.

"I should be, seeing as I've only slept with Aaron without a condom, and he's supposed to use protection whenever he sleeps with anyone else. He's never given me anything before, so I trust he's been careful about that. Last I checked myself was after I'd slept with you, and you're my most recent one-night stand. Result came out clean. Doubt Aaron has given me anything in the meantime. Are you?"

He blinked. "*I'm* your most recent one-night stand?"

I frowned. "You sound surprised. Is that truly so hard to believe?"

He shrugged. "No offence, but yeah."

"But offend, you did," I muttered. "Just because I've had an open arrangement with Aaron, it doesn't mean I sleep with strangers frequently."

He shook his head. "That's not how I meant for it to seem. I've never had that impression of you."

I steered my eyes to the ceiling above my head. "Frankly, I

should be the one surprised between us. Last time we had sex, you said you only had one partner. Was that Violet?"

"Yeah."

"So Francesca came after that?"

"Sort of."

I turned to look at him again, intrigued. "Elaborate."

"Francesca and I were undefined at the time. There was always a question over whether we'd meet again. Violet was a stable, regular thing."

"Right."

"Anyway, I got myself checked after I ended things with them – all clean."

My lips twisted with my amusement. It wasn't like him to beat around the bush, so why was he now? "Are you trying to say that you'd prefer not to use a condom?"

He rubbed the back of his head. "Yeah. Feels better. But only if you're alright with it."

I grinned. "I'm alright with it."

"Great." He beamed. "Though, I'd appreciate it if you took a test anyway, just to be sure. We'll proceed without condoms from now on, because waiting three weeks for the result when we're ninety-nine per cent sure you're clean seems a bit unnecessary, but I still think it's prudent to take a test just in case Aaron's been careless. I'm aware the chances are slim, but…if you happen to have anything, it's better we pick up on it sooner rather than later in terms of getting treated."

I nodded. "Yeah, that's probably wise. I'll get myself checked later this week, yeah?"

He glanced at me with affection. "Thanks." As he opened the door, the music pounded into the room, so he shouted, "Jason! Turn down the bloody music!"

"Finally!" Jason roared back, impatient. "Took you long enough! Jesus Christ, man! How long do you last?"

The music stopped.

"Why? You jealous of my stamina?" William replied, poking his head out the door.

"Piss off."

"Unless you want to see my cock, I advise you to look away. I need a shower."

"Fucking animal," Jason muttered. "Is she even still alive in there?"

"Barely," William answered as he headed into the bathroom, audibly smug.

Thoroughly amused by the way they spoke to one another, I giggled where I lay.

William had been gone for about a minute when Jason announced his approach. "Incoming."

Immediately, I dragged the duvet over my battered body and turned my head to welcome him.

Once he entered the doorway, he leaned against the doorpost and folded his arms. A look of great amusement covered his face while he analysed my lazy figure. "I gather you made up, then?"

I smiled, basking in the glory of the delicious aftermath. "You could say that."

Sparkles of joy danced in his light-blue eyes. "Yeah? Are you happy, then?"

I sighed, delighted, and dared not imagine how smitten I looked. "I *really* fancy him, Jason," I shyly confessed.

He grinned. "I can tell. Have you told him?"

I shook my head. "Not in those exact words, but I'm quite sure he already knows."

"He's an arrogant bastard, so I'm sure he does," he replied, visibly amused.

I giggled and stretched my hands towards the ceiling. "What time is it?"

"Nearly three."

I gasped. We'd been at it for ages! "Oh my God."

"Yeah," he nodded as he read my thoughts, "I thought you'd never finish."

I blushed profusely. "I'm so sorry."

He cocked his head from side to side. "Was a bit of a shock waking up to that. Then again, suppose I might as well get used to it. Next time, I'll use my headphones. Unfortunately for me, they were out of battery this time around. So, if we receive complaints from the neighbours, it's on your shoulders, because there wasn't a chance I was going to listen to that."

"Yeah. I accept full responsibility."

He chuckled. "Anyway, I'm happy for you."

My heart tingled upon his statement. That was heartfelt and, seeing as William was his brother, his blessing meant a lot to me. "Thank you."

"Are you hungry? I saw you'd started on an omelette, so I finished cooking it."

"Aw, thanks, Jason. I was making it for Will. I'm sure he's starving."

"William!" he shouted then.

"Yeah," came his loud reply.

"Are you hungry?"

"Famished!"

"Shall I order sushi for dinner?"

I heard laughter from the shower before it was switched off. Soon after, William opened the door to say, "Go ahead. Why not move to Japan, Jase?"

"I'd love that."

"I'd love it if you did, too."

Jason frowned in his direction. "Cunt."

"I'm done showering, Cara," William yelled to me.

"Right," I murmured. "Unless you want to see me naked, close the door, Jason."

He scoffed. "As if I haven't seen you naked countless times before. Guess you dating my brother changes things, though," he responded, amused, and shut the door between us.

"You've seen her naked?" I heard William question, appalled.

"Cry me a fucking river, Will," Jason replied, his voice monotone.

"Dickhead," William muttered before he ripped the door open again just as I was climbing out.

I couldn't help my besotted grin. I was reeling, and my insides had melted into a gooey mess. Truly, I had never felt more ecstatic. I felt liberated. After what had been a dreadful process, I could finally allow myself to enjoy him. I could hardly wait. Already, I wanted to explore the entirety of him. Friday couldn't come soon enough.

"Will you spend the night?" I asked, and my question appeared to take him by surprise.

"Would you prefer it?"

"Yes."

He nodded. "Then of course. However, I haven't got any clothes here, so I'll have to leave earlier in the morning to fetch my things before work."

Uncertain, I frowned. "Are you sure? Or is that terribly inconvenient?"

He shook his head. "I'm an early-bird."

"Settled, then."

"Yeah."

I grinned. "I like this."

A coy smile found his mouth. "Good. Me too."

29

· · ✦ · ·

STRONG POINT

*L*IVE AT THE *APOLLO* WAS ON THE TELEVISION WHILE William, Jason and I slouched on the sofa as we recovered from our food coma. Jason's favourite comedian was on stage, and I'd started suspecting that he was William's, too, after hearing the sound of his guffawing, which he had then confirmed when I'd asked.

I'd always found their favourite comedian rather hilarious myself, and the chance to laugh was exhilarating after all the chaos of the weekend. However, despite my good mood, I was checking my phone now and then to see whether Aaron had sent me anything, but he'd been dead silent, which was unlike him. He wasn't one to let anger fester, so I was slightly worried about his silence, since it spoke much louder than words. I wondered if perhaps he expected me to reach out to him instead. After all, I'd been the one to kick him out. Nevertheless, I decided I'd give him some space for a few days. If I still hadn't heard from him by Tuesday, I'd reach out to settle our dispute.

The thought of him inspired me to recount last night's events, which ultimately murdered my good mood. While I hadn't been sober, I still recalled most of what had happened. The thought of how wounded he had looked after being enlightened about my affair with William made me tense against William's side, as I was lying snuggled between him and Jason.

I could understand Aaron's discomfort. I wouldn't have appreciated being launched into such a scenario at all. He'd been completely blindsided, so I supposed that could justify some of his behaviour. Totally unprepared and influenced by the alcohol in his blood, he'd become defensive, which was understandable considering William's ruthless attempt to provoke him and stir an argument between us.

The latter memory made me frown. Like Aaron, William had been quite upset, and understandably so. However, what didn't sit right with me was William's attempt to ruin my friendship with Aaron by twisting my words to make it seem like I didn't care about Aaron at all. Acting like that, it was evident that he had placed his own wounded feelings first – certainly before mine – and it irritated me, because the more I thought about it, the more I realised he'd been prone to it ever since we first met.

In every situation where our opinions and actions had differed, he had self-victimised due to his injured feelings, and while I certainly felt bad for him, I was also aware that I hadn't behaved like that myself; I had respected his boundaries as much as I could, a favour he hadn't returned most of the time, and never had I played the victim. On the contrary, I had taken and accepted blame where it was due.

His tendency to act righteous and entitled bothered me, and the more I considered it, the more I realised it was a red flag which needed to be acknowledged and dealt with. I was happy that we had finally reconciled and that we were about to start dating each other seriously, but considering his past conduct, I was also slightly alarmed. If he intended to continue self-victimising every time I stood up for myself and my opinions, we were going to have a severe problem.

I wasn't one to hold grudges, and I believed in giving people a chance to mend their ways, but for William to do that, I would need to bring the issue to his attention. It wouldn't be reasonable of me to expect him to change his ways if he had no idea his behaviour was problematic in the first place.

Overall, I liked to think I was a forgiving person, but I couldn't deny I was growing slightly wary of him. Consequently, I would be on the lookout for more red flags. While we explored our chemistry, I intended to devote myself to him fully, but if he proved unable to respect my boundaries and place me first the way I did him, we simply wouldn't work out. I was eager for us to succeed, but that did not mean I was willing to settle for anything that didn't make me happy.

"Right, Will," Jason suddenly said while he leaned forward to pour himself a glass of water. "This is going to sound proper weird, but after hearing Cara talk about your performance in bed and witnessing the duration of it first-hand, I've got to know – how the hell are you able to last that long?"

Instant giggles poured out of my mouth, and when I turned my head to study William's reaction, I found him grinning from ear to ear, eyes firmly set on his younger replica. I was grateful Jason had asked while I was present, because I was curious to know, too.

"Are you a minute-man, Jase?"

I rarely saw Jason blush, but his face turned completely pink.

"No, but I'm not an eternity-man either."

William shook beneath me while he struggled to stifle his laughter.

"Come on, Will," Jason pushed. "What's your secret?"

"I've got several, as it happens."

"Spill them."

"I want to know, too," I said.

"I'll probably sound insane," William murmured, nose wrinkling somewhat.

"We already know you are," Jason bantered.

"True," I chimed in. "Nothing would surprise us at this point."

"Right," William said with a sigh. "Well, first of all, I've read plenty of books on the female anatomy relating to sex. Since you're nearly a doctor, J, I doubt you'll need to do the same. However, it certainly taught me a lot. That said, every woman is unique, so I like to ask my partners what they like, where things feel best, things like that, to create a sort of map in my head."

Jason's eyebrows arched, and so did mine. "Damn," he said, "that's some dedication."

"Definitely," I agreed, impressed.

"Still doesn't explain your endurance, though," Jason continued.

William chuckled. "Well, when it comes to endurance, there are several things you can do to last longer. First of all, rubbing one or several out in secret before you have sex will improve your endurance rather a lot. If that's not an option – I didn't today, for example – I like to pull out every time I'm close to coming to proceed with giving her oral attention instead. Once my arousal recedes somewhat, I continue.

"However, there's one more thing I tend to do, which I doubt most men do in general, but it certainly aids my endurance overall."

"And what's that?" Jason probed and finally dared to look at him.

"Kegel exercises."

I chortled. "Kegel exercises? I thought only women did that?"

Condescension was written across the arch of William's brow when he looked at me. "That's stupid. They're a great exercise for men, too. Can help treat several problems, like erectile dysfunction, overactive bladder, premature ejaculation, the list goes on." He looked back to Jason's gawk. "However, this requires that you do it frequently, which I do. Consistency is key here. I even go so far as to get erect, and then I tie some weight to my erection and try to lift it using only my penis. Progressive overload, you know? It's a brilliant method to improve your endurance."

The image in my head caused blood to flood my cheeks and prickle across my scalp.

"Jesus Christ." Visibly amused, Jason shook his head to himself. "You're right – you are actually insane."

"I like sex," William justified with a shrug, "so I prefer to last for as long as possible. Besides, getting my partner off is something I take great pleasure in, so I go out of my way to achieve it."

"Cara, you ought to appreciate his dedication."

"I do," I squeaked, embarrassed.

"Well then. Cat's out of the bag," William said with a grin. "Happy wanking, Jason."

"Fucking hell."

"Let me know how it works out."

"Sure."

"I can send you a few links on it, unless you'd like to research it yourself."

"No, send the links. I'll do some research, but you're clearly doing something right, so your sources seem credible."

"They are."

"Do you guys talk about everything with each other?" I asked inquisitively. "I hardly ever talk to my sister about sex."

"Yeah, everything," Jason confirmed.

"Yeah," William agreed. "Well, not everything," he corrected, "but if asked, always."

"That's what I love most about us," Jason murmured after a sip of water and turned his head to give his brother a fond grin. "The full transparency."

"I love you too, Jase," William replied, charmed, and reached over to push his head playfully. "Glad I can help you better your sex life. Though, to put it to good use, you've got to start dating."

"Yeah, yeah. I'll get to it as soon as I find the time."

William snorted. "If Cara – of all people – can find the time, then surely you can, too."

That summoned Jason's laughter. "Touché."

§ § §

Exhausted after the weekend, we went to bed at ten. Yet, despite how fatigued I was, sleep wouldn't find me. I was anxious about Aaron, and I was overthinking his silence. We'd never fought before, so I had no idea how to treat the situation. I'd never witnessed Aaron as distraught as he had been last night, and because of it, I wasn't sure what to expect or how to proceed. I had no experience dealing with his anger – did he prefer silence? Was he expecting me to reach out first? Would he remain angry for a long period?

Worse, had this been a disruptive event in our friendship? Had the disclosure made him reconsider our friendship overall?

I couldn't imagine what was going through his head, but I hoped he didn't feel betrayed. After all, the sole reason I hadn't told him about my affair with William was that it was part of our agreement. Surely he had to see that.

It was nearly midnight when I slipped out of William's hold to reach for my phone. He seemed fast asleep, so I was careful not to wake him as I checked my phone for any messages, but there were none.

With a sigh, I decided to write to Aaron. I couldn't stand this silence between us. He was one of my best friends, and our argument made me more anxious than I could bear. I hated the possibility that I might have hurt him inadvertently.

> I'm sorry about how last night turned out. I wasn't aware he'd be there, and I'm sorry he treated you like that. You didn't deserve an ounce of it. Call me when you're ready to talk, yeah? x

Switching between my social media and my messages, I waited five minutes for him to see it, but since he didn't, I placed my phone back on my nightstand and decided to use the loo.

Once I'd returned to bed, I snuggled into my duvet and sighed again. Sleep seemed far from my reach, but I had thought William had found it, so when he suddenly asked, "Everything alright, Cara?" I nearly gasped.

"Sorry, did I wake you?" I replied, startled.

His arms reached for me. "No. What's wrong?" He tugged me

into the spoon of his embrace.

I tensed. Part of me wanted to discuss my issues with his past behaviour, but at the same time, I was reluctant to keep him awake. It wasn't so pressing that it couldn't wait another while. "Just can't sleep."

Silence ensued, and I found his nearness oddly distant all of a sudden.

"I can hear the gears of your mind turning," he eventually said. "Talk to me, please."

Unsure, I chewed on my lower lip. "It can wait. Get some rest, Will. You've had little of it this weekend, and you've got work tomorrow."

"Cara, no. Now that I know something's bothering you, I won't be able to sleep until you tell me."

I exhaled loudly. "I don't know where to start."

He was quiet for a beat. "Please don't tell me you've changed your mind about us."

"No, I haven't," I reassured him at once. "But, if you really want me to talk, I should turn on the light."

"Shit," he mumbled. "Is it related to me?"

I grimaced in the dark. "I'm afraid so."

"Alright, spit it out, then."

Obliging, I reached over to switch on my night lamp before I sat up. Crossing my legs, I faced him and fiddled with my fingers. "This is going to be quite the speech," I warned. "But please, don't interrupt me."

Clearly apprehensive, he avoided my eyes while he pushed up to slide towards the headboard of my bed, which he rested his back against. Folding his hands on his lap, he inhaled deeply and then blew out his cheeks.

"Okay, bring it."

Nervous, I scratched my cheek while my heart hammered. "While I'm grateful we made up today, there are a few things that are bothering me, which I feel are important to make clear if we're going to work out."

Finally, he met my eyes, and a slow nod followed. "Go on."

"I've been thinking about your conduct – your pursuit overall – and I've noticed an alarming pattern, which is that you tend to always put yourself first, Will. You've behaved quite selfishly, and if you mean to continue with that, we're going to have a problem."

He frowned. "Would you mind elaborating on why you're under that impression? Have you got any examples?"

I nodded patiently. "I've got several. Would you like to hear them all?"

"I'd prefer it, yes."

"Then please don't interrupt till I've shared all of them."

"I won't."

"Thank you," I said and reached for his hand, and I was grateful he gave it to me. While tracing my thumb along the edges of his neatly trimmed nails, I started, "When you messaged me on Instagram that first time, were you genuinely seeking to befriend me?"

He grimaced, and I saw shame at the root of it. After a reluctant shake of his head, he admitted, "No."

"Was it part of your pursuit?"

"Yes."

I'd expected it, and while it annoyed me, I reminded myself to be constructive about this. "Thank you for your honesty. I appreciate it."

He averted his eyes with a nod.

"Anyway," I continued, "you failed to respect my wishes when you did that. I specifically told you I wasn't interested in anything else, and you disregarded that and decided to put yourself and your own feelings first."

Seeing my point, he nodded again.

"Then, after you walked in on Aaron and me, you got very angry with me, as if I'd committed a crime."

"That wasn't right of me," he agreed.

"It wasn't. Either way, you still punished me for it. I know you were drunk that night – when you brought Jason home after he'd had too much to drink – but you threatened to destroy my friendship with Jason just because you were angry with me for sleeping with Aaron. While you were at it, you insinuated that I'm the type of woman who uses men solely for my own personal gain, and that was very unkind of you. I'm not like that, and I found it extremely disrespectful that you would treat me like that. How do you think I felt in the wake of that incident? I hated that I'd hurt you, but at the same time, I'd told you I wasn't interested in anything else, Will. I didn't deserve your spite."

Air poured out of his mouth for a long while, and I watched as his chest deflated with it. His gaze dashed to the ceiling then, and it remained there.

"Again, you placed your own hurt feelings first," I told him, which he nodded to. I continued, "I have another question, and again, I'd appreciate it if you were honest with me. I'm not looking to punish you here. On the contrary, my point with bringing all this up is that I want us to work out, so I'd like to recognise and treat the problem before it gets a chance to worsen."

Seeming to realise and appreciate my intentions, his fingers wrapped around my hand. Still, he refused to look at me.

"What's your question?" he quietly asked.

"The shoe cabinet... Did you tilt it over on purpose? To stop us?"

His jaw clenched. "I might have overdone it."

I groaned. "William, you had no right."

"I know," he admitted shamefacedly, hand squeezing mine. "I just couldn't bear it, Cara. I'm sorry."

"I understand, Will – really, I do – but the pattern remains the same. You were hurt, so you put yourself first. I wouldn't dream of doing something similar in that sort of situation. As it happens, I even went and collected Francesca for you despite my notion of her reason for being there. You put your wounded feelings before my right to do such a thing in my own home, even when I had no idea you'd be there.

"And, speaking of Francesca, that brings me to the scheme you pulled. I had made myself very clear with you by then, several times over, and yet you made it seem like you fucked her just to elicit a reaction from me. You showed no consideration for how much that might have hurt me, and you also showed no consideration for the fact that I had told you not to pursue me. I mean, poor Francesca! You took advantage of her there."

He winced. "Hardly. I dragged out the time a bit, and perhaps I did some questionable things, but what she doesn't know can't hurt her, Cara."

I scoffed. "That's funny. That was my view when I asked you not to tell Jason about us, which you scolded me for... which also brings me to my next point."

He groaned. "Christ, how long is the list?"

"William." My tone was strict. "I'm trying to be constructive here."

"Sorry. It's just embarrassing to remember all this. I hardly recognise myself, and hearing it out loud is making the gravity of what I've done real to me. It's uncomfortable."

A sympathetic smile curved my lips. "Well, that's good. That's the point of all this."

He sank somewhat. "Carry on, then."

"I shouldn't have kissed you on Friday," I murmured with a pout. "It was selfish and reckless of me, but I was very drunk and, all along, I've been very attracted to you, so I fell for temptation, and it was ruthless of me. However, you also had a responsibility to make sure I wouldn't be overstepping your boundaries. You should have made sure we were on the same page as much as I should have. You *knew* I wasn't interested in anything more – I'd told you time and again – and yet you went ahead anyway. I am to blame for some of the hurt that scene caused you, but you do share some of the blame, William. You're a grown man. You should be able to look out for yourself."

His chest expanded and deflated with his loud, deep breath. "You're right. It is partially my fault."

This conversation was exceeding my expectations. He was being unusually attentive.

"I'm glad you're able to see that," I said and lifted his hand to my mouth to kiss it. "Anyway, what happened after that is also a bit problematic. While I agree it was selfish of me to ask you not to tell Jason about us, you did in fact agree to it. So, that you decided to tell him without warning me first was completely unacceptable. I understand you were angry with me and wanted to hold me accountable for my actions, but at that moment in time, you put yourself first – *again* – by telling him without my consent."

"I'm very sorry about that," he insisted. "In my defence, I knew Jason wasn't going to care – that he'd prefer the truth – so it just seemed nonsensical to keep it from him at the time."

"I get that, but it wasn't nonsensical to me, which is what you should have respected. Your view on something isn't the only one that matters, Will."

"I know," he mumbled. "I'm sorry. I'm actually mortified listening to this."

"Really?" My eyes narrowed as I tried to gauge whether he was being sincere or not, but it was apparent he was.

"Really."

I sighed. "Well, there's one more thing left, and this is going to get very uncomfortable, I think."

He retrieved his hand. "I think I already know," he said, but it was barely audible.

"Last night, you were very upset, and I completely understand why you were. Really, I do. However, I would *never* have insulted Francesca if the roles were switched around, and I would *never* have tried to get between you by attempting to ruin your friendship. What you told him about my 'air' comment was completely offensive, Will. It may not have been your intention to destroy our friendship by saying that, but it might still have been a consequence. You twisted my words in order to hurt him. You didn't consider my place in that situation at all, but you should have. Instead, you minded your own stakes, and those alone, and it's not okay. You can't keep doing that.

"So, ultimately, the pattern I've noticed is that you keep putting yourself first. While your ulterior motive might justify some of it – the fact that you saw the potential for us working out – you've still disregarded and disrespected my boundaries and placed your selfish desires first. That can't continue in the future. I won't enter a relationship with someone who's prone to such toxicity. I've tried time and again to respect your feelings and keep my distance, but you've made it *really* fucking hard, William. You've intentionally provoked me, so when you argue that I've contradicted myself, please reconsider who's to blame. You're at fault as well, not just me.

"You say I'm inexperienced, and I know I am. I've tried to warn you about it several times. However, I'd argue that you can be very immature yourself. When you've had no claim whatsoever, how entitled you've acted can be considered quite childish, you know.

"I understand you've been hurt, and I understand you've been confused since I've told you I have feelings for you, but I have also told you I didn't want anything, and those are also my feelings, Will, which you have repeatedly disregarded. You can't just pick and choose what to listen to and what to ignore. The overall point was that I did not want your romantic attention, and you disrespected that.

"I know you've meant well – your intention and heart were in the right place – but you can't keep doing it. I consider it a major red flag, Will, which I'll be mindful of as we start seeing each other. I won't settle for someone who won't respect me and my autonomy."

I nearly stopped speaking when I saw tears surface in his eyes. "I'm sorry," I said, but he shook his head and continued to avoid looking at me.

"Please, continue. I'm fine," he insisted.

Yet another sigh escaped me, and my pout intensified. "You're twenty-eight, Will. You've been in a long-term relationship before, you've got a stable career, your friends are at a point where they're considering children. Typically, all you've left to do is find a woman to settle down with, and that frightens me a bit because I'm nowhere near that point in my life. I'm still trying to establish myself. I don't even know if I want children. I'm really far behind you, and you need to bear that in mind. If you want to date me, you'll need to be patient with me. I've agreed to start seeing you, and I obviously hope we'll work out, but the pace is a serious concern of mine. We'll have to take things slow. If you can't respect that, you *need* to find someone else – and this is your last warning. I mean it."

He nodded vehemently. "Okay," he said feebly. "I'm glad you brought this up. With hindsight, I agree with everything you've said. I've been extremely selfish, and it needs to stop. I swear I'll fix it. I've just…" He blew his cheeks out again, and I could tell he was struggling to keep his tears at bay. "I've just wanted to give you everything. I've been so eager that I haven't been able to think clearly."

I leaned forward to roll onto him. Hugging him, I wrapped my leg over his and rested my cheek on his chest. "I know what you mean. I've been confused, too. Feelings are a bitch that way."

"Cara, I'm really sorry. Hearing this, I'm shocked you want to give me a chance at all."

Wearing a faint smile, I left a prolonged kiss on his chest. "Well, it's because I see hope for what is at the root of it all. Like I said, your heart's been in the right place, but how you've gone about it can't continue. So, while I'm glad we are where we are, it won't justify things if you repeat this pattern."

"I won't. I promise." His arms came around me, and while he squeezed me against him, he pressed his lips to my hair and kissed me repeatedly.

I let out a breath of relief. "Thank you for listening to me and for taking it so well. And, with all of that said, I want you to know that I'm sorry, too. I never meant to hurt you, but I did, and I'm sorry for it."

"I'm glad you told me. If you have thoughts like these again, I'd appreciate it if you brought them to my attention at once. I want this to work, so I'm grateful you're helping me manage it."

Crawling up his body, I stopped just before I reached his mouth, and a tender grin spread my lips apart when I saw that his tears had retreated. "The fact that we were able to talk about this so constructively is a great sign, Will. Huge star in my book."

He smiled faintly. "Mine too. Communication might turn into our strong point."

"Let respect be, too."

"Agreed."

I pecked his mouth. "With that out of the way, I think I'll be able to sleep now."

He glanced at my alarm. "Good. It's quite late."

"It is." Reaching for my night lamp, I killed the lights.

When he pulled me back to him to wrap his limbs around me, I smiled in the dark. He was so warm and big, and he smelled so good. Nothing could beat this feeling. I'd never felt so at home in an embrace before – like I belonged.

"Good night, darling," he cooed and kissed my cheek.

Snuggling closer, I released a contented sigh. "Night, Will."

"That's my name."

I laughed. "Like I could ever forget."

30

INTO THE NIGHT

WILLIAM HAD LEFT BEFORE MY ALARM RANG THE NEXT morning, and while I'd been asleep when he did, I had a vague memory of his lips on my cheek, and the sensation of it remained in my mind all the way to work. It was a lovely thing, but despite it, I was nervous today. Everything had changed this weekend. I was now seeing my boss, and how to handle it was completely unexplored terrain for me.

I'd no idea what to expect, but I was sure about two things: when at work, I expected us to behave professionally towards one another, and I also expected us to keep our affair a secret from our colleagues, with two exceptions. In the end, I expected that both Andy and Violet would learn the truth since they were among William's most cherished friends. That didn't bother me all that much because I trusted their loyalty towards William. However, following this past weekend, I feared Elisabeth had her suspicions too, but I would confirm nothing if she did.

While I liked her rather a lot, I was aware she was prone to gossiping, and I wasn't interested in being a subject of it. So, as soon as William arrived, we'd need to discuss how to proceed with our affair. I would ask him to request Violet and Andy's silence, and I would also ask him not to tell anyone else till I'd finished work in September.

As chance would have it, Elisabeth called, "Morning, Cara," just as I was about to enter the lift.

"Morning, Ellie," I called back and pressed the button to hold the doors open for her till she arrived by my side.

"What happened to you on Friday?" she asked while the doors slid shut, head turning to regard me. "I got worried. Sent you a text, but you never replied."

"Shit, Ellie," I grimaced, "I'm so sorry. I had such a rough night, and plenty of plans the day after, so it honestly just slipped my mind to reply." I hoped my sincerity showed in my voice, because I truly felt sorry for making her worry. Knowing her, it wasn't something she only said to be polite.

"Rough night? What happened?"

"I got far too drunk. Will found me and had to bring me home. It was awful. I'm still absolutely mortified. After I lost you, I ordered a few shots of tequila, and – you know – things just got a wee bit out of hand," I explained, embarrassed.

Elisabeth blinked, and then she pursed her lips to stifle a smile. "Your boss had to bring you home? Good thing he's your flatmate's brother, eh? Christ, Cara."

"Please don't tell anyone. I'm still so embarrassed."

"Of course I won't. Has Will given you a hard time for it?" she asked. "I know he tends to look down on people who don't drink responsibly. Either way, it was after hours. Might be unprofessional, but you had every right."

I cocked my head from side to side. "He wasn't exactly impressed." To change the subject, I continued, "On another note, one of Brian's friends tried to force me to kiss him."

Elisabeth gasped, and a look of horror crossed her face. "What?

Which one?"

"I don't remember his name, but he had somewhat long hair, brown, side parting, neatly groomed stubble. Brown eyes, too."

Her nostrils flared. "Fucking Guillaume. He's such a cunt! I don't know why Brian hangs out with him. Then again, he's more Jake's friend than Brian's. I'm so sorry you had to go through that, Cara. Trust me to have a serious word with him." She was seething. I'd never seen her like this. It was maternal protectiveness unleashed, like that of a lioness.

"He could do with a correction," I replied with a nod. "And I suppose every squad has their uncontrollable idiot," I added, to defend Brian.

"Did Will see it?" she queried worriedly.

"He came to my rescue, actually, like a knight in shining armour. But I didn't tell him that the bloke was Brian's friend."

"Thank god. Will would have given me a thorough earful had he known, and it wouldn't have been necessary. He has no patience with that sort of thing. But trust me to deal with Guillaume."

I shrugged. "Sure. Thanks."

The doors slid apart on our floor, and after five steps, the second lift opened as well. Turning, my eyes were immediately captured by William's, and instantly, my heart leapt to my throat.

"Ellie, good to see you," his sensual voice murmured for a greeting. "How are you? We lost you on Friday."

Halting, she turned to acknowledge him. "Hi, Will. Yes, I heard about your adventure. Sorry about that. I did text you where we were located, but I suppose we moved before you had a chance to find us."

He frowned, eyes flickering in my direction. "Adventure?"

"I heard you had to take Cara back to hers."

His eyebrows arched. "Oh. Yes. That was quite the scene. She puked her guts out."

I wrinkled my nose and regretted the fact that he'd been forced to see me like that. I didn't want to imagine how dreadful I must have looked.

Ellie giggled beside me, probably at the mental image. "Poor thing."

William gave me a smile. "Yes, she was rather helpless."

"You're a gentleman for helping her home, Will, but you always take care of the weaker ones."

"Do I?" There was a smirk in his tone.

"You do. I've seen it."

"I'm not weak," I muttered.

"Sorry, I didn't mean it like that."

"She surely isn't," William asserted. "Anyway, we need to get to work, Cara," he said and walked past us to lead the way to his office. "We've got plenty of things on the agenda."

"I'll see you for lunch, Ellie," I told her fondly and proceeded after him.

Since his hands held two cups of coffee, he opened the door with his elbow before he cocked his head to indicate I should enter first. Passing him, I gave him a shy smile and glimpsed the coffees in his hand.

"This one's for you," he said to stall me. Wrapping my hand around it, I turned it to study the writing on the side.

Behind every strong man is a stronger woman, it read, and it made me grin. "Aw, how sweet," I said as he closed the door after us. The instant it drew shut, he lowered his head in search of my lips, but I hesitated due to our situation. However, knowing no one could see us, I decided to make an exception and stretched up on my toes to offer him a peck.

"That was a reluctant kiss," he remarked as I pulled away.

I chuckled. "I've meant to bring this up with you."

He groaned. "I already know what you mean to say."

"Don't you agree, though?" I walked towards his desk.

"For clarity's sake, tell me anyway."

"That we should remain strictly professional while at work?"

"No, I agree, but a kiss now and then can't hurt, can it?"

I smiled. "Alright, how about this? At work, you get two kisses a day. One for hello, and one for goodbye, but it's a requirement that they are shared in secret."

Smiling, he nodded to himself and walked round his desk. "I can work with that."

"Another thing," I murmured.

Dropping his bag on the floor, he met my eyes. "Yes?"

"Violet and Andy know about us, don't they?"

He looked slightly ashamed. "They do."

"I'm alright with that," I said, "but can you please ask them not to tell anyone?"

"That's not even necessary, but since you want me to, I'll do it anyway."

I released a sigh of relief. "Thank you. I just don't want to take any unnecessary risks."

"Understandable."

"As for Elisabeth, I think she's starting to suspect."

"Me too."

"Still, can we agree not to confirm anything to her?"

"I never tell Ellie anything at all regarding my private affairs," he assured me. "She's a darling, but her tongue is a tad too loose."

"My thoughts exactly. Glad we're on the same page."

Descending into his chair, he smiled up at me. "Was that all?"

I paused for a moment, thinking. "Yes, I think so."

"Right. Let's get started on work then, shall we?"

"Yes."

§ § §

At quarter past five, I had finished everything William had asked me to do today.

"I've done everything you asked me to. Am I free to leave, or do you need me to stay longer?" I asked while the cursor lingered over the cross to exit the windows on my computer.

Glancing in my direction, he smiled. "You're free to leave. Though, before you do…"

"Yes?"

"Practical question," he said while he continued to study the screen of his desktop Mac.

My brows furrowed. "What's that?"

He cocked his head from side to side, and I despised how handsome he looked even while doing normal human things like that. What was wrong with me? The sight of him cocking his head from side to side shouldn't send my heart racing like this. This was becoming ridiculous.

"Well," he murmured and tucked his chin into his hand so that his index finger repeatedly tapped on the cupid's bow of his lip. All the while, he was wearing a devastatingly sexy frown on his face. I wanted to slap it off him, just to spare my ovaries the grief.

"Yes?" I prompted.

With a sigh, he reclined in his seat, large hands gripping the ends of the arms of his chair. When he finally blessed me with his attention, I saw his jaw flex while his fingers tensed around the material of his chair.

While blatantly ogling me, he asked, "Do you *have* to look so appealing, Cara? Couldn't you wear burlaps or something of the sort, just to spare me the pain? I mean, honestly, wearing a dress like that, you're an occupational hazard."

Confused, I blinked back at him before I dropped my gaze to study my attire. I was wearing a grey dress, and while it did cling to my curves, it was a sophisticated dress, like that of a secretary during the sixties, and it showed no cleavage at all. It was square at the top, hiding the golden necklace Mum had gifted me for my eighteenth birthday.

"Is that seriously your question?" I asked disbelievingly, and I was slightly offended by his request. "If you can't control your erection, that's not my problem."

He chuckled and spun his chair around. "It's going to become your problem, I assure you."

I rolled my eyes. "I will not change how I dress."

He continued to spin his chair while he gazed up at the ceiling, much to my amusement. Carefree William Night was a sight to behold.

"It wasn't really a request. It was a cheeky, indirect compliment – nothing else. As for my question – practicalities. We could be traditional for our date on Friday, meaning I'll take you to some expensive restaurant, or we could settle for something more… casual. Which do you prefer? And while I know you're a feminist – as am I, by the way – I won't let you pay for a single thing. I'm not budging on that. Call me old-fashioned if you want, but I fancy the traditions of a gentleman."

"You're hardly a gentleman," I twitted.

His feet charged down to the floor to halt his spin. With a wicked gleam in his eyes, he watched me with a wry smile on his tempting mouth. God, that mouth, and all the things it could do. "Well, pardon my manners, but something about you turns me into a caveman."

I had to fight back my urge to giggle. Flattered, I looked away from him with a poorly suppressed smile on my face.

"So, then. Which is it? Stiff or casual?" he queried and rested his handsome head on his fist.

"I like you stiff," I teased, "but for a date, casual first, then stiff once we get home."

Visibly aroused by my reply, he chewed on his lower lip. "Sounds perfect." With a chuckle, he spun his chair around again. Once he'd gone full circle, he stopped the motion by resting his long legs on his desk and then proceeded to cross them. Next, he entwined his fingers across his torso and watched me for a few breaths.

"I've got time for a snog," he teased. "I'm spending the entire evening here. Consider it my goodbye-kiss."

I laughed. "You idiot," I said, but I ascended from my chair to oblige anyway. "Is the door locked?"

"Yes. We should make a habit of that."

"Agreed."

Striding round his desk, I gripped his grey tie, straddled his lap and brought his perfect mouth onto mine. While I still wasn't well-versed in the unique motion of his kiss, I smiled at the fact that it was slowly becoming increasingly familiar. One day, I hoped kissing him would feel as familiar to me as my own skin.

I'd only intended to give him a quick kiss, but before I knew it, I had lost myself in the taste of him. I struggled to restrain myself – his expert tongue was seducing me. It moved so skilfully, casting a spell that confined me to him, trapped me in this moment with him. His hands roamed across my body, worshipping every curve while he pressed me tightly against him, his mouth despatching passion that made me feel lightheaded. I yearned for more of his flesh. I wanted to feel him within me again. Between my legs I could feel him grow harder, his erection straining against the material of his trousers and poking my entrance. My vaginal walls were throbbing for him, begging for his intrusion, begging for his clothes to be gone so he could slide right in and complete me again.

Aroused, I inhaled sharply, taking his seductive scent deep into my lungs. Drugged by it, I felt my fluids trickle out of me, generously saturating my underwear. A groan escaped my mouth when he trailed his hand from my hip to my thigh, slowly, and then inwards, sliding further towards my beckoning wetness. His touch was electric, charging through my skin and into my bloodstream. Then, his talented fingers skimmed my soaked thong, brushing up and straight across the area of me where he knew I was the most sensitive. The acute sensation led me to break our kiss with a gasp, and as soon as I looked at him, I was reminded of our situation.

"Oh my God!" Mortified, I stared at his smug expression. He looked so pleased with himself that smacking him was tempting.

"God, what a mess I've made," he said with a smile and pressed the pad of his thumb precisely against that awfully susceptible spot. The sensation bolted up my spine, making me stiffen. Intense heat slapped my face as another gasp leapt out of my mouth. "Allow me to clean that up for you."

Panicking, I clasped his wrist. "Will," I pleaded, out of breath.

"Don't."

He grinned, his hand remaining in place. "I could." Sudden pressure on my clit made me catch my breath. Digging my nails into his skin, I watched him beseechingly. "So easily," he purred.

"Don't."

Laughing, he withdrew his hand to run his palms across my bum instead. "Meet me at Leicester Square on Friday, at seven."

After puffing out a breath of relief, the excitement for our date left a joyful smile on my mouth. "Sounds good. Will I see you out of your suit?"

His brow curved while a crooked smile dominated his mouth. "Why, Cara, you've already seen me out of my suit."

Rendered momentarily speechless, I felt another wave of heat hit my face. "I set myself up for that one, didn't I?"

"You did," he confirmed, amused. "But, rest assured, you're welcome to help me out of my suit at any time."

"You're incurable," I moaned and retreated from his lap.

"And you're my disease."

§ § §

I had promised myself I wouldn't be a nuisance to Aaron, but since William and I were going to start seeing each other, and since I hadn't heard a word from him despite my text, I would have to break that promise. So, on Tuesday, I found myself outside Aaron's building, arriving straight from work. We needed to talk, and I had a feeling that it wasn't going to be pleasant.

After pressing his name on the doorbell, I waited impatiently for either Tyler or Aaron to answer, though neither of them had picked up when I'd tried to call them earlier. It was perfectly possible that they weren't home, but I had decided to take my chances.

"Yeah?" I heard Tyler's voice greet me.

"Tyler, it's Cara. Is Aaron in?"

He hesitated for a beat. "No, he isn't, but have you tried calling him?"

"Yes, and he's not answering. Nor were you," I grumbled.

"Well, sorry, love, but last I checked, Aaron was angry with you, and that's putting it mildly. I didn't want to get in the middle of things."

The confirmation that he was still angry led me to inhale sharply. "Well, you are now. Will you let me in? I'll just wait for him to come home."

He hesitated again.

"Tyler, I'll either wait here outside, or you can let me in. It's up to you. I'm not leaving until I've talked to him."

I heard him groan before the door buzzed.

I dragged it open. "Thank you."

Tyler and I had decided to order pizza while we waited for Aaron to come home. We hadn't discussed William at all, which I was grateful for. Tyler had always been shy of conflict, so I hadn't really expected him to probe me either.

I raised my slice high above my head, and with my tongue I rescued a chunk of melted cheese that had threatened to fall just as Aaron entered through the front door. Our eyes met and, taken aback, I blinked for a second. With haste, I closed my mouth and swallowed my mouthful. Meanwhile, my heart raced. Thankfully, I'd had two beers by now to calm my nerves.

His warm eyes rolled as he took in my presence. "Look what the cat dragged in," he muttered, annoyed, and dropped his bag in the hall.

Tyler snatched three slices onto his plate before he scurried out of the room like a rat afraid of the cat. "Good luck!" he exclaimed as he charged out.

"So much for moral support," I muttered to myself and had another bite. "There's pizza for you," I mumbled behind my hand and cocked my head towards the box.

Aaron sighed as he sauntered into the room and then slumped down in the chair Tyler had vacated opposite me. Trying to gauge his thoughts, I studied him intensely. He still seemed angry, and it wasn't like him. Aaron was never angry, and definitely not for extended periods of time as far as I was aware.

"How was work?" I asked after swallowing another bite.

Without looking at me, he raised a brow and grabbed a slice. "Fine. Why are you here, Cara?"

I frowned. "Why do you think? You've been dead silent for three days straight, and you left me on read after I texted you on Sunday. It's not like you. I know I fucked up, no pun intended, but you know I didn't mean for that to happen. I didn't know he was going to be there, and—"

"Yes, I know that," he interrupted and finally met my gaze. His eyes were blistering, and they paralysed me for a moment. I'd never seen him like this.

"Th-then what's the problem?" I stammered. I was growing increasingly nervous. My hands had started to shake a little.

"I don't know. I'm still trying to figure it out," he quietly replied and looked away from me again. My appetite swiftly vanished, and my heart clenched. I could barely breathe. This wasn't normal. I could feel him slipping through my fingers, and I hated it.

"You're still trying to figure out why you're angry with me?" I enquired, perplexed. "You don't know?"

He grimaced and then frowned angrily to himself. "No. I don't know, Cara."

My breath hitched. "I don't get it. I didn't mean for you to get trapped in that situation, and I'm sorry he insulted you. You didn't deserve it at all. I also never meant for you to find out, so I'm sorry you learnt the truth in such a horrible way. If I could go back, I would've—"

"Cara, it's not that!" he snapped, unusually impatient. "It's the fact that you've fucked him that's bothering me!"

His brutal declaration struck me like a cannonball to the chest, making me jerk into the back of my seat. Pale-faced and with lips parted, I watched him in utter confusion and despair. "Because it's him?" I dared to ask.

He tossed his slice of pizza back into the box and leaned backwards. "Yes. No. I don't know."

What did he mean he didn't know? "Aaron," I said softly. "Please, we need to talk about this. I'm getting scared." In my lap, my fingers toyed with each other, betraying how anxious I was.

"Cara, was he the lad you mentioned? That man who had wanted you to give him a chance a while back?"

I gulped. "Yes," I revealed, upset.

His eyes maintained a distance from my gaze while he nodded to himself. "I thought as much. When did you first sleep together?"

I hadn't expected this interrogation, and it was taking me aback. Unsure of how to proceed, I eventually decided upon transparency. "In April."

Evidently unimpressed, his brow arched again. "That time you went for drinks with Livy?"

I released a painful breath. "Yes."

He nodded. "So, when he walked in on us, you'd already slept with him."

Shielding my face with my hands, I nodded.

"That makes a lot of sense," he murmured. "I always had a weird feeling about him."

"Aaron, it's part of our agreement not to tell each other about things like this."

"I know." He stood from his seat and started pacing round the room while rubbing his neck. "Cara, I think you should know something. During the three years we've spent together, I've only slept with one other girl."

My lips closed so that I could swallow the lump in my throat. What the hell? Where was he going with this? How was that relevant?

"O-okay?"

He turned towards me and nodded repeatedly. "Yes, that's right. One. It happened about three months into our arrangement, and afterwards, I felt like vomiting. I felt bloody disgusting, and that feeling has prevented me from doing it again ever since. And it wasn't the girl, Cara. She was perfectly sweet. It was because of you."

Tears started welling in my eyes as my fear increased. "M-me?"

I stammered again and studied him blankly.

"Yes, you," he moaned and rubbed his face.

"I see," I mumbled and looked away. "I'm sorry to hear that, Aaron. I haven't meant to stand in your way."

"Cara!" he yelled, exasperated, and I flinched at the volume. "Please, don't make this any harder for me than it needs to be."

I rushed to save a tear that had spilled over. He'd never shouted at me like this before. It was shocking me. "I just don't understand how this is relevant," I mumbled, upset. But I was starting to. I just didn't want to believe it.

Despairing, he moaned and shook his head. "Cara, the three years we've been sleeping together, I've essentially been monogamous. I haven't minded the idea of you with other men before because I haven't really known that it was happening. And, every time we've met, you've been so attuned to me that I've found it hard to believe that you could have been like you are with me with someone else. But I can't…I can't overlook this. I can't ignore it. I can't pretend like I don't know this happened the way I could with others, because I've seen him, and I know it's happened, and I can't get the images out of my head!"

I recoiled at his last shout and covered my face with my hands again. Was this truly happening?

"And what makes it even worse," he continued, agitated, "is the fact that he's your fucking boss! You'll be seeing him every day for the next three months, and from the look and sound of him on Saturday, he harbours no intention whatsoever of letting you go! I can't stand that, Cara. I can't stand knowing he'll be trying to get between your legs, day after day, and I especially can't stand it when you've fucked him before! You're obviously attracted to him! And whatever happened between you on Friday, I don't want to know, but the two of you are clearly unfinished business!"

I pressed my lips together to prevent a sob from spilling. Beside me, I heard Aaron sigh before he dropped down onto the sofa. Minutes of silence elapsed between us. We were both processing.

"I don't think I can do this anymore. I'm sorry," he eventually stated, voice calm and defeated, and the sound led a crack to form in my chest. "The way I see it," he continued, "we can either upgrade this to an actual relationship, exclusive at that, or we'll have to settle with being platonic. And, if you decide on the latter, you should know I'll require some time to move on, so we shouldn't be in touch for a while."

I started sniffing and nearly choked on my row of stifled sobs. My entire body quivered. I couldn't believe this was happening. He was giving me an ultimatum, and I hadn't seen it coming for the life of me. To make matters worse, I didn't return his feelings. I had wondered a few times in the past if what we shared was actually love, but meeting William had disproved it. Aaron had never given me butterflies, he'd never made my heart soar in my chest, and he'd never made me crave him the way I craved William.

But there was still love. Just not the romantic variety, and that was why this agonised me so. I'd have to break his heart, and it would break mine to have to do it.

I sensed him watching me for a long while before he sighed again. "Right. You don't need to say it. If you wanted to be with me, you would've said it by now, so just get out, Cara. Please."

I shook my head from side to side, disbelieving of reality. This wasn't what I had expected. It felt like I was about to implode from all the emotions that clawed at my chest. I'd never felt so despicable. How could I have been this blind? I'd never noticed his feelings for me, but then Aaron had always been good at maintaining his composure.

It was obvious that my obliviousness had cost me one of my dearest friends, and I worried our friendship had been broken beyond repair. I'd never seen him like this, and the revelation that he'd been in love with me this entire time made me question whether we'd ever truly been friends at all.

"Cara," he pleaded. "I don't want to be mean, but I'd really appreciate it if you left. Looking at you right now is making me want to cling to you, and that's not good for me in the long run.

I'm running out of strength here."

While sniffing, I pushed my seat out and headed straight for the hall without looking at him. I couldn't bring myself to say a single word. I was much too rattled, and I worried it would just unleash my inconsolable sobs.

So, without a word, I closed the door after myself and left into the night.

ABOUT THE AUTHOR

C.K. Bennett writes to challenge the norm and people's perspectives – including her own. She endeavours to contribute something new and different to the genres she writes within. She loves to learn, thus she spent 3 years studying Business Administration before she started her LLB (Bachelor of Laws). Bennett is now finally on her way to acquiring her LLM (Master of Laws) and aspires to become a lawyer – an ambition she has pursued since she was 12 years old.

She has lots of hobbies, including but not limited to writing. Strength training and taking long hikes are two of her favourite pastimes. Coffee is her elixir, and she's very curious about the world and how it works.

If you want to know more about her, check out:

https://ckbennettauthor.com/about

Bennett loves interacting with her readers, so don't hesitate to reach out to her on Instagram, where her username is @ck.bennett.

ABOUT THE COVER

C.K. Bennett made the cover herself, although the artwork is by the brilliant artist Caracolla (how uncanny is that? *Cara*colla? Bennett was meant to find this artist). She discovered Caracolla's work online after having searched for what felt like an eternity – definitely months. Bennett struggled to find something that was aligned with her own ideas but, the moment she saw Caracolla's art, she knew it was the perfect fit.

Bennett wanted a non-cliché depiction of the night theme. She could always have used a starry night sky, or made one herself, but the idea didn't resonate with her. It was too straightforward; Bennett enjoys more thought-provoking concepts, so she opted for an abstract portrayal of the theme instead.

If you take a look, you can see the blue crashing against the light, much like a wave crashing against the shore. The light represents the day, and the blue sweeping over it is supposed to imply that the night is emerging to consume the day, which is a reference to what Cara states in the book:

"I wanted him to consume me the way the skin of the night consumed the light of day to reveal infinity. Like the night sky, I hoped his devotion would be infinite. There in the dark, I could strip to my core without fear of judgement, for eternity."

The darker shades make it appear as though the universe is breaking through – think loads of galaxies, or even just the pattern of the Milky Way. Bennett wanted the cover to be artful, so the gold scattered across it is not actually stars but is instead supposed to imitate them.

The light shade of blue is the colour of William's eyes, being reminiscent of "a serene ocean surrounding a warm paradise". Bennett thought this made the artwork particularly apposite, as she sees it as the night reflected in the ocean.

The titles in *The Night* series are progressive, meaning they go deeper and deeper as the story evolves. In *Skin of the Night*, you are meeting William's surface. Bennett wanted to make a point of this by alluding to his eyes on the cover; it simulates an ocean and the night sky simultaneously. Moreover, Bennett decided to make the font seem written in "skin" to highlight more of William's exterior. It is supposed to represent William's handprint, as he surely leaves his print on Cara in more ways than one. He is also the Night, so it seemed optimal to Bennett to incorporate his handprint in the font.

As Bennett was making the spine and backside, she flipped the artwork. So, if you spread the book apart in the middle and look at it from above, you might notice that the dark-blue/black resembles a bird with spread wings. Bennett's logo is an owl with its wings spread, so she thought this was a cool little detail.

Overall, this abstract theme is something Bennett will be continuing with for all the remaining books in the series, though with different patterns and colours. Hopefully you will find that the complete series will complement your shelf.

If you're interested in more of Caracolla's art, check out:
www.instagram.com/caracolla.art

Curious about the hardcover design? Check out:
https://ckbennettauthor.com